COMING THROUGH THE FRONT door, Anne was hit by Sara, who flung herself into her mother's arms. The others rushed forward, Max sobbing, Steven shaking, his fair skin splotched with red patches.

"What is it?" she asked, bending down to her children, gathering them in.

"It's Tom," Sara cried. "He's crazy."

SUCH
NICE PEOPLE

by

Sandra Scoppettone

FAWCETT CREST • NEW YORK

*For Gloria Donadello, who
knows all the reasons why.*

SUCH NICE PEOPLE

Published by Fawcett Crest Books, a unit of CBS Publica-
tions, the Consumer Publishing Division of CBS Inc., by arrangement with G.P. Putnam's Sons

Copyright © 1980 by Sandra Scoppettone

ISBN: 0-449-24420-2

Printed in the United States of America

First Fawcett Crest Printing: July 1981

10   9   8   7   6   5   4   3   2   1

"I'm shocked. He was always a nice quiet boy."
—Stan Paxton
The Logan *Times*

"It's hard to believe. They were such nice people."
—Mrs. Helen Wykoff
Old Hickory *News*

"A terrible, terrible tragedy, I mean, they were people just like us."
—Lois Fisher
Pennsylvania County *Gazette*

Wednesday, December 18

1.

Tom couldn't believe how elementary it was, but his orders had been given. He was going to kill them all. Except, of course, for his sister, Kit. Kit was different, special. Besides, she would be needed. She was coming home from school on the twenty-third. He would have it all done by then. He would kill his mother, father, younger sister and two brothers on the twenty-second. When Kit arrived home on the twenty-third, it would be over. Mess cleaned up. They would have a terrific Christmas alone.

Perfect.

He would make a wonderful dinner. Then, candles lit, wine poured, he would explain SOLUDA to her. Kit would understand. After all she was a graduate student, had her Masters and in another year she'd have her Ph.D. Of course, she wasn't as intelligent as he was.

Few were.

Kit was twenty-four and he was seventeen, but chronological age had nothing to do with anything. That had been proven over and over down through the ages.

Tom rolled over on his back. The morning light trickled across his pillow, dimpled his cheek. Recently, he'd begged his mother for black shades to keep out the light. But, oh no. Why couldn't she understand that the first sign of light awakened him? Typical response. She said the little bit of light that got through the blue Levolor blinds couldn't possibly disturb him.

But it did.

Why couldn't she accept the truth of what he said? Who knew better what disturbed him? MOTHER knows best. Bullshit. Mother knows nothing. Stupid. He smiled, twirled a piece of his blond hair around his finger. She thought he didn't know about her and that goddamn innkeeper. She thought it was some big deal secret. Of course his father, being the boob he was, *didn't* know. And the other kids didn't know, but he wouldn't expect them to.

Only he knew.

As it should be.

And now he would punish her for it just as SOLA wished him to, told him to.

He was good. Did what he was told.

He moved to the far edge of the bed against the wall, out of the burning solar rays. Facing the white wall he flashed a picture on it. It was SOLA. Phosphorescent blue robe flowing, blue eyes flashing, piercing, knowing.

SOLA knew all.

Always.

SOLA's purple hair began to blow in a breeze, become tangled. The strands twisted and turned. They expanded, each one blowing up, becoming elongated and round. Each end turned up and he saw the two slimy eyes, the head, the darting tongues reaching out at him. Every strand of hair had turned into a deadly poisonous snake, hundreds of them, pulsating, undulating, beckoning.

He could hear SOLA laughing. The deep laugh.

SOLA's voice boomed throught the room. AS LONG AS THEY LIVE, YOU WILL BE IMPURE. More laughter.

"All right, all right," Tom whispered. "Soon. Only a few days more." Surely SOLA would understand. Plans had to be made. You couldn't just do something like this half cocked. "Understand?" he asked aloud.

SOLA's laughter penetrated Tom's brain, the pain almost unbearable. DECEMBER TWENTY-TWO, SOLA said.

"Yes."

The image on the wall began to fade.

He closed his eyes. His breathing, moments before coming in great gasping chunks, slowly returned to normal. The blue pajamas he wore were soaked with sweat.

His headache diminished.

Tom lay on his back, arms at his sides.

It had happened again.

The weirdness.

Afterwards he was always shaky, confused, spent. The claminess of his pajamas depressed him.

What should he do? These . . . things, whatever they were,

9

were happening more often. How long had it been going on? He couldn't quite remember when it had started. A month? Two months? At first SOLA spoke to him only once in awhile. But lately....

The knock on the door made Tom jump. He pulled the covers up around his neck so she wouldn't see his soaked pajamas. Shaking slightly, he tried for control. Couldn't let her know. Enough on her mind.

The door opened and Anne Nash stepped inside.

He smiled at her, softening his eyes, hiding his fear.

"Morning, Tom," she said sweetly to her son. "Breakfast in ten minutes."

"Thanks, Mom."

"Did you sleep well?"

"Fine." He prayed she didn't notice his hair limp with sweat.

"Good. Get up now, honey. Don't fall back to sleep."

"Don't worry." He winked at her. His pal.

She winked back, smiled, showing her one dimple, eyes creasing at the corners.

"Hurry now," she said, closing the door.

Tom took a deep breath. Part well played. He frowned. Part well played? Why must he play a part? What was going on? He tried to remember what had happened ten minutes earlier. He'd been given some kind of order or something. He could never fully remember these sessions. There was something about Kit. Kit would no longer be his sister. What did that mean? He would be Grand Duke and she Grand Duchess.

Tom sat up in bed, unbuttoned his pajama top, took it off and wiped his chest and underarms with it. Cold.

I am the SUN of SOLA, he thought. Wondered what that meant. No time now to untangle these thoughts. Breakfast. School. Jennifer. Whatever this was about he could deal with later. Always later. Still, funny thoughts pierced his brain like shrapnel.

Swinging his long legs over the side of the bed, he hit the floor with a bounce. Five more days, he thought, then Death.

No time to stop and figure out what that meant.

Keep going.

2.

At the top of the stairs Anne gripped the banister, knuckles turning white. Something was wrong, odd. It had seemed odd for a while now. Or was she imagining it?

Slowly, she descended the long wooden staircase, sliding her hand along the oak banister she'd painstakingly unearthed from beneath layers of paint. As she walked through the hall toward the kitchen, she heard them all beginning to move around upstairs.

Even now, after all these years, it still shocked her sometimes that she had five children. She'd been so sure she'd never have more than two. Being the second of four she felt she knew the pitfalls of shared love.

Breaking an egg into a bowl, Anne reviewed her exchange with Tom. On the surface there was nothing remarkable about it. It was what he didn't say, his eyes, smile. Everything was slightly off, like a record played at the wrong speed, a film out of sync. How to explain that to Cole? He'd say, "You read too much crap." "Overworking that imagination again."

All Cole ever worried about was his children's safety. Physical jeopardy his big concern. Car accidents, drowning, falling, illnesses, something breaking, someone dying. The emotional nuances of his children were beyond him. He related only to what he could see.

When Kit had started school he'd insisted Anne walk her back and forth four times a day (she came home for lunch) even though the sixth graders, members of the Safety Patrol, were posted on every corner. And Anne had done it for the whole year, Kit crying and pleading, feeling like a baby, a fool.

Before Kit began second grade, Anne had fought fiercely

with Cole. He expected her to continue accompanying the child. Anne knew it was impossible. Made Kit hate going to school. So she went up against Cole. Won. But not without a threat. "Anything happens to that child, you'll pay for it," he said. Couldn't help himself. She understood. Anne took the responsibility of Kit's safety. Had to. Kit needed that particular independence. Besides, nothing would happen. Nothing did.

Poor Cole. The agonies he suffered over his offsprings' imagined cuts, bruises, plagues, deaths. Yet, sometimes the children passed through his life like plastic pieces in a board game. When he was called upon to relate, love, in a regular father-child way, he was hopeless. If she'd only known how he'd be. Oh, not that again, not now. Not ever. No point. Done.

The bacon spit and hissed as though attacking the pan. Anne backed away thinking, as always, that she must buy one of those mesh covers.

When had she first noticed the difference in Tom? Two, three weeks? And what was it, after all? Who could understand boys of seventeen? Surely that was it. His age. Hadn't it all happened before? Familiar.

She and Kit had been the best of friends. Spending hours together talking books, refinishing furniture, shopping, sharing stories, problems, life. Even after Tom and Sara were born, the relationship went on, perhaps growing even closer. Anne never wanted to slight the older for the younger.

Then, about a year after Steven was born, when Kit was fourteen, it all changed. Overnight. So it seemed. She avoided her mother as though she were a leper. All sharing stopped. Conversation was at a minimum. Kit spent all her time at home in her room. Anne was bewildered. Cole, of course, thought Kit was sick. He insisted she be checked over twice in four months and was forever shoving a thermometer under her tongue.

It was Dr. Blackwell, their G.P., who'd clued Anne in.

"It's just a stage," he said. "All girls go through it."

"What kind of a stage?"

He sighed deeply, not wanted to crush still another mother. "She doesn't like you right now. It's her way of becoming independent, breaking away from you."

"But I've always been her support, her protector."

He smiled sadly. "I know, dear, but it's just the way things are. Don't you remember going through something like this with your mother?"

She started to say no, remembered. Of course. When Anne had been around thirteen, fourteen, Dorothy Clifford could do no right. Anne smiled, remembering her constant refrain through those years: Oh, Moth-er, please don't.

Still, Kit's behavior hurt her terribly, and she'd cried herself to sleep some nights.

Finally she'd broken a cardinal rule she'd made for herself: No snooping. Especially no reading of her children's private papers. But she'd lost control.

Kit's diary. She told herself she would only read the entry made the day before. It had been enough.

Mother started in again tonight. She makes me sick. She wants to know every little thing I'm thinking. Doesn't she have anything else to do? What a creep. I really hate her.

I really hate her. The words had been like little steel knives in her belly. She'd backed off then, leaving Kit alone. Trying to. Couldn't always. And she'd never pried into any of her children's private things again. Good lesson.

At about the age of eighteen, Kit had made her way back to her mother. Good friends now.

Was that what it was with Tom? A stage? Did he hate his mother? But Dr. Blackwell had said, all *girls* go through it. Did boys go through it too? And did they start later? After all, Tom was seventeen. Was it all very normal or was it something else? Ah, Cookie, she said to herself, ya read too much crap! Then for a second a flash of Tom's quick broad smile, trenchant blue eyes. Her center lurched. Gone.

As Sara hit the bottom step, Anne poured the eggs into the pan. Sara's heavy tread broke Anne's heart. Controlling her daughter's diet at home was useless. It was clear she ate between meals elsewhere.

Sara thudded into her chair asking, "Eggs and bacon?" Disappointment transparent.

"Eggs and bacon," Anne confirmed.

Sara blew noisily through her lips. "I hate breakfast."

"I know." Anne also knew that if she were serving pancakes or waffles Sara would love breakfast. She wondered if her daughter ate a second breakfast of carbohydrates somewhere else? Did she have a second home, another food-giving

mother, lardlike and loving, spooning dumplings and dough-
nuts into Sara's waiting mouth? Madness.

Steven skulked into the kitchen, green sweatshirt inside
out, fly only half-zipped.

"Well, you look lovely!" Anne said.

He tugged at his sweatshirt, pulling it out from his stomach as though this would somehow rearrange things, accord
with his mother's high standards.

"Your fly's open," Sara said, milk moustache curling up
from the corners of her small mouth.

"So's yours."

Quickly she glanced down, forgetting she was wearing the
blue pants that zippered in back. Too fat for her jeans.

"Gotcha," Steven said, laughing. Surreptitiously, he zipped
his fly.

"Mommy," Max said, sliding into his place at the long pine
plank table, "Coco scratched at my door all night long."

"I don't think so, honey," Anne said. "Coco slept with me
last night."

"She was mewing and scratching all night and I didn't get
any sleep and I don't see how I can go to school today."

"Oh, here we go again, gang," Steven said, crunching bacon between chiclet white teeth.

"Max," Sara said, "just wait until you're a freshman and
then you really won't want to go to school."

Steven said, "Big deal," and ran a hand through his pale
yellow hair.

"First grade is hard," Max said.

"Big deal."

Sara looked at her empty plate, foraged for invisible bits
with her fork, gave up the hunt, sighed. "You don't even have
homework, Max. Just wait." She rested a plump cheek on the
palm of her hand.

"I hate school," Max said.

"We know." Together.

Anne poured coffee for herself, wondered again how her
children could be so different from each other. But that was
the fun, the point. She half listened to the inane conversation
of these three, blonde heads, blue eyes the only similarity
among them. Was Thomas at all like Steven when he was
twelve? Was Steven like Max at six? No way was Kit like
Sara. Beauty Kit.

Tom loved school. Steven tolerated it. Max hated it. The
girls were fine, good, bright, but then girls were different

14

about school. Girls shone in the classroom, played dumb in life. But, no, it wasn't that way any more. That had been her time. *Never let a boy know how smart you are, Anne. Two years of college are plenty for a girl. Always let the man lead the way, dear. Men like girls who look up to them.* Oh, Lord! She'd bought it all. But not her Kit. Kit was her own person. Pretty soon Dr. Catherine Nash. Catherine Nash, Ph.D. Little Kit, grown Kit. Woman. So smart.

"Dreaming?" Cole asked.

She hadn't heard him come in. Smiled for an answer.

"Cereal?"

"Yes." Cole tousled Max's hair, slid his hand down his cheek, automatically feeling for fever. Trying to hide it.

Fooled no one.

Sara and Steven caught the gesture, rolled their eyes, allies for a moment.

"How's everybody this morning?" he asked.

Grunted replies. No one wanted to engage in anything that might bring on questions of health.

"Daddy," Max said, "I didn't sleep all night 'cause Coco was scratching and sniffing at my door."

"Is that right?"

"How can I go to school when I didn't sleep?"

"Don't you feel well?" Cole asked.

"Well...." Max knew his man.

"He feels just fine," Anne broke in, putting a bowl of cereal in front of Cole. "Pay no attention."

"I hate school, Daddy."

Cole picked up his spoon. "Sometimes we have to do things we hate."

"Why?"

"Oh, Max," Sara said, "don't start that again." She eyed Max's plate, bits of bacon left untouched.

Anne caught her daughter's line of vision, carefully removed Max's plate.

Sara slumped.

Steven cleared his throat. Careful approach. "Dad?"

"Yes?"

"I've made a decision. I'm going out for Little League in the spring."

The muscle in Cole's cheek jumped. He wiped his mouth.

Swallowing, Steven said, "You hear me, Dad?"

"I heard."

Tom joined them. Fresh, clean, sparkling.

15

Nothing wrong there, Anne thought, sitting, looking at Tom. You're imagining things. She turned her attention to Steven. She saw that he twisted his napkin on his lap. Poor tyke.

"What position?" Cole asked.

"Pitcher," he said softly.

Cole's marble blue eyes narrowed. "Pitcher?" As though the boy had said he was going to sky dive.

"What's wrong with that?" Tom asked. He knew the answer. Had to fight his own sports battles with his father. He'd won. Most of them. Not football. Didn't like it much anyway.

"Could be dangerous," Cole answered.

"Oh, Dad," Steven said.

"Get hit in the face. Line drive."

Sara was bored with talk of sports. "Daddy, did you know that a senator named Huey P. Long was assassinated in 1935?" Father and daughter shared an interest in American History.

"Please, Sara," Cole said sharply.

Sara bit the inside of her upper lip. Stung.

Anne reached out, gently touching her daughter's leg. Abruptly, Sara pulled away.

No question where Sara stood on the I-hate-mother front. That had been going on quite awhile now. Somehow it didn't bother Anne the way it had with Kit. Funny she hadn't thought of it earlier. Nothing like what she saw in Tom. That again.

"I don't like the idea, Steve."

"Dad," Tom said gently, "you've got to let him try it."

"Why?"

"Tom's right, Cole," Anne said.

He gave her an icy look. Turned back to Tom. "You didn't play in Little League."

"I know and it was lousy. I wanted to. You wouldn't let me."

"Because you were too young. So is Steve. Nothing's changed."

"Dad, I've been playing sports for the last four years and nothing's ever happened to me."

"Basketball, swimming, tennis. I don't like those much either, but at least they aren't as dangerous as baseball and football."

Sara wanted to throw over the table. Too heavy.

"Better move kids," Anne said.

"I'll think it over," Cole said.

"Okay," said Steven. But it didn't matter. He was either going to play Little League or run away from home. That was all.

The children rose, dashing for coats, hats, gloves. Hurry, you'll miss the bus. Same words morning after morning. 'Bye. Don't dawdle. Have a good day. Careful. Kiss from Max only. Door close.

At the table they drank their coffee.

Cole dabbed at his thin mouth delicately, napkin folded precisely.

She didn't have to look to know. Twenty-five years of marriage, you knew. Anne thought about Tom again. Speak. Try. "How did you think Tom seemed this morning?"

He looked up from his coffee, questioning. "Tom? Why? He sick?"

Lord. "No, he's not sick. I mean, no virus or anything."

"What then?"

She didn't know how to say it. Cole lived by the tangible. How could she explain to him? What would he say to her thoughts on the look *behind* Tom's eyes, the *undertone* of his voice, the tension in his neck? Or the *feeling* she had lately when she was around him. How to phrase it so Cole would understand. She poured him another cup of coffee. "He doesn't seem, I don't know, *different* to you?"

"Different from what?"

"From usual."

He thought. "No, I haven't noticed anything."

But, of course, he wouldn't. No point.

Cole slipped his napkin back through the tortoise shell ring. Only one who did. Standing, he finished his coffee. "Something bothering you, Anne? About Tom?"

Let it go. "I guess it's growing pains," she said, knowing this would be acceptable. It was.

"Stage. They all go through different stages." He'd read or heard that somewhere. Made him feel like he knew. Like a father. "Well, see you later." He kissed her on the cheek.

She watched him through the door to the living room as he walked to the closet, got his coat, hat, gloves, boots. Still the same proud walk he'd had for as long as she'd known him. Now older, body thicker, not by much.

When he'd gone, she sat at the table, poured herself the last cup of coffee. Touched her cheek where his lips had

17

grazed. When had the morning kiss gone from lips to cheek? Long time.

She lit a cigarette.

First time she'd seen him, she'd gone to mush inside. He was gorgeous. At least six feet tall with blue eyes the color of the sky. For weeks before the girls had speculated about what the new man would look like. He was being transferred from the Old Hickory, Pennsylvania, branch of Brandt, Brandt & Todd to this one in Chatam, New Jersey. Anne had seen his resume and knew he was a Lehigh man and had been in the Korean war.

She'd fantasized about him. Dates, marriage, even a family. Crazy. Probably wouldn't give her a tumble. And maybe she wouldn't even like him.

But she did.

To her, he was an older man. She was only nineteen. Right out of Centenary Junior College. Even so, she felt sophisticated. Smoked. Drank. But she was still a virgin. Once a guy from Princeton had said, "What are you saving it for, toots?" She'd thought about it a lot. Wondered. Why was she hanging on to the archaic virgin-when-married idea? She really didn't know. She petted. Below the waist as well as above. Why not go all the way? But she couldn't. Didn't want to. Even though sometimes she thought she might die of stomach cramps.

When she saw Cole Nash for the first time, she knew why she'd been saving it. For him. And she was glad.

Of course, Cole had no knowledge of this great gift that awaited him. Paid no attention to her. Not that he paid attention to any of the other females. Came in, did his work, had lunch with a few of the other men, did his work, went home. It was that way the whole first summer.

She was in despair. But determined. In 1952 there was one aim in life for a young woman. Marriage and family. And Anne Clifford was just like all the rest. She had no career aim, never had. Husband and children were all she'd ever wanted. Been raised for it. Hadn't Daddy said it all her life? *"Cookie, you're going to make some lucky guy a wonderful wife."* How many times? Hundreds.

There were other boys that summer of '52. Although with the war still going on, the pickings were lean. Still, she dated. She was a good looking girl and the boys that were home were glad to have a chance to date her. But that was just the problem, as far as Anne was concerned. *Boys.* She wasn't interested in boys. They were silly, had little to say and the end of the evening was always a battle. She wanted to date a *man*. And that man was Cole Nash. He'd been through college and the war. There was no way he could still be a boy. God only knew what he'd seen over there!

She tried everything. New clothes, new hairstyle, different shade of lipstick. And she kept her mind active, too. Of course there was no way to know what Cole was interested in but she made sure she was informed about sports and current events and she read the latest novels, just in case. Naturally she didn't want to be too well-informed, just enough to be able to hold an intelligent conversation. He could really explain it all to her. That was the way it was supposed to be. But Cole Nash went through the summer as though Anne Clifford didn't exist. Not that he was rude. He always smiled, said good morning and good night. But that was it.

By the beginning of September she'd given up hope and turned her attentions toward Russ Garrison, a twenty-year-old who had a deferment because he was sole support of his widowed mother. Russ was a perfectly nice guy, good looking, fun, had a pretty good job at the bank and didn't push her sexually. She liked him a lot. But no magic. She'd been raised on the movies and sometimes she wondered if her standards were formed by Errol Flynn, Tyrone Power and Robert Taylor. When her head was in the sky, her father always brought her back to reality. *"Can't wait around for Prince Charming, Cookie. You're not God's gift, you know."* Zap. Daddy drunk.

Still, she continued to believe there could be magic. And there was. At the end of September, out of nowhere, Cole Nash asked for a date. She couldn't believe it. She already had a date with Russ and although her mother's words, *"Make a boy wait. Never say yes the first time he asks"* rang in her head, she had no intention of losing this opportunity. She said yes. Broke the date with Russ.

Cole was almost everything she'd imagined. Mature, gentlemanly, wise. He wasn't much of a talker (she'd kept the conversational ball rolling) and there was something a little mysterious about him. As though he had a secret. Anne chalked it up to his war experiences. People were always talking about how guys who'd been in the war, any war, were often shy, reticent. She remembered all the movies made about soldiers returning from the Second World War, and Cole fit the bill. That would change, she told herself.

She dropped Russ and dated Cole exclusively. She was mad for him. He made her feel grown up. Encouraged her to

19

talk. Liked the fact that she had lots of interests. He didn't seem to have many except American History (she boned up), but she was glad to keep him entertained.

As far as sex went, Cole was totally different from any other man she'd ever been out with. It was he who kept things in check. She would have gone to bed with him if he'd asked, but he never did. Just as things got hot and heavy he'd pull away, light a cigarette. Even though she almost went crazy from desire, she thought he was wonderful to have so much control.

In February of 1953, when he asked her to marry him, she didn't give it a moment's thought. There'd never been any question in her mind.

And if he was a bit removed, withdrawn, moody, well, that was okay. She'd bring him out of his shell in time. Marriage would change him. Children (he wanted at least four) would do the trick. She wished he might be a little more spontaneous but a girl couldn't have everything, could she? After all, he was handsome, intelligent, kind and had a good solid future. What more could she expect? *You're not God's gift, you know.*

They were married on April 16, 1953. Her father didn't like Cole, but he put up a front. And Cole didn't like him, although he never let on about that until much later.

They had a big wedding, four bridesmaids, her sister Liz her Maid of Honor. Cole asked his father to be his Best Man, but he refused, saying Cole's mother would be all alone at the wedding if he were. So Cole's boss, Wayne Moore, stood up for him. Anne told herself that Cole didn't have any friends because his very best ones had all moved away—far away. It was pure fiction, but she believed it. Had to.

Their honeymoon was to be in the Bahamas, but with the first night at the St. Moritz in New York. She felt like she was in the movies. Until she got into bed in her green lacy nightgown.

Cole, in blue pajamas, lay rigidly next to her. Sounds of horses and carriages from the park below penetrated the room. She waited, but nothing happened. She said his name. He didn't respond. Everything she'd ever read, heard, told her he was to make the first move. Clearly he wasn't going to.

Was it her? Was there something wrong with her? Was she so totally undesirable that he couldn't bring himself to touch her? She wanted to call her mother, ask her what to do in this situation. But she could hear her: "A nice girl waits

20

for the man to make the first move, dear. You don't want to ruin his self-confidence. Just wait. Keep waiting."

Should she say nothing? The whole thing was terrifying. "Cole, I'm frightened," she heard herself say. Then bit her lip. No response.

Feeling deeply wounded, she moved to her side of the bed, clinging to the edge. It was an almost sleepless night, with a few winks here and there between silent tears.

In the morning she was a wreck. They flew to the Bahamas and that night he made love to her without a word.

There weren't any skyrockets and she wondered what all the fuss was about. She ended up with the same stomach cramps she'd always had. But at least he was gentle. Afterwards she'd wanted to lie in his arms, but he'd immediately gotten up, showered and when he came back to bed he kissed her forehead, said goodnight, turned his back and went to sleep.

Later she'd tried to talk to him about their wedding night, but he refused, becoming angry, then sulking. She dropped it. Forever.

It was all there. A microcosm of their future lives together. Cole distant, afraid of intimacy. Anne trying to get closer, failing. It was all there if she'd wanted to see it.

She didn't.

But she saw it now. Had for quite some time. She sipped her coffee. Cold. At the sink she poured the coffee down the drain, stared out the window. The sun was out, but she knew it was freezing. Cold coffee, cold weather, cold life.

Until now. Jim.

He'd come into her life by surprise and now everything was beginning to change. Was it an infatuation or love? She thought of him constantly and, although she had to deal with guilt, Jim O'Neill made her feel like a lovely woman again.

Wrapping her arms round herself she thought, you've got to make a move, get out. Any woman with guts would do it. Ah, Cookie, you're a gutless wonder, face it.

She faced it.

3.

From the house in Logan, it was five miles to Cole's office in Old Hickory. The roads were winding and, with snow on the ground, it took him about fifteen minutes. At the intersection of Liberty Street and William Penn Avenue, if he took a right, he'd go into the little town of Summerseat where his parents lived.

He looked at his watch. Eight forty-five. There was nothing pressing at the office until ten-thirty when he was to meet with Lt. Charles "Chollie" Buck to discuss the alleged accidental death of Harrison Foster, who held a double indemnity policy with Cole's firm. Cole liked visiting his parents early in the morning; he liked exercising his right to come into the office when he wanted to. After all, it wasn't Brandt, Brandt, Todd & Nash for nothing.

He took the right turn.

There weren't many houses along Liberty Street, but those few were decorated with wreaths, candy canes on the doors, candles in the windows. He liked that.

Turning left on Solebury Lane, he had to slow the car to about ten miles an hour. The snow was piled high on each side of the narrow road and he could barely see over the tops of the drifts. Only a little past mid-December and already it was a bitch of a winter. Sometimes he wondered why he'd come back to Pennsylvania. Not that he'd ever lived anywhere but the East. Of course he'd been to Korea, but you couldn't call that living, could you? That was more like hell. And in the States he'd gone to boot camp at Parris Island in South Carolina. Hardly *living* either. Still, it was warm. Hot. The memory of boot camp made him begin to sweat. He turned down the car heater.

Parris Island, July 1950. It stank. The heat was unbearable yet they bore it, sometimes vomiting, sometimes fainting. One pink-faced kid getting prickly heat, becoming the butt of endless jokes. Later there'd be a scandal at Parris Island, men dying. No reason. But then it was just brutal training and *wanting* to die. At least Cole had wanted to. He prayed for God to take him, thinking he couldn't stand another day, hour, minute. But he kept on standing it, insides roiling.

At night, lying in his bunk, muscles aching, sweating, sick to his stomach, he tried to remind himself why he'd joined. His father. Stuart Nash had been in the First World War, a hero. His war medals were mounted on purple velvet, hung in the living room. All his life he'd heard his father's war stories. At first he'd loved them; all little boys love their father's stories. Later, in high school, he heard them as a reproach. Stuart was brave, Cole a coward. Never said, still there.

When the Korean thing happened, Stuart, loud and clear, let Cole know what a man would, should do. He hadn't wanted to go, wanted to start his career and, being an only son, he would have gotten a deferment. But Stuart would have been ashamed of him. God forbid. The thought of sharing bathrooms, among other things, with other men made him feel sick. He'd spent his whole school life avoiding that kind of intimacy. Neat trick. But Cole's privacy was essential to him. At Lehigh the other boys had insinuated he had a small penis, and that that was why no one had ever seen him naked. The night they raided his room, stripped him, they found out their suspicions were far from true. After that, they left him alone, started calling him "Three-legged Nash" behind his back. He heard about it, of course. Didn't think it was funny.

But in the barracks and on bivouac privacy was impossible. Still, he never got used to it. And there were worse things. Like being forced to spend endless hours of time with the same person.

Nick Dowdeswell. Buddy. Chum. Friend.

It was hard to know where you were with the snow everywhere, and Cole almost missed the turn into his parents' driveway. The mailbox that said *Stuart Nash* was completely covered. He eased the car back slightly, careful not to get stuck, turned in, stopping as soon as he was off the road. He walked down the driveway to the house.

The house was small, cottage-like. The front door covered

in aluminum foil, a silk red ribbon stretching catty-corner down its length, sprigs of holly where the big bright bow was tied in the center. Even at seventy-nine his mother kept up with the seasons. Cole knew his father had had nothing to do with the door decoration. The Christmas tree was his only contribution. Which reminded Cole they'd have to get *their* tree on Saturday. A big family outing. The whole bunch. Daddy's brood.

Nick Dowdeswell. Tall. Reed thin. Long, narrow face, as though it had been pinched in a giant clothespin. Brown hair, clipped military short. Wire-frame glasses before they were fashionable. Dopey looking. But not. Talk was he was a fag. Cole never believed it. Didn't care anyway.

Goddamn Nick Dowdeswell. Lousy bastard.

Cole shook away the image of the gangly young soldier. Not now. Christ. He went up the two brick steps.

The door was unlocked, as always. If he'd told them once, he'd told them a thousand times to lock their damn front door. Sure the crime rate was low, but you never knew when some pervert might take it into his head to beat up on some old couple, thinking they hid their cash in their mattress or something. God, it was aggravating. They were like a couple of irresponsible kids.

A light came from the kitchen in back. They were eating breakfast. It occurred to him to sneak up on them, not shout his usual hello from the door. Scare the bejesus out of them. Serve them right. On the other hand, he wouldn't want to be responsible for a heart attack or a stroke.

"Halloo," he called.

There was a murmuring from the kitchen as he walked through the small livingroom, down the hall.

They sat at the round table, shrunken, old. Close together. Nothing changed.

Clara Nash, eyes almost obliterated by the thick lenses of her glasses, fussed her hands together like tiny birds. "Cole, what a surprise."

Never mind that he stopped to see them at least three times a week; it was still, always, a surprise to Clara. Unwanted?

"H'lo, boy," Stuart Nash said sticking out a scrawny, trembling hand.

Formality. Cole took his father's hand in his, perpetually shocked and revolted by the dryness of his skin. Age sapped the vital juices, all right.

"Want some coffee?" Clara asked, starting to rise.

"I'll get it."

It was on the stove in the yellow pot. First, he went to the cabinet for a mug. He took one of the brown and white ones. It didn't matter; he couldn't match the ones they drank from. Theirs were pale blue and hers said CLARA in black script and his said STUART in the same style. There was no mug that said COLE. Never had been.

"How's the weather out there?" Stuart asked.

"Cold," he answered, sitting down across from his father. He wondered how many lines criss-crossed the old man's face. Maybe he could run a contest, have people guess for a prize, like so many beans in a bottle. "I like the door, Clara." He stroked the lower part of his long face between thumb and fingers.

"Well, it's not as nice as last year, but it'll do."

She always said it wasn't as nice as the year before.

"Ya see Clara's decorations in the living room?" Stuart plucked at the cuff of his black, green and white flannel shirt.

"Didn't notice. Just walked through."

"It's nothing," Clara said, a modest shake of her head.

Cole started to rise. "I'll look."

Clara said, "Oh, not now." As though he were stupid. "See them on the way out."

"How's the family?" asked Stuart.

"Fine." The question still startled him sometimes. Stunned to realize he had a family of his own.

"Be nice to see Kit. I miss her." Clara tucked a loose strand of white hair behind her ear. "She's a winner, that girl."

"A real looker, too," Stuart said, making a clucking sound meant as approval. "'Course, she didn't lick it off the ground, as they say."

Cole smiled crookedly, for a moment foolishly thinking Stuart meant him.

"Should have seen Clara at Kit's age."

"You didn't even know me then, Stu," she said beginning to twinkle, tilt her head coquettishly.

Cole lowered his eyes, the thin scalloped lids hiding embarrassment.

"Seen pictures. Anyway, you were just as pretty at twenty-nine, when I married you and broke a lot of hearts all over the county." He chuckled. "Morgy Bennet's *still* pining for you."

25

"Oh you," she said, touching his hand, giving his arm a poke.

Cole felt sick to his stomach.

"Want some more coffee?" Clara asked her son.

"No thanks. I can't stay. I have an important meeting. Double indemnity case." He began to tell them about it. Harrison Foster was a bigwig in Old Hickory, socially prominent, politically affiliated. People liked gossip about his type, about him, in fact. Now it looked like he'd killed himself and had hoped to dupe the insurance company. Unusual for the area. Anybody'd be interested, keen to know the facts, fascinated to be connected with the man handling it. Anybody but Clara and Stuart. Halfway through the tale, he could see their interest had waned. He was losing them…to each other. Clara pushed another muffin at Stuart and he pretended she was feeding him and it was all they could do to keep from laughing. All this sideways and in the mime as they pretended interest in what Cole was saying. They didn't want to be completely rude, after all.

He wound up the story fast. No point. They didn't even care that it was important in his career, to his company. Hell, they didn't even care that he *had* a company. The night he told them he'd become a partner served only to remind Stuart of when *he'd* become a partner of his firm which brought him around to the man he'd replaced who, of course, had been madly in love with Clara and so on.

Cole put his mug in the sink. "I'd better be going."

In the living room, he oohed and aahed over her decorations which covered every available surface: tables, mantel, shelves. They ran the gamut from the Three Wise Men to Rudolph the Red-nosed Reindeer. Clara didn't miss a trick. The tree stood bare in the corner waiting for Stuart to do the lights. He'd get around to it by Christmas eve, Clara nagging him until then. They knew their parts; no rehearsal necessary. He knew his part, too.

"Good-bye," he said. "I'll come get you Christmas morning."

"We'll see you before then, won't we?" Clara asked. Bored?

"Maybe not. I'm busy this week."

"I see," she said, knowing he'd be there.

"Christmas morning, then," Stuart said. Hopefully?

The cold hit him hard. When he got to the car, he didn't bother to look at the house, wave. No one would be in the doorway or window.

He backed out slowly, carefully. In his mind he saw them again at the kitchen table, hands, fingers entwined, eyes locked together, throwing bouquets at each other, his visit wiped from their brains as surely as if he'd never been there.

Three was definitely a crowd.

As he started toward Old Hickory, Nick Dowdeswell was back, sitting next to him in his memory.

It was after six weeks in basic, six weeks of doing everything side by side, that Nick first confronted him.

"What is it with you, Nash?"

"What do you mean?" He didn't look up. Kept digging. Foxhole. Pretend.

"I don't get you."

"Who says you're supposed to?"

"Oh, shit. That's just what I mean." He reached out a large thin long-fingered hand, grabbed Cole's wrist. "Hold it for a sec."

Cole stopped digging, looked up into the big brown eyes. "What is it, Dowdeswell?"

"You're a robot, you know that. You're a fucking zombie."

"Thanks. You finished?" He tried pulling out of Nick's grip, but the man was surprisingly strong.

"No, I'm not. You and I've been working together, sleeping together, for Christ's sake, for six weeks and all I ever get out of you is yes, no and maybe. And it's not just me. I mean, if you were buddies with some of the other guys then I'd say, well, hell, the fucker just doesn't like me and okay, that's life. But you don't talk to anyone."

"So?" The sun was beating down at over a hundred degrees and Cole was starting to feel sick.

"So it's not normal, bud."

"What do you care?"

Nick laughed, cackled almost, dropped Cole's wrist and wiped the back of his hand across his mouth. "I'll be damned if I know. Guess I just hate to see a guy so frigging miserable."

"I'm not miserable." Now he was feeling dizzy.

"The hell you're not."

Cole resumed his digging. Something was going on inside him. Not just the nausea from the sun. Miserable. Yes, it was true. He hadn't allowed himself to *know* it, although he'd been feeling it.

That night, lying awake, he became acutely aware of his misery. But he couldn't determine its origin. It was beyond

27

him why he should feel so awful. So miserable. Damn Dowdeswell for putting the idea in his head.

Another week went by before they exchanged any more than perfunctory and necessary words. This time it was Cole who started the conversation. He'd been unable to go back to the unknowing state he'd existed in for so very long.

It was during a war game and they were huddled in their foxhole.

"Dowdeswell?"

"What?"

It pained Cole to have to ask this guy anything but he had to know. "Why did you say I was miserable?"

"Je-sus," he mumbled.

"Why?"

"Because you are. You're the most miserable bastard I've ever met."

"I've never done anything to you." Sweat trickled down his temples. Heat or nerves?

"I doubt if you've ever done anything to *anyone*. That's just the point."

The point? Cole was bewildered. He pressed on, hating Nick for making him ask. "What do you mean?"

"You're stupid as well as miserable. The point is," Nick said like a grade school teacher to a slow student, "you're not human. Humans need other people. They have conversations with them. Do things with them. I bet you've never even had a girl?"

Cole's mind leaped to Patsy Linton. Old Hickory. Behind the Mill. Parked car. Two dollars a shot. But that wasn't having a girl, was it?

Nick went on. "It's like something's been cut out of you. Something essential. Like the human part."

Cole was glad it was night because the words stung and tears were forming in his eyes. He couldn't speak.

It was as though Nick sensed what the silence really meant. His voice became more gentle. "The thing of it is, Nash, I think you're goddamn lonely."

Lonely. Was that it? Was it as simple as that? Lonely. Yes. Could it be so simple? Oh, my God. He started to cry.

Nick heard him. After awhile he said, "It's okay, Nash."

After that night, little by little, Cole started talking to Nick. At first he was reticent, didn't really know how to express himself, but once he got going there was no stopping him. Sometimes, laughing, Nick had to tell him to, "turn it off, you're driving me nuts."

In September, they were shipped to Korea. Nick and Cole were now inseparable, grateful that they were assigned to the same platoon. Near the end of September, they helped recapture Seoul.

Cole felt human for the first time in his life. Even though he was involved in killing, his relationship with another person made him overlook what might have sent him into despair. It was strange. Opening up this way could have made him more sensitive to what he was doing and, in a way, it did. But Nick helped him through it, getting him to talk about his feelings rather than bottling them all up the way he always had.

And they made plans for after the war. Nick was from a small town in upstate New York so the idea of moving to Philadelphia was big time to him. They'd open their own insurance office. Equal partners.

In October, they started marching toward the 38th Parallel. Nobody really knew what the hell was going on. They just knew they were driving into North Korea toward the Yalu River.

On November twenty-fifth things were quiet as Cole and Nick waited in a trench for their orders. Nick had spent the last hour talking about his mother, father, sister and brother. Cole felt he knew them better than his own parents, looked forward to meeting them after the war. They sounded like the family he'd always dreamed of. Now Nick was going on about the family he wanted. Four kids. Two boys, two girls. Girl, boy, girl, boy.

"I know everybody wants the boy first," he said, "but I always wanted an older sister. Anyway, who wants the same old thing everybody else has? Don't know what I'll name the first girl, but I'll name the first boy Thomas after my...."

Even with the blast, Cole filled in the word. Father. A word Nick Dowdeswell would never say again. Not that word, nor any other.

It was the beginning of the massive Chinese invasion which would drive the U.S. forces south of the 38th Parallel by the end of December.

Miraculously, Cole survived the invasion. But he might as well have been killed for all he cared. The only friend he'd ever had was dead and Cole Nash couldn't imagine what there was to live for.

And he was angry. Angry at Nick for dying. For ever having lived at all. For touching Cole, opening him up, for making him human.

Whatever misery he'd felt before knowing Nick was nothing compared to what he felt after his death. Goddamn Nick Dowdeswell. Lousy bastard.

Cole pulled into the parking lot behind his office. Over twenty-five years ago and it could still get to him. He opened his brown leather briefcase that lay on the passenger seat, reached in, pulled out the small vial. He unscrewed the cap, dropped a 10 milligram Valium into his hand, popped it into his mouth, swallowed it with the saliva he'd built up (he was expert at taking them with no water, had been doing it for years), screwed back the cap and replaced the vial in his case.

Now he was ready to face the day.

4.

Tom traced his finger along the lines of the heart etched in the deck. No matter where he sat, there was sure to be some dumb heart with initials inside. Or sometimes it was just initials separated by an "L". He wondered why people found it necessary to advertise their feelings. Of course, it wasn't as bad as what was in the BOYS bathroom.

Joy L. has big ones
If you want good head call 555-6512

And so on.
He hated it.

The initials in the heart he was looking at now were "S. S. and L. C." He wondered how long ago they'd been scratched in the pine desk? Had a boy or a girl done it? What was used? A knife, a key, a nail file? Did "S. S." and "L. C." even know each other now? They were probably married to other people and never gave each other a thought. Or maybe one of them was dead, maybe both.

He looked away, out the window. The sky was gray, cold looking. Tom wished he were in bed, under the patchwork quilt his Grandma Clifford had made, light on, snuggling with a book. Then he remembered he couldn't read anymore. It had been about a month, maybe more. Each day it got worse. Couldn't concentrate. A longing for the days of curling up with a good adventure story sent tears up behind his eyes. Quickly, he began to do the nine multiplication table so he wouldn't cry.

What was happening to him? Something was very wrong. Maybe he should tell his mother, after all? But here it was a week before Christmas and she had dozens of things to think about. Besides, she seemed preoccupied these days. He tried to remember why that was. Somewhere he knew. Couldn't remember right now. Anyway if he told his Mother she'd tell his father and he was bound to go ape-shit. That was all he needed, his father dragging him to Dr. Blackwell every minute. Or making him stay home at night, not letting him use the car. He wasn't going to ruin his own Christmas vacation just because he had some dumb headaches and sometimes felt a little weird. Maybe after the holiday, if he was still feeling funny, he'd say something.

Not being able to read, concentrate, made school harder. He'd been an A student for so long that none of the teachers bothered him. No one had noticed. There were just three more days to get through. These last days before the holiday were never tough. Everybody was full of Christmas spirit and very little work got done. Except for this class. English. Mr. Grant. He was his homeroom teacher as well. Today they were discussing, as they had for the last week, *I Heard The Owl Call My Name*. Tom had read it a long time ago, so he wasn't in any danger here. If Grant asked him anything, he'd most likely be able to answer. But Grant hadn't bothered him for awhile now.

SOLA said books were evil.

There it was again! It gave him a chill. SOLA. What was SOLA? A person? If so, who? And why, every once in awhile, did the name pop into his head? And not just the name either. Sometimes it was a piece of philosophy or a statement. Like a moment ago. *Books were evil. SOLA said.* If SOLA said, then he must be a person. Why was Tom assuming it was a *he?* It made his head ache. He wondered if he should ask some of the other kids if they knew anybody named SOLA. *Books were evil.* That was ridiculous. Whoever SOLA was, if he thought books were evil, Tom didn't want anything to do with him. And he didn't want to think about him anymore either. It made him uncomfortable and restless.

He ran a finger under the crewneck of his purple sweater. It itched. He shifted in his bench-chair, the material of his jeans feeling tight across his thighs. When he turned his head to his left, he saw that Lisa Anderson was staring at him. She was one of the most popular girls in the senior class.

She smiled at him. A strange smile, eyes doing something weird, lashes flicking.

He smiled back.

She turned away.

Tom looked back down at his desk, studied the initials again. Lisa Anderson went steady with Mark Bickel, who was captain of the baseball team. He'd heard guys talking about her during gym class. They said she balled a lot and that Mark didn't know she'd spread it for anyone who wanted her. Tom hated it when they talked like that.

SOLA said he shouldn't listen.

Jesus! Again.

His head was pounding, vision blurring.

Would Lisa Anderson spread it for *him?*

He felt like vomiting.

Out of control. Thoughts. Actions. He was out of control and he was scared.

He reached into his pocket. The small knife Steven had given him for his birthday felt smooth in his hand. He could feel the green of the handle. Slowly, he pulled it out, hid it in his fist which rested on the desk as he stared at the blond hairs on his knuckles. Carefully, he brought fist and knife to his lap, his left hand joining his right. He leaned forward, mid-section against the edge of the desk. Not looking, he opened the knife, ran a finger across the blade, honed just yesterday to perfect sharpness. He couldn't feel the cut, but knew it was there; he knew that blood was burbling slowly up between pieces of sliced skin. He wiped the finger on his jeans, pressed down hard. Then he raised the open knife, still concealed in his large hand, to the top of the desk.

Very carefully, he shifted the position of the knife in his

hand so that his fist closed around the stem. The blade, sharp and shiny, protruded from his curled pinky. He was ready to do it. Goddamn.

Phil Grant was counting the hours until Old Hickory High rang the last bell before Christmas vacation. It wasn't that he disliked teaching or was bored by his English classes, although some of them could have had a little more juice. The thing was that in about sixty hours he'd be in New York City at the Plaza, tucked in a big double bed ramming the most beautiful girl in the world. Thinking about Sheila made it hard for him to concentrate on Margaret Craven's book, good as he felt it was. Get yourself into it, man.

Glancing around the room as Karen Winters droned on about symbolism, Phil's eyes rested on the Nash kid. What a life he must have! Phil remembered back to his senior year. A misfit. Big nose, glasses, kinky hair. Hair wasn't in style yet. But this Nash kid, blond, blue-eyed, smile wide as a mile, teeth perfect, white, good build. Jesus, he had the world by the balls.

But Phil had noticed something odd about him in the last few weeks, something he couldn't put his finger on. Probably having love problems. Some chick giving him the old heave-ho maybe. Nah, not him. He'd be the dumper. Aha! Right! You sure called it, Phil old man. Look at that. The Anderson snatch giving Nash the old bedroomy eyes. Oh, catch those flashing teeth. Let her have it, boy.

"Thank you, Karen," he said quickly, realizing she'd stopped talking. "Anyone else?"

Melissa Gillespie started talking and Phil nodded a few times before he let his eyes travel beyond her back to Nash. What was he doing now? Fooling around in his lap. Probably had a hard-on. Couldn't blame him. Phil had had a perpetual hard-on in high school. But he was making up for all those years of taking care of himself. Now his curly hair and moustache, his glasses, were in. Girls couldn't stay away. The Nash kid should get all he could now because his type might just go out of style. No, those WASPS never went out of style.

What now? What was he doing? Hunched over the desk. I'll be damned. Scratching something into the wood. What'd he have there, a knife? Two offenses. Zettick wanted teachers to report knife carriers and definitely to stop kids from carving up the desks. Phil couldn't see it. What the hell difference did it make? He wondered what Nash was carving. Probably "LISA."

When the bell rang and the room was empty, Phil slowly walked to the back of the room where Tom Nash had been sitting. He'd been able to note where the boy was carving. Right hand corner. Phil moved around to behind the desk.

"SOLA."

What the hell was SOLA?

He couldn't think of any girl with that last name. Probably initials for something. A secret organization? Some sex code? Shit. Kids were a pain in the ass. SOLA, for Christ's sake. Then, suddenly, he started to laugh. They *were* initials. What the hell else could it be?

SOLA....Suck out Lisa Anderson:

That Nash kid was a pisser.

5.

Kit left the early morning session with Dr. Clay, her therapist, feeling exhausted. It wasn't always that way. Sometimes the sessions were bombs. Nothing happening. Today, however, it blew her mind. But then it was one of *those* sessions. About *him*.

She crossed the Carrington campus, trees, bushes, lawn covered with snow, and walked down the shoveled path toward the cafeteria. The tips of her fingers tingled with cold. Only a few students were out this early and the ones she passed she didn't know. Probably from the undergraduate school.

In the cafeteria, she put her briefcase on a table near a window, took off gloves, parka and her red ski cap, the long, wavy blonde hair tumbling out, over her narrow shoulders.

At the cafeteria counter, she avoided the eyes of the boy

34

doling out the pancakes. She knew if she looked at him, he'd give her a lewd smile. It never failed. Sometimes she wished she were plain, even ugly, yet knew plenty of problems went with that as well.

Back at her table, she removed her breakfast from the tray. Orange juice, cold cereal, pancakes, sausage, coffee. Kit loved to eat, never gained an ounce. From her large shoulder bag she took a small jar. It contained pure maple syrup. She'd become convinced, in the last year, that refined sugar was a killer. Never used it. It was appalling to her that mental patients were stuffed with it, their diets in hospitals ignored. When she'd visited the State Hospital during a research trip, she watched even the sickest patients gobbling down desserts, dumping packet after packet of sugar into their coffee. When she'd said something to the staff doctor about it he'd looked at her as though *she* should be admitted. It ought to be studied. Maybe she'd explore it later on. For now, she warned people against it whenever she could, almost to the point of fanaticism. Friends laughed at her. Teachers shook their heads. Her lover, Noj, groaned a lot, but cut out sugar to please her.

She poured the syrup over the pancakes and replaced the empty jar in her bag. Must remember to refill it. Kit had breakfast in the cafeteria twice a week after her sessions with Dr. Clay and always had pancakes. True passion.

Kit's mind darted back to her session. How she hated dealing with her father. Had to, though. Funny the things one remembered from childhood. Some were etched on the brain forever; others, even important events, forgotten like old clothes. Not because of blocking, either. But she remembered the lying incident because it was important, Dr. Clay said.

She'd been in the first grade. That awful year when he made her mother walk her back and forth to school. All the kids made fun of her. She tried to ignore them, pretended to herself that she was a special princess and her mother a bodyguard. Still, when the kids called her "sissy" and "baby," it didn't help much. It wasn't until years later that she learned how her mother hated doing it, fought him on repeating it in her second year. She'd assumed, during that first year, that Mother went along with the idea. Resented them both.

Cole had never paid too much attention to Kit, even though she was an only child until she was seven. Unless, of course, she got sick. Then he was there, hovering around, touching her head, ministering, feeding her soups, bringing her presents. She'd been sick a lot during her grammar school years. They'd never caught on. Sometimes, if no one was in the room when her temperature was being taken, she'd remove the thermometer from her mouth, put it against a hot light bulb until it went up a degree or two, stick it back in her mouth. She had to be careful because once or twice she left it on the bulb too long and it rose above one hundred and six degrees. She quickly shook it down before Cole came back in the room. But all that was later, when she was nine, ten, eleven.

During her sixth year she hadn't quite caught on to the "sick" act and needed something to gain his attention. At first the lies were small, reasonable.

At four-thirty she would come in from playing, restlessly watch her television programs until five-thirty, then sit at the window waiting for him.

When he drove in, always putting the car in the garage, Kit would run to the back door, eager for him, having rehearsed her story many times by then. He would kiss her forehead, pat her hair. Patiently, she waited while he changed clothes, made a drink and settled into his easy chair in the living room. They didn't have a den in that house.

She sat at his feet on a green and brown hassock, looking up into eyes she could never fathom. Still, she swore that when she grew up they would be married.

She waited for him to take the first sip of his drink, an unspoken signal for her to begin.

"Today in school," she started, "we were all sitting in our seats, listening to Mrs. Fisher read us a story."

"What story?"

"The Wind in the Willows." She wondered if he knew this story, waited to see what he'd say.

"Go on."

"So, we were listening." For a moment, she forgot where she was going.

"And?"

"Oh, and then there was this funny noise in the back of the room."

He nodded.

"So we all turned around."

"At the same time?"

She was confused, giggled, shrugged. "I don't know."

"Go on." He sipped his drink.

"So we turned around and there was Herbie Brockleman dropping his pens and pencils, one at a time, on the floor."

"Why?"

"Huh?"

"Why was he dropping them on the floor?"

"Because he's bad."

"I see."

"Mrs. Fisher said," and here Kit did her best imitation of a grown up, "'Herbie Brockleman stop that.' And Herbie said, 'I don't want to.'"

"Yes?"

"Well," she said, rising and putting her hands on her hips, now going for the big finish, "You just stop that right now, Herbie Brockleman."

"Did she call him Herbie or Herbert?"

"Herbie," she said, wondering why he'd asked.

"Go on."

She sat down. "Well, he wouldn't stop and wouldn't stop. He just kept throwing these pencils on the floor."

"Herbie has a lot of pencils," he said flatly.

"Yes. So, anyways, Mrs. Fisher finally marched over to him and pulled him out of his seat and sent him down to the principal."

"And?"

"And that was that," she said, smiling.

"I see. Well, that was quite a story. Thank you for telling me." He picked up his paper and began to read.

She always felt slightly depressed after these stories, lies. But she'd had his attention for a little while, so it was worth it. As the days and weeks went on, she found that to hold his interest she had to make the stories a little more elaborate each time until finally, about a month or so after she'd begun this little ritual with him, she told her last Herbie Brockleman story.

"... and then Herbie took out this pen knife, blue and silver, and he snapped it open. The blade was at least a foot long. George Mercadante's eyes got real big and he started shaking all over."

"And?"

"And then Herbie jumped at him and stuck the knife in George's chest." She squeezed her eyes shut, shook her head with horror and just for a moment wondered if she was going too far. But she went on. "There was blood all over and George fell on the ground. Then Herbie stabbed him again and again.

37

Then Mr. Driscoll came running onto the playground and he pulled Herbie off George. Then the ambulance came and took George away and the police came and took Herbie away." She sighed, tired out. It had been a long story. She looked at her father, waiting for his reaction. Surely he'd want to discuss this one further. It was the best story she'd ever told.

He stared at her, a muscle jumping in his cheek. His eyes narrowed and his lips pressed together in a tight line. Then he spoke, voice icy. "You are a liar. Day after day you've been telling me these goddamned lies. Do you think I'm a fool?"

She stared at him, immobilized, color rushing to her cheeks.

"Liar!" he repeated.

Anne ran in from the kitchen. "What's going on?"

"She's a goddamned liar," he said, pointing a finger at Kit.

"Cole, please."

"Go to your room," he ordered Kit.

She burst into tears, ran hard into her mother's legs, clutching.

Anne took Kit into the kitchen, consoled her, but told her it was wrong to lie.

Later that night, Kit heard her parents arguing.

"You don't speak to a child that way," Anne said.

"Why not?"

"Because she's just a child."

"She lied like a trooper."

"Cole, she's six years old."

"She's a liar."

"All right, she lied. But we should find out why, talk to her about it."

"I hate liars," he said.

"Doesn't it make any difference to you that she's a baby?"

"She's a liar."

That naturally ended Kit's private times with Cole in the evening. The next time he paid her any attention was six months later when she got the mumps.

Kit finished her bowl of cereal. The pancakes sat on her stomach in a lump. Shouldn't think about this stuff when she was eating. She tried washing away the leaden feeling with a swallow of coffee.

Dr. Clay said Cole didn't know how to differentiate between children and adults. They were all the same to him. Aliens. It was horrible to think you were an alien to your father. And infuriating to think she'd spent all her life trying

38

to win him with never a hope in the world of succeeding. If she'd known that earlier, would she have stopped trying? Probably not. What child would believe that nothing they did would *really* matter to their father?

Kit finished her coffee and looked at her watch. Time for her first class. Statistics. She hated it. Sometimes she wondered if she liked anything about this field. But she'd yet to meet anyone who *liked* statistics.

As she left the cafeteria and headed toward the Follett Building, she wondered if she'd really ever give up trying to win her father, real or symbolic?

Maybe in time.

With help.

6.

Tom tore the wrapper from a Clark bar and took a large bite. It was after lunch and he and Jennifer walked through the halls holding hands.

Jennifer was talking on and on; Christmas vacation, parties, skiing. She was a pretty girl with long dark hair, almond eyes, small nose. They'd been going steady for more than a year. He'd had other girls before her; seemed he'd always had a girl since the fifth grade. But Jennifer was the first girl he'd ever made love with.

Suddenly he thought: SOLA hates Jennifer.

The same shock he'd experienced before rippled through him. Then, while she talked on, he let his mind go with the thought. Thoughts. *Prettiness is unimportant. Useless. In the new world, looks will be meaningless. SOLA is interested only in brains. Did Jennifer have brains? Not many. She was frivolous. Superficial.*

Then the thoughts stopped. He noticed he wasn't quite as

39

frightened by them as he had been. More curious. What, for instance, was the *new world?*

"You're not listening to me, are you?" Jennifer said, squeezing his hand.

"Sure I am." He chewed his candy bar, tried to appear relaxed.

"What did I just say?" She stopped walking, looked at him. He dropped her hand. "Don't start."

"I don't know what's wrong with you lately."

His blue eyes narrowed. "What's that mean?"

"Just what I said. You've been acting so peculiar lately. Like you're spaced or something. It's a real drag."

"So don't see me anymore."

"Oh, stop. God, every time there's any...you just can't stand conflict, can you?"

"I don't know what you're talking about." He wanted to know what she'd meant by 'peculiar.'

"I hate blue eyes. I have no idea what you're thinking."

He took a chance. "What do you mean, 'peculiar'?"

"I don't know."

"Yes, you do." He took her hand again, pressed hard. He had to know, but he didn't want to alarm her. "C'mon."

"Sometimes you look at me in a funny way. Lately." She shook her head as if to dismiss something unpleasant.

"How funny?" He finished the candy bar, crumpled the wrapper, held it.

"You get a weird look on your face. Sometimes I feel I don't even know you." She began walking again, didn't want to look at him anymore.

They passed a large green trash can and he flipped his wrapper inside. He had no idea how to respond to Jennifer, so he said nothing.

Softly, she said, "Is something wrong, Tom? Something to do with me?" Maybe he didn't love her any more, didn't know how to tell her.

"No."

She stopped again, faced him, took his other hand. "Do you still love me?"

He smiled. "Sure." Wondered if he did. He couldn't feel love right now.

"Not very reassuring."

"I love you," he whispered, trying to remember how to make it sound right.

"I'd just die without you."

Die, he thought impassively.

The bell rang to begin classes.

"Would you die without me?" she asked.

"Jennifer," he said, embarrassed at the excess of this question.

"Boys are different, I guess. My mother says they don't care the same way."

"Better get to class."

"Will I see you later?"

"'Course." He leaned down, kissed her quickly.

He watched as she walked along the corridor away from him, then turned in the opposite direction toward his locker. On the way he passed a poster advertising a sleigh riding contest. He'd passed it dozens of times in the last weeks, but now it made him remember his first sled. His mouth twitched and he shook his head.

She was a beauty. A Red Flyer. He was seven and he'd gotten it for Christmas from Nana and Pop Nash. It had been a real funny winter that year. No snow. He waited all through vacation, but nothing happened. Then the second week of school, after the holiday, it started snowing during the night—heavy, thick. All the kids knew that when it stopped they'd be taking out their sleds and going down Hartman's Hill, the street the Nashes lived on then. Tom couldn't wait.

The school bus was late and then it crawled along at a snail's pace. Finally he got home, raced up the hill and, in the house, changed his clothes for play. As he was getting the sled from the garage, his mother appeared in the doorway.

"Tom, darling, come inside a minute, will you?"

"Oh, Mom." Why did grown ups always want you when there was something important to do?

"Please dear, I have to talk with you. It'll just take a minute."

"Okay." Reluctantly he put down his sled, walked into the house.

Anne sat on a chair so she was on a level with him, pushed back the hood of his snowsuit.

Why was she acting so funny. "What?" he prodded her.

"Tom, it's about.... Oh, Lord." She shook her head from side to side, started again. "It's about sleigh riding."

He grinned thinking of it. "It's neat snow for it. All the kids are coming over here to go down *our* hill."

"Are you planning to go *all* the way down, Tom?"

"Huh?"

"All the way down?"

"Well, sure, a course. We'll turn in at the bottom, into the O'Briens' driveway."

"That's too far down, dear. Daddy wants you to go no further than the Barnetts'."

He was stunned. The Barnetts' drive was *less* than halfway down the big hill. "Whattayou mean?" he cried.

She touched his cheek.

He pulled back, mouth pursing. "What, Mom?"

"Look, darling, that's a nice long ride." There was no conviction in her voice.

"It's no ride at all." His face flushed with anger. "I'm goin' down to the O'Briens'."

"No, Tom. You can't. I'm sorry, really I am. It's either turning in at the Barnetts' or nothing."

"But all the other kids...."

"I know," she said gently, kindly, "I know. But it's what Daddy wants."

"What do you want?"

It was a long time before she answered, and when she did she looked away from Tom. "I want the same thing."

"I hate you," he yelled, running from the house. "I hate you both."

He took his Red Flyer from the garage out into the backyard and flung it as hard and as far as he could. It landed up-ended, the front of its new red runners pointing skyward. It stayed that way all winter long. Rusting.

At his locker, Tom wondered what ever happened to the sled. Had they taken it with them when they moved to the new house a year later? Couldn't remember.

Taking his books for his next class from his locker, he realized it was Kit he had to thank for getting as many liberties as he had. His father's nuttiness on personal safety almost made them all nuts. The locker clanged shut. Sometimes he wondered why his mother didn't take more of a stand. Was she afraid of him?

Then he thought, *Doesn't matter, all be over soon.*

As he walked to class, his mind turned back to Jennifer. She'd seen something in him, something weird, she said.

SOLA hates Jennifer.

He smiled.

His next thought seemed perfectly natural. Didn't frighten him at all.

42

Jennifer Wheeler had to die.
SOLA will be proud.

7.

Chapter One was Anne's favorite store in Old Hickory. And
Finch Bond, the owner, was one of her favorite people. Finch
was busy with a particularly annoying customer, so Anne
browsed through the *New Fiction Hardcover* section although
she'd bought a book last week, and her Christmas book buying was done. Cole would make a scene if she bought another
so soon. Even when she spaced her purchases, in what she
considered a frugal way, he always had to comment. *I'll never
know why I had to marry an egghead. Get a load of the big
intellectual.* It was absurd. There was nothing intellectual in
her choices. She read popular novels, suspense. Some of the
new women writers—she wanted to keep up with Kit—and
an occasional non-fiction title.

But any book was a threat to Cole. He simply didn't read.
Except for the newspaper and a few magazines. Reading had
always been important to Anne, to the whole Clifford family.
The highlight of any Christmas or birthday was new books.
Anne had tried to make that true with her own children and
sometimes it was a fight.

"Why the hell do you want to load the boy up with these
goddamn books?" Cole would ask.

"There's nothing wrong with reading. You act like it's
subversive or something."

"Waste of time reading novels. You want them to read at
least give them something they can learn from."

"That's not the point."

"Crap."

But in the end she'd had her way. Only Steven resisted.

43

And even he read an occasional adventure story. Steven said he was anxious about starting books because he feared they might be boring. She'd tried to assure him that it was all right not to finish a book if you didn't like it, but Steven was compulsive about finishing what he started. Admirable in most cases.

Anne felt a ping of excitement as her eye caugh the blue and gold jacket of a book she'd been waiting for. She picked it up, ran her hand over the lustrous cover. It felt good. Opening the book she fanned the pages, taking them in as though through osmosis. She turned to the inside front jacket. Ten dollars and ninety five cents! Impossible. Cole would make an incredible scene. Why had books become so damn expensive? Well, she'd just have to get this one from the library or wait until it came out in paperback. After reading the first page, savoring each sentence, she closed the book, caressed the jacket once more, put it back in its place.

She'd buy a new paperback to compensate. Cole wouldn't notice. She took paperbacks out of her weekly food allowance.

Turning away from the hardcover fiction, she went to the paperback section. Here fiction and non-fiction were mixed together. Her attention was caught by a book on alcoholism she'd not seen before.

Alcoholism: Causes and Cures.

Anne smiled, shook her head. They were still writing about cures. When would they learn? She picked up the book, flipped its pages seeing nothing. On the back cover were various quotes. As she read them, her mind drifted.

Maximillian Clifford had been a drunk all his life. Died a drunk. Probably born a drunk. At least, he'd been a nice drunk. Most of the time.

But, of course, it had taken its toll on his wife, children. It always did. Her mother's behavior affecting them just as much. She remembered the nights at the dinner table, Dorothy Clifford pretending they were Ozzie and Harriet or some damn thing.

"And how was your day at school, Ross?"

Ross, the oldest, looking at his plate, chewing his food, then answering, playing his mother's game.

"Good, Mom. Got a ninety-five in Algebra."

"Well, twenty-three skiddoo!" Daddy, hand clutched around a large coffee mug. As though they didn't know what was really in it.

44

"Wonderful, darling," Dorothy said, pretending Max wasn't there, or that his comment had been appropriate.

Anne always tried to emulate her mother, thinking she was brave and wise. Unlike Liz, her younger sister, who hated her mother for it.

"Why doesn't she throw the bum out?" Liz would say to Anne.

"Because she loves him," Anne would answer. "She's weak, that's all."

Anne couldn't see it that way. Not then.

Walter, the baby, five years younger than Anne, never said anything. No one ever knew what he was feeling. But then who knew what any Clifford was *really* feeling? Except maybe for Liz. Not that either parent ever instructed them not to show their true feelings. What parent ever did that? But it was there, implicit in every word, gesture. Show a smiling face to the world, even to each other. What's the point in making things worse? And if we *act* like everything's all right, maybe it will be. Maybe the bad things will just go away. And Anne bought it.

"So, big shot," Max said, his normally fine features screwed over to one side, eyelids drooping, "tell us all about your hotshot ninety-five." Gulping from the coffee mug.

Dorothy said, "Yes, dear, tell us." Father Knows Best.

Ross, lock of hair falling in his eyes, unable to look up, said, "There's nothing to tell. I mean, there's no story. Got a ninety-five, that's all."

"You bet your bottom dollar there's nothing to tell," Max said slamming a small fist on the table. "Boring as hell."

"Oh, Christ," Liz said, jumping up, chair falling backwards. "It just makes me sick."

Anne reached out a hand, trying to stop her from leaving.

"You're such a namby-pamby, Anne. God." Liz left the dining room, managing to slam into things as she went, creating a noise no one could ignore.

"Well, what the hell's the matter with her?" Max asked. Hurt.

"Now, dear, don't pay any attention to her. It's just growing pains."

God Almighty. The lies. None of the other children dared look at each other for fear of acknowledging the subterfuge, of becoming allies, facing feelings.

Max rose from the table, his short, frail frame swaying as though he were going to fall any moment. But he never did

45

in those years. Later. "Well, she's got some helluva nerve." Lifting the mug to his lips, draining it. Using Liz's departure as an excuse to go get more. "That girl needs a good talking to."

"Now, dear."

"Don't *dear* me, I'm her father, ya know."

Nobody watched as he left the room. Nobody tried to stop him, knowing he had no intention of talking to Liz. Filling his mug his only aim.

"Don't be angry with your father. He's sick. We mustn't ever get angry with him; he can't help it." Dorothy always said the same thing after one of Max's scenes.

Don't ever be angry.

That was it all right, all right. Anne had learned the lesson well. Anger was hard for her. Sometimes impossible. And if it did come through, she suffered. Guilt.

But Dorothy had one part of it right even if she didn't really know it. He *was* sick. Alcoholism was a disease. Anne learned that over the years, through the countless books, articles, papers she read.

Poor Dad. He'd try not to drink. Once went as long as two years. What heaven life had been then. But he couldn't keep it up. Something always got to him, they never knew what. Now she understood that that was the way alcoholism worked. He didn't *need* anything real to pick up a drink. He was an alcoholic; any old thing would do. If only he'd been able to get into the AA program. Tried one meeting. Said, "Oh boy, not for this guy. Nice people, Cookie, but you and I couldn't take them for very long. Know what I mean?" A wink of the soft blue eye.

Oh, how she loved him. Drunk or sober.

At the end, he asked only for her, his favorite.

He lay, small and yellow, in his hospital bed, tubes sticking out from everywhere while his liver crumbled. They'd warned him, the doctors. But you can't scare an alcoholic. Not a good dedicated one like Max Clifford.

She held his bony hand in hers. He looked up, eyes watery, voice barely a whisper. "You're my goody-girl," he said.

She was thirty-three then, with four children. "Don't talk, Daddy."

He tried to wave his other hand, as if to say, what's the difference? Couldn't lift it. "Always been my favorite," he whispered. He motioned with his head for her to come closer, put her ear next to his mouth. "You mad at your dad?"

46

"No, of course not." She squeezed his hand, careful not to hurt him.

"Could you do me a favor, Cookie?"

"Anything, Daddy." She was trying not to cry, not to show her feelings. Of course.

"Good girl. Do ya think you could get me a little drink?"

She sprung back, away from him as though he'd whispered an obscenity. Good Lord! She couldn't believe she'd heard correctly, almost started to ask him to repeat, then knew she'd heard absolutely right. "Oh, Daddy," she said.

"Just one," he whispered, looking old, desperate, pathetic. *Just one.* The alcoholic credo.

She quickly decided she'd get him his drink. After all, what difference did it make? If that's what he wanted, then he should have it. She told him she'd get him one.

He smiled up at her, the gaunt face looking like it might crack. "Ah, Cookie, I knew ya would."

When she came back with the pint of whiskey, he was dead. It was only later that she realized his call for her wasn't because he loved her so much, wanted to see her one more time. No, it was because she was the softy and he knew he could get what he wanted from her. Selfish to the end.

It hurt, but it didn't make her angry. Of course not.

Anne put the paperback in the rack. This book wasn't going to tell her anything new. She was interested because there was a fifty percent chance that the children of alcoholics would be alcoholics. Only Liz had had the disease. So ironic that she should be the one. But she was sober, and in AA six years now.

And she worried for her own children. There was a good chance any of them could have the disease. Tom! Was that it? Was he drinking? But wouldn't she smell it? Wouldn't it be clear? Or maybe it was other drugs? But he'd never seemed the type. She'd always thought Steven would be the likely candidate. Still, it was a possibility.

The bells on the bookstore door jingled. The annoying customer had left.

Finch rolled her eyes as Anne approached the desk.

"Jesus," she said, "what a pain in my arse! That bitch sticks it to me at least once a week. She buys a Harold Robbins book, reads it, then returns it 'cause it's too dirty. Ganef. Can ya believe it? I swear t' Christ, Annie, I'm gettin' out of this business."

"Sure you are," Anne said, smiling. How many times had she heard that?

Finch squinted at her, thick black eyebrows joining. "What's up, little gal? Ya look beat or somethin'."

Anne marveled at the way Finch read her. Always had. They'd been friends since the day Finch opened the shop, ten years before. It wasn't just a love of books that had made them close, although that was a definite part of it, but a mutual interest in the community and a caring about things as remote as the killing of baby seals in Canada. And they respected and cared for one another.

They shared things. Secrets, fears, hopes. Why hadn't she told Finch about Jim?

"Take a seat." Finch gestured toward the bentwood rocker in front of the counter. "Want a cup of java?"

"All right."

"Why is it when somebody indicates trouble, my tendency is to offer a cup a coffee like it's some magic elixir or something? Jesus, you'd think I'd sprung fullgrown out of a soap opera."

"I guess hot coffee is comforting."

"Guess so." She handed Anne a cup. One sugar. No milk. "So what's the scoop, kid?" She ran her thick hand through one side of her coarse gray hair.

Anne smiled, knowing Finch's way of talking, was her way of insulating herself against locals. Finch was Jewish, and the locals didn't like Jews. If Old Hickory hadn't been a tourist town, Finch would have closed her doors long ago. Her return to the speech of her native Bronx was a way of giving the locals the finger. With Anne, she slipped in and out of it.

Anne said, "Oh, I don't know, Finch. Do I look that tense?"

"Just a bissel."

Anne looked at her quizzically.

"A little," she translated. "Give."

Anne hesitated. She wanted to ask about Finch's boys when they were Tom's age, but it always made her uncomfortable to bring them up because of Bob, even though Finch assured her she didn't mind talking about him. After all it was almost twelve years now. Bob had been killed in an automobile accident. Finch was driving. Wasn't her fault, but Ray, her husband, never forgave her. They'd finally separated four years ago.

"When your kids were growing up, did you ever notice...I mean, was there ever a time when you felt a drastic change?"

48

"Day in, day out. Sometimes hour in, hour out."

"No, that's not what I mean. I know that phenomenon. One day they want to be a surgeon, the next a jockey. That's not what I'm talking about."

"So spell it out."

"It's Tom."

The bookseller shifted in her leather chair. Tom Nash was one of her pets. One of the few young people who read real books. She nodded, indicating that Anne should go on.

Anne laughed, uneasy. "It's probably nothing."

"Probably. But let's hear it anyway." She lit a Nat Sherman, brown.

As though she were reading braille, Anne explored her pretty, delicate face with fingertips. She cupped her nose with both hands, leaning her brow against the prayerful forefingers. Surrendering to her thoughts, she dropped her hands to her lap.

"I don't know what it is, that's the trouble. If only I could put my fingers on something, be more specific."

"You mean he hasn't done anything...well, odd, peculiar?"

"Not really."

"Oi, vey, how I hate *not really*. What the hell does *not really* mean? He has or he hasn't." A long stream of smoke curled between them.

"I can't help it...*not really* is what I mean. There've been no big acts. That's just the point. I know this sounds silly but it's...a look, his smile maybe. Something's changed, Finch. I know kids go through stages, God knows I had a helluva time with Kit for a while, but there's something different about this."

Finch took a gulp of coffee and wondered if Anne was imagining this to take the focus off herself. Anne didn't know it, but Finch knew about her and Jim O'Neill. For the thousandth time, Finch wondered if she should mention it.

"Do I sound crazy?" Anne asked.

"Crazy? Nope. But I was just wonderin'...is there somethin'...anythin' else making you anxious?"

Anne was startled. Did Finch know? Did other people? Anne had wondered. Even though Jim lived thirty miles away, it was all small town stuff. She'd wanted to tell Finch, share it. Sometimes it became an awful burden. She needed a friend who'd understand. Yet something stopped her. She trusted Finch. Still, you never know. If she was ever going to tell her, this was the time.

"No, nothing," Anne said, deciding against it again.

Finch accepted the answer. It was Anne's right to confide in her or not. But Anne's hazel eyes looked so sad, worn. Anne Nash wasn't a happy woman, although she had everything that was supposed to make a woman happy.

So much for that myth.

No news to her.

Anne bowed her head slightly, her honey hair falling into sheets eclipsing her oval face.

Finch reached out, touched her friend's hand. "Anne, what is it? What is it, really?" One more try.

Her armor of hair still protecting her, Anne said, "I feel like I don't know him anymore. I've always been so close to Tom. I thought we had something special going." She raised her head, looked at Finch, begged with her wistful eyes for an answer.

Finch gave up the ghost of getting the Jim O'Neill story and squeezed Anne's hand, searched within for some answer, some comfort. Remembering, she smiled, a mesh of wrinkles forming at the corners of her eyes. "Listen, kid, when Billy was Tom's age, I thought I'd die from the loss of him. I mean, he was there all right, in body, but he might as well not have been for all the time of day he gave me. He didn't need his Mommy! But now we're as close as two peas in a pod."

"I know that stage. I had it with Kit. I have it with Sara."

"I'm not talkin' about active hate. Indifference is what it is. Nothin' hoits woise, kid."

Anne closed her eyes, head back, sighing. "I wish it were indifference. That's not it."

Finch felt helpless. "What then?"

Anne leaned forward, trying for some answer, some better explanation. "It occurred to me a little while ago that maybe he was taking drugs. I'd know, I realized, if he were drinking. But I don't think it's that."

"Tom taking drugs? Never."

"When he looks at me, it's like he's not there. But not always. It seems to come and go."

"Sounds like he's preoccupied, honey."

"Damn! I wish I could be more specific. It's more than preoccupation. I know that look."

"Is he mad about somethin'?"

"I know," she said, getting a clear image for a moment. "Sometimes when he looks at me his eyes are . . . they're cold." She shuddered, inwardly remembering.

Finch couldn't imagine Tom Nash with cold eyes. That was one of the special things about the boy. His warmth. And part of that came from his eyes. "Really? Has Cole noticed it, too?"

Anne looked directly at Finch, cocked her head to one side, as if to say: *are you kidding?* She'd confided in Finch about Cole.

"Right. So how about talkin' to the kid himself? Ask him if he's got somethin' on his mind? 'Course knowin' kids, he probably won't give with any info...but at least he'll know you cared, noticed. Ya know?"

"I suppose. Oh, Finch, I guess you're right, he's just going through his not needing mother stage and I can't stand it. Sara's hostility is hard enough to take."

Finch stubbed out the thin cigarette. "Yeah, it's rough. But you know it'll pass. Sara, too. It can never be as bad as it was with Kit 'cause you know the outcome. It's like losin' a first love, ya know? Ya think you'll die and then ya find out ya don't. It can never hurt like that again, no matter what." She tried looking straight into Anne's eyes, giving her one last chance.

Ah, but it can, Anne thought. "I'll try and talk to him."

Finch said, "I haven't been one goddamn bit of help, have I?" She pulled at a long earlobe.

"Of course you have. It's just good to get it off my chest. I needed to tell someone.... You're the only one I'd feel comfortable telling."

And yet she won't tell me about O'Neill. Funny. "I'm glad you trust me, Anne. I'd never betray you."

"I know."

There was a moment between them when Anne thought she'd tell and Finch thought she'd ask. Then it passed. They were both relieved. In a way.

"I may be a flop at advice, but I'm trustworthy." Finch grinned, her small even teeth advertisement white.

"You're not a flop at anything."

"Would that that were true, kid."

The image of Bob's ruined and lifeless body turned the corners of Finch's mouth downward.

Anne knew her friend well enough to know what she was thinking. She touched her shoulder. "Don't do that to yourself."

"Yeah, sure." She rose heavily, blinked away tears, images, walked behind the counter.

How wise Finch had been, Anne thought, to open the store when she did. Get her mind off the death of her child. Surely the worst pain of all. How did people live through it? Running a comb through her shoulder length hair, she said, "I'd better get to Verna's or I'll miss my appointment. You know how touchy she is."

Finch patted her mannish haircut. "Haven't seen her in years. And can't say that I miss her. My hair may not be the most *au courant* but it beats listenin' to Vera stick it to everybody in town."

Laughing, Anne put her cup on the counter. "Thanks for the java."

Finch nodded. "The new Crawford book is in, the one you've been waitin' for."

"I saw it." She shrugged, resigned. "I can't. Cole would kill me."

"Cheap bastard."

"You got it."

Finch reached under the counter and pulled out a copy of the book. "Here. Take the jacket off and don't bend the spine too much. No one'll ever know."

"Oh, Finch, I couldn't."

"'Course ya could. I do it all the time. You've bought books I've read and ya never knew. Take it. Don't spill any booze or plum pudding on it. That's all I ask." She pushed the book against Anne's breasts. "Take it...don't be a dope."

Anne wrapped a hand around the book. "Thanks."

Finch nodded.

In the car, Anne looked down at the book on the seat beside her. Finch's generosity touched her deeply. Even if she hadn't been such a good customer, hadn't spent a ton for Christmas books already, she knew Finch would have lent it to her. She was a damned good friend.

Anne turned the key, stepped on the gas. When Christmas was over, when everything died down again, she was definitely going to tell Finch about Jim. After all, if things went according to schedule, she and Jim would be lovers in the true sense of the word. For a moment, she imagined what it would be like to make love with him, to go beyond the kisses that touched her center, made her weak. Lord, she'd need to talk to someone more than ever once they'd crossed that line.

She'd never be able to carry *that* alone.

Too much.

Finch was elected.

8.

After the last bell, Jennifer Wheeler walked to her locker, deposited some books, took out others, put on her red and yellow parka, scarf, red woolen hat, hair tucked up under it, and walked down the long back hallway to the rear entrance to wait for Tom. They would, as usual, hitch a ride with one of their friends and go into town to The Queen of Sheba where they'd hang around and have Cokes.

Her clothing was beginning to make her warm after waiting for five minutes. Then she spied Tom ambling down the hall toward her as though he were on his way to nowhere. She could have killed him. He was becoming so annoying lately. Sometimes she wondered if it was worth it. This relationship. Next year they'd both go to college and she was smart enough to know that that would be that. But it was important to have a boyfriend now for dances, parties. Not that there weren't at least three or four other boys who'd be glad to take Tom's place. But it was such a pain to start all over again with someone. And for eight months tops, if you counted the summer.

Tom, his plaid scarf wrapped around his face so that his mouth and nose were covered, gave Jennifer a salute and opened the door.

She glanced at him, irritated. Outside, they walked to Michael Schultz's Ford Galaxy. Super car. Low to the ground, a purple and silver stripe down each side. Michael, his girl Jane, and four other kids were in the car waiting. Jennifer sat on Tom's lap in the back.

"Get a load of 'The Cheetah'," Michael said, referring to Tom. "What are you supposed to be, the 'Masked Maniac'?"

Michael called Tom "The Cheetah" because he said Tom was the fastest living mammal.

Michael was Tom's best friend.

Tom smiled at Michael with his eyes, acknowledging the "Masked Maniac" joke.

Michael gunned the car, but moved slowly because of the snow. It took a long time to drive down Ferry Street. It seemed like everybody was talking at once. The din hurt Tom's ears.

Jennifer pulled at his scarf. He jerked out of her reach.

"What's wrong with you, Tom? I want to talk to you. Take that humungus scarf off. You're really tacky. I hate you." She shifted her body and stared out the window, trying desperately not to look sulky. Trying to look indifferent, sophisticated.

Tom stared straight ahead, his eyes resting on the back of Jane's red hair. He loathed redheads. Especially redheads with freckles. Like Jane. They had a peculiar freckle smell; nothing that he could describe. He wished that his eyes were guns, that he could shoot bullets from them. Two small ones right in the back of Jane's head.

Funny, he thought, I used to like her.

For a moment, he wondered what had changed, then forgot what he'd been wondering.

At The Queen of Sheba, all eight of them piled uncomfortably into a booth until the waitress said it was unlawful, as she did at least four times a week. Then they broke up, four and four, into two booths.

Jennifer and Tom sat with Michael and Jane. They talked about basketball, the Christmas dance Saturday night, the parties before and after, Pat Staten's New Year's party, gossip about various friends and enemies.

Tom was quiet.

When Michael and Jane left the booth to sit with some other friends, Jennifer leaned her chin in her palm and asked Tom what was wrong.

"Why do you keep asking me that?"

"Well, for one thing," she said, lowering her voice, "we haven't done it for two-and-a-half weeks."

"So?"

"So that's not like you." She thought that if they did it now, under the present circumstances, she might at least be

54

able to enjoy it. After all, you couldn't get pregnant when you already *were* pregnant.

He shrugged, crunched some ice on the right side of his mouth; he couldn't do it on the left.

"Stop that," she said, wincing, squeezing shut her eyes.

"Sorry."

For a moment, she toyed with the idea of telling Tom. She might enjoy the look of shock that would come over his face. On the other hand, he was acting so odd lately, so unlike himself, who could say how he might react. "Don't you want to do it any more?"

"It's not right," he said.

She almost laughed out loud. "Are you kidding?"

"No."

"Well, since when? Since when isn't it right?" She ought to tell him, the nerd. But if he was into this number, she was surer than ever that he'd make a fuss about her having an abortion and want to marry her or some wimpy thing like that.

"It's wrong," he said shielding his eyes from the light.

"Why are you squinting like that?"

"The light hurts my eyes."

She'd noticed him doing that before, meant to ask him about it. "Have you seen an eye doctor?"

"No. After Christmas."

She nodded, returned to the conversation at hand. "So what's all this stuff about it being wrong, Tom? Huh?"

Suddenly, he put his head in his hands, began to cry. Jennifer didn't know what to do. She looked around to see if anyone was staring. No one was. She'd never seen him cry before except once in a movie when an animal had been killed. She reached across the table and touched his hand. He jumped.

"Tom," she said gently, "what is it?"

He stopped crying as suddenly as he'd started, pulled a handkerchief from his back pocket; wiped his eyes. When he looked at her, he was smiling.

"What is it? Please tell me."

"Forget it."

"Forget it? Listen, Tom, how can I forget it when you first tell me it's wrong to do it after we've been making it at least twice a week for the last eight months and then you just break out crying like that. I mean, honestly. I'm worried about you." And she was.

55

"We've been fooling ourselves, Jen. I know now it's been very wrong."

"Who says so?" she asked. "I mean, Tom, I know you don't believe in anything and...."

"Who says I don't?" There was a new light in his absent blue eyes.

Surprised, Jennifer said, "You did. I know your family's Presbyterian, but you told me it was a lot of shit. Remember?"

"Yes, I remember," he said softly.

"Well, then?"

"There are other things to believe in Jennifer. You'd be surprised."

"Don't tell me you're a Moonie or something."

He shook his head, the white gold hair shimmering, looking at her as if she were a poor pathetic creature who'd never be enlightened. He took her hand in both of his, smiling enigmatically. "Jennifer, don't worry about what it is I believe in. I wish I could share it with you, I really do. Maybe someday I'll be able to. But for now you'll simply have to trust me. Okay?"

"Okay," she said. But she'd never trusted him less. She wanted to pursue this, find out what he was talking about. But when Tom said he wasn't going to talk about something, he wasn't going to talk. Not that he was ever your big talker; her parents always said what a nice quiet boy he was. But she hated his silences. Especially when she wanted to know something.

He grabbed her wrist.

"You're hurting me."

"Sorry." He eased up, held on. "Sunday. The twenty-second."

"What about it?" He looked positively demented, she thought. Eyes all slitty and everything. Honestly, what was happening?

"I want to see you."

"We're going to the dance and parties the night before." Idly, she sipped at the last dregs of Tab. Watery now.

"I know. So what? What's that have to do with anything?"

"Well, I don't know. We'll be tired is all." It wasn't like him to seek a date this way, so far in advance. Dates with them were quite casual, last minute. "Anyway, it's a Sunday night."

"It's vacation." He started chewing on his unopened straw.

"Well, what's so important about Sunday night?"

56

"Nothing, forget it." He got up, went to the men's room.

Jennifer groaned. Now what? Sunday night she'd been planning to stay over at Jane's. The day after Christmas, they were going into Philadelphia to get Jennifer an abortion. The important details, like who was going to do it and where they were going to stay overnight, were all arranged but they still had lots to talk about. It wasn't every day you had an abortion. Honestly. But if he was going to sulk and make everything awful for Christmas if he didn't get his way, which he sometimes did, she'd stay over at Jane's on Monday instead.

When he came back to the table she told him. "If you really want to go out that much on Sunday night, okay."

At first she thought there was a peculiar look in his eyes when she said it. But then when he smiled that way, that special way he had, she was positive she'd imagined it.

9.

The snow was tapering off. Kit looked out the third story window and watched as the flakes grew smaller, lighter. It was still bleak outside and all the neighboring houses were dotted with lights even though it was three in the afternoon. She hoped this would be the last snow before she started for home on the twenty-third.

Her papers were spread out on the kitchen table, a cold half cup of coffee waiting to be replaced.

She lit the burner under the coffee. Noj was taking a nap. Crawling in bed beside him was becoming a more tempting idea each moment. The paper she had to read next was *Intrafamilial Environment of the Schizophrenic Patient: VI. The Transmission of Irrationality*. Who the hell cared? She did. But not at this moment.

Kit stood in the doorway of the bedroom. Noj was on his back, arms out and above his head. God, he was beautiful. He wouldn't like that, of course. Gingerly, she sat on the bed looking down at his face. His jaw was almost classically square. Though his eyes were closed, she'd looked into them enough to know they were the same soft brown as his hair. Leaning over she kissed his silky lips. He stirred, but didn't awaken.

The tan and black Blass comforter they'd bought together was tucked securely under his chin, nothing but his head showing. Kit knew he was naked underneath. She needed to feel his arms around her, to touch his warm skin, lose herself. She'd known for some time now about her addiction.

Sex with the one she loved was her drug of choice.

Alcohol was sloppy. Grass made her dopey. But during sex she could really lose herself. Let go, breakout, escape.

Ray Linzer had been the first. She'd dated many others before, touched, fondled, everything but intercourse. It was some dumb idea she had that if she didn't have intercourse she remained pure or something. But in her sophomore year, when she met Ray, who was a year older, he'd pointed out the fallacy in that. It was just semantics, he told her. And besides, pure for what?

Lovemaking with Ray had been pedestrian although at the time she didn't know that. At the time, it seemed quite wonderful, new and exciting. And, of course, she thought she was in love with him. Then, suddenly she didn't think so. There was no explaining it; it just stopped, went away, like melting snow. She didn't hate him, wasn't repelled by him; it simply faded, dried up, vanished. For months she tried to pretend it was still there, even faked her orgasms. When she couldn't pretend anymore, she told him it was over. He couldn't believe it, wouldn't accept it, hung on. Eventually, when nothing else would convince him, she told him she'd been faking for months. She hated to hurt him and he cried, but it worked. They split. He never spoke to her again. That was the hardest thing to accept. They'd spent two years together and Kit couldn't understand how someone could just walk out of your life like that, never looking back. After all, hadn't they been friends?

Sometimes, when she thought of the possibility of life without Noj, it sickened her. She asked him to promise that no matter what happened he'd always be her friend. He simply

58

smiled and said he wasn't going anywhere. But Kit knew how transient love could be.

There was no one special for awhile after Ray. All spring she'd thrown herself into her work and during the summer she only went out on an occasional date.

Then back at school in the fall, she'd met Larry Carruth, as opposite from Ray as possible. Kit couldn't help thinking she'd picked him to punish herself for sleeping with Ray. Larry wasn't a nice man. He was cold, self-involved. No matter what happened, what problems she had, all roads led back to him. He kept her always slightly off balance, insecure, made her wait for hours, broke dates, stood her up.

But then again, she never slept with him. That was her weapon. Larry had the reputation of having any woman he wanted and Kit, one of the most beautiful undergraduates at Carrington, was considered a prize. Everyone assumed they were sleeping together. Why wouldn't they be?

Larry tried everything with her, but she couldn't, wouldn't. Something inside her said sleeping with Larry would be terribly destructive. It was punishment enough just to be around him. He abused her in public, liked to make people think she was nothing but a sex object and a lousy lay at that. He knew she wouldn't reveal there was nothing sexual between them. If she'd tried to deflate him, lay him bare to cronies, friends, who would have believed her? Sour grapes, they'd have said. Kit Nash, beauty beyond belief, model-like, was a flop in bed. So she'd had to say Larry Carruth, cocksman, couldn't have her. Power and control. The whole thing was sick and Kit hated it. Probably as destructive as if she'd let him penetrate her.

She dropped him in May.

He pretended to drop her.

She let him.

It was the beginning of July before she felt whole again. Clean. Larry had made her feel tarnished. Amazing. She knew now if she'd actually had intercourse with him it would have been less sordid. It had been a disgusting, degrading affair.

On the fourth of July, at her parents' annual party, she met Doc Mancinelli. Or re-met. She'd known him for years. He was forty-two, an ex-football player, married, father of three, a friend of her parents and simply gorgeous. She couldn't believe she'd never noticed.

Male friends of her parents had flirted with her before,

but she never took them seriously. Never flirted back. But when Doc smiled as he handed her a gin and tonic, looking directly in her eyes, an electric shock sailed straight down the center of her body, frightening as well as exciting.

She'd become obsessed with him for days, imagining his mouth on hers, arms around her, more. But, she'd assumed his flirting with her had been idle. In town, a week later, she'd bumped into him in the drugstore. They said hello, stared at one another. He waited while she paid for her suntan lotion, walked out with her, took her arm and guided her to his car. It never occurred to her not to go with him. Neither cared who saw them, who talked.

Insanity.

In the car, they said nothing. Doc drove out along the highway for several miles, then pulled into a motel. Awash with excitement, she waited in the car while he registered.

He came back to the car, drove to the room.

Once inside he picked her up, carried her to the bed. Without a word, he undressed her, undressed himself. She experienced no apprehension, inhibition, shyness; she was completely relaxed, free.

Doc took her.

He devoured her with his mouth; she had never felt anything like it. One after another, tiny explosions rippled through her body. His hands seemed to be everywhere at once, fondling, stroking, probing her depths. She was mesmerized.

When he entered her, it was as if everything within her cascaded; whirling, turning, lights flashing, sounds of drums, the bleat of horns. Every cliché she'd ever heard or read she now experienced.

And when it was over, she wept.

He held her, crying too.

Even then, they didn't say much to each other. They acknowledged the danger and insanity of their situation and admitted to helplessness over it. Again they made love, this time slower and more gently. It was even better than the first time.

When they drove back to town, before he let her out, they made plans for their next rendezvous.

For the three days following, Kit thought of nothing but Doc and their lovemaking; completely obsessed. She pretended he was there, had conversations with him, made love with him. She had no desire to go out with friends, do anything. She just worked at her summer job and waited to be alone to fantasize until she would be with him again.

The next time was even more exciting than the first. Unbelievable. The summer became time alone *thinking* of Doc and sex or time *with* him and sex.

And everyone knew. But neither of them cared. They couldn't stop.

Near the end of the summer, Anne came to her room.

"There's no point in pretending I don't know about you and Doc Mancinelli, Kit. And there's no point in pretending that my heart isn't breaking. School starts in another two weeks? What are your plans?"

Kit was stunned. Even though she considered she and her mother good friends, they'd never had a conversation like this before. Kit couldn't deny the affair; she tried to forget her embarrassment, as though she and her mother talked this way every day.

"I'm going back, if that's what you mean."

"And what about Doc?"

She shrugged. "What about him?"

"Are you in love with him?"

Kit had never thought of Doc in those terms. Obsessed, yes. "Look, Mom, I know I have to go back to school and I know I have to get over him, so don't worry."

"Don't worry?" Anne said angrily. "You've got to be kidding. I've done nothing but worry all damn summer. Are you aware that everybody in town knows what's going on? And what do you think you've done to Barbara Mancinelli?"

"I haven't been able to think about her." Shame crept along her edges.

"Well, maybe you should. It's outrageous what you've done, Kit. That woman is...."

"Please don't, Mom. I wish it hadn't happened, but it did. It'll be over soon. I'm sorry. I couldn't help myself."

Anne looked at her daughter, shook her head. "One can always help one's self, Kit. At least be responsible for your actions."

"You don't understand."

"Of course not. Mothers never do."

They hadn't talked about it again. Ever.

At the end of that summer, she and Doc had gone their separate ways. It was agony getting over him.

In February, she met Noj.

61

Looking down at him, she touched the hair hanging over his high forehead.

She kissed his lips.

Noj opened his eyes, long lashes fluttering for a moment. "What's up?" he asked, putting a hand on her thigh.

For a second she felt guilty, having thought of Doc while she sat on the bed with him. Foolish. Useless. She dismissed it. "Good morning, Jon Hampton, sleeping prince." She kissed him, sweetly, friendly.

"What time is it?"

"After three."

He stroked her cheek with the back of his hand.

She took the hand with her own, kissed his knuckles, fingertips. He had beautiful hands for a man. Long fingers, delicate, sculptured. Her tongue flicked over his palm.

Noj squirmed. "You're asking for trouble."

"Am I?" She continued.

There was movement under the quilt, yet both his hands were in view. Kit knew Noj wanted her as much as she wanted him. She stood and began to unbutton her shirt, slowly, deliberately.

Noj watched.

The plaid shirt slipped back over her shoulders, down her arms, dropped to the floor. Her large breasts, nipples growing erect, heaved with her increased breathing. She unbuckled her belt, slid it out of its loops, snapping it in the process. It jointed the shirt. She unzipped her fly, inched her jeans over her small hips and ran her tongue over her lips as the jeans slowly fell lower and lower.

Noj smiled, noting the underpants she was wearing.

He'd given them to her as a joke. They were tan with blue lettering which said "ACTION ALLEY."

Catching his eye, smile, Kit looked down, realized. "Oh shit," she said.

Stepping out of her jeans, she fell across him as they both laughed.

Noj threw his arms around her, rolled over, laughter growing.

"You'll never make a proper stripper," he said between giggles.

"Well, not with you as an audience."

When their laughter subsided, they lay on their backs, Noj's arms tucked under her neck around her shoulders. The

62

quilt was thrown back and Kit saw that Noj was no longer ready. "Laughter's a killer," she said.

"Not permanently." Reaching over he peeled down the offending underpants and ran his hand over her blonde, soft hair.

She shuddered, leaned into him, found his lips, tongue. Their legs intertwined, chests touching. She felt Noj growing hard as he pressed against her belly.

In a few moments, she was transported, oblivious, absent. Her desired state.

10.

One part of Sara hated coming home to an empty house and another part loved it. Alone in the house, she could eat what she wanted. No one the wiser. It wasn't often that her mother was absent; Anne didn't like Max to be alone. And you never knew when the others would be delayed. But today Max had gone to his friend's for the afternoon and Anne would be picking him up. Sara didn't know when Steven would be home, possibly any minute.

She headed immediately for the kitchen.

The refrigerator was a hell-hole. Nothing but vegetables, luncheon meats, dinner stuff, milk, juices. Pyuck!

The pantry was much better. Cookies. Candy. Pasta. Why was it that everything good was fattening? Oh, well, who cared? And who cared if the pantry was supposed to be off-limits to her? Who'd know? Did the Hideous Witch count every cookie, candy? She probably did. Just thinking about her mother made Sara grab a fourth Oreo when she was only planning to take three.

She sat on the window ledge chipping away at a cookie,

running her tongue over the white icing between the two dark round sides, thinking about her mother. Hideous Witch.

It hadn't always been that way. Once she loved her mother. Sara closed her eyes remembering. It was almost as though she could feel Anne's arm around her, sitting in the wing chair in the family room while she read to her from *Winnie the Pooh*. Oh, so warm and cozy. Safe. Nothing could happen to her as long as Mommy was there. Mommy always protected.

And then she didn't.

Yes, that was when it started.

Sara was ten.

All the kids in the neighborhood went out without their parents on Mischief Night, the night before Halloween. Anne had fought with Cole year after year to let the kids go. He said it was dangerous. Anything could happen. Everything was dangerous to him. Sara hated him in those days. How things changed. But finally, after nights of arguing with Daddy, Mommy won that battle. And not only that. She said she'd help them get ready for the big night.

The Cunninghams were the most important target. They lived to the left of the Nashes, about half a mile down River Road. And they were evil! All the kids said so. Their house was dark and gloomy and whenever you walked by you felt all cold. It was said, if you didn't whistle as you passed the Cunningham house, something bad would happen to you.

They were, Mr. and Mrs. Cunningham, at least a hundred years old. Everyone said so. Every Mischief Night, kids planned to get them. They stuck pins in their doorbell and soaped their windows and strung fishing wire across their steps so they'd fall. Just to go up on their porch was scary. Everyone said so.

This being Sara's first time out on Mischief Night, she wanted to do something special to the Cunninghams. Something different. And Anne said she knew just the thing.

Down the basement, where the old coal bin used to be, they made their weapons, Anne directing.

They were paper balls.

Day after day, after school for the whole week preceding Mischief Night, Anne, Sara, Steven and two friends worked in the basement. They took old newspaper, soaked it in water and carefully built layer upon layer of wet newspaper into balls the size of oranges. Anne told them how she'd done this as a child and how it made an incredible cracking sound when it hit glass, but was not hard or strong enough to break anything.

When Mischief Night came, Anne sent them out at six with their bags of paper balls. Cole was late that night, so he didn't see them go. They were all glad not to have to listen to a safety lecture.

Half an hour later, they were squatting in the dark, terrified and excited. Sara, since she was the daughter of the inventor of this ammunition, was the leader. They crept closer and closer, hearts beating. When she gave the signal, they started throwing the balls. Anne had been right. They made a terrible sound, and not a single window broke.

Then the door opened and old Mr. Cunningham, fist raised, ran out onto the porch, yelling. They kept on throwing. One hit him on the forehead. He screamed, grabbing for his head, and ran down the steps in their direction.

Sara threw one more before she yelled for them all to run. When she turned to escape, her feet slid in recently rained-on grass and she fell. Before she could get up, the old man had grabbed her by the collar.

As they walked toward her house, Mr. Cunningham holding her arm in a tight vise of his bony fingers, swearing at her, threatening her with the fires of hell, Sara was secure in the knowledge that her mother would protect her from anything Cunningham promised.

But it didn't work out that way.

In the living room with her father, mother, Steven and Cunningham, Sara was stunned as her mother remained quiet while the old man demanded the children be punished.

"What do you mean, paper balls?" Cole asked.

"Just what I said. Goddamn paper balls, big as watermelons. Look at this cut on my head," Cunningham said pointing to a tiny scratch on his shiny forehead.

They looked.

It could barely be seen. But it was there, skin broken.

"Hard as rocks," Cunningham said. "My wife has a heart condition. Whatta ya think happened when them things started hittin' our windas? Huh? She almost had an attack, thas what."

Sara looked to Anne, waiting for her Protector to say something. To order him from the house. Anne said nothing.

"I'm very, very sorry Mr. Cunningham," Cole said. "I'll make sure it never happens again."

"Are ya gonna punish these brats?"

Now her mother would speak up, Sara thought.

Nothing.

"Don't worry about that." Cole patted Cunningham on the shoulder and started leading him toward the door. "And please extend our apologies to Mrs. Cunningham."

The old man grunted.

Well, thought Sara, her mother had to be quiet while Cunningham was there. After he left she'd tell her father the truth and they'd all have a good laugh. Sure, that was it. She winked at Steven, who was trembling in fear.

When the old man was gone, Cole came back in the room, glaring at them. "I don't know what's wrong with you kids? Are you nuts or something? And you, Anne, how could you let them do that?"

Now, Sara thought. Now Anne would explain it all.

"I didn't know what they were up to," Anne said.

Sara's mouth dropped open. She couldn't believe it. Looking at Steven, she saw that he, too, was shocked.

"Well, you should have. You should know what they're up to." Turning to the children, he said, "I'm disgusted with you. Especially you, Sara. You're old enough to know better. You're both grounded for two weeks. Now go upstairs to bed. No dinner."

Sara was unable to move. She couldn't really believe that her mother wasn't going to save her at the last minute. Finally she said, "Mommy?"

Anne turned to her. "Do as your father says."

Sara saw a strange look on her mother's face. Was it fear? Fear of her father? Steven started to say something and Sara grabbed his arm. If her mother wasn't going to say anything on her own, she didn't want him giving it away. What was the point?

Upstairs in her bed, Sara sobbed herself to sleep. It had nothing to do with her father's punishment, although she was very, very hungry. She cried because she'd been betrayed. Betrayed by the person she'd trusted most. And why? She couldn't understand it.

In the morning, her mother came to her room.

"I'm sorry, Sara. I know you don't understand."

"But why?"

"It's hard to explain."

"Does it have to do with Daddy?"

"Yes. He'd be very mad at me.... Is there any way you can understand that?"

66

"I guess," she said. But she didn't. So what if Daddy was mad at her mother? What about him being mad at her and Steven? Instinctively, she knew there was no point in going further with it. The truth was clear. Her mother had betrayed her to save herself. There was no other explanation, no other truth.

And that was how it had started. A large chink in her trust.

Little by little, she'd pulled away from Anne until in the last year she'd grown to hate her. Hideous Witch. But sometimes, sometimes when she felt awful and lonely, she wished she were little again. Wished she could sit in the big wing chair, her mother's arm around her while she read to her from *Winnie the Pooh*.

Sara sighed knowing it would never be again.

Devouring the last cookie, she reached into the far left corner where Anne put the Hershey Bars. What an asshole she was! Did she really think they wouldn't be found? Well, Sara would deny to the death that she'd eaten any.

Just as she began to tear the brown wrapper, she heard the front door slam. Quickly, she flung the chocolate bar back in its corner and closed the pantry door. When Steven entered the kitchen, Sara was standing at the table holding the salt, trying for nonchalance, failing.

"Aha!" he said. "The Incredible Bulk And The Salt! Episode 22!"

Sara's face began to mottle, eyes narrowing. "You shut the hell up, Steven, you asshole." She slammed the salt on the table.

"Nice talk. What's to eat or wouldn't you know?" He walked to the pantry, small compact body secure in every move he made.

"I wouldn't."

"I just think I'll have some yummy cookies and milk."

"Do you think I care?" she said, looking at the ragged nails on her stubby hand.

He poked his head around the wainscotted pantry door. 'Probably not, because you've stuffed your fat face already, right? Hmmm?" He ducked back into the pantry.

"You're a horror show." She thought about slamming the door shut on him and leaning on it—she outweighed him by about twenty-five pounds—then changed her mind and left the kitchen.

In the family room, she turned on her favorite soap, kicked off her shoes, sprawled on the flowered couch. Coco was sitting on the nearest arm, her white front feet curled inward touching each other. Perfect symmetry. She was a tiny cat calico, pink nose the size of a baby's nail. Sara stroked her from head to tail and Coco's hindquarters automatically rose. Cats were so peaceful, she thought. Restful. She wished she were a cat. No problems. Also, they only ate when they were hungry.

On the soap, Stacey was telling off her mother, Elisabeth. Sara wished she had Stacey's nerve. Anne was always nagging her. Weight. Uncombed hair. Bitten nails. Sloppy room. The best Sara could do was to show her contempt by ignoring her mother, making a face. Occasionally, she gave her an argument. But she'd never actually told her off. Someday. You wait.

"You lookin' at that dumb thing?" Steven asked, coming into the room. His mouth was crammed with cookie.

Sara ignored him.

"How come you look at that, huh?"

"Shut up."

"Shut up," he mimicked, falling onto the couch beside her, his foot smacking hers.

She moved it.

He inched closer, banged the foot again.

"You're asking for trouble, Steven."

"Big deal."

"You have the most limited vocabulary of any person I know."

"And you have the fattest face."

There was a beat, a stillness, then Sara turned, slamming Steven in the face with her open hand. Hard.

Stunned momentarily, he recovered and lunged, grabbing her around the neck, pulling her to the floor.

The tussle was short-lived.

Within moments Sara had him on his back, straddling his chest, knees planted firmly on his shoulders.

"You fat pig," he wheezed, voice almost cut off by her weight.

"I could easily kill you now. You know that?" Sara spoke evenly, spacing her words.

"So why don't you, you whale?"

Tears formed in her eyes. Infuriated, she desperately tried to hold them back, could not. One rolled out, down her cheek.

Steven's trim, pink mouth fashioned a smile.

Sara slapped him.

His head snapped to the side, the cheek immediately turning red.

"What's going on?" It was Anne.

Sara, tears full blown now, spun her head around.

"Get off him right this minute, you...."

In her head, Sara supplied the rest of Anne's sentence, *you fat slob*. She'd never hated anyone more than she hated Anne at that moment. What she felt for Steven was minor by comparison. Slowly, trying for some sort of dignity, she climbed off her brother and stood rigidly, staring at Anne.

Steven raised himself to a sitting position and ostentatiously rubbed his cheek.

"Now tell me what was going on?"

Sara pressed her lips together, hatred silencing her.

"Steven?"

"Ah, forget it, Mom. It's between us."

The soap blared.

"Turn that damn thing off," Anne commanded.

Obediently, Steven snapped the switch.

Anne said, "I know it's between you, that's quite clear. I want to know what it *is* between you."

Sara wound her long, brown, uncombed hair around a chunky hand and pulled it across her face, covering her mouth.

"Do you hear me, Sara?"

"I hear you," she answered in a muffled voice.

Impatiently, Anne grabbed her daughter's arm, pulling her hand from her hair.

"OW," Sara cried. "You hurt me."

Good, Anne wanted to say. "I'm waiting for an answer." Instead.

"Oh, Mom, forget it, okay? Me and Sara'll work it out."

Simple for him to say, Sara thought. What was to work out? Her fat a forever, easy target.

"You two are at each other night and day and it's a big fat bore."

Fat. Always a reference. Sara seethed.

Anne ran a finger under her pink turtleneck, tucked her red and gray flannel shirt into her jeans. Stalling. "I'm sick of your stupid squabbles. You give me a headache. Lay off." She glared at each one, withdrew.

When she was gone, Steven gave Sara the finger and she

reciprocated with a crazy, forced smile, batted her eyes, blew him a kiss.

"Fat cow," he hissed, heading out the door.

Sara managed to laugh derisively.

Alone, she fell back on the couch. Tears threatened again, but she checked them, not wanting to acknowledge the feeling, even alone. She wished her dad were there. He'd hold her. But that was a lie. He hadn't held her in years; not since she'd gotten so fat. Maybe she could lose for him. There was no one else to lose for. Even if Cole didn't hold her on his lap anymore—after all she was fourteen—she knew he loved her. Only one who did.

A thought sprang into her head; she hadn't had it in years. Accompanying it was shame, embarrassment. When she'd been five or six, the thought had been comforting, right. Now it made her uncomfortable. Still, she couldn't chase it from her mind.

She wished they were all dead except Daddy.

Daddy and her.

And that was the truth.

Upstairs in the kitchen, as Anne unpacked her groceries, she thought about the fight between her two children. It pained her terribly to see them go at each other like that. Was it normal, the growing up process? Someday would Sara and Steven be the best of friends? Like she was with Ross? But she and Ross had never indulged in mortal combat the way her children did.

She used to try to be like her mother, unruffled, in control. Lately she'd come to see her mother's actions as controlling, rather than calm and collected. She didn't want to be controlling, that was a terrible way to be. You were called tyrannical and ball-busting, depending on whom you were controlling. Ball-busting was an epithet often tossed at a self-sufficient woman. But that was something else. She'd stopped falling for that one when she'd joined the Consciousness Raising group several years before. Sorry it had disbanded. Missed it. But she'd learned a lot while it lasted.

Inside the refrigerator she juggled things around, making room for the new supplies. Sometimes life seemed like endless filling of a constantly depleted fridge.

She'd been lucky. Measles, mumps, the usual. And none of them seemed to have serious problems. Oh, there was Sara's weight and Kit's insecurity and Steven's arrogance, but none of those things seemed insurmountable. Kit was a woman working on her own problems. Sara would grow out of it. And Steven. Well, he'd get put in his place sooner or later. Nothing serious. Max was too little to know about yet and her mind zig-zagged around thoughts of Tom.

Her mother had been lucky, too. They'd all turned out pretty well, considering their alcoholic father. Could have been worse. Only one alcoholic offspring and she'd dealt with it. Of course the years Liz was drinking weren't any picnic, but then her mother didn't have to see it, hardly knew about it.

But there *was* Walter. If Dorothy Clifford had known her youngest son was a homosexual would she have considered herself a lucky mother?

As she put the last egg in the bin, she suddenly had a startling thought. Was Tom gay? Was that it? But what about Jennifer? Walter had had girls in high school. Jennifer's presence was no proof. If that was it, he'd naturally become secretive. Wouldn't he automatically pull away from her. For fear she'd find out.

Should she call Walter? And say what? Should she ask Tom? It was ridiculous. There was no evidence of his being gay. She was grasping at straws now. Making mountains out of molehills.

Everybody was fine. Perfectly fine.

Including Tom.

11.

Cole stared down into the cavern of keys of his blue and white Smith-Corona. The case of Harrison Foster was not going to go his way. Chollie Buck said there was no way to prove that Foster rammed the telephone pole on purpose. And yet there were no skid marks. He hadn't even tried to stop himself. The theory was that he'd fallen asleep at the wheel. But usually when that happened, the car slowed. Foster's car had been going between eighty and ninety miles an hour. It was as though he'd gotten the car up to the fastest speed he could on the somewhat winding Ferry Road, then just pointed it at the telephone pole. But there was no way to prove it.

Cole could identify with the impulse. He'd thought about it a number of times himself; he even started to do it once.

The problem now was how to avoid paying off a two hundred thousand dollar policy. The police were definitely declaring it an accidental death unless Cole's company could come up with some hard evidence. And that was unlikely, although he had his best man on it. Daley would dig and scratch and run down every avenue until there weren't any left. He had to trust Daley.

"Staying all night?" Harry Todd asked.

"Just closing up shop," Cole answered, putting the gray plastic cover over his typewriter.

"Want to have a drink?"

"Why not?"

The Coach House was nestled in a grove of trees at the edge of the river and in the winter it was a popular bar with the local businessmen. In the summer, it turned gay and the businessmen of Old Hickory and surrounding areas stayed away in droves.

Cole and Harry said hello to various business associates, Rotary members, as they passed through the bar to a table overlooking the water, icy and gray.

Harry Todd, with a leonine head of gray hair, long thin nose and smoke gray eyes, was in his early fifties, a few years older than Cole, but looked in his middle sixties. Until 1969, the firm had been Brandt, Brandt & Todd; then it added the Nash. The Todd had been Samuel Todd until 1967, when Samuel died and Harry took his place. Harry still carried a resentment about it. As far as he was concerned, it should have been Brandt, Brandt, Todd & Todd long before 1967. He didn't think he should have had to wait until his father died to become a partner and even though his father had been dead for all these years Harry couldn't forgive him. The anger had given him bitter lines around his mouth.

Both men ordered vodka martinis on the rocks with a twist.

72

"We're going to lose the Foster case, aren't we?" Harry asked.

Cole smoothed back the white at his temples, nodded. "I think so, Harry. Unless Daley comes up with something and frankly I don't see how he can."

"Shit."

"Yeah."

"It's a big loss."

"I know. What can we do?" Cole popped a peanut in his mouth.

Harry shrugged, pulled at his tie, opened his collar; a mass of black curly hair revealed itself like a small animal hidden under his shirt. "A fucking shame."

The waitress put down their drinks.

Harry smiled, showing long white teeth. "A sister of mercy." He patted the waitress's arm.

She pulled away, tactfully.

Harry didn't notice, he never did.

Cole noticed and was embarrassed.

"Fucking shame," Harry said again. "You know as well as I that Harrison Foster killed himself, right."

Cole nodded. "Has all the earmarks. But Eleanor Foster isn't going to tell us anything. We can count on that."

"Why the hell should she? Would you? I mean if you had a D.I. policy on Anne and she bought it on her own, would you tell?"

The jolt Cole felt thinking about Anne's death surprised him. After all, it wasn't as though he loved her. "I guess not. No, I'm sure I wouldn't."

Well, he certainly wouldn't if it were *his* wife, Harry said. And from that he launched into what a dried-up prune she was anyway and that was why he always made sure he had some "babes" when he went to Philadelphia or New York on business. Cole nodded, made appropriate sounds, but he didn't listen. Didn't have to. He'd heard it all before.

While Harry did his monologue, Cole thought about freedom.

His freedom.

It was a certainty that he couldn't kill himself. That was a kind of freedom, he supposed, but not what he had in mind. And Anne and the children weren't going to disappear.

Or die.

His parents might die; in fact, *would* die fairly soon. At least, if statistics could be trusted. And Cole lived by statistics. Probably in the next five or ten years and certainly before his wife and children.

The point was *he* was dying. Metaphorically, of course. Life was passing him by. Staring discreetly past Harry's head he looked at himself in the blue tinted mirror behind their table. In another year, he'd be fifty. Almost too late. Not quite.

Right now he was a good-looking man, his hair was still thick and black, except for the temples. Nice. Distinguished. Skin good, clear, never sallow. Healthy. The lines were spare, well-placed. Two at the brow, two on either side of his patrician nose, two at the corners of his curved, full lips. Solid chin, almost square. A manly growth of beard, still had to shave twice a day. Proud of it. But the key to his looks, he'd always thought, were his crescent-shaped, startlingly blue, eyes. Like Paul Newman.

"See something good?" Harry asked.

Embarrassed, Cole went for his tie, straightening, adjusting. "I'm listening. Go on."

His eyes on Harry, he continued nodding, thinking his own thoughts. In a few years, the firmness of his angular body would be gone, his cheeks would become jowls and more lines would appear, eyes growing dim, lackluster. Why should he waste these last years of being sexually attractive, appealing, with a wife he didn't love? No reason.

On the other hand, how were things any different now than they were seven years ago? Except that he was older. Wiser? Doubtful. More defeated, perhaps. If he hadn't been able to leave then, with Julia, would he ever leave? Certainly, it was different. Running off with someone and going off alone, activating THE PLAN was something else.

THE PLAN was haunting him again. Three times over the years he'd plotted his escape. Each time, at the last minute, he'd found one excuse or another as to why he couldn't act. But in the end he knew only one thing held him back. Fear. This time would be different though. This time he'd do it.

Disappear.

Thin air.

Others had done it. Why couldn't he? He thought about the banker who'd gotten on a train in New York a few years ago to go home to wife and kids in New Jersey, then simply vanished. As far as Cole knew, they'd still never found him. Guts. That's all it took. Simple. He'd worked out the details many times and with a few changes, a little polish, THE PLAN would be in working order again.

Something had to give; he couldn't go on like this.

Leaving, vanishing, was the easy part. Guilt, the hard part. What would happen to his family? The major part of their savings would be left for them, but how long would that last? Anne would have to go back to work. What kind of job could she get after all these years? At her age. He wouldn't miss her, but in a way he felt for her. Stuck at forty-five with five kids. Well, four. Kit was on her own.

And what about Tom? If Cole left, he'd be cheating the boy out of a college education. Without his salary, there was no way Anne could afford to send him, not at six thousand dollars a year. A flash of anger scored him.

Why couldn't Tom get a scholarship?

Work his way through?

The anger subsided as he realized that that was exactly what the boy *would* do. He was that kind of kid. Not one to shirk or avoid responsibility. Still, it was a lousy thing to do to a seventeen-year-old boy. More guilt.

And Sara, Steven, Max?

Just kids. They'd be all right. In time, Max would forget him. Max. If only she hadn't gotten pregnant for the fifth time. It spoiled everything. He should have stopped sleeping with her after Steven instead of after Max. Then it all would have been right. Just the way Nick wanted it. Girl, boy, girl, boy.

Never mind. Not again. Twice in one day.

And Kit? Grown woman. Sometimes it shocked him when he saw her. Not just her beauty. Although that in itself was startling. But that he had a child this grown, this formed. It made him feel old.

He didn't know how to talk to her. Had he ever? First born. Surely he'd tried with her. Had he spent time with her? Smiling, he saw her on her first two-wheeler, him holding the back of the seat, one handlebar. He frowned. Something had happened. He saw her falling. Nothing serious. Looking all around.

"What are you looking for?" he asked.

"People."

"People?"

"Did anyone see me falling?"

"What if they did?" Harsh.

Tears welling up, shrugging. "I dunno."

75

"You care too much what other people think."

Chin up, shoulders back. Proud. "I don't care what anybody thinks."

"Now you're contradicting yourself."

"What's contradicting?"

"Never mind."

Cole shook his head. No, he'd never known how to talk to her. He'd wanted to, tried, but couldn't ever master how to talk to a child. Especially her. Something about her that always got to him. Put him off. Riled him. Still that way. They'd start off nice, and inevitably end in a shouting match. Every time. He guessed that she hated him. Maybe they all did. Did he hate them?

No. He didn't hate his family; he just hated responsibility. Being free, without ties of any kind, was his idea of heaven. To report only to one's self; to never *have* to do anything, care for anyone, need anyone. The Gauguin dream. He'd heard plenty of men talk about it at Rotary after a few drinks. Hardly a unique idea. But so what? The unique thing was to act.

Would he do it this time? Or would he someday sit, shriveled, peeing in his pants, wondering what life would have been...if only? Goddamnit, why was he so afraid? That was the damn trouble; he was afraid of everything. Always had been.

The waitress was putting a second martini in front of him.

"What's your name, honey?"

Tuning in, Cole heard Harry speak to her.

"I don't think we've seen you before."

"Bertha. I'm Sylvia's sister. She's sick."

"Bertha? You hear that, Cole? Bertha. I haven't heard that name since my old aunt went to her great reward. Are you an old-fashioned girl like your name, honey?" He looked at her lewdly.

Cole wanted to smash him. Harry was truly disgusting.

"Very old-fashioned," Bertha said pointedly, unconsciously plucking at the front of her uniform. She put their empty glasses on her tray and left.

"No sense of humor," Harry said. "Imagine giving a beauty like that the name Bertha. Jesus."

"Maybe she wasn't such a beauty when they gave her the name."

Harry laughed. "You got a point." He raised his glass, sipped. "So where was I?"

76

Cole drank calmly, knowing Harry would find his way back.

Cole drifted. Julia. Fear had sabotaged him then, too.

She'd been so young. Twenty. But he was younger then. Forty-two. Still, it was a big age difference. He was constantly thinking things like: when I was graduating from Lehigh she wasn't even born, or, when Nick died she was a few months old, or, when my second child was born she was ten. Stupid game. Yet he couldn't stop playing it. Except when they were in bed.

Julia was dark. Skin, eyes, hair. He loved her hair, long, thick, curly. Her brown eyes were large and seemed luminescent, though of course they weren't really. Some might have thought her mouth too large for her face, but Cole thought it sensuous, perfect. She couldn't have been more different from Anne, in fact from them all. He reacted to her as though he'd been subjected to blonde, blue-eyed creatures long enough.

He'd met her in the summer. It was late afternoon. He'd left the office early and had gone to Mia Casa, a small quiet bar and restaurant on a side street. He was sitting on the deck when she came in. Alone. He was struck by her dark beauty immediately. Appreciative of her looks, youth. Nothing personal occurred to him.

And then she smiled at him.

Surprised, he found himself smiling back.

She got up from her table, bringing her drink.

"Mind if I join you?"

What could it hurt. Besides, he was flattered. "Not at all."

She was a talker and Cole liked that. Less for him to do. She told him all about herself, background, present, hopes for the future. She'd come to Old Hickory to do summer stock at the River Playhouse. This was her day off, the theater closed. Her parts were going to be small this summer, but she was sure when she went back to New York in the fall the experience here would be invaluable. He was enchanted by her as one might be by an energetic, charming child. At least, that's what he told himself.

Until the next Monday when he found himself looking at his watch all afternoon and then at four picking up and leaving, driving to Mia Casa, feeling a strange excitement.

He'd almost given up hope when she came in.

Grinning ingenuously she said, "Oh, I hoped you'd be here. I thought about you all week."

77

He almost said, "You did?" But instead, just smiled enigmatically and ordered her a drink.

It took another two weeks and four more meetings and then it was Julia who asked *him*.

"Don't I appeal to you, Cole?"

"You're charming."

"I don't mean that."

He was embarrassed. She certainly did appeal to him, but he hadn't really let himself entertain those thoughts. She could be his daughter. Kit was only three years younger. He simply didn't know what to say.

"Listen, this is the seventies and we're grown up people."

He tried not to smile, couldn't help himself.

She saw it and her eyes flashed with anger. "I'm not a child."

"You are to me," he said.

"You mean there's nothing about me that's womanly to you?"

Involuntarily, his eyes flicked over her large, beautiful breasts.

She laughed. "Come on, Cole, get off it. I know you want me."

"I'm married. I have five children."

"What's new?" She put her hand on his thigh. "I want to make love to you, not marry you."

He was shocked. As a boy from the forties and early fifties he was unused to girls talking like this. But he was aware that a change had taken place. Things were different now. When the shock passed, excitement took over.

They went to her room.

And she did make love to him. He'd never experienced anything like it. It was wonderful. Immediately after, he decided he was in love with her.

By the end of the summer, she was in love with him. Instead of going to New York, she got a job as a waitress so she could be near him. The pay wasn't enough to keep her going so he helped her.

In November, lying in his arms, she confronted him.

"You're never going to leave your wife, are yóu, Cole?"

He'd never said he would, but he'd implied as much. Now it was clear Julia needed more than she was getting from him. If he admitted the truth, that he simply couldn't leave, that he was afraid, he knew he'd lose her. He tried to stall with an old gambit. "I need some time, Julia. There's a lot to arrange."

It seemed to work. But it hadn't.

When he arrived at her apartment three days later, she was gone. Moved. He was devastated. And relieved. He could have found her, sure she'd gone to New York. But he didn't try. What was the point?

A few months after Julia left, he'd made love to Anne, trying to revive something. It was then she'd gotten pregnant with Max.

Years later when Kit was having the affair with Doc Mancinelli, he'd wanted to kill the bastard. But he thought of himself and Julia and ignored it all instead.

The years after Julia were the worst. He had felt more isolated than ever. He knew how to deal with his wife and children even less than before. Sometimes he tried to take clues from television or movies on how to behave as a husband and father. He had no instincts.

Feeling more and more incompetent every year, he began thinking about escape. Getting away. Alone. He devised THE PLAN to disappear. Just thinking about it kept him going. And even though he'd tried to act on it three times and failed, he always hoped one day he'd have the courage.

"Cole, you hear me? Huh?"

Harry was looking at him, head to one side, eyebrows bunched.

The feeling that he'd been caught at something dirty took a few seconds to vanish. "I hear you."

"You had an odd look on your face."

Cole smiled, showing even, white teeth a touch too small for his face. He guessed that Harry had still been talking about "babes." "Just enjoying the talk, Tiger," he said. "You're giving me a stiff one." He winked.

Damn, he thought. I've got to do it this time.

12.

Sitting alone in a back booth at The Court Coffee Shoppe, Noj tried to concentrate on a paper by Gregory Bateson but his mind kept flying off on tangents. Most of them, in the direction of Kit.

He'd had a lot of women in his twenty-eight years, but no one like her. It wasn't just that she had the most perfect body he'd ever seen outside of a stroke magazine; it was everything about her. Sometimes he couldn't believe she loved him, wanted him. Not that he had trouble getting women; none of the Hampton men had that trouble. In fact, it was just the opposite. Both his brother Barry and his father had trouble keeping women away. Noj didn't give a damn about Barry; he'd never liked Alice, Barry's wife. But it bothered him with his father. He *did* like his mother.

Betty Hampton was mad about her husband, but Hallock Hampton was a ladies' man. Always had been. Whether Betty knew or not was a moot point. She continuously looked sad. And those times when Noj knew his father had been with someone else he felt his mother's eyes become even more despondent.

When Barry had begun to womanize after his marriage, Noj caught his father and brother exchanging notes.

"I think you're pigs," he'd said.

Shocked, Hallock flushed, regained his composure and said, "The Hampton men have always been good fuckers, Noj. What the hell's the matter with you?"

"I guess I'm old-fashioned. I think once you're married it's no longer a viable alternative."

Father and brother laughed.

"That's because you're not married," Barry said.

80

"My grandfather, your great-grandfather, died on the street of a heart attack after goosing some red-headed chicken. He was ninety-two."

Noj said, "You both make me sick."

And they did.

It was true he'd never been married, but he was sure that once he did marry that would be that. He wasn't naive enough to think that a sexual attraction lasted forever at the same pitch. Even Kit, who brought out something in him that he'd never felt before, would eventually lose the magic she held for him now. He wasn't a complete idiot. But when he married her, and love changed, sex diminished, Noj knew the answer wasn't other women. At least not for him. He didn't care what other men said. He was convinced there was no way to have an affair without it affecting your marriage.

There was his mother, living proof.

Queen of the Downers.

Ah, Shit!

He didn't want to think about her now. Pill junkie.

Pushing the Bateson paper aside, he gave in to his need to think about Kit. Beautiful woman. Sexy woman. Oh, so sexy. He'd never seen anything quite like her. Some women were studied, calculated, but Kit's sexuality flowed from her naturally. Nothing overbearing. Just an unconscious promise of everything sensual, erotic. All done simply with a turn of the head, a seemingly innocent gesture, a quick intake of breath. Watching her sip her coffee could cause Noj to project hours of tactile pleasure. She was ingenuously carnal.

And had been from the beginning. He'd first seen her in a lecture class not quite a year before. What struck him immediately were her eyes. He'd never seen eyes like them. Emerald green. Really. It crossed his mind that she might be wearing some kind of tinted contact lenses. It was hard to believe that anyone could really have eyes that color.

She'd been wearing jeans, a loose lavender turtleneck. Even so he could see that her breasts were large. He knew instantly that her body was wonderful. But it wasn't that or her eyes that got him. It was her hands; the way she reached down into her purse and pulled out a pen, then held it poised above her pad. Ridiculous. There was this woman with an extraordinary body, fabulous breasts, an absolutely beautiful face and he could feel himself growing hard looking at her hand and the way she moved it. But that was the way it had been and was now. Not that those other things didn't turn him on. Clearly they did. He loved her body, savored it. When skin met skin as it had that afternoon, when he felt the length of her against the length of him, his mouth on hers, everything was right with him. Nothing else mattered.

Like the first time they'd made love. About a month after they'd started dating. Kit was wary, hadn't wanted to get into anything. She told him she was getting over someone. So they'd gone fairly slowly.

They were in her apartment, lying side by side on the daybed in the living room, kissing. For a long time. Noj was beginning to feel a little frantic.

"Please," he said.

She swallowed, looked deeply into his eyes. "I'm afraid."

"Why? Do you think I'll love you and leave you or something stupid like that?"

She shook her head. "I'm afraid you won't like me."

"Oh, my God," he said hoarsely. "Kit, don't you know? I mean, Christ Almighty. Like you?"

"Maybe I won't be good enough for you."

He kissed her eyelids, mouth. "You'll be wonderful. Look, if it helps any, I'm scared, too."

Her eyes widened and she looked at him quizzically. "You're not serious? You?"

"What do you mean, *me?*"

"I don't want to be just another one. I know that's not terribly sophisticated of me, but it's the way I feel. After . . . after the last man in my life, I decided that I'd have to be really sure the next time. I'm starting to think of myself as promiscuous and I don't like it. And I don't care if it's *in* or chic. It's not me, Noj . . . it just isn't."

"I know that. Let me tell you something."

He talked about his father and brother, his great-grandfather.

"I don't want to be like that. I just don't believe in it . . . maybe I'm not sophisticated either. It's true that I've slept with a number of women . . . I guess I want to get it out of my system now. But, I'll tell you this, Kit. There've been three serious affairs in my life and while I was involved in them there was no one else."

"True?"

"True."

He kissed her. Then they pulled away and looked steadily into each other's eyes.

"I want you very much," he said.

82

"What if you don't like me, the way I feel...."

"Oh, baby, you're crazy."

Later, as he drew himself up along her body from between her legs, right before he entered her, he said, "You're perfect. I knew you would be."

Their love-making that first night, although slightly off, was wonderful for them. They were both experienced enough to know it could never be absolutely right the first time. But enough was right to show them what their sexual future held.

Now, ten months later, they were absolutely in tune. Their rhythms perfect. They knew each other's bodies well and wanted, needed, no one else.

Noj loved Kit. He wanted to marry her. She was reluctant and it made him crazy. She was afraid of losing her identity. He'd promised everything she'd asked for: no children, her own career, fidelity. He'd even acquiesced to her keeping her own name, though he hated the idea.

Still, she wouldn't say yes.

Well, he had it all figured out. After spending the first five days of the holiday with his family, he was to drive down to Logan and be with Kit for New Year's. What was more corny than New Year's Eve? Nothing. Except giving a woman like Kit an engagement ring on that night. Manipulative. Maybe. But what the hell. She needed a nudge. A diamond push!

It was all very old-fashioned, but that was the way Jon Hampton was made. So was Kit Nash. And that was the bottom line for both of them: one of the million reasons they belonged together.

Noj sipped his coffee, cold now. He simply wouldn't take no for an answer. He'd be old-fashioned that way, too. And to make it really corny, they'd get married in June.

And live happily ever after.

13.

SOLA was everywhere.

Tom sat at the maple desk in his room. A history book lay open, a photograph of James Curley staring up at him.

But it wasn't James Curley.

It was SOLA.

SOLA was everywhere.

A sickening fear danced across Tom's middle, slid over his arms, legs. Turning away from the book, he looked across the room at his matching maple highboy bureau.

It was moving. Undulating.

He thought he might vomit and swiveled in his chair to face the bed.

Moving.

The red and blue stripes of the sheets shimmered and glowed, casting brilliant lights on the wall.

The wall was SOLA.

Tom slid from his chair to the floor. He lay spread-eagle on the rug; nose, mouth, chin pressing into the soft nap. Inside he could feel everything turning to water.

The rug began to move.

Eyes open, he could see the intricate design of the rug begin to change.

Day-glo colors replaced the muted blues, browns, reds and blacks.

Each unit moved, formed, changed.

Small, yet perfect.

SOLA.

Everywhere.

He had never been so terrified.

Surely now he was going to die.

SOLA. SOLA. SOLA.
Everything moved but him.
Because he could not.

14.

Family room.

Anne, unable to sleep, stood in the doorway taking in the room's comfort, casualness. Looking at the easy chairs, one red, one tangerine, picking up the colors in the flowered couch, all worn now. She recalled how important it had been more than ten years ago to make this room work. Family room.

She smiled to herself, shook her head sadly, walked to the coffee table, opened an art deco cigarette box. She lit her cigarette, inhaled, slowly blew the smoke into the still air. How long since the family had spent time here together? All of them. She couldn't remember.

Even with her father the way he was, it seemed to her that they had all spent so much more time together. At least, the brothers and sisters had. A memory of summer nights at the cottage, around the table on the porch. Monopoly. Ross, serious, hair falling in his eyes. Always winning. Complaints. Sometimes Liz made a fuss. But no one really cared. The game itself was the thing. Was mother there? On the wicker couch, reading or sewing. Her brood under control. But they were together.

Had times changed so much? Was it just part of the seventies for a family to be so alienated from each other? Or was it *her* family. *Her* children.

And what *was* going on with Tom? Tonight at dinner he seemed further away than ever. And then that odd thing after dinner. He'd just gotten up without a word and started to leave the dining room.

"Hey?" Sara said.

Tom kept going.

"Hey, Tom!"

He stopped, turned, looked at her blankly.

"It's your turn tonight."

"Turn?" he asked.

Anne noted the odd expression on his face, glanced at Cole to see if it registered, but he was finishing his dessert and wasn't watching.

"Your turn to clear."

"Clear?"

Sara rolled her eyes, groaned, looked to Anne for help. "Mother?"

"Tom," Anne said gently, "is something wrong?"

"No. Why?"

"Well, it's your turn to clear the table. The dishes. That's what Sara means." As though he were a Martian.

"Oh. Oh, yeah, sure." He touched his fingerips to his right temple, blinked his eyes and came back to the table.

"Is something wrong, dear?" She hesitated to ask if he was sick. Didn't want Cole to start up.

"No, Mom. Sorry. It's just a project. On my mind."

Even his speech seemed odd to her, but he'd immediately started clearing, behaving in an ordinary, normal fashion.

Normal. What was normal, after all? Oh, not that old saw. Wasn't that just a way of avoiding looking at things? Foolish or not, tomorrow she was going to go see Dr. Blackwell and tell him about Tom. Tell him what? Never mind. She'd tell him what she could. He was always so understanding, never made her feel like a stupid female as some other doctors did. Besides, he'd delivered Tom, knew him well.

She thought of the morning of Tom's birth, born on her own birthday. Cole standing over her, smiling.

"Very good," he said, "just right."

What did he mean? He'd said the same thing when Kit had been born. When she asked what he meant, he waved her question away, shook his head. She was too weak to ask now.

"Thomas will be his name."

Not a question. A statement. She'd been so sure it was going to be another girl she hadn't even thought of a boy's name. Sara was all she had in mind.

"Thomas? Why?"

"Because I like it. You named Kit."

"You said you didn't care, Cole."

"That was so I could name this one."

So childish, she thought. Didn't he know if it was so important that they could have discussed it like adults instead of playing some dumb secret game of taking turns. She didn't mind the name Thomas so she agreed.

When Sara came along, he again said it was perfect, right, and was agreeable to the name, little interest. And Steven was in some secret plan of his too. But the name hadn't mattered.

But when Max was born and she asked about a name, he'd said mysteriously, "It doesn't matter. It's all ruined anyway."

No matter how she pleaded, he wouldn't explain and finally she gave up. Max had been the turning point anyway. If they'd had their problems before, his birth was a definitive line between *some* communication and none. They were just two people who shared a house, a bed. But nothing ever went on in the bed. She'd tried a few times after Max was born, but Cole feigned tiredness, headaches, the things women were supposed to use as excuses. And the last time, he'd made her feel like a whore.

"Is that all you think about?"

"Hardly."

"There are other things in life, you know."

That was it, she'd never tried again. Nor had he. Six years. Long time. Would she remember how? Would it all come back? Like riding a bicycle? Scary. Can't think about it. Not now.

Standing in front of the low bookcase, she crossed her arms, ran a hand over the smooth velvet of her robe, staring at the row of framed pictures, awards, memorabilia of family.

An early group picture. Max not even born. On the lawn of the old house, before the move. Steven in her arms. Toddler Sara. Thin. Tom, skinny little boy, glint of sun catching in his hair, smile dazzling. Cole, somber, no gray in his hair, body stiff, erect. And she? Was there a hint, even then, of disappointment, disillusionment? Or was there still self-deception?

Anne's eyes moved on hastily to the next picture: baby Max. Chubby, pinchable cheeks, pursed mouth, inevitable blue eyes. Between pictures were the trophies, mostly Tom's. Tennis, basketball, baseball, swimming. Kit's captain of cheerleaders letter, poetry award, valedictorian citation. Tom's would undoubtedly be added in June. Steven's Captain of Safety Patrol scroll. Nothing from Sara. Sad.

Her own Mother of the Year Award. County-wide. Oh, God. Some Mother of the Year. Only two years ago and now she was an adultress. Almost. Friday. Maybe.

Turning away from the artifacts of a life, the tired tales, untruths all, perhaps not then, but now, Anne plopped down in the red wingback chair, feet up on the brocade hassack. Stubbing out her cigarette, she leaned back, thinking of Jim O'Neill. A week since she'd seen him, two days since they'd spoken.

Startled, Anne jumped. Coco had landed in her lap.

"You scared me, Coco."

The cat looked up at her, purring, mindless of Anne's sensibilities, eager for stroking.

Anne obliged as Coco settled on the purple robe.

Jim.

Where would she be now if she hadn't gone to the Inn that day last April? Asleep? Did love create insomnia? Had she slept better before? Life in a vacuum.

What if?

If only.

Did she really feel regret? Or was it simple fear of the unknown, the future? Each action brought her closer to the dissolution of Family. But it was all a lie anyway; a charade born of myth and novelists. Still, any change was difficult.

It was that desire, the need for change, that had brought her to this juncture. If she hadn't wanted a change, she'd never have gone by herself to the Koehler Inn in the first place.

The twenty-five-mile drive, mostly on the Post Road, from Logan to Williams, had been beautiful on that day. Lush green of spring. Forsythia, butter color, blazed along fences, railings, filing her with a sense of well-being, love, gratitude at being alive.

The Inn, perched at the edge of the water, was white, stately yet inviting, columns grandly holding up the second floor roof. It was five of twelve when she pulled open the heavy oak door. A dining room on either side of a narrow hall; at the end, she could see part of a bar. Feeling nervous, foolish, to be there alone—oh, why hadn't she called a friend?—she fussed with the waist of her powder blue skirt, patted the bow of her white silk blouse.

Her breath came quickly, in short, small takes. Dizziness made her reach out to touch the wall.

At that moment, he appeared in the doorway of the bar. "Hello. Can I help you?" Smiling. Seeing her bracing herself, he took five or six long strides toward her. "Are you all right?"

She wanted to die of embarrassment, disappear. "Yes, of course." She removed her hand from the wall, hoped she'd remain upright.

"Am I too early?" she inquired.

"No, not at all. Are you lunching?" he asked.

"Yes."

"A table for two on the water?"

"No." Meeting his eyes, she said cryptically, "A table for *one* on the water."

He nodded, smiling from one side of his mouth.

"Follow me," he said turning.

Follow me.

She had, of course. Why not? There was no way to know then what would happen. He was simply the owner of an inn. Handsome and charming. Naturally. Yet she noticed every detail of him. About three inches taller than she with a trim, neat body. Face craggy, dark eyebrows, sad brown eyes. The suit he wore, gray, was fashionably cut and the blue of his shirt almost matched her suit. A foulard tie and matching handkerchief were the perfect accessories. She guessed him to be about forty-six, -seven, even though he radiated a kind of boyishness. Later she learned he was forty-two, three years her junior.

Lunch had been wonderful; shrimp cocktail, sole almandine, broccoli with hollandaise, salad, strong coffee. Luxury. Freedom.

And then he was standing by her table, the charming one-sided smile meant only for her. "Did you enjoy your lunch?"

"Very much. This is a beautiful place."

"Thank you. Forgive me, I'm Jim O'Neill."

She told him her name as they shook hands. What was that feeling? Nervously, she said, "I read about the Inn in the *County Gazette.* I've wanted to come for a long time."

"I'm glad you finally did." He looked directly in her eyes. Schoolgirl, she thought.

"May I offer you a complimentary cordial or brandy?"

I shouldn't, her first thought. I will, her second.

Crème de cacao, real cream on top.

He joined her. She wasn't surprised.

89

It hadn't been intimate conversation. Fact of life. Her husband, loss of his wife, children, jobs. Time evaporated.

He walked her to her car. "Come back," he said, eyes imploring.

"I'll try. I don't get out much. Today was...unusual."

"Yes," he said meaningfully, "it was."

Innocent? Simple? And here she was eight months later about to sleep with a man other than her husband. A first.

Jim had booked a room in Philadelphia.

She lit another cigarette and Coco, whiffing the sulfur, jumped to the floor. Anne brushed the hairs from her lap, crossed her long legs. So why not? Why shouldn't she? It wasn't exactly like she owed Cole anything.

She ached for Jim O'Neill. Yet that act, that loving act, could change her whole life. Was that so bad? Scary, yes. Bad, no.

Were vows made at twenty applicable at forty-five? Not when the other half didn't care. Was she to bury her sexual feelings forever?

Crushing out her cigarette, she rose. Sleep.

In bed, next to Cole, she held her pillow, pretending it was Jim. Tomorrow she'd call, make final arrangements. In forty-eight hours, her life might be completely turned around. Well, that was better than no life at all. Wasn't it?

Ah, Cookie, put up or shut up.

For sure.

15.

"Let's go, Noj," Kit said for the fifth time.

"In a minute, babe."

It was nearing midnight and the crowd at the New Amsterdam was at its peak. Smoke and the smell of beer were starting to make Kit feel sick. She had her last class in The Psychology of Crime at eight-thirty the next morning and she didn't want to feel lousy for it. It was a course she found stimulating, fascinating, unlike so many of the others that were dry and dull.

Noj and Ben Davis were arguing the value of individual versus family therapy for a seriously disturbed child. It was an argument they'd had before, would undoubtedly have again, and Kit was bored. It occurred to her that this could be a preview of her future life if she married someone in the field. It was wonderful to have things in common, but there was the danger of becoming insulated, one-dimensional.

But what really jolted her was the recurring thought that psychology was not for her. What then? She'd been over and over this, mostly in her undergraduate days, trying to pick a future. How lucky people were who had a talent. She'd never had any. Bright, yes, but where did that get you? The world was filled with bright people. Her roommate in college had urged her to become a model.

"Oh, Sally, you can't mean it."

"You bet I mean it. If I looked like you, I wouldn't give it another thought."

Sally Little was plain. But she could write. Knew what she was going to do after school. The great American novel. Never mind if it didn't sell. She had a direction, desire, talent.

"Being a model is so empty. Why would you want to do that, with your talent?"

"Come on, Kit. Talent. I'm one in hundreds. Thousands. Millions."

"You're good, Sal."

"So what? So are a lot of people. Anyway, with your looks and your knockers...."

"Disgusting."

"But true. Hell, you look like Cheryl Tiegs. Better."

"Well, I just couldn't." The idea of displaying herself after years of trying to play down her looks, body, was appalling to her. "Besides, there are lots of good-looking women in the world."

"Not like you, sweets. You know, looking like you do is a *kind* of talent. I mean, if you use it right."

Sally knew how Kit envied talent. But physical beauty was not a talent to her, no matter what anyone said. Maybe if you could combine something with it. Like acting.

But she didn't have acting talent or any other. So she'd

chosen psychology by default. Would she really be able to stand listening to one patient after another, day after month after year? And what if they were boring? Surely every patient's problems couldn't be interesting. Would the reward of bringing a patient to a cure, or more likely an adjustment, be enough?

And then to share her life with another psychologist! But what other person would she want to be with?

An insurance man like her father? The thought of being married to someone like him was frightening. Of course, his profession was not the reason for his personality. There had to be other men in insurance who were more interesting, warmer, alive.

When she thought of her father, a kind of coldness crept through her. More than once, she thought she'd identified him in her studies. But she'd quickly dismissed those moments, chalking them up to her hostility toward him. Still, her father kept appearing in the pages of her textbooks. It was disturbing. And if he was as neurotic as Kit suspected, what did that say about her mother? Even more disturbing.

More than once she'd wondered why her mother stayed with him. It was clear they weren't in love any more. Had they ever been? On the other hand, talking with friends, she'd learned that most of their parents seemed distant, uncaring with each other. Well, how could romance last all those years? She was naive to think it would be any different for her. Of course there was Nana and Pop Nash. But *they* were the oddballs. And how healthy was that in the end? Surely their consuming passion and interest in each other had had some effect on her father. So what was the right way for parents to be?

Jesus, she thought. I don't want any brats. Too much responsibility. And what's the point? They'll just grow up to hate me and end up in some psychiatrist's office! A vicious circle.

Look at Sara, for instance. Loathing her mother. Eating herself into oblivion. She wished she could help Sara, but whenever she tried to get close, Sara seemed to go further into her shell. She would try again this holiday no matter what defenses Sara put up.

Well, at least there was Tom. A model son and brother. Sometimes she wondered if he wasn't too perfect. Secretly, she hoped he smoked pot or something. She wondered if he was still a virgin or if he and Jennifer were getting it on.

She hoped so. Tom and Max were her favorites. Tom because he was gentle and sweet, bright and affectionate. Max because he was the baby. Steven, so different from Tom, was a bit of an enigma to her, although she loved him. She'd have to make an effort to get to know him better this trip.

She longed to see her mother, needed to talk to her, wondered how open she could be.

"Ready, Kit."

She looked up. Noj was standing, smiling. She hadn't heard the end of the discussion or noticed him rise.

"Something wrong?" he asked.

She shook her head.

On the drive home, Noj tried to pin down her agreement with his side of the argument: family therapy was the only way to help a disturbed child. Kit was tired, uninterested.

"Hey babe," Noj said, "this stuff is going to be your life. You act like you don't give a damn."

"I don't. Tonight. I'm sorry."

"Do I bore you?" he asked defensively.

She squeezed his arm. "Of course not."

But she wondered if he did. She thought she adored him, but maybe, once again, it was just sex. Maybe she couldn't sustain a mature relationship. Maybe she was disturbed herself.

Dr. Clay implied she was afraid of intimacy. But Kit thought she'd made progress in that area, living with Noj. Some things were in the marrow though, she supposed. Too tired to think of it now.

Climbing the stairs to their apartment, Noj's hand on her shoulder, Kit realized she was depressed. Very depressed. Was it because she'd be going home in a few days? The family syndrome?

Oh, shit, she thought, putting her key in the lock, sometimes I wish I were dead.

But just for awhile.

16.

He had survived.

Somehow Tom had managed to get to his bed. Lying there now, the house hushed, except for the usual nightly noises, he couldn't remember how he'd gotten from rug to bed. He was still soaked with sweat. For the last half hour or so, the movement had ceased.

He kicked off the handmade quilt, wiped his body with the striped sheet. There was no question in his mind now. Something terrible was happening to him. But *was* it terrible? Sometimes he thought it was and other times...The experience he'd had tonight was frightening. But wasn't it also important, necessary? He didn't really know what that meant. But he felt it.

He'd completely abandoned the idea of telling his parents. Not just because of the holiday. Not because his mother had things on her mind. His father would probably ground him. There was another reason.

SOLA

Yes, SOLA didn't want him to tell. And that was fine with Tom. More and more, he liked his time with SOLA. Less and less, the time without. Everyday time. His world as he'd always known it was disappearing, replaced by a new and better world. Who was he to question it? He was only a pawn. A conduit. Nevertheless, important to the success of SOLUDA. SOLA said so.

What had it been like before SOLA?

Everything had been so simple, easy. School, sports, friends, parties, Jennifer. Quiet. Dull. And then what happened?

Pain. Bright light. Did the headaches come first or was

it his eyes that were affected? Perhaps both at the same time. Speed. Racing. Thoughts, ideas tumbling, crashing over and into each other. Dizzy. Nausea.

Suddenly, SOLA was there. Life changed. Good. Now there was reason, purpose, meaning. SOLA was his guide to a better life. He couldn't handle anything without SOLA.

SOLA said he must pretend to be the boy he'd always been. Until it was time, he had to keep them off the track. SOLA said he could do it.

He was less tense now, but knew that he probably wouldn't sleep. Sleep was something lost to him forever. Gone. It didn't matter. SOLA had explained that sleep was unnecessary for Tom.

The usual things didn't apply.

Food, too, was obsolete.

Only water was of consequence.

And only what he had to do was important.

SOLA had explained it all. Each step of the way.

Like getting a gun.

Tom had completely forgotten about it. This was proof that he needed SOLA, proof that the world would be a better place when everyone understood SOLUDA.

SOLA had reminded him of the closet in Jennifer's basement. She'd shown him the gun months before.

At the time, he hated it. Now he loved it.

YOU MUST LOVE THE MEANS TO YOUR END, SOLA told him.

Tom did. And he would follow SOLA'S instructions to the letter. Tomorrow he would get it. SOLA promised it would not be hard and SOLA never lied.

At this time tomorrow night he would have it.

SOLA said it was beautiful. And it was.

The gun.

With SOLA'S superior knowledge and guidance, he would secure the gun from the closet in Jennifer's basement. And the box of ammunition.

Then making way for SOLUDA, he, the chosen, Thomas Stuart Nash, Grand Duke, would happily and proudly do SOLA's bidding.

He would pull that trigger.

Over and over and over until it was done.

All dead.

He sighed deeply.

Thursday,
December 19

1.

In the town of Logan, where the Nash family lived, there were only thirteen houses facing the Delaware River, all large Victorians set far back from the road, a good distance from each other. The Nashs' two neighbors on River Road were approximately a half mile apart on each side. The loathed Cunninghams were on the left and on the right, facing the water, was the Durham house.

Esther Durham, nearing sixty, was a small wiry woman with steel gray hair, worn in an attractive bun. Her brown eyes were large and round, giving her an owlish look. Her nose and mouth formed a neat, taut triangle. Two deeply etched lines ran from the corners of her mouth to the bottom of her chin, not unlike those on a ventriloquist's dummy. The rest of her face had eluded wrinkles, except for a delicately-laced network in the hollows under her eyes.

Dressed in gray wool slacks and a heavyknit green turtleneck sweater, Esther was on her way to town. Grocery shopping, cleaners, library. She'd stopped at Anne's in neighborly fashion to see if she needed anything. Now the women sat drinking coffee from blue willow mugs.

Esther, mother of three married daughters, thought of Thomas Nash as the son she never had. As far as she was concerned, he was everybody's ideal boy. And she didn't hesitate to tell Anne Nash that every chance she got.

This morning was no exception.

"And how's that wonderful son of yours?" she asked.

Defensively, Anne said, "I have *three* sons, Esther."

"Oh, dear heart, don't be like that. I love Steven and Max and I'm sure when Tom leaves us and goes off to college, I'll be seeing the virtues of Steven." She didn't really believe

98

anyone could take Tom's place, but she went on to appease Anne. "Then Max...if I live that long."

"Of course you will...live that long, I mean." Anne sincerely cared for Esther.

"God willing. Anyway, how's Tom? I haven't seen him for awhile. He usually stops by once a week or so just to see how I'm doing. Not many boys his age would bother with an old lady like me."

Anne smiled ruefully. Esther wasn't telling her anything new. If she let her, Esther would run on about Tom forever.

"When did you see him last?" she asked, feeling warm, rolling up the sleeves of her blue button down shirt, exposing the sleeves of the white cotton turtleneck underneath.

"Well, that's just it, Anne, he hasn't been by in a dog's age. Maybe as much as three weeks. Thought I mentioned it to you awhile back."

She had, of course. The last time they'd talked. Anne knew Esther wanted her to urge Tom to visit. But she hadn't; she wondered why.

"Anne, you hear me?" Esther blew a plume of smoke into the air.

"Yes, you *did* mention it. I guess he's busy, the holiday season and all."

"Not that I expect anything of him. I mean, the boy owes me nothing and I *do* know how young people are."

"I'm sure he'll be by soon. When are you going to stop smoking those awful cigarettes?" Anne clucked her tongue, inwardly hearing her own mother in the sound. That happened a lot lately; annoying, embarrassing.

Esther waved away Anne's irritating question. "I like my Camels. It's the one pleasure I have left."

She'd stopped eating salt a year before when she discovered she had high blood pressure. It had always threatened, but now it was serious.

"Sure it is," Anne said, eyes on Esther's coffee mug.

"Leave me be, Anne Nash." Changing the subject, Esther said, "George wanted to get Tom a target pistol for Christmas."

Anne felt something sink inside her. "Tom hates guns."

"I know. I told that to George. 'Course, he can't understand that. Says all boys like guns but I said, our Tom is different. I remember when Cole's father gave Tom that .22 a few years back." She sucked in her breath. "Lord, Anne, that was a terrible thing. Remember?"

99

"Who could forget?"

"I thought Cole was going to have a stroke. That was Tom's thirteenth birthday, wasn't it?"

"Yes." This was the last thing she wanted to think about today. It had been such an awful scene.

Esther went on, as though, having brought it up, she now had to recall the event in its entirety, bad as it was. "There we all sat watching the boy open his gifts. I'll never forget the look on Cole's face when Tom opened that package and took out the gun. If George'd been there that day there'd be no way he'd suggest a gun for Christmas, I'll tell you."

"No, I suppose not. But surely he knows how Cole is about things like that."

"You know George, sees what he wants to see, knows what he wants to know. Anyway," she went on recalling, "you would have thought that the old man had given Tom a live cobra or something the way Cole looked at that gun. Then he turned on his father, face all red, eyes kind of piercing the way they do sometimes. Oh, it makes my blood run cold to think of it." She clucked her tongue.

"I know, I know," Anne said. "Look darling, I'm sure Tom'll be by soon, so don't feel hurt or anything, okay." She didn't want to remember. Not at all.

Esther paused. Clearly, Anne didn't want her to go on about that awful incident. Why would she? "I expect so. Well, anyway, we're giving Tom some shirts from Barth's. Seems to like them, doesn't he?"

"Yes, he does. But you spend much too much money on the kids, Esther."

"Oh, hell. We enjoy it. It's once a year and what do George and I do with our money, anyway?"

"Well, you have family of your own."

"There's plenty to go round, Anne. Don't worry. George Durham may look like a hick, but he's a smart man when it comes to a dollar." She stubbed out her cigarette.

Anne smiled. Everyone knew the Durhams were worth plenty, even if they didn't show it. That's one of the things Anne liked about them so much. No pretensions.

"Well, still," she said, "you spoil our kids."

"Fine. That's all I'm good for anymore...to spoil other people's kids. You'll see, Anne, when you have grandchildren. Which reminds me...is Kit bringing that nice fellow home with her? What's his name...funny name if I recall."

"It's Noj. Jon backwards. No, he's going home to his own family."

"I hope that's not over or anything. He seemed like such a nice boy." Remembering Doc Mancinelli, Esther wanted Kit married and safe as soon as possible.

"As far as I know, everything's fine."

"You think they'll be getting married?"

"I don't know, Esther. Kit hasn't said anything about that."

"Well, I hope they do. I like that boy even though I think calling him Noj is about the dumbest thing I ever heard."

Anne laughed.

"Well," Esther said, rising, stretching her short arms overhead, "guess I'd better get on with my errands. Sure you don't need anything?"

"Not a thing."

At the door, Esther pulled on her red and black lumber jacket, zipped it up the front, put her red earmuffs in place.

"When are the kids arriving?"

"Sally and Company'll be the first on Monday. Margaret's gang Tuesday and Janet and her brood early Christmas morning."

"Well, then let's have our Christmas Sunday night. Why don't you and George come over about seven-thirty?"

"We'll be there. Say hello to all and tell that handsome boy I miss him. No, on second thought, don't. I don't want him visiting me out of guilt and he would, too. Just tell him I said hello."

Esther crunched through the snow to her eight-year-old Oldsmobile. George Durham couldn't see the point of trading in a car when it gave perfect service like "Bathsheba" did. Esther would have preferred something a little newer, but George held the purse strings.

Cold as it was, "Bathsheba" started up immediately. Driving along, Esther's mind went back to the .22 rifle incident four years ago.

Stuart Nash had seemed stunned by his son's reaction. Must have been like George, knowing what he wanted to know.

"How could you?" Cole asked his father.

"What's that? What do you mean?"

"Christ almighty." He spun around, grabbed the gun from Tom's hands. "How could you give a child a gun?"

"He's thirteen," Stuart said.

"What's all the fuss?" asked Clara.

Ignoring her, Cole went on yelling at his father. "You know how I feel about things like this, like guns, weapons. Good God."

"You can't protect the boy forever, Cole."

"As long as he's a boy, I can."

Esther remembered Tom sitting on the floor, head bent low, not watching the scene.

"You're living in a dream world. These kids have to face reality sooner or later."

"Guns don't have to be a reality." Cole held it out as though it were about to explode. "Take it."

"It's Tom's," Stuart said.

"No, it's not. Take it." He tried shoving it in his father's arms, but Stuart backed up.

Tom had raised his head then. "Dad, don't."

"Keep out of it," Cole said. "Take this gun," he demanded of his father.

Stuart stood his ground. "It's not my gun. It's the boy's."

Cole started to say something else, stopped. His knuckles went white as he gripped the gun. He walked to the front door, opened it and threw the gun outside as far as he could.

Tom, crying, ran upstairs.

When Cole faced his father, Stuart said, "You're one son of a bitch, Cole. Come on, Clara."

They'd left and Anne had told Esther it was more than a month before Cole and his father spoke again. And then they hadn't mentioned the incident.

When Tom had come visiting a few days later, Esther asked how he was feeling about the whole thing.

"I wish my father would let me be like other kids. The dumb thing is that I never would have used the crummy gun. I couldn't kill little animals or anything. But if I had a gun, well, I'd be like the other kids, you know?"

Esther had tried to minimize Cole's obsession. "It's just that he loves you and worries about you."

"Does he?"

"Worry about you?"

"Love me?"

"Why, of course he does. What a question. You don't really think he doesn't love you, do you?" The thought of anyone not loving Tom was absurd.

He shrugged his shoulders. "I dunno. I guess he does. Just sometimes it's hard to know."

Well, that was all water under the bridge and everybody had survived the incident, awful as it was.

Starting up Hogan's Hill, Esther shifted into second. She hoped Anne would give Tom a hint about visiting after all. He was the nicest, sweetest young man around and she missed him like all get out.

2.

Jim O'Neill couldn't keep his eyes off the clock behind the bar. Why hadn't Anne called? He knew her family was out of the house by now.

He walked behind the bar, removed a glass from the rack above his head, squirted himself a Tab. Perhaps he'd been wrong to press her into a final action. But how long could a grown man go on talk, kisses, promises? If there was no hope of consummation, he knew he'd have to end it.

The thought made him sick.

He sat at the end of the bar, faced the water. Except for the whine of the vacuum coming from the rear dining room, the Inn was still, the rest of the staff not due for half an hour. This quiet time was his, as well as the time after closing, alone in his apartment upstairs, time to think.

Jim plowed a hand through his thick, dark hair. It was different now, three years after Marilyn's death. Then he'd dreaded time alone, tried to fill every moment. Avoiding grief. Stupid.

Four months ago he'd put away her pictures and now sometimes he'd forget what she looked like. It frightened him. Yet he knew she wanted him to go on; she said as much.

"Don't deny the future, Jim. Life goes on and it needs you."

She'd expected him to fall in love, marry again. Why were her expectations so hard for him? Guilt undercut all his feelings.

He saw her charcoal eyes burning out, the clear white skin degenerating to yellow, hands dry, bony.

She was gone. He was alone. After the business of the funeral, he stayed long hours at the magazine; time spent superfluously, his staff understanding.

Quite suddenly, he quit and left New York.

Home to Doylestown with his parents.

How kind they were. Father, inarticulate, remote, trying with a thumping clap on the back to show he understood. Mother, indulgent, soft-spoken, eyes always brimming over.

He'd had to leave. An apartment of his own.

Driving aimlessly one day, he'd seen the sign for the Inn.

The six months of renovation kept Marilyn out of his thoughts, his life. But after the first two months of business, he'd collapsed internally. Only then, two years after her death, he allowed himself to grieve, doing so for almost a year.

Until Anne walked into his life.

The moment he saw her standing in the hallway, one hand braced on the wall, something inside, something he'd forgotten existed, stirred.

Five weeks stretched between their first and second meetings. She'd almost begun to fade from his thoughts. Then there she was in the doorway between hall and bar. Neither could speak. Wordlessly, smiling, he led her to the same table she'd had before.

When the lunch crowd was gone, he brought her a crème de cacao, joined her.

After some trite, inconsequential talk, he leapt in.

"I'm so happy you came back. I've thought of you...many, many times. I didn't know if I'd ever see you again."

"I tried to stay away. Every day I had a new resolve and it worked. Until now."

He covered her hand with his, but she gently pulled away.

"I must tell you I don't understand this and I don't really know why I'm here or what I want. I feel quite crazy," she murmured.

"So do I."

"I've been married for twenty-five years. And I've five children."

He nodded.

"And I don't believe in adultery."

Jim smiled, the great craggy lines deepening. "I didn't think adultery was something one believed in."

She laughed, embarrassed, covered her face with her hands. "I'm an awful fool."

"No. I understand. I really do."

And goddamn, he thought he did. But he'd had no idea it would go on like that.

They'd come so close so many times.

If she'd loved Cole, Jim would have accepted it, gracefully. Removed himself. But she didn't. She wanted him; he knew that. If he didn't believe that, he'd given up long ago.

But his patience was thinning out, nearing an end. They were going nowhere. Either they had to stop or go forward and there was only one way to go forward.

If Anne couldn't go with him to Philadelphia tomorrow, he'd made up his mind to end it. The Inn was doing beautifully and right after New Years he'd take a trip. Stay away as long as it took.

If she did go, made love with him, he knew she'd be his. Not because he was a great lover, but because that was the kind of woman Anne Nash was.

He wanted her. Wanted to marry her. In thirty-six hours, he'd know.

Good Christ, he thought, know what? She hasn't even called. Probably won't.

Merry Christmas, jackass!

3.

Blood gushed from his nose as though someone were pushing a button.

"What the hell is wrong with you, Nash?"

The basketball had hit him hard, in the center of the face, knocking him down. He was sitting up now, head thrown back, feeling the blood pour over his lips, down his chin.

"Are ya in some kind a trance or somethin'?" Bob Harris, the coach, asked, shoving a handkerchief up to Tom's nose.

He felt as though he were being engulfed by blood; swallowed alive by his own chemistry. It both frightened and excited him. Harris was talking to him, but he couldn't hear. He pushed the handkerchief hard against his nose, a horrible pain boring through the bridge, between his eyes.

Two of the boys lifted him under the arms.

"Take him to the nurse," Harris ordered. "Keep your goddamn head back, Nash, you shmuck."

As they walked down the hall his teammates asked lots of questions. He didn't answer. Couldn't.

"It was just like you didn't see the ball coming, Tom, but you were looking right at it. What happened?"

"You didn't really see it, did you?"

"He was looking right at it, you turkey."

"Yeah, I know, but sometimes you're looking and you're not looking, you know what I mean?"

"Something wrong, Tom? You seem out of it, lately."

"Is Jennifer giving you blue balls or what?"

Mrs. MacNish had no one else in her office. She took him immediately. His friends left. He lay on the cot, head tilted back, listening as Mrs. MacNish clunked across the room to the small refrigerator. In a moment she was leaning over him.

"Take the handkerchief away, Thomas. I'm going to give you an ice pack. It'll stop the bleeding and take down the swelling."

When he opened his eyes, she was leaning over him, her large bosom encased in the white uniform almost directly over his mouth.

The ice pack felt terrible.

"What happened?" Mrs. MacNish asked.

"Ball hit me," he managed to say.

He heard her make a tsking sound, then, "Violence all the time, sickening. All right, keep that ice pack on there, head back." She pulled the green curtain all around him.

Alone.

The truth of the matter was he'd no idea what had really happened. Of course he'd seen the ball coming toward him; seen it leave Raeburn's hands. Fast. Hard.

Then what?

He wanted to remember. He was sure it was important. He tried to picture the ball, round, red, white and blue spinning, spinning toward him. Had he begun to lift his hands for the catch? Where were his hands? Hanging down at his sides? Of course not. As always they were waist high, out, slightly ready, waiting. But he hadn't lifted them, not even a millimeter.

He remembered.

Instinctively his hands, arms were tensed ready for the pass. And then his orders came.

Loud and clear.

SOLA.

DO NOT LIFT YOUR HANDS.

But why? Why would SOLA want him to be hit in the face? Hurt? Bleed?

A roar that sounded like an angry lion's almost threw him off the cot with fear.

It was SOLA. Shouting.

He'd forgotten. "I'm sorry," he whispered. "I'll never do it again."

Reluctantly, SOLA forgave him.

He must never, never question SOLA's reasons again. SOLA knew best. It didn't matter if he *never* knew why SOLA wanted him to be hurt and bleed. SOLA had his reasons. A mere messenger like Tom could not expect to know everything. Later, when he was a Grand Duke, he would be permitted to understand more. Now he was just a lowly subject and must do what he was told.

SOLA was all powerful.

Tom was nothing.

4.

Damn Esther Durham for bringing up that old gun incident, Anne thought. She hated thinking about it. She'd been so ineffectual. But what could she have done, really?

She began making Max's bed, brushing cookie crumbs and cat hairs into her hand. Clearly, Coco had been there again. What could she ever do against Cole when it came to safety. He almost always beat her down.

She thought of Kit, four years old, in the hospital to have her tonsils out. It was necessary, the doctor said. Anne and Cole had spent the early part of the evening at Kit's bedside, cheering, reassuring.

At three in the morning, Cole had sat up in bed, turned on the light.

"What is it?"

"Get dressed. We're getting her out of there." He swung his legs over the side of the bed, unbuttoning his pajama top.

"Cole, what are you talking about?"

"I'm talking about Kit. I'm not letting that butcher near her."

"But Cole, the doctor said it's necessary. She's going to have a lot of trouble if she doesn't have them out."

"What the hell does he know? I can't go through with it, Anne. Don't you understand?"

"No, I don't."

"Something might happen to her," he said softly. "A slip of the knife. Problems with the anesthetic. Anything."

"Oh, Cole, please. Children have their tonsils out every day."

"Not my children. Are you coming or not?"

"Can't we wait until morning?"

"No."

She'd gone with him, of course, knowing Kit would be frightened, them barging in like that. She'd need her mother. They'd taken her out of the hospital and Kit *had* had trouble for years. The doctor had refused to treat the Nashes anymore. Kit still had her tonsils. But Cole had relieved his panic at the thought that something more than colds and sore throats would happen to his daughter. And Anne had been unable to stop him, change his mind, alter anything.

Had she tried to interfere during the gun incident, it would have been pointless. Cole was a madman at times like those. She mustn't blame herself. No one could've stood up to him. Could they?

She left Max's room, went to her own. Even as she told herself this, Anne knew it was cowardice that paralyzed her. And thinking of lack of action, she noted the time. Jim would be wondering why she hadn't called. Then she thought of the promise she'd made to herself the night before to call Dr. Blackwell.

Was it really necessary? Yes, damnit. For once take some real action, follow your instincts, she told herself. She picked up the white receiver, dialed.

After making the appointment for later in the day, she dialed again. She felt jittery, unsure of what she'd say, but when she heard Jim's voice, her resolve was confirmed.

"I thought you weren't going to call," he said.

"I'd never do that to you." And she wouldn't. "Oh, Jim, I miss you so."

"Darling," he whispered.

She knew he was waiting for her final decision, knew he must be in pain. "I'm going to be there tomorrow. Nothing will stop me."

There was a pause. "Jesus," he said. "Oh, Jesus. I don't know what I would've done if you'd said no. I want you so much."

"I want *you*." These words, both his and hers, sent tingling sensations through her body. She was instantly aroused.

"What time do you think you'll get there?"

"I hope by eleven-thirty."

"Are you afraid?" he asked.

"Terribly."

"It'll be good, Anne. But it's all right to be afraid. I am too. We've waited so goddamn long."

The thought of making love with Jim produced in her a kind of excitement she hadn't known in years.

"We've waited *too* long," she found herself saying.

"Oh, my darling," he said. "You don't know what it does to me to hear you say that."

"I think I do, Jim."

"I love you," he said.

"I love you, too."

When she hung up, the full implication of her action struck her. Commitment. There was no turning back now. But that was ridiculous. Of course, there was. Still. She'd told Jim she'd be there. And she would be.

Anne walked to the window, looked down at the solid white snow, sun reflecting, hard on the eyes.

Anne Clifford Nash is taking an action, she thought. She was asserting herself. Helluva way to do it! What would her mother think, father have thought? Oh, God, why did she always think in terms of her parents' evaluation of her. Would she ever grow up enough to let go of that? Then she thought, Daddy would be glad!

"You're sure you want to marry this fellow, Cookie?" Max Clifford had asked her more than twenty-five years before.

"Yes. Why Daddy? Don't you like him?"

He'd raised his ever-present coffee mug to his lips, taken a swig, licked his lips. "The truth? No, I don't."

"Why?"

"Wish I could tell ya. I mean, I wish I could say, it's this and this and this," he said, making points in the air with his forefinger. "It's just a feeling. There's something missing."

She told herself her father was tight, ignored the feeling inside herself that accorded with his for just a flickering moment. "I don't see why a feeling you can't even put into words should make you not like him."

"Shouldn't, I guess, but it does. Besides, he doesn't look me in the eye when he talks to me. And his handshake's a bit weak."

"Oh, that's so old-fashioned, Daddy." She laughed.

"Maybe so. Well, all I want is for you to be happy, Cookie."

"I'm going to be."

"Good. But, darling, if it doesn't work out, don't be afraid to come home. We'll always be here for you."

But she had been afraid to go home. *You can't go home again.* How could she have gone home to her parents with the children? But the point was that her father had been saying she didn't have to stick it out no matter what. Only *she* had told herself that.

And stuck she had. Now, damnit, she owed herself a new chance. Had the right to be loved. Whatever stupid allegiance she thought she had to Cole was over. Done with. And her father would have been glad. I'll end my marriage for Daddy, she thought, then realized the insanity of that thought.

No. For me.

And my children.

5.

Kit heard the phone ringing as she raced up the stairs. She was positive that no matter how fast she ran, got the key in the lock, it would stop ringing just as she reached it. An unwritten rule. But this time she was wrong.

Out of breath, she said, "Yes?"

There was a pause, then, "Kit?"

"Yes?"

"It's Mom."

"Oh, hi. I didn't recognize your voice."

"You sound funny."

"I'm out of breath. I was just coming back from class. Ran up those back-breaking stairs. What's up?" It was odd for Anne to be calling so close to Kit's trip home.

Another pause. "I....Nothing dear. I just wanted to say hello."

Kit sat on a kitchen chair, unzipped her red parka, pulled

off her striped woolen cap. "Mom, forgive me, but I don't believe you. I'll be seeing you in five days."

"Oh, Kit," Anne said sadly.

Kit was concerned. "What is it?"

Silence.

"Mom, please. You're scaring me." It wasn't like her mother. Not at all.

"I'm sorry, darling. I don't know what it is. How's the weather there?"

"Oh, no, you don't."

"Would you believe me if I said it's nothing I could put my finger on?"

"I'm not sure. Is it Daddy?"

"Daddy? Why do you say that?"

"I don't know." Kit realized she always half expected to hear her father had flipped out.

"It's no one. Just blues, I guess."

Kit smiled. *I have the blues.* It was really her grandmother's generation who used that expression. Her mother had gotten it from Kit's grandmother. Depressed, was what she meant.

"Are you okay, honey?"

"I'm fine." She began wriggling out of the parka, juggling the phone.

"And Noj?"

"He's fine, too. Mom, don't you have any idea what you're depressed about?"

"I didn't say I was depressed."

"Okay, okay. Do you have any idea why you have the blues," she corrected.

"I'm going to see Dr. Blackwell later."

Kit felt frightened. "What is it? Are you sick?"

"No, no, I'm fine. It's Tom."

"Tom? What's wrong with him?"

"I'm sure it's girl trouble or something equally earth-shattering. No doubt this is Christmas excitement on my part. Oh, I don't know, Kit. Little things. Suddenly he's complaining about the light in his room hurting his eyes. He says he wants black shades. The other afternoon I found him sitting at his desk wearing dark glasses."

"Maybe you should have his eyes checked." Carrying the phone, she walked to the refrigerator.

"I thought of that, but I couldn't get an appointment until the twenty-seventh."

"God, I hope nothing's wrong with his eyes," Kit said, opening the door.

"It's not just that," Anne said. "It's complicated. Lately he's been acting different."

"How?" It wasn't like Anne to see things in her children that weren't there. Kit had always appreciated how planted in reality her mother was. "Can you give me an example?"

"Oh, it's absurd. I don't know why I'm calling you. Pay no attention to me."

"It's not absurd. I know you. There's something wrong if you made an appointment with Blackwell. Now if it were Daddy, I wouldn't be concerned? What does he say?"

"Nothing. He doesn't seem to have noticed. It's not physical. I guess that's why I called you. It's mental, Kit. He's odd. Vague. Sometimes he looks at me strangely. A look I've never seen before."

"What kind of look?" She took a quart of milk from the refrigerator.

"It's a cold look."

"Have you talked to anyone else about this?"

"Well, I mentioned it to Finch."

Good. Finch was sensible. "What did she say?"

"She said he was probably going through a stage."

Gently, Kit said, "Mom, she's probably right." But she wondered. Tom, so warm and giving, eyes cold? Unless her mother was imagining it. Unless something was wrong with *her* instead of Tom.

"Yes, I guess."

Kit decided to take a small chance. "Have you been sleeping, Mom?" Walking to the cupboard, she removed a glass, poured the milk.

"Sleeping? Yes, why?"

She pressed on. "Have you been feeling all right? I mean other than this thing about Tom? Do you feel all right?"

"Yes, fine. Why?" Anne laughed. "Oh, Kit. You think it's *me*, don't you? You think something's wrong with *me*."

Kit was embarrassed. Smart lady, her mother.

"I don't know what I think." She returned the quart of milk to the refrigerator, kicked it closed with her foot.

"Darling, please don't worry. I'm fine. Honestly. It's...look, Kit, there are things...damn! I hate phones."

"I know."

"I shouldn't have called. I don't want to worry you. It was selfish of me. I always get anxious around...."

"Mother, you started to say something. You said, 'there are things'... What things?"

"We'll have a long talk when you get home. I promise. It's nothing urgent. Okay?"

"Are you sure?" She took a swallow of milk.

"I'm sure."

"Will you let me know what Dr. Blackwell says?"

"If there's anything to tell. I'm positive he'll assure me it's nothing, but I think I'll feel better if I hear it from him."

"I know you're right but in case, you'll call, won't you?"

"Of course."

"And if you need me, Mom, I can leave today, you know. I can be there late tonight."

"Oh, no. No, don't."

The answer came quickly, too quickly. Disquieting.

Softly, Kit said, "All right. But if you change your mind.... If you need me, please don't be afraid you'll upset my plans. My schedule's flexible. Really."

"Thanks, Kit. Don't worry. I'm fine. It's just Christmas jitters."

"Christmas is a killer," Kit said. "Do you know that more than half the population hates it and yet we persist. Crazy."

"I don't hate it. It just...there's so much to do, that's all."

"Well, take it easy. Don't knock yourself out. Wait for me, I'll help."

"I will. I'd better go." She giggled oddly. "Got to get going."

Kit started to tell her to take it easy again, stopped herself. She knew her mother would do whatever it was she had to do and the last thing she wanted was to come on like a mother.

"I love you, Mom."

"I love you, too."

Calling Finch Bond had not been an easy or arbitrary decision for Kit. She'd always been a favorite of Finch's, but she knew her first allegiance was to Anne. And, it was possible nothing would be gained from the call; it might only serve to make Finch anxious. It might also irritate her mother if Finch found it necessary to tell her. But in the end Kit knew she had to phone. Even if Finch couldn't tell her anything, at least she would have tried.

At first Finch dismissed Kit's questions, playing the whole thing down. Then, unable to ignore the obvious concern and worry in Kit's voice, she relented. Agreed this focus on Tom was nonsense, probably a substitute for something else.

114

Then Finch indicated she knew what the something else was. And after cajoling, impressing on Finch that her mother's mental health might be at stake, she got the truth.

Sitting at the kitchen table, staring down into a mug of coffee, she remembered words her Grandmother Clifford had said to her when she was a nosy five-year-old. "Don't ask so many questions, Kit, you might find out something you don't want to know."

She had.

Unbelievable. But why? Because it was *her* mother? If she'd heard the same thing about Noj's mother or anyone else's mother, would she find it so improbable? Certainly, she wouldn't find it so disturbing.

Her mother.

Her mother.

Her *mother*.

She said it out loud, as though trying it on for size. "My mother is having an affair."

Absurd.

Inwardly, she flinched at her sexist thinking. Had the idea of her father's affair been absurd? Horrifying, yes. But par for the course. In one sense, acceptable. All men did that. Women didn't.

She hadn't thought of Julia Paige in years. But now her mind drifted back in time, ashamed, embarrassed. She'd been very young and the young are often ridiculously moralistic, she told herself. God knew she had been.

Rob Fitz, her boyfriend during her senior year in high school, was the first to tell her.

"I don't believe you, Rob. And I think you're a creep to say it."

"I thought you'd want to know. I'm sorry. I mean, everyone else knows, so I thought you'd want to know."

"Who's everyone?"

"I dunno," he shrugged, "just everyone. I heard my mother telling my father."

"Well, so what if he is," she said defensively.

Rob looked at her blankly. "I dunno."

"Men always do that, have affairs. It's just their way and it's been going on down through the centuries." She only half believed what she was saying. Feminism had not touched her yet, but instinctively something rang false. "Who'd you say the girl was?"

And Rob told her again about Julia Paige and where she lived.

Kit spent the next few weeks watching Julia go in and out of the restaurant where she worked and in and out of her apartment building. She couldn't decide what to do, but felt it was her duty to do something. Her father was hurting her mother, making a fool of her, and somebody had to protect her. Even though Kit wasn't that crazy about her mother right then, it worried her that she might find out and leave Cole. Then what? Who would send her to college and what would happen to the family?

Then one day it occurred to her that her father might leave her mother. She knew she had to act.

Terrified, she knocked on Julia Paige's door.

"Yes?"

Kit was surprised. She'd never seen her so close before, hadn't quite realized how young she was. "Miss Paige?" she stalled.

"Yes. Who are you?"

"I'm Kit Nash."

The two young women stared at each other for a moment. Then Julia asked her to come in.

As frightened as she was, Kit knew if she was going to be effective she couldn't let Julia know. She decided her best stance was an aggressive one. "Does my father pay for this?" she said, gesturing around the small, hardly elegant apartment.

"Some of it," Julia said, unashamed.

"I suppose you know why I'm here," she said, throwing back her shoulders and trying to appear mature, imitating someone in a movie.

"I have no idea," Julia said. "Would you like a drink? A Coke?"

Immediately Kit got the sarcasm, refused. She resolved not to mince words with this whore. "I think you're disgusting."

"I'm sure you do. But you don't understand, you're too young."

"And how old are you?"

"I'm twenty."

Twenty! Kit was shocked. Julia was only three years older than she. She'd thought she was at least over twenty-one. "You're only three years older than I am," she said angrily.

"Those particular three years make a big difference. Someday you'll see."

Kit felt herself losing ground, getting off the track. "Look, I know all about you and my father."

Julia smiled. "Obviously. What is it you want, Kit?"

"I want you to give him up. Did you know he was married?"

Julia nodded. "And I knew about you and the others."

"Then how *could* you?" Kit thought she'd never met anyone as heartless or as immoral.

"I fell in love," Julia said calmly.

Kit was repelled. And her father in love with this tramp? She couldn't bring herself to ask. Didn't want to know. "Well, it's killing my mother," she lied.

"She knows?"

Kit noted that Julia seemed disturbed. "Yes. She found out this morning."

"I see." She lit a cigarette.

"Will you give him up?"

There was a pause and then Julia smiled in a strange way. "Yes. I will."

Kit was stunned. She really hadn't expected it to be so easy. She guessed that Julia realized it was a hopeless cause now. How smart she'd been to say her mother knew.

She'd left Julia's apartment that day feeling victorious, powerful. And when she learned the next day that Julia had left town, she was ecstatic. She'd saved the family.

Almost eight years later, she found herself again wondering about the family for the same reason. But now she knew she couldn't interfere. Blushing at the memory of her earlier interference, she knew now that her meeting with Julia hadn't caused the woman to leave town. What had, she'd never know, but surely it hadn't been the visit of an arrogant seventeen-year-old. Would a visit from one of Doc Mancinelli's kids have changed things for her?

Hardly.

When she'd found out about her father and Julia, she'd been forced to think of Cole as a sexual being. Separate and apart from her mother. It had almost been impossible. It was hard enough to think of her parents together in a sexual contact.

When she was six, a boy told her what the word *fuck* meant. Maybe his parents did dirty things like that, but not hers, Kit protested.

Later, when she asked Anne about it and was told prop-

117

erly, told it was part of love, beautiful, also how babies were made, she tried to picture her parents in the act and couldn't. When she was eight, she walked in on them one night.

Pounding her father's back, she shouted at him to stop hurting Mommy. It wasn't until Cole carried her back to bed, angrily slapped her behind, that she realized what had been going on.

In her early teens, she always knew when they were having sex. It wasn't often. Her room next to theirs, she could hear through the wall. Springs creaking. Grunts. She hated it; hated that it often excited her. After the Julia incident, she didn't hear it and then she went away to school. But Max was born that next summer, so obviously, they still did something.

Since then Kit hadn't given any thought to her parents' sex life. Now she had to reconcile herself to the idea that her mother was having an affair. Was Anne in love? Who was Jim O'Neill? Would there be a divorce? Here it was again. Even now, the idea of the family splitting frightened Kit. Crazy. She was a grown woman. But what about the little kids? Steven, Sara, Max? Especially Max.

Would O'Neill take on the kids? Who'd get custody? Oh, God, it was so awful. People in Logan thought of them as the ideal family. What would they think now?

And there that was again, caring what other people thought. Didn't Dr. Clay tell her it was one of her biggest problems, trying to keep up the fiction that her family, mother, father, siblings were perfect and loving? When the truth was that there was plenty wrong.

Hadn't she really known for years that her parents weren't in love anymore? And not just because of her father's affair. There was something very wrong between them. On the surface, everything looked good. They all looked good, including her. But, Dr. Clay said, there was a cancer underneath, eating away at the fabric of all their lives, and if Kit didn't face it, deal with it, she'd suffer later on.

She had to get her mother to talk with her. *"There are things."* Her mother must have meant the affair with O'Neill. But Kit had promised Finch not to say anything. She'd have to wait for Anne to bring it up. After all, her mother didn't even know Finch knew.

She smiled, thinking maybe it wasn't true any more that the Nashes looked so good to the outside world. According to Finch, a number of people knew about Anne's affair. And hadn't people known about her and Doc? And her father and Julia? Maybe it was just her. Maybe she alone had the need to think they were the perfect family. What a laugh.

So her mother was having an affair. Okay. Part of the perfect picture had crumbled. Dr. Clay would be glad. And Kit would deal with it. Besides, there was nothing she could do about it. She wasn't seventeen and she had no intentions of paying a visit to a Jim O'Neill. But when she got home she would try to make it clear to her mother that she could trust and confide in her. She would be her mother's friend.

Rising from the table, putting her mug in the sink, she gave a sigh of relief. At least nothing was wrong with Tom.

Thank God for that.

6.

Cole was getting ready to go to lunch when Harry walked into his office, ostentatiously loosened the knot of his splashy striped tie, turned a chair around and sat facing Cole.

Something was up.

Harry lowered his head, looked at Cole from under his eyebrows. "Going to lunch?"

"I was."

"With anyone?"

"No." He'd been looking forward to this lunch alone. He wanted to think further, about his disappearing act.

"Good. We have to talk." He took a Pall Mall from the pack, tapped one end on his large, yellowing thumb nail. "We can go to lunch or...."

"What is it, Harry?" There'd be no way he could eat until he knew what was on Harry's mind.

"I don't want you to skip lunch."

"Don't worry about my stomach. What's up?"

"Cole, we've got big trouble." He pressed his lips together, nodded his head several times, full white hair springing outward with the motion.

Cole could have put his fist through Harry's face. Now he had to ask 'what trouble?' Why couldn't Harry just spit it out? But he never could. In all the times Harry'd played this game, Cole had never been able to determine why it seemed so familiar. Now he did. His father used to do this to him when he'd done something wrong.

Cat and mouse.

What would Harry do if he didn't ask? But he couldn't help himself. Programmed.

"What trouble?"

A piece of tobacco flew from Harry's lip when he spoke. "Big trouble," he said again, shaking his head from side to side.

Cole tried focusing on the piece of tobacco which had landed on some yellow paper near the edge of his desk. When his father had done this to him, the anxiety was so great he usually ended up confessing before he was accused. But he had absolutely no idea what Harry was leading up to.

Gripping the sides of his chair so he wouldn't scream, he said, "How about telling me?" His voice even.

"I feel sick about this. Just sick. Well, I guess I'd better get to it." Harry smacked his hairy hands together in a loud clap and leveled his gaze at Cole. "You know the Harrison Foster case?"

Cole thought he might tip over the desk and crush Harry beneath it. Instead, he said, "Of course."

"Daley got an interview with the daughter. Laura Howland. She's married to the D. A., Tim Howland."

He nodded.

"Well, this Howland babe, who incidentally, is not bad for a broad in her late thirties, gave Daley an earful." He pinched the bridge of his thin nose.

Cole leaned forward. Was it possible there was a break in the case? No, Harry had said they were in 'big trouble.'

"What kind of earful?" Cole asked dutifully.

Harry rubbed his face with both hands, shook his head again. "It's really something. Well, Cole, I guess I'd better hand it to you straight."

They were looking at each other, Cole waiting. He wondered what cue line Harry wanted now. Suddenly he felt as though he didn't know his part, panicked. He managed to get out, "What?"

"This is tough. Look, let me tell you the way Daley told me. He couldn't come to you, you understand."

"No, I don't understand, Harry. Will you just spit it out, for God's sake." His voice rose.

"Take it easy, boy." Harry held up a hand. "This is a delicate matter."

"*What* is a delicate matter?" he asked through clenched teeth.

"I'm about to tell you, if you'll only listen." Harry was put out. "Okay. Yesterday Daley got an interview with the Howland broad. He sort of hinted around maybe her old man had bought it on his own, you know? Maybe he came down too hard on that... well, who knows. Anyway, according to Daley, she gets pissed off and kind of turns on him."

Harry blew a smoke ring, rested his chin on the arm he'd draped across the chair back.

Cole recognized his cue, gave his line. "What do you mean, turned on him?"

Harry let his expression change from one of deep intensity to something like concern. Perhaps sympathy?

"Cole, this isn't fun for me, you know."

Cole almost laughed out loud. Playing his part, he knew he must nod in understanding. "Let's hear it."

"Now, the thing of it is, Cole, the Howland babe might be lying. It's possible. So don't go flying off the handle."

Cole bit his lower lip, waited.

"She says to Daley, 'How dare you'... don't you just love these types?" He laughed deep in his throat. "They always come on with the *how dare you* act. Kills me. Anyway, she says her *how dare you* to Daley. Then, and this is the kicker, she says, 'I think before you make any insinuations about my family you'd better look to your own house.'"

"What's that supposed to mean?"

"That's what Daley asked her. Or something like it."

"And?" he asked impatiently.

"Well, after a back and forth which I won't bore you with, she makes it clear that his 'own house' is us. Brandt, Brandt, Todd & Nash... especially Nash."

"What do you mean, Harry?"

"Christ, this is hard. Look, I wouldn't tell you this if I didn't think it was, well, important. I mean, I know how much the company means to you and... oh shit, Cole. This cunt

121

Howland said Anne's shacking up with some goddamn Mick. I'm sorry."

All Cole could think to say was, "Mick?"

"Yeah. An innkeeper down in Williams. Name's O'Neill."

"O'Neill?" he repeated stupidly.

"I'm sorry as shit, Cole. I mean, to tell you like this, but I knew you'd want to know. And we can't have this kind of thing thrown back at us. Right?"

"Right."

"Now it may not even be true. Christ, we all know how these things can get started over nothing."

Cole knew Harry didn't believe for a moment that the rumor was unfounded. He also knew his reason for telling Cole had nothing to do with the health of the company. What a bastard Harry Todd was.

"But if it is true...well, you've got to put a stop to it, Cole."

He nodded. After all these years, Harry was having his revenge. He couldn't get back at his father, so he'd punish Cole. It made him want to laugh.

"Are you all right?" Harry stood, one hand resting on the desk.

"I'm all right."

"I know it's a shock. It is, isn't it?"

"Yes."

"You have any idea who this O'Neill bastard is?"

"No." He wished Harry would leave.

Sounding like something out of a B-movie, he said, "I could have him taken care of if you want, Cole?"

It was all Cole could do to keep from guffawing. "What the hell does that mean?"

Harry straightened, embarrassed. "I...I have friends ...friends who'd talk to him."

He shook his head, tried not to offend. "I'd like to be alone now."

"Oh, right, sure." He started to leave, stopped. "Before you do anything crazy, you'd better check it out. Could be a pile of shit, you know. The guy's name is Jim O'Neill. The inn is in Williams, The Koehler Inn on the Post Road."

Cole nodded, noting that Harry had already done some checking.

At the door, Harry tried to look sincere, caring. "Tough break, boy."

When he'd gone, Cole's mouth slowly broke into a smile. It was funny. But only for a moment.

It wasn't funny at all.

If it was true.

He opened the top drawer of his desk, reached way in the back, fished around and pulled out a small tin box. He kept an extra supply of Valium in the tin that was used for aspirin many years ago. Cole popped two, started to close the tin, thought better of it and took one more. Just in case. To be sure. You never knew.

Grinding his teeth together, the muscle in his jaw jumped. As far as he was concerned, she could screw anybody she wanted. But he didn't want the whole county knowing it. It made him look like an ass.

He put on his coat, wrapped his scarf carefully around his neck. Why let this mess up his lunch? Two martinis would help him sort it out. Right this minute he had no idea what he was going to do about Anne and this O'Neill character, but he'd put it together. Figure out an angle.

One thing he knew for sure. He'd be damned if he'd just sit on his duff while the rest of the world laughed behind his back.

Not on your life.

7.

"You look just awful," Jennifer said.

Tom nodded. He'd looked in the mirror before lunch, seen the skin underneath both eyes was turning black.

"I just can't understand how it could have happened to you." She picked up her cup of cottage cheese.

If he hadn't needed her desperately, he would have picked up the cottage cheese and pushed it in her face. She was always on a diet; always picking at her food. Pushing it around her plate. Sifting through it as if it were sand.

"Did you hear me?"

"I heard you. What d'you want me to say?" He tried to keep the edge out of his voice.

"How did it happen?" she whined.

"It just did. Okay?"

Cocking her head to one side, she looked at him from under long lashes. "You're embarrassed about it, aren't you?"

"Let's drop it." He could have wrung her neck.

She pursed her lips, started to say something, stopped.

Tom concentrated on his food, listening as Jennifer began to talk about their friends. Gossip. He tuned her out, nodded, grunted at appropriate times. She'd never know he wasn't really listening.

After school he'd go to her house and when she left the room, he'd check out the gun, make sure it was in the same place. When he broke in on the twenty-second, he didn't want any problems. Thinking of this made him laugh.

"What's so funny?" Jennifer asked.

"Huh?"

"What's so funny? I tell you that Bunny's breaking up with Don and you laugh like some nerd."

"Laugh?" He was stalling, ears burning. Obviously, he'd laughed out loud, hadn't realized it. Had to watch himself.

"What's *wrong* with you, Thomas Nash?"

"Would you get off my case, please? Can't a guy laugh? Is it suddenly a criminal offense to laugh, for God's sake?" He slammed down his fork.

"There's nothing funny about two people breaking up." She looked at him in her most serious manner. "A great deal of pain is involved."

"If you have to know, I wasn't laughing about that." He was getting in deeper.

Jennifer looked at him with suspicion. "You mean you weren't listening to me?"

He couldn't afford to alienate her. "Look, Jen," he said in his sweetest tone, "Christmas is coming and a guy's girlfriend shouldn't be asking a lot of questions. You know what I mean?" He was banking on her greed.

It made no sense. But Jennifer accepted the explanation because it felt good.

"Should I go on with the story?"

"Sure," he said.

The bell rang.

He was relieved.

So was she.

They made the usual date to meet after school and went to their separate classes.

Close. Not that Jennifer could really figure anything out. If he laid his plans out for her, she probably wouldn't get it. Not that she wasn't bright. She was. By ordinary standards.

By SOLA's standards, she was a moron. The only standard that mattered. She'd have to be eliminated.

Tom sat in the back of the classroom. Normally, he sat up front. He always wanted to hear what the teacher said. Now he didn't.

SOLA had explained that these teachers knew nothing. He'd been taken in by them for years. This was his next to last day of school.

After the twenty-second, SOLA would be his only teacher. SOLA was all he needed.

"Well, Nash," Mr. Rosner said, "what hit *you?*"

Everyone turned and looked at him.

He wished desperately for a machine gun. "A basketball," he answered, smiling.

There was laughter.

"You look like a panda," Rosner said, shooting for a cheap laugh.

He got it.

Tom grinned. A good sport. When the laughter subsided, he said, "I can think of worse things to look like."

"I guess," Rosner said. "Okay, people, turn to page 212."

All heads turned back to their books.

Allen Rosner. Should he exterminate him? Ask SOLA. No. SOLA would be against expanding the operation at this time. Tom knew that instinctively. Rosner could be dealt with later.

Only those people who could interfere with the advancement of SOLUDA should be removed.

The family.

Cole was the first on his list. SOLA said it was important to get him out of the way, as he was the strongest. But there were always variables. Things, people he couldn't predict.

One step at a time.

First, the gun.

Today he would begin.

125

8.

Dr. Stanley Blackwell sat behind his large oak desk, hands fondling an unlit cigarette. He would play with it, but not smoke it. Four weeks had passed since he'd had his last one, and it wasn't getting easier.

Blackwell, in his mid-sixties, had been in practice for over forty years and as he listened to Anne Nash's complaints about her eldest son he wondered if he'd ever hear anything new again. Realizing she'd stopped talking, he smiled, passed the wilted cigarette back and forth twice between his two hands and nodded thoughtfully.

"Well, dear friend, I have to tell you I don't hear anything alarming."

Anne felt her stomach muscles unknot, then tighten again. Relief was only momentary. If there was nothing wrong with Tom, then was she imagining things? "You think what I've told you is normal?"

The doctor adjusted his glasses, the hearing aid irritating his right ear. "Let's just say I've heard it all before. Par for the course, as they say. Seventeen-year-old boys are, in one way, very complex. In another, simple." Perhaps, he thought, I should have this little speech typed up and mail it out to all the mothers of adolescent sons. He went on. "They're not yet men, although they think they are and their sexual development and interests force them to leave their boyhood behind. It's a confusing time for them, therefore it confuses you."

"You think it's got to do with sex then?" Thinking about Tom and sex made her uncomfortable.

Blackwell shrugged, his thin shoulders like narrow wings.

126

"Of course I can't say absolutely, but chances are, yes. Has he got a girlfriend?"

"Yes. She's very nice. Jennifer Wheeler."

"Oh, sure, I know her well." He bobbed his head, a smile creasing his face. "Sure, sure. That's undoubtedly it. Oh, my."

"What? What is it, Stanley?" She was eager for a solution to her anxiety.

"Jennifer is a very old-fashioned girl, Anne. Her mother, Annette, is also old-fashioned. Strict, you know. Not like some of these mothers around here who come in with their daughters for birth control pills or to fit them with diaphragms." He held up a bony forefinger. "Not that I have anything against birth control. But for a fourteen-year-old girl?" He shook his head. "I don't know, maybe I'm just an old geezer." He laughed.

"Not you, Stanley. I can't imagine bringing Sara in for birth control pills." The thought of Sara and sexuality was too much for her. "But what do you mean about Jennifer being old-fashioned?"

"Ah! Yes. If I know the kids I deal with, and I think I do," he said, trying his best to look modest, "Jennifer Wheeler is still preserving her virginity. This fact alone, I'd bet, is making Tom a nervous wreck."

Anne thought of pointing out that Tom didn't appear *nervous*, that wasn't a symptom. But she didn't want to contradict the doctor. After all, he knew more about these things than she did and she *had* told him everything that bothered her. Surely he had taken that into consideration. "You mean, he's frustrated?"

"Exactly. Sexual frustration can cause boys of that age to act in extremely peculiar ways. Don't let it get to you, darling. It'll work itself out. If he can't break Jennifer down, and between you, me and the lamp post I don't think he will, he'll find another outlet. There are other girls around here who'll help him out."

She wondered if he meant prostitutes, but didn't ask. Didn't want to know. Typical, Cookie.

Blackwell rose, the cigarette still in his hand. "You feel better?"

Anne, following his lead, got up from her chair. "I guess."

"I know, it's hard to think about them in a sexual light. Makes you feel old knowing they're growing up." He put an arm around her, patted her shoulder. "Can't stop the clock, sweetheart."

127

"No. You can't."

He walked her to the door. "But you look well. The rest of the family? Everybody all right?"

"Just fine."

"Good."

"I'm sorry I took up your time, I..."

He held up his hand. "Don't be silly, darling. I'm glad you came in. It's good to talk about these things, air them. We go back a long way. If you can't talk to me, then who?"

She kissed his cheek. "Thanks. You've made me feel a hundred percent better."

He opened the door. "Good. Have a wonderful holiday."

"You, too."

Outside, in the car, Anne sat for a moment. Was it true? Did she feel one hundred percent better? Well, who knew about percentages? But she was relieved. In one way. She was very glad that there wasn't anything seriously wrong with Tom, but she hated to have to think about his sex problems. So why did she?

She didn't.

Dr. Blackwell had said, *it would work itself out.* She didn't have to think about it for one more minute.

Tom was fine.

Normal.

A growing boy. Enough. She'd done what she could and been reassured.

Now she could devote herself to her own problems.

And God knew she had enough of them!

She started the car, pulled out of the parking lot and headed for home.

There were things that had to be done before tomorrow morning.

Tomorrow morning.

Jim.

Oh, God.

Oh, yes.

9.

When the crowd thinned, Finch Bond turned the store over to the capable hands of Linda Allen, her employee. In the back room, Finch sat in her old overstuffed chair, eyes closed, cup of coffee on the small table by her side, legs up on a leather hassock, giving her varicose veins a break.

Since her conversation with Kit, she'd desperately wanted this time to herself. The Christmas shoppers had delayed her reflection. But through those hours a gnawing sensation in her stomach had been a constant reminder.

Lighting a cigarette, Finch recalled the first time she'd heard about Anne's affair.

The store had been empty when one of her best, though not favorite, customers came in. Whenever she saw Laura Howland, she experienced mixed feelings. Glad for her patronage, loathe to deal with her.

Laura Howland was a bitch.

After the usual exchange of local information, book talk and as Laura was writing out her usual large check, she said, "Well, what's this I hear about your good friend, Anne Nash?"

Clearly, it wasn't good. Laura's tone implied that. But there was no way for Finch to ignore the question. "What do you hear about Anne?"

"Oh, come on. Don't tell me *you* don't know." Laura handed her the check for eighty-four dollars, a fantastic sum in the off-season.

Finch shrugged. "Sorry. Don't know whatcha mean, kid."

Laura looked around, making a show of being discreet. As though she'd care if the whole town overheard her. "She's having an affair."

Shock made Finch laugh oddly, a high trill, unlike her usual bellow.

"You think it's funny?"

"I think it's absurd," Finch said.

"Darling, *everyone* knows." Laura lit a cigarette, her long, pointed red nails two slashes across her lips. "Except, obviously, for you."

Finch was angry. Of everyone she knew in the county, Anne was the least likely to have an affair. "I think it's bull. Anne Nash is a very moral woman."

"Ha! Moral shmoral! She's screwing her brains out with one James O'Neill of Williams, Pa." Laura blew a satisfied stream of smoke past Finch's ear.

"Oh yeah, and I suppose you've been in the room with them and watched, huh?"

"Darling, don't be such an innocent. God, you sound like one of those people who says, 'but how do you know that Mamie Eisenhower's a drunk?' Honestly, Finch, people know these things. And in a place like this, as only *you* know too well, I might add, no secret is safe."

Finch argued it with Laura until she'd finally left the store, disgusted.

Over the following months she'd heard it here, there; whispered at cocktail parties, alluded to at dinner gatherings, even laughed about in some circles. Still, she couldn't confront Anne directly. As a good friend, she should have told her everyone knew, was talking. But she couldn't help feeling that to bring it up first, before Anne was ready, would be an intrusion.

Now look what she'd done.

Sighing, she picked at a hole in the chair, pulled out some stuffing, rolled it into a small ball and threw it across the room at the wastebasket. Missed.

If only Kit hadn't sounded so desperate.

Bullshit!

There was no excuse for telling Anne's daughter. She didn't know why she'd done it. Couldn't pin down her motive. Self-examination, self-knowledge, was one of the most important things in the world to Finch. She'd work on this damn thing until she understood it. Betrayal. That's all it felt like at the moment. But perhaps, if she could understand, explain it, it would somehow be less horrifying.

"Finch?"

It was Linda.

"The store's a madhouse again."

"Coming."

She pushed herself out of the chair, smoothed down her hair. Kit had promised to say nothing until Finch could speak to Anne. They'd agreed there was no point in ruining Christmas. Come hell or high water she would speak to Anne about it on the twenty-sixth.

She wouldn't let it go a minute longer.

10.

Max Nash, chin held up in the center of his two small palms, sat across from Steven at the work table in the basement. Swinging his short legs back and forth, he stared at the crown of his brother's blond head, bowed over the work in front of him. They all had blond hair. All his sisters and brothers. Why was his brown? He pulled a piece out in front of him, scrutinizing it carefully, searching for blond touches. Brown. He drew the hank of hair under his nose. Clearing his throat loudly, he hoped to get Steven's attention, make him laugh at the fake moustache.

Totally absorbed in the building of his model airplane, Steven didn't look up. Max dropped the swatch of hair, sighed audibly. Still no response. Absently, he began clicking the metal clasp on his blue-striped overalls.

Without looking up, Steven said, "Cut it."

Attention. "Huh?" Clicking away.

"The clicking. Cut it."

"Oh, yeah." Stopped. Sat. Bored. "Steven?"

"What?"

"I wish we could play run-away."

"Huh?"

131

"Run-away," Max repeated. "You know." It was his favorite game. Scary. But fun.

"Are you crazy?" Steven went on with his work.

"Maybe." He giggled. "Why can't we?"

"Because everything's covered in snow, dopey."

"Oh." It was true. They'd never played run-away in the snow. Sometimes they pretended they were running away from home and sometimes they pretended they were burglars escaping from the window onto the roof and over to the tree and down to the yard. Other times the roof was part of a prison and the tree a flagpole and they were convicts. And the tree had been a ship's mast too, when they were pirates. But none of it in the snow. It was a secret Max shared with Steven. If Daddy knew they climbed out on the roof and down that skinny tree, he would've been real mad.

Max tried to think of another game they could play indoors. Couldn't. Truth was Steven didn't play with him much anymore. Max wondered why. Absentmindedly, he reached out his hand and touched the corner of a piece of wood.

Slamming the flat of his hand on the table, Steven affected a warning stance without lifting his head.

Max jumped, pulled back his hand. He tugged at the neck of his red turtleneck, twisting a flap of the material in his stubby fingers. This was no good. He felt awful. Why did Steven hate him? There was no one in the world that Max wanted to be like more than Steven. He was nuts about him. But for awhile now Steven was always too busy for him. He couldn't understand why. He supposed the only thing to do was ask.

"You hate me, don't you?"

"Oh, for God's sake, Max. Leave me alone. I'm trying to do something here."

"What?"

"Are you blind?"

"Yes."

"Huh?"

"I'm blind," Max said trying again for a laugh.

"You're stupid, too," Steven said sullenly.

Max stared at the wood, glue and tiny pieces of plastic in front of Steven. Of course he knew Steven was building a model airplane. The body, one wing and one piece of tail were in place. Steven was cutting out something from the balsa wood with his X-acto knife.

132

"It's an airplane, huh?" He grinned, showing small neat teeth, a wide space between the top two front.

"Brilliant!" Steven said.

"You going to fly it?"

Steven groaned. "It's not the kind that flies. You've seen them before."

"I never did."

"Oh, Max, I have tons of them in our room."

Max lay his head down on his crossed arms. Couldn't think of a joke or anything else to get Steven's attention. He wished Sara would come home. She played with him sometimes. He knew Sara liked him. Tom never paid any attention to him anymore; he hardly knew his sister Kit. Of course, Mommy loved him. And Daddy, too. He guessed. Especially when he was sick. Then Daddy paid a lot of attention to him and brought him presents. But Sara was really nice. She hugged him a lot and he liked that. Even if she was a girl, Steven hated Sara.

"You hate Sara, don't you?" He picked at the balsa shavings, puncturing pieces of the soft wood with his nails.

"She's a pain."

"Why?"

"She just is. So are you."

Max wondered why Sara was a pain to Steven. And why he was. He couldn't understand it. "Why?"

"Why what?"

"Why am I a pain?"

"Because you're always asking questions, that's why. Now shut up."

Max stuck his hands under the straps of his overalls, and tried thinking about this. He didn't know what to think. This made him mad. He started to ask Steven what was wrong with asking questions. Stopped. Another question. He was all mixed up. He didn't want to make Steven mad, but he didn't know what else to do.

In the center of his tummy, he felt something burning. Then it happened all at once. It was as though he'd blacked out. He didn't even know he'd done it. Until he saw the look on Steven's face and knew he'd better run.

Right before he turned, he glanced at the work table and saw the smashed pieces of balsa wood.

He prayed he'd make it to the bathroom where he could lock himself in before Steven caught him.

11.

Sara had missed the bus. She couldn't believe it; she never missed it, was always on time for everything. But today she'd done something she'd never done before and this was the result.

She'd hung around outside Mr. Fleming's room hoping he'd come out so she could accidentally bump into him, talk for a moment. Sara thought Richard Fleming was the most handsome, most exciting, most brilliant, wonderful person who'd ever lived. She'd been in love with him for three months and knew she'd never, ever love this way again.

The rest of the world could have their John Travoltas and Shaun Cassidys and Henry Winklers; to her they were nerds. Immature. Revolting. Richard Fleming was glamorous, mature, fascinating. At least twenty-six or -seven. But that didn't matter. She'd figured it all out. When she was twenty, he'd be thirty-two and what was wrong with that? Ab-so-lutely nothing. Plenty of people, happy couples, had an age difference of twelve years or more. And the gap would narrow as time went by.

So she'd waited outside in the hall, walking casually back and forth, pretending she had a reason to be there. He hadn't come out. She'd allowed herself fifteen minutes. But either her watch was wrong or the bus had left early, because when she got outside, it was gone.

She'd hitched a ride to the center of Old Hickory with some seniors who treated her the way seniors always treated freshman. As though she weren't there.

But that was nothing new for Sara. Most kids treated her as if she weren't there. Unless they were making fun of her. It had been a long time since she'd had a friend. A friend she really liked. Now there were Robin and Susan. Even as far as Sara was concerned they were nerds. The only reason she hung around with them was because they were the only kids who'd hung around with her. But she didn't like them much.

Amy had been her last good friend. Fifth grade. She'd loved Amy. They'd had so much fun together and then right before they'd started sixth, Amy's mother and father broke up and Amy, her brother Kevin and her mother moved away. Just like that. They'd written to each other for about a year and then gradually the letters stopped. Sara wondered where Amy was now and what she was doing. Maybe she'd write to her tonight at the old address. She might still be there. But, what if Amy was there, got the letter and didn't answer? Some things were better left alone.

Now she stood looking in the window of Krausse's Fudge Store, mouth watering. She had enough money in her jeans for half a pound of maple nut, her favorite. She looked at her watch. Plenty of time.

Inside the store, Sara was in heaven. The smell of sugar was ambrosial to her. Someday she'd have enough money to buy a pound of every kind of fudge. Someday the Hideous Witch would have nothing to say about what she ate. When she was married to Mr. Fleming he'd bring her boxes and boxes of. . . . She stopped. What if Richard hated fat? Everyone in the world hated fat. Why would he be different? But he *was*.

She knew that. She could just tell. She ordered her half pound of maple nut.

Out on the street again, she crunched through the snow, walking along as though it were the middle of summer. Chomping on her fudge, she was oblivious to the cold, the high snow drifts lining the street.

When she was part way through the half pound, she went into the drugstore, to a phone booth.

Anne answered on the third ring.

"I missed the bus and I'm in Old Hickory. I need a ride."

"How did you miss the bus?" Anne asked, annoyed.

"I don't know, Mom, I'm sorry."

"Honestly, Sara, you're really trying, lately."

"I said I was sorry."

"All right, all right. It'll take me about twenty-five to half an hour. I'm in the middle of something. Go to the book shop. I'll meet you there."

Sara was thrilled. She'd have plenty of time to savor the rest of her fudge before she had to go to Finch's.

As she was about to step outside, she saw Tom and Jennifer walking down the street. Quickly, she closed the door, stepped out of sight. She could see them, but they couldn't see her.

In Sara's opinion, Jennifer Wheeler was a creep.

Thomas Nash an even bigger creep!

Well, not really.

Watching as they walked hand-in-hand across the street to Michael Schultz's car, she ate a piece of fudge. Tom had his green ski band around his head, his hair white-gold in the winter sun. Sara thought she could see his extraordinary blue eyes from this distance, realized she was filling them in from memory. For just a moment old, wonderful feelings about Tom came back.

Oh, how she'd loved him. And he'd loved her, too. He was the sweetest, kindest boy on earth.

He'd always stood up for her, trying to help her to do the things he'd not been allowed to do. Oh, how he'd begged his father to let her go to summer camp. Of course he hadn't succeeded. Still, he'd tried. And then there was the time with the cat collar. That was only a year or so ago.

Tom had taken her shopping with him at Woolco, a special treat. Once inside they'd separated and Sara had stolen a red cat collar for Coco. It had a nice little bell on it. She'd never stolen anything before, didn't know why she was stealing then. Just did it.

When she met up with Tom and they got on line to pay, her heart was beating fast. As she removed her wallet from her purse to pay for the new brush she was buying, there was a jingle as the collar fell to the floor. Tom caught her eye, saw her blush. He bent down and picked up the collar, said nothing.

When it was his turn to pay, he added the collar to his things. Outside as they walked along, he asked her why she'd done it.

"I don't know. Are you going to tell?"

"Not if you promise never to steal again."

"I promise."

"It's wrong to steal, Sara. You could get in a lot of trouble, besides," he said, putting his arm around her.

"I know. I won't ever do it again."

She never had. And he hadn't told. He was her good friend. Always keeping her out of trouble.

Then he'd met Jennifer.

Even so, he'd still been kind of friendly. Sure, he was busier. Anyone with a girlfriend would be. She could understand that.

But lately.

Lately, he was impossible. Never talked to her, looked at her or anything. She licked her gooey fingers. The Schultz car drove off.

Funny. She'd never minded that he was everyone's pet. He'd been her pet, too. When someone was as neat as Tom, you just couldn't be jealous. At least, she couldn't.

But he wasn't so great any more. Maybe he didn't like fat either. She ate the last of the fudge, crumpled the white bag and threw it into a corner of the store.

Slowly, she walked the block to Finch's.

The bells tinkled when she opened the door. The store was crowded, but Finch saw her, waved.

"Hiya, kid. Got a neat new Danziger book for you."

"Fab," she said, smiling. Inside, she mourned the loss of Tom and wished she had more fudge.

12.

Anne was annoyed. She'd been in the middle of shaving her legs when Sara called. Now one leg was shaved and the other wasn't. She'd wanted to have that done by the time Cole came home. Somehow the idea of preparing for another man while Cole was in the house bothered her. Well, maybe she'd get it done in time.

It was as though something was against her. First Max acting up and now Sara. Damn. She simply didn't need this.

The last thing she wanted to do was go out in the cold and drive to Old Hickory. She'd been out once today. Enough. As much as the township kept up with cleaning and salting the roads, there were still danger spots.

Concentrate. Finish her legs.

Anne tried to keep her mind from leaping ahead to the next day. It was almost impossible. Now all she could think was that by this time tomorrow it would be over. She would be driving back from Philadelphia. Her whole life changed. It made her think of an old song: *What a Difference a Day Makes*.

Ah, Cookie, you sentimental fool.

Fortunately, there was a space on the corner near the book shop. She wasn't in the mood for trudging through the snow.

Finch looked odd, Anne thought. Overwrought. Not like her. Perhaps it was the last-minute Christmas rush.

"She's back in the sci-fi section, I think. Damn brat dragging you out." She smiled.

"You all right?"

"Sure. Why?"

"I don't know." Anne shrugged.

"Christmas rush," Finch said, avoiding Anne's eyes.

"Right."

Anne found Sara sitting on the floor, leafing through a magazine with horrible bloody people on the cover. "What, in God's name, is that?"

Sara looked up, startled. Her brow creased into a frown.

"Punk People," she said disdainfully.

Pulling herself up with effort, she shoved the magazine open, to a particularly nasty picture, under Anne's eyes.

"That's revolting." Anne grabbed the magazine, snapped it shut.

"I know," Sara said, smiling.

"Why were you looking at it?" Anne wondered if she knew this child at all.

"Curious."

"Well, let's go." She touched her daughter's shoulder, felt her shrink at the contact. That stung.

There was a crowd around the checkout desk, so Anne waved goodbye to Finch.

In the car, Sara sat against the door, her eyes fixed on the dashboard. Glancing over, taking in Sara's bulk, Anne thought her heart might break. If only Cole would pay for a therapist. She'd begged him. He thought it was nonsense.

"You make too much of it. It's baby fat. You read too many of those stupid women's magazines."

Anne knew it was a lot more serious than baby fat. She also knew that Sara suffered because of the way she looked; trying to pretend she didn't care about being overweight. It didn't fool Anne.

Jim O'Neill would have sent his daughter for help. A certainty.

Perhaps after the first, no matter what happened, Anne should get a job and use the money to pay for a doctor for Sara. There was nothing Cole could do about that.

Could he?

Or maybe Jim—

She couldn't finish the thought.

Meantime, she should try to help her daughter herself. Talk to her. But she felt so empty. She had to try.

"Sara?" she said.

"Yes?"

Say the perfect thing. What is it? Anne paused, then gave in to failure.

"How was school?" she asked, and hoped she wouldn't cry.

13.

Sitting on the soft, checked couch in the Wheeler basement, arm around Jennifer, Tom felt close to choking with impatience. Wasn't she ever going to go to the bathroom, go upstairs? He had to check the closet for the gun. It was getting late.

They were listening to records. The Undertakers singing their hit tune, *Long Time Feeling Pain*.

After the line, "I think I'll die without you...nothin's been so bad," Jennifer turned her heart-shaped face up to Tom's. "That's the way I feel."

"What is?"

"I'd die without you."

Wondering why she'd speak so lightly about death, he thought of telling her about her own. Something made him hold back. SOLA wouldn't like it.

"Do you feel that way about me, Tom?"

"What way?"

"Oh, honestly." She pulled away from him, ran her fingers through each side of her long hair. Maybe she *should* tell him she was pregnant; she bet he'd wake up then.

"I don't like talking about death." A small insolent smile.

Jennifer missed it. "You're weird." She rose, stretched. "Be back."

When the bathroom door closed, he strode across the room and carefully opened the closet door. The enclosure was deep and "L"-shaped. He was afraid to turn on the light. If he remembered correctly the gun was on a shelf to the right. Leaning in, his eyes roved the packed shelves.

"What are you doing, Thomas?"

He whirled around.

Mrs. Wheeler screamed.

It frightened him. He jumped.

He touched the small bandage that saddled his nose, smiled winningly, "I'm sorry I scared you, Mrs. Wheeler."

Annette Wheeler, forty, was a brown-haired, angular woman, her pallid skin smooth, unlined. High cheekbones set off a delicate nose and dark button eyes. Her mouth was a thin neat line. She wore tight Sassoon jeans, purple sweater, no bra.

"What happened to you?" she asked Tom.

"What happened?" Jennifer echoed as she came out of the bathroom.

"I frightened your mother. My eyes." He closed the closet door.

"He got hit with a basketball," Jennifer said languidly.

"I see. Well, it's really quite startling. I bet your mother'll be happy to see those shiners! Nice for Christmas."

Tom nodded sympathetically. "I know. I don't look forward to her reaction." He couldn't care less. That was the truth.

"Of course, it's not like you got in a fight or something." Annette made a move toward the stairs, remembered why

140

she'd come down. "Could you turn the volume down, Jen. It's driving me nuts."

"Sure, Mom. Sorry."

On the stairs, Annette stopped. "Tom, what were you doing in the closet?"

Jennifer looked at him. "Closet?"

His mind whirred. Help me SOLA. Smiling. "The truth?"

"Always," Annette Wheeler said.

"I cannot tell a lie. I was peeking." He shrugged boyishly, charmingly.

"Peeking for what?" Annette said tersely.

"Nothing special. I guess I'm a sucker for closed doors. I don't know, Mrs. Wheeler. I know it was wrong. I'm really sorry." He gave her his softest look. As he gazed at her, he was shocked to see a vivid pink ring, somewhat like neon tubing, appearing around her entire body. It was hard not to react, hard to keep his ingenuous smile in place. A growl from SOLA kept him in check.

After a moment, Annette said, "I know what you mean. I have the same problem."

Tom wondered what problem she was referring to.

"But we really mustn't look in other people's private places. Not that, that dump," she pointed to the closet, "is very private."

Jennifer said, "You've seen inside that closet, Tom."

"Not me," Tom said. The glow surrounding Mrs. Wheeler was making him dizzy.

"I distinctly remember showing you...."

"Must have been some other guy," Tom interrupted, looking at her, glad for the excuse to look away from her mother.

"I'm sure...."

"Does it matter, honey?" he said sweetly.

Jennifer shrugged.

"Maybe you two could spend some afternoon cleaning it out," said Annette.

"Oh, Mother." Jennifer flopped on the sofa, long legs spread in a "V."

"Sure. We'll do that." It hurt to look at the pink ring. Tom wished she would leave.

"Some rainy day," Annette said and went up the steps.

Tom smiled, recognizing his power.

"You really don't remember me showing you inside the closet?" Jennifer asked.

"I don't, but what's the difference?" His mind still vibrated from the intensity of Annette's aura.

"You don't remember the gun?"

"Gun?" His insides lurched.

"Tom, you really are getting to be a weirdo. I showed you Daddy's gun and you got all funny. You didn't want to hold it or anything. Now don't tell me that wasn't you."

This was perfect. Now he could see exactly where the gun was. "Honestly, Jen, it wasn't me. Show it to me. Maybe it'll bring back memories."

Jennifer started toward the closet door, stopped. "Oh, damn. I just remembered. Daddy sold it a couple months ago."

The blow felt almost physical. Fear invaded him. SOLA would be furious. "Sold it," he said dumbly.

"Yeah. I forget why or who to. Anyway, I know you saw it and...What's wrong? You look funny?"

"I don't know. My stomach. I feel sick."

"Well, sit down." She moved to the sofa, patted one of the cushions.

"No, I think I'd better get on home." He had to be alone. To think, plan. Somewhere, somehow he had to get a gun. It would be impossible to do it all with a knife. Too risky.

She helped him on with his jacket.

"It's probably from the blow to your nose."

"Probably." He went to the stairs.

"Aren't you going to kiss me good-bye?"

He looked at her. "I feel sick." And he did. The orange glow around her body was nauseating.

"Maybe *I* make you sick," she said petulantly.

"Come on, Jen," he managed. He had to look away.

It wasn't until he'd crossed the living room that he realized Jennifer had not come upstairs with him. Just as well.

Outside, the sky was growing dark. As he walked, his breath puffed out ahead of him. Turning a bend in the road, the Durham house came into view.

He stopped. Smiled.

Of course.

George Durham loved guns.

So simple.

GOOD BOY, SOLA said.

14.

"**Well,** I'll be damned." A grin spread across Noj's face.

"It's not funny," said Kit.

"Of course not, honey. It's just.... I mean, I only met your mother once and although she's a very attractive woman, she just didn't seem the type."

Kit bristled. "What's that supposed to mean? The *type?*"

"The type to have an affair. What are you getting so mad about?"

"And just what is the *type* to have an affair?"

He reached for her hand; she pulled away. "Kit? What's wrong?"

"Would you say that about a man?"

"Of course."

"I'll bet." She knew her anger was ridiculous. She'd thought the very same thing herself. Looking up from the table she saw the hurt in his soft brown eyes. "Oh, hell, I'm sorry, darling. I'm just so confused. By the feelings it's evoked in me."

"I think you should call your mother right now and ask her if you can help her in any way."

"You mean tell her I know."

"Why not?"

"Oh, Noj, I don't know. It might embarrass her. And be-sides, I promised Finch."

"Well, then, sort of give her an opening to tell you. You know, say you've been thinking about her phone call this morning...it's bothered you. You know what to say."

"You think?"

Noj pulled his chair closer, took her face in both his hands, kissed her gently. "I do, babe. Go on."

Kit looked at her watch. It was a good time; Cole wouldn't be home.

Tom answered the phone.

His hello sounded odd, strange, unlike him.

A kind of prickliness danced across Kit's belly.

"Well, Duchess," he said, "pretty soon you'll be home, huh? So how come you're calling? Something on your mind? It'll be good to see you, won't it? When do you arrive? On the twenty-third, isn't it?"

"Tom, what's wrong?" She'd never heard him speak so quickly.

"Wrong? What do you mean, wrong?"

"Is Mother there?"

"No, Duchess."

She tried to sound relaxed, amused. "What's this Duchess stuff?"

He ignored the question. "It's good to hear your voice. I look forward to your arrival on the twenty-third. Everything will be perfect then. I have so much to tell you." He was speaking more and more rapidly.

Seeing the look on Kit's face, Noj came closer, took her hand.

"Where's Mom?" She leaned against Noj. Anxious. Uneasy.

"Don't know, Duchess. Wasn't here when I got here."

"Are you alone?" Her hand was sweaty on the phone.

"Alone?"

"In the house? Is anyone else there?"

"Kids. Max, Steven. I'm going to change your life with what I have to tell you, Duchess." He giggled.

"What are you talking about? What's the matter, Tom?"

"You mustn't be afraid of knowledge. Knowledge is everything. Shall I give you a hint."

Noj was listening now, sharing the phone with Kit, his ear next to hers.

"Tom, has something happened?"

"It's an important new discovery, Duchess. I will change your life. *It* will change your life. Listen carefully."

Noj and Kit exchanged a puzzled, worried glance.

Pause.

Then loud and clear through the telephone came a sonorous, masculine voice.

144

SOLUDA IS KNOWLEDGE, it thundered.

A click. The connection terminated.

"Jesus," Noj whispered, "who the hell was that?"

15.

Very quietly, Steven backed out of the kitchen. Everything in him was shaking. He had to get out of there before Tom turned around and saw him. He knew this instinctively.

Once in the living room, Steven wasn't sure where he should go. Max was in their room and he didn't want to see him. For sure. To go back to the basement meant going through the kitchen. He couldn't stay where he was because Tom might come there at any moment.

So?

If Tom came into the living room now, he wouldn't know Steven had heard him, so why was he afraid to confront his older brother?

He just was.

Quickly, silently, he ran up the stairs. He would go in Sara's room for awhile. To think.

He looked around not knowing where to sit, finally chose the floor, a corner. The beating of his heart began to slow, but the dancing feeling in his belly continued.

Who had Tom been talking to? Who was Duchess? Was it Jennifer? And why was Tom talking so funny, so fast? And then the worst part. That voice.

Scary.

Just thinking about it made Steven's skin go to ice.

"Soluda is knowledge," Tom had said. What did that mean? What was soluda? And what was that voice? He'd never heard Tom sound like that. It was very deep. And strange. Hollow.

Steven squeezed his eyes shut as if that would block the

remembered sound. It didn't. The voice echoed in his brain. He pulled his knees up against his narrow chest, hugged them with his arms.

Something very bad was happening. He'd known it for a while now. He couldn't identify what the bad part was. Still couldn't. Not completely. But he knew something awful was happening to his brother.

Ever since he was five years old, he'd wanted to be like his big brother. And his big brother had, most of the time, been very nice to him.

Sure, there were times when Tom had shooed Steven away like a pesky fly, wanting to be alone with his friends, and now that he had Max following him around, Steven understood that. But a lot of the time Tom had included Steven in what he was doing. And he'd taught him things. Like sports. And stood up for him against his father. Tom told him about sex. Shared comic books when he was younger. Given Steven his saxophone when Tom had switched to the clarinet. And best of all there were lots of times he took him to the movies with him and his friends, even let him ride around with them. Then when Jennifer came along, things changed. It had been hard for Steven to understand why Tom would rather be with Jennifer than riding around with his friends, but he tried, especially when Tom explained about love.

Then awhile back things really started to change. How long ago? Steven wondered. Maybe six weeks, two months. At first, Tom just seemed distracted, absent. Steven had noticed a faraway look in his eyes. Not all the time. Just once in awhile. Then, as time went on, more and more.

And Tom's patience got shorter. He'd snap at Steven for no good reason. Something he'd never done in the past. Steven wondered if Tom was on something, but he doubted it. He was sure he'd know if that were the case.

Now this. Weird. The thing was, should he tell anyone about it? He didn't want to betray Tom. If he said anything to his parents, especially his father, he was sure to rush him off to some doctor and that was a real drag. Might even ruin Tom's Christmas holiday. Maybe he should just tell Mom? But why worry her? It wasn't like Tom had actually *done* anything *bad*. No, best keep it to himself.

What a pain. He wished like hell he had a joint, but he'd smoked the last one yesterday. He'd have to score before the holidays so he'd have a supply for vacation.

Who could make the Christmas-Family scene without their dope?

Not him.

Definitely not.

16.

When Anne put down the phone, she hesitated a moment before returning to the dining room. She needed time to absorb what Kit had told her. It didn't make sense. There was nothing particularly unusual about Tom this evening. Except for his black eyes.

If Kit had asked about Cole again, that might have been a different matter!

Every time Anne looked at him, he was looking at her. The tiniest smile threatened the corners of his mouth. His eyes seemed to hold a new dimension. Whatever it was made her decidedly uncomfortable. Perhaps because of her plans with Jim she was paranoid. Still.

But this business about Tom was what she had to deal with now. She'd assured Kit he was behaving in a normal manner, promised to ask about the phone call. And what was that name? Soluba? No. Soluda. That was right.

"Well," Anne said, trying to sparkle, "that was Kit." Her eyes were on Tom. Nothing changed in his face.

"When's she coming home?" Steven asked.

"Monday."

"How come she's calling?" asked Sara, her plate already empty.

Picking up her fork, Anne said, "Oh, just to.... Well, as a matter of fact, she was worried about the conversation she had earlier with Tom. How come you didn't mention it, dear?"

147

Slowly, Tom raised his head. The blue eyes, surrounded by bruised flesh, met hers. "What conversation?"

Panic began inside Anne. Covering, she said, "The conversation you had this afternoon."

"I didn't have any conversation with Kit this afternoon." He looked bewildered.

Steven, watching Tom, experienced an inner fear he couldn't explain. The conversation he'd overheard had been with his sister! Why was Tom lying about it?

. Anne knew Kit couldn't have made it up. Besides, Noj had confirmed. Tom was blatantly lying. It gave Anne a sickening feeling. And great concern.

"Kit called to speak to *me* this afternoon when I was out picking up Sara. You talked to her, Tom," she said evenly.

"Not me," he answered, smiling. "Steven? Was it you?"

He couldn't believe what he was being asked and didn't know what he should say. For some reason, Tom didn't want anyone to know. Steven guessed not giving Tom away was his chance to repay his brother for all the times he'd stood up, covered for him. "Nope," he said, "wasn't me." Quickly, he looked back at his plate.

"Maybe it was Max," Tom said.

"I think Kit would know the difference between your voice and Max's."

"Gotcha," Tom said. "Kidding, Mom. Anyway, I haven't talked to Kit in...I don't know, since Thanksgiving."

Anne chose the moment because he was looking directly into her eyes. "What's soluda?"

It was almost imperceptible. If she hadn't been looking for it she probably wouldn't have noticed. But she *was* looking. Carefully. And she saw it. Like the shutter of a camera clicking closed, then open, ever so quickly.

"I have no idea," he said. "What is it?"

It was horrible. She knew he was lying. Clearly, he had knowledge about this soluda business. Clearly, he wasn't going to talk.

But she couldn't let it go, it would look too odd. Something was very wrong with Tom. All her suspicions, fears, of recent weeks, were reactivated, converging in this moment. "I suppose you have your reasons for...."

"Leave the boy alone," Cole said.

"But, Cole?" Anne said, surprised he'd cut her off that way.

"What's all the fuss over a phone call? These kids have

148

their secrets. It's time you learned that, Anne. Everybody has secrets." He smiled at her, knowingly.

It was as though he'd slapped her. She felt startled, undone. Could he possibly know about Jim? If he did, she didn't want to know, didn't want to force him into confronting her. Not now. Not yet. But what about Tom's conversation with Kit? Could she, should she let it drop? If she pursued it would Cole pursue whatever was on *his* mind? Oh, God.

Steven looked at his parents, waiting. Something was going on there, too.

Sara watched her father.

Tom ate his dinner, oblivious.

Max had been fed early and put to bed for wrecking Steven's plane.

"Let's change the subject," Anne said.

Ah, Cookie, your strength is overwhelming!

Cole said, "Let's just eat in peace."

Silence.

"What do you want?" Sara asked, looking up from her desk.

Steven stood in the doorway. He'd decided to share what he knew with Sara, even if she was a pain. He needed her. "I want to talk to you," he said, softly, nicely.

She turned over what she'd been writing. A love poem to Richard Fleming. "What about?" she asked suspiciously. She didn't trust Steven. Why should she? He tormented her almost daily with barbs about her weight.

"Can I come in?"

Sara swiveled round in her gray desk chair to face him. There was an odd look on his face. What was it? Worried? Was she going to fall into some mean trap of his, get suckered into something, then *zap* he'd lay it on her? "What do you want, Steven?"

He closed the door behind him. "I have to talk to you. About Tom."

She was interested. "Okay." The first bad thing he said to her, she was going to throw him out.

When he'd finished telling her about the phone call, she shared some of her own observations, although nothing as dramatic as Steven's revelation. They agreed something was wrong with Tom. They also agreed not to tell their parents.

Yet.

If something else happened, something worse, they'd have

to. They even shook hands on it and each of them, though they'd never have said so, felt closer and kindlier toward the other.

It felt good.

Anne soaked in her hot tub, water laced with soothing bath oil, softening her skin. At least that's what the ad said. And who was she to doubt Brut?

She lay back, eyes closed. After the children had gone to bed and Cole was ensconced in front of the television, mind tuned out by the sit-coms, she'd dialed Kit.

Obviously, Tom had lied about the phone call. Putting all the pieces together, Anne, Kit and Noj came to the conclusion that he was involved in some sort of cult. Something called Soluda. And one of the members, perhaps even the leader, had been in the house today, had spoken to Kit and Noj. "Soluda is knowledge," he'd said.

Again, Kit offered to come home. Then they'd agreed things should go on normally. As planned.

The idea of a cult scared the hell out of Anne. She thought of nine hundred dead. How could someone like Tom—loved, straight as an arrow, popular, intelligent—be sucked into one of these cults? The followers, disciples, were deficient in the ways Tom was strong. Weren't they? But it certainly would explain his odd behavior of late.

Confronting him, Kit said, might push him into making some sort of move. A waiting game was necessary. Mustn't put him further out of the family's reach. When Kit came home, they'd all sit down and talk.

Anne tried to still the anxious flutters inside. Kit was the psychology major; she understood these things best. In this area it was pragmatic to follow Kit's advice. Her child, yes. Woman, too. Surely, Anne could feel confident.

She'd thought about calling Stanley Blackwell, but realized that if indeed Tom was involved in a cult, a psychiatrist would be needed. There was one in Old Hickory. If he wasn't any good, she'd take Tom to Philadelphia or New York or wherever was necessary.

For now, she'd watch Tom carefully. Relax, she told herself.

Anyway, what could happen in three days?

The late movie began.
Force of Evil, with John Garfield.

Cole had seen it before. Couldn't remember what it was about. Didn't matter. Coco was sitting on top of the set staring at him. Damn cat.

White wine was his new passion. He sipped from a long stemmed glass. The wine was cool, dry in his mouth. Third glass. Something to take the edge off. Television alone didn't do it anymore. Neither did the valium. The movie, black and white, droned on.

Earlier, he'd listened into a conversation between Anne, Kit and Noj. Concern over Tom. Cult talk. He didn't believe a word of it. The boy was breaking out, that's all. About time. All boys broke out. The kid had always been perfect. Steven was going to be more interesting. Max, too. Too bad he wasn't going to be around to see it.

The news of Anne's affair had decided him absolutely. This time he'd go. Disappear. No note. No nothing. But first he was going to make her pay.

Perhaps on Saturday night, as they trimmed the tree.

"So, Anne," he'd say, "I understand you're shacking up with Jim O'Neill?"

What would that do to the kids?

Maybe say something in front of Anne's mother. Saying it in front of the kids would hurt them too much. The moment had to be right.

Three days to go. That was his plan. Monday after the office party. Drive right out of the town, county, state. Never come home.

He turned the glass in his large hand, the eerie light from the set radiating through the wine, sharpening its golden hue. Squinting, he stared, as though the wine were a crystal ball. Would he really go this time? Did he have the balls? The answer wasn't in the glass. It was inside him. He drank.

The money was there. For years he'd had a secret account. Just in case. Seven thousand dollars. Nothing to stop him. And everything. Fear. Number one.

He'd chosen Arizona for his first stop. Didn't know why. Arbitrary. This time he had to go. Goddamnit. Nothing to stay for. The bitch was cheating on him. He knew it was true. Instinct. No need to check. He finished his wine.

John Garfield was going on about something. Garfield wouldn't hesitate. He'd beat it. But first he'd knock the shit out of her, screw her. Cole smiled.

He got up, snapped off the set.

151

Fucking bitch.

He headed upstairs.

Cole snapped on the light.

Anne jumped. "You frightened me."

"Frightened you by turning on a light? You must have a guilty conscience." He smiled.

Anne fussed with the covers. "What's that supposed to mean?"

"Never heard that saying?"

"Is it a saying?" He looked odd. Tight?

"Sure. When's your mother coming?"

"She's driving down Saturday morning. Why?"

"Just wondered. How long's she staying?"

"Oh, for about a week. You know that, Cole."

"Forgot." He began undressing, dropping his clothes on the floor.

Anne watched, puzzled. It wasn't like him. Cole was neat. Compulsively so.

And what was all this talk about her mother? Cole acted as though her mother's visit was something new. Since Mr. Clifford had died in 1966, her mother had spent a week at Christmas with each of her children. A different one each year. Four years since she'd been with them.

"Do you resent Mother's visit?"

"Resent? No. She's never been my favorite person, as you know."

And you've never been hers, Anne thought. "It's only once every four years."

"Did I say anything? I just asked how long."

True. "Well, you'll be at work during most of her visit."

Cole, naked, flopped on the bed, flung back the covers.

Anne was shocked.

"It's been a long time," he said.

She couldn't believe it. Why tonight?

Embarrassed, she said, "Cole, why?"

He laughed oddly. "Why? What kind of question is that?"

"I mean, you're right, it's been a long time. Do you have any idea how long?"

He shrugged.

"Years." God help me, she thought. I can't. "Since Max was born."

"Then it's about time." He slid on top of her. .

She felt his erection. Everything inside her went numb.

152

Never refuse your husband.

They were her mother's words. But how long ago? She'd been in her teens when her mother had said that. And wasn't there more to that line?

Never refuse your husband if you want to keep him.

Cole began to push up her nightgown.

Well, she didn't want to keep him, did she?

She felt his hand on her pushing her legs apart.

"Please, Cole, don't."

"What do you mean, *don't?*" With his fingers he began probing her. Dry. He withdrew his hand, wet his fingers with his tongue, returned them to her vagina.

Anne thought she might vomit. "I can't. I don't want to," she said, trying to push him away.

"Well, I do." He'd never felt quite like this before. His cock seemed enormous; he wanted to split her in two with it.

"This is rape," she said.

He laughed. "I'm your husband."

She felt his hard penis against her, trying to ram its way inside. She simply couldn't allow this. The anger that had been building slowly inside her exploded in a tremendous burst.

"How dare you?" With one push, she sent him flying to his side of the bed. Quickly, she jumped up.

"You disgusting pig."

Slowly, he raised himself to a sitting position. "I'm your husband, goddamn you. I have rights."

"You have *no* right to rape me," she said, shaking.

He thought of hitting her with the O'Neill thing, knew it'd hurt more in front of her mother. He could wait.

But what about this? His penis was still hard, throbbing.

Anne picked up her velvet robe.

"Where the hell are you going?"

"I'm going to the guest room. I'll sleep there tonight." She started toward the door.

Cole leapt from the bed, grabbed her arm, hurting her. "You're going nowhere."

She took a deep breath. Never had she defied him openly. A change was already occurring; she had already crossed a line.

"Cole," she said, her voice even, firm, "if you don't let me go, I'm going to scream this house down. I will tell your children that their father was trying to abuse me. I mean it."

Weighing her words he decided she would. Anything to not have to fuck him. He let go of her arm.

"Thank you," she said.

"And thank you," he said, sarcastically. "What the hell am I supposed to do now?" He gestured toward his erection.

Anne tried not to laugh. "Do whatever you've been doing for the last six years, Mister. Take it to the lady you've been sticking it in or take care of it yourself. I couldn't care less."

The door closed behind her. Cole stared at it dumbly. He'd never heard Anne so crass. Well, he'd get even.

Saturday or Sunday he'd expose Anne to her mother.

Then Monday he'd be gone.

Perfect.

Climbing back into bed, he realized his penis was limp.

Relief flooded through him.

17.

Tom was furious with SOLA. He'd never felt that way before. Things were getting out of hand. SOLA was giving him directives; he was carrying them out.

And not remembering.

It was frightening.

Sleep wouldn't come tonight, hadn't for so long. But he didn't need sleep.

SOLA said so.

What had happened?

He tried piecing it together from what he'd been told.

Kit had called. He had answered. He'd said things, alarmed her. But SOLA must have told him to say these things.

Why?

Obviously, he'd said something about SOLUDA.

SOLA must have told him to.

Why wouldn't SOLA let him remember?

It was too early to tell Kit about SOLUDA. His time schedule was getting fouled up. Should he change it?

He waited for a signal from SOLA.

Nothing.

He'd have to go by his own instincts. His own timetable. Tomorrow he'd visit Esther. Check out the gun situation. Saturday he would play it cool, tight, watch his step.

And Sunday was K-Day.

He hoped SOLA wouldn't pull any more tricks on him.

Fear. Almost overpowering. He sat straight up in his bed. What if Kit came home early because of the conversation they'd had? That would ruin everything. He needed Kit for his Duchess. Most of all, he didn't want to kill her.

There was only one thing to do. In the morning, he'd call Kit, correct whatever impression he'd made. She just couldn't come home early.

But if she insisted, if she got here before the twenty-third he would have to kill her, too. He'd have no choice.

So sad.

Friday,
December 20

1.

Noj had Kit pinned beneath him, arms stretched out above her head, hands held down at the wrists.

"Listen to me," he said breathlessly, "all I want to do is talk about it. You're hysterical."

"I'm not hysterical. Goddamn it, why is it men always call women hysterical when they show a little emotion? Now let go of me."

"Can we talk?"

"Let go."

"I want to talk, Kit. You're not going to go running out of here without talking it over."

"Who the hell do you think you are?" Her green eyes becoming emerald.

"I'm your lover. And I love you and want to help. And I honestly don't want to play this game." He let go of her wrists, rolled off.

Lying next to one another on the bed, they stared at the ceiling, the sound of their breathing filling the room.

Noj reached across the narrow chasm between them, took her hand.

After a moment she entwined her fingers, squeezed. "I'm sorry." she said.

"It's okay. Can we talk?"

"Yes."

"Tell me what Tom said."

"He said I'd lost my sense of humor. Didn't I know when someone was putting me on?" She let go of his hand, pushed some hair from her face.

"Did he sound normal? Damn, I wish I'd heard."

"He sounded like he always sounds, but there was something wrong with it. You know as well as I, yesterday was no joke."

"Did you ask him who the other guy was?"

"Yes." She sat up, her thin arms around her knees.

"He didn't answer right away. Then he laughed, sort of mumbled and said he was a friend. So what's soluda? I asked."

"And?"

"He said he'd tell me all about it when I got home...that it was *neat* and I'd love it. Then he said he had to run because he'd be late for school, not to worry and for God's sakes don't rap to Mom. His tag was I should find my sense of humor before I came home. That was it."

Sitting up, Noj touched her hair, put an arm around her shoulders. "And that made you want to pack your bags?"

She sat up. "Jesus, Noj. Are you still asleep or something? You heard him yesterday. That was no joke."

Of course it was no joke. He'd never forget that voice. Weird. Creepy. But hadn't they worked all this out last night? The kid was into some cult, some religious group. Patience.

"I don't see what's changed from last night. We agreed to go on as we were."

"It's his denial," she said, getting up.

Sunlight bounced off the white formica parson's table under the window. The plants had a bright, crisp greenness. They gave an illusion of spring, and for just a moment Kit felt lighter. A cloud, passing in front of the sun, brought grayness to the room. Again her spirits plummeted.

Kit looked at Noj, cross-legged on the bed. "Denial," she repeated softly.

"So he doesn't want to go into it right now, Kit. Big deal."

"Then why yesterday, huh? Explain that?"

"I can't. Except that today he changed his mind."

"He's acting crazy."

"Come on." He reached over to his night table, grabbed the pack of Mores. "He's not crazy. He's a teenager."

She shook her head from side to side, hands on hips. "Christ, talk about denial. *You* are something."

"What does that mean?" He lit the brown cigarette, blew out the match.

She grabbed a heavy red sweater from the back of a chair. "It means, you know perfectly well, that it's more than his being a teen-ager." Angrily, she pulled the sweater over her head. "You just don't want me to leave for vacation early."

The truth. He didn't know what to say. But, actually what

could she accomplish by going home three days ahead of time? It wasn't as if Tom were going anywhere. He said that to Kit.

"And how the hell do *you* know that?" she asked.

"Because he told me. And you."

Her brow creased, she cocked her head to one side, questioning.

"He keeps telling you he can't wait to see you, to tell you all about it. If he was going to bolt, he wouldn't say that. From what you've told me the kid's close to you, so he probably wants to drag you into the cult or whatever it is. He'll be there when you get home Monday."

Watching her face, he could see he'd made sense to her.

But she wasn't ready to surrender. "Anything could happen between now and then."

"Like what?"

"Like anything. Have you forgotten Jim Jones?"

"Oh, Kit, don't overdramatize." Should he get up, go to her?

Sitting in a chair, she put on her yellow construction boots, began lacing them. Her cheeks were flushed with anger. "You make me sick."

"Thanks."

Bent over the boots, she raised her head. "You don't give a damn about Tom. You just want to make sure I don't go before your precious party with Professor Block. Well, fuck you, Mister."

She stormed out of the room.

"Where you going?" he shouted.

Giving him his answer, the front door slammed.

Noj crushed out the cigarette and lay back down. Run after her? No. She needed time to think this thing through. There was no doubt in his mind that she'd come back. Seeing it his way. It was true he didn't want her to go home. He also knew that jumping the gun was pointless. Nothing bad was going to happen before she got there Monday.

Nothing at all.

2.

Sitting in study hall, dark glasses in place, Tom kept his eyes trained on the open book in front of him but saw nothing of the printed words. Even if he'd wanted to read, he couldn't have. The print swam before him. He didn't care. Schooling was finished for him.

SOLA was his sole educator.

SOLA. SOLE. SOUL.

Kit told him SOLA had spoken to her.

She didn't know who SOLA was, but it was clear he'd spoken. Tom was surprised. He'd never known SOLA to speak to anyone else. At least not in his presence.

But was he present?

Obviously, his body had been present, not his mind. SOLA didn't want him to remember that conversation with Kit. SOLA refused to reveal why he'd forced Tom into the conversation with Kit. SOLA was incommunicado. Tom was baffled.

Was he also jealous that SOLA had spoken to Kit?

THE EMOTION OF JEALOUSY WILL BE REMOVED FOREVER. THIS IS PART OF SOLUDA.

SOLA had promised.

Understanding, he unconciously snapped his fingers.

Marvin Birkenmier, the boy sitting next to him at the study table, turned to look at Tom. "What's up, man?" he whispered.

It was a moment before Tom understood that Marvin was responding to his snapped fingers. He said a quick, silent prayer to SOLA, asking to appear as he always had.

"Nothing," he said to Marvin, feeling the old Tom seep back inside him. "What's up with you?"

"I thought you was snappin' at me, ya know?"

"I just thought of something, that's all."

"Cool."

"Quiet," Mrs. Spector said.

Tom and Marvin grimaced at each other, turned back to their books.

Tom thought about exterminating Marvin. In his mind he saw a gallon jar. Invisible ink. He poured it over Marvin. Marvin vanished. Tom giggled into his hand.

The voice almost knocked him off his chair.

SOLUDA FORBIDS IDLE EXTERMINATION.

It was SOLA.

Tom could feel the beginning of interior tremors. He apologized.

YOU MUST FOLLOW MY ORDERS ONLY.

The tremor turned to shuddering.

Marvin noticed.

DO NOT QUESTION MY DECISIONS OR I SHALL DESTROY YOU.

His teeth chattered.

Cynthia Porter, sitting on the other side of Tom, registered the sound, looked to her right.

Tom's breath came in gasps.

"Hey, man, what's wrong?" Marvin asked.

Tom didn't hear him.

CATHERINE NASH WILL ONLY SURVIVE IF SHE ACQUIESCES.

The vibration of his body shook his glasses from the bridge of his nose onto the table.

"What's wrong with him?" Cynthia said to Alison who sat across from her.

YOU ARE RESPONSIBLE.

The snakes were everywhere. They were crawling along the study table, huge and menacing. Tongues flicking. He must get away.

When Tom pushed his chair back, rose, his body jerking spastically, Marvin and Cynthia stood up also. They were frightened. They, and the rest of the study group, had never seen anything like this. Neither had Mrs. Spector. She came toward Tom as though she were in slow motion.

Just before he fell over sideways onto the floor Tom heard: K-DAY. KILL DAY. K-DAY. KILL DAY. K-DAY.

For at least five seconds after he passed out, his body continued to twitch.

When Tom came to, he knew immediately he was in the Nurse's office again. But he didn't know *why* he was there. Nothing hurt.

Voices came from beyond the green curtain. He listened, hoping for a clue.

"No, I don't think it's epilepsy, Mrs. Spector. Certain symptoms are missing," said Mrs. MacNish.

"Well, what then?" she clucked nervously.

"I don't know. I'm going to call his mother."

Epilepsy? Some sort of fit? As he listened to the dialing of the phone, he desperately tried to remember.

"I think," Mrs. MacNish said, "the sooner we get him out of school, the better. God knows, we don't want to be responsible."

"It was simply awful," Mrs. Spector said. Cluck.

The last thing Tom remembered was Mrs. Spector telling him and Marvin to be quiet.

Mrs. MacNish said, "Damn. She's not home." She hung up the phone.

"Try the father."

Oh, no, Tom thought, sat up and pulled the curtain aside. The two women turned to look at him.

"My father's out of town on business," he said, smiling sweetly.

"Dear, dear," MacNish said. "Your mother's not home."

"I know. She's gone for the day." He swung his legs over the side of the cot, faced them. "It's okay. I feel all right now."

"Has this ever happened to you before?" Mrs. Spector asked.

Nurse MacNish glared at her, feeling usurped. "You can go back to class now, dear. I'll handle this."

The teacher took the hint, nodded, left the office.

Mrs. MacNish pulled over a chair, sat down near Tom. She hated repeating Mrs. Spector's question. Had to.

"No, it's never happened," he assured her. "I think it must have to do with the other day. You know, the basketball hitting me."

She doubted it. "Maybe. Never heard of such a thing. Any epilepsy in your family?"

"No." He was worried. Would the nurse call his mother later? He should have said they'd both left town until Monday. School would be closed then. MacNish wouldn't do anything during vacation.

"How do you feel now? Dizzy?"

He tried looking in her eyes, using his charm. "No. I feel fine."

"Can you stand up?"

"Sure." He prayed to SOLA for help. Stood. Perfect.

MacNish nodded. "Walk across the room."

He did. Fine.

"Well, I think you ought to rest anyway."

"All right." He didn't want to make any trouble, give her cause to pursue calling his parents. He lay down on the cot.

"When will your mother be home?"

"Late tonight."

"You'll tell them, won't you, Tom? What happened today? I think you'd better see your family doctor."

"Oh, sure, I'll tell them." He gave her his most sincere look.

Mrs. MacNish nodded. She had no reason to believe he wouldn't. He was a good boy. Nice. Besides, if the parents weren't going to be home until late tonight, what was *she* supposed to do? Starting at three today she was on vacation and she'd be damned if she was going to spoil the first night of the holiday by getting into some phone conversation with parents. If they were off galivanting around, and not where they should be to get the news at the proper time, then it wasn't her responsibility after three. Angrily, she pulled the curtain around Tom.

Tom closed his eyes. Relief. He knew MacNish wasn't going to tell them. And, of course, neither was he. The best he could hope was that whatever had happened wasn't going to happen again.

He prayed for SOLA's protection. Surely SOLA knew if it happened in front of his parents it might ruin everything.

SOLA KNOWS.

Tom smiled, hearing SOLA'S answer.

Funny the way things worked out. If his mother hadn't been having an affair, she would have been home when MacNish called. For the first time, he found himself glad that she was. He hadn't been the day he found out.

He'd heard his mother on the phone. Home early one day. She hadn't heard Tom. He'd gone into the kitchen, lifted the receiver, listened.

Shocking. His mother talking in that low, sexy voice. First shock, then fear, then anger. He never doubted they were lovers. Before the conversation ended he'd put back the re-

164

ceiver, gone outside, waited ten minutes. Then back; pretending he was arriving for the first time.

Had he imagined it? Imagined hearing her? Sometimes he wondered.

And then he'd searched for something more concrete. It was SOLA who had told him where to look.

There were four notes tucked way in the back of her closet in a box, under some clothing she had stored for the Salvation Army. He read only one. One was plenty.

Darling.

Your letter came today and I have read and reread it, swallowed in your words, held the paper in my hands like your sweet face. I love you. I will see you very soon, hear your voice, feel your smile.

Sometimes I wonder if you really know how I long for you. To have my arms around you, to make love to you. How could you possibly know how much I ache for the very touch of you. Anne, my darling, you are everything to me (is that unhealthy? Well, who gives a damn...I'm alive again), and I live for the day we can be together...always.

                                                            J.

"J." It was for Jim. Tom didn't know the last name. But he'd heard his mother call him Jim on the phone.

And now Jim had saved him. And saved his mother. For death.

It was time to get things rolling. The last bell of the day, of the season, would be the beginning. When it tolled, it would be his signal.

He would leave school forever.

And take his first step toward K-Day.

It was time to visit Esther Durham.

3.

First Anne had spilled the container of milk all over the kitchen floor. Then she'd dropped and broken a beautiful Staffordshire plate her mother had given her. In the bathroom, her talcum powder slipped from her hands, spraying the blue toilet seat cover.

Finally, she had to laugh at herself. Not since she'd been a girl had she felt so nervous, not even before her wedding.

Cole's behavior the night before helped her with any guilt she might have had. Clearly, once the holidays were over, she must end this sham of a marriage. God knew, she'd given it her best shot.

At breakfast, Cole had looked at her in a new way. Undoubtedly, he was shocked by her rejection the night before. A first in twenty-five years. But his face reflected something beyond anger, hurt, humiliation. What was it? Did he know where she was going? What she was going to do?

Tom, on the other hand was cheerful, joking, almost like his old self. Not quite. A tiny hint of strain played at the corners of his mouth. To anyone else he would have appeared the perfect boy he'd always been. Thank God he was at least making an effort. Relief. Whatever reasons he'd had for lying about his phone call with Kit could be put on the shelf for the moment. And if he was involved in some cult, he apparently wasn't going to take any action now. Christmas vacation was soon enough to deal with it. Kit would help.

Anne looked at herself in the full-length mirror which hung on the back of her closet door. She'd chosen a rose-colored wool skirt and matching paisley blouse, the neck a low "V", showing her ample cleavage. Was it too obvious, too sexy? Too sexy for what? After all, she wanted to be sexy for Jim, didn't she?

Her honey hair curled softly around her face. At that moment, she knew her mouth was definitely too large and too wide! Convinced it stretched the width of her face, she pursed her lips, trying to make it smaller, succeeding only in giving herself little whistle marks above her upper lip. Quickly, she relaxed her mouth. She had enough of those lines already. One in particular looked like a deep scar. Damn! And why was her nose like that? Slightly crooked, off-center. Never straight or perfect, it had never seemed bent in so many directions! My God, she thought, have you ever seen such beady little eyes? What she usually called hazel appeared today as washed-out brown.

Cookie, you are simply a mess!

And then she laughed.

Closing the closet door, she remembered Jim thought she was beautiful. He loved her wide mouth, her hazel eyes, slightly crooked nose. And he didn't give a damn about her lines. Nerves.

Downstairs, she checked the stove, switched off the lights, inspected the ashtrays. House secured, she put on her brown dress coat, fur boots, brown leather gloves.

As she was closing the front door, the phone began ringing. She started to go back in, stopped. If it was bad news, it might change things. Delay. Cancel. If it was good news, it might do the same. Or take too much time. If she hadn't spent two minutes looking in the mirror worrying about herself, she would have been gone by now. Wouldn't have been able to answer anyway!

Deciding no news was good news, she shut and locked the door on the ringing phone.

4.

Try as he might, Jim O'Neill couldn't get engrossed in the story on Arabs and oil in *Time* magazine.

Tossing the magazine on a chair, he began to pace. As motel rooms went, this one was fine. Even had a small pine table and two chairs. And a half refrigerator where he'd stashed a bottle of white wine. On the table, he'd placed a bouquet of yellow roses.

Suddenly, he felt an uncomfortable twinge. Marilyn loved yellow roses. Buying them had been unconscious. Was he trying to replace her, even after all this time? Or was it just a reflex? Next time, he'd make the roses red. Would there be a next time?

Would there be *this* time? Sitting on the edge of the bed, he knew he was waiting for the phone to ring. Waiting for Anne to back out. He looked at his watch. If she didn't cancel, she'd be here in less than an hour.

He lay back on the bed, trying to relax. What if he was impotent? Extraordinary but true: he'd not had sex for three years. If he failed, Anne would understand, be patient. The important thing was they loved each other. They weren't children. Apprehension was stupid. Things would work out.

He checked his watch. If Anne wasn't going to keep this date, she would've cancelled by now. A new confidence warmed him.

But only for a moment.

Leaping to his feet, he paced.

And paced.

5.

"Find anything out?" Harry Todd asked Cole.

He could have killed him. Had to look up. "I'm taking care of it, Harry. Don't worry."

"I'm not worried. Too bad things didn't happen differently." Oily smile.

Cole thought, here we go again. "What things?"

"Daley broke the Foster case." He whistled admiringly. "He's some slick operator, Daley."

Excited, Cole asked how.

"He got to the Howland kid. Foster's granddaughter, Betsy. There was a note."

"I'll be damned," Cole said. It was a terrific break. But what the hell did he care? Company business didn't affect him any more. At least, it wouldn't after Monday.

"So you see, if Daley had gotten to the kid sooner, the whole thing about Anne wouldn't have come out. Too bad." Harry tried not to smile.

"Yeah. Well, better I know."

"I guess so. Want to celebrate later?"

"Sorry, I'm leaving early. Got some Christmas shopping to do."

Harry nodded. "See you Monday."

Loose ends, Cole thought. Nice to wrap things up.

Maybe he should go see this O'Neill character. Just for the hell of it. Another loose end. Why should the guy go scott free? He looked at his watch. Too late to drive down there today. Perhaps tomorrow.

He stood up. Today he had shopping to do. But even as he thought it, he knew that wasn't what he was going to do. He was changing his habits, patterns already. It was afternoon and he was going to break out of his mold. He would get a jump on his new life.

Why not?

6.

For a moment, after Anne pulled into the parking lot of the motel, she couldn't remember whether Jim had said room five or fifteen. At least she knew there was a five in it. Feeling dizzy, she discovered she was holding her breath. Then like some great revelation, it dawned on her to look for Jim's car.

A red BMW was parked in front of room five. She drove to fifteen, spotted the tan Pontiac stationwagon, swung her car into a spot reserved for visitors.

Anne turned off the motor, sat. She was sure she felt her blood running through her veins at high speed. In the rearview mirror, she gazed at herself. Ran a comb through her hair. There was nothing she could do about all the flaws. If he wanted her, he'd have to take her the way she was, damn him! Now she was angry at him for *her* thoughts. She smiled, shook her head, opened the car door.

Jim jumped when the knock came. After taking her coat, hanging it in the closet, he led her to the table and chairs. The formality was excruciating. Ridiculous. They sat, backs straight, looking as though they were waiting for someone to pour tea.

Unnatural. Stilted. "How was the trip." "Were you waiting long?" "Glad it didn't rain."

Jim broke first.

"Darling, *what* are we doing?" He reached across the round table.

Feeling his touch, her breath caught again. This time from excitement. She wanted to feel his arms around her.

Jim stood, walked around the table, guided her to her feet. Gently, he touched her hair, looked into her eyes. "I adore you."

Self-conscious, aware of the stretchmarks from five pregnancies, she asked him not to look when she undressed. Disappointed, he said, "I want to be able to remember." But eager to put her at ease, he complied.

They lay under the sheet, side by side, his arm around her, his other hand holding hers. For the first time, they could feel each other's bodies, skin.

Anne, trembling, wondered if she'd survive his touch.

Slowly Jim turned, raised up, kissed her, his tongue exploring her mouth, his hands touching, feeling, as though they had lives of their own. Then he felt her tense. Before she could stop him, he said in a husky voice, "I'm deeply in love with you, Anne, and you're in love with me. Don't run away now. It's right, it's good. Anne, please, trust me. Listen, my darling, I need to be inside you."

"Oh, God," she said, "yes." Her arms flew around his neck as she drew his mouth down to hers.

All thoughts of everything, everyone but each other, vanished.

7.

When Esther opened the door, she gasped.

Tom had forgotten to wear his dark glasses.

He grinned. "Oh, gosh, seems I'm scaring women all over the place lately. Yesterday Jennifer's mother freaked. Got them in basketball. Sorry, Esther. Didn't mean to frighten you." His smile was radiant.

Holding a hand over her heart she said, "Land sake's, Tom, those are really something."

The pleasure of Tom's visit began to take precedence over the shock. She motioned him in.

He wiped the snow from his feet, pulled off his headband, unzipped his parka. "I just can't seem to remember I've got these two neat shiners." He kissed her cheek.

"Basketball, huh?"

"Just a freak accident." He hung his things on a wooden peg near the door.

"Well, they're humdingers! Come on in, take off your shirt and pants, like they say." She clamped a hand over her mouth. "Whoop, I shouldn't be saying that to you, I guess. Well, forgive. You know what I mean. Want some hot chocolate?"

He could swallow that. "That'd be nice, Esther."

She stopped, turned around, looked at him. It wasn't what he'd said. There was nothing wrong with the words. *That'd be nice, Esther.* Something in the tone maybe. Something....

"What's the matter?" he asked.

She shook her head. "Nothing. Come on in."

The Durham kitchen was Esther's pride and joy. A dream of a room. The counters had been made from the center cuts of pine trees, the shape of the tree still obvious. At one end was an enormous fireplace, its fieldstones making up the entire wall. A fire blazed, lighting the room.

Esther started to turn on a light. Tom gently stopped her.

"Cozy," he said, stepping in front of the fire. "It's pretty nippy out there."

"Sure is." Esther stared at his back. Something was definitely off kilter. Nothing she could identify. But even the way Tom held himself seemed odd, irregular.

Sitting at the round, oak table with their mugs of chocolate, a dollop of marshmallow floating on top, Esther decided to ask. "Something wrong, Tom?"

"Wrong?"

"You seem, well, I don't know...kind of on the fritz, if you know what I mean." She hoped she wouldn't offend him. After all the boy had taken the trouble to drop by. Had Anne told him to?

Tom cocked his head to one side, smiled candidly, trying to remember what he'd always done to charm Esther. He thought this look was the one she liked. "I guess it's just these black eyes that make me look so funny."

Now that was her Tom. Wasn't it? "I guess it probably is. Well, I suspect you've been real busy lately."

172

"Christmas," he said vaguely. "But I thought I'd better not let you languish, Esther. I mean, you're my best girl, aren't you?"

She grinned, patted her gray bun, tucking in loose strands. "The truth? No. Far as I know a little gal by the name of Jennifer Wheeler has taken my place."

"She can't compare to you." It was difficult keeping his eyes from the glass gun case.

Esther followed his gaze. "Nasty things. I hate them here in the kitchen. I mean, it's such a homey place except for those guns. But, it's George's house too. Marriage is a compromise, after all."

"Oh, I don't mind guns. I could even hold one." He jumped up, opened the glass door, took out a pistol. "See," he said, turning around, pointing it at her.

Esther jumped. "Don't, Tom. Don't point it at me, for God's sake." She was frightened.

"Sorry," he said, lowering it.

Stupid. Foolish.

Was it? He could kill her now, take the gun, hide it. No one would ever suspect him.

Yes. Much simpler than creeping over in the night. Risking discovery.

Again he raised the gun, and pointed it at Esther's chest.

8.

Kit was furious.

She'd forgotten her gloves, couldn't go back. Goddamn Noj. All he cared about was himself, *his* needs. That he wanted to show her off at a party made her sick. Was she just a body? Was that really what it was all about?

At first she walked aimlessly, but soon found herself heading toward Professor Bell's house. Gloria Bell was Kit's Abnormal Psych. lecturer.

She'd never just "dropped in" on Professor Bell, although Gloria encouraged her students to visit any time. Standing in front of the small frame house, Kit wished she'd phoned first. It was at least half a mile back to the nearest phone and it was icy cold. Still, it might be worth the walk. She wouldn't feel she was barging in. Gloria Bell opened the door, surprising Kit.

"Come on in." She smiled, waved an inviting hand.

Blushing, as though she'd been caught at something terrible, Kit walked the shoveled path to the door.

"I don't mind drop-ins," Gloria said, reading Kit's mind.

"Thanks."

Inside, Gloria took her into a den where a fire was in the beginning stages. Two brown velvet chairs were angled toward each other and the fire. A black and red coffee keeper sat on a table between the chairs along with two red mugs.

"You were expecting someone." Kit felt even more uncomfortable now.

Gloria shook her head, touched the rim of her round wire-framed glasses. "I always keep an extra cup ready. Like some?"

"Yes, please." The chair was plush and comfortable. She began to feel at ease for the first time that day. Watching Gloria pour the coffee, Kit was struck by the small delicateness of the woman. Tiny, almost to the point of frailty. But obvious inner strength beneath that. Her stylish short cropped hair was black with patches of gray in front. Her ears pierced, sported tiny diamond earrings. She was in her early fifties, but looked younger. Always wore shades of brown and today was no exception: dark brown corduroy pants, taupe turtleneck, tan checked blazer, collar turned up fashionably.

"You look troubled," Gloria said.

"Do I?"

"Yes."

"Noj always says I'm the most transparent person he's ever met."

"What's wrong?"

Immediately, Kit found herself telling Gloria Bell everything. Tom's two phone calls, the revelation of her mother's affair, her desire to go home and Noj's wanting her to stay. Easy. The words just tumbled out.

174

When Kit was finished, Gloria smiled kindly and said, "I can understand your anxiety, Kit. What you've told me is enough to make anyone feel anxious." She lit a cigarette, stuck it in a short black holder. "Do you think you could be of some use at home?"

Kit closed her eyes, rested her head against the back of the chair. "I don't know. Maybe I'd just make things worse...you know, alarm everyone. Of course, I could always say I came home because . . . I don't know . . . I guess I could say almost anything."

"But you're hesitant because it would upset Noj?"

"Yes. Is that wrong?"

"Of course not. It's not a matter of right or wrong. You have to do what makes you most comfortable." Smoke spiraled upward.

"You're very direct."

"Why not?"

Kit shook her head. "No reason, I guess. Alvin's rather circumspect."

Gloria nodded. "Our approach is quite different."

"Do you see patients?" she asked suddenly.

"Clients," Gloria corrected her.

"Yes, of course."

"I do. Why?"

"Could you take me on?"

"Don't you see Alvin Clay?"

"Yes, but it's not working. I don't want to see a man."

"Well, I'll have some time when we get back from holiday. Of course, you'll clear things up with Alvin before we begin."

Kit nodded. "Is this a session?"

"A chat." She ejected the cigarette from the holder, blew a fat puff of smoke from it.

"Do you think I should go home? What would you do?"

"More coffee?"

"No thanks." She waited eagerly for Gloria's reply.

"I would try and feel what was going to make me the most comfortable and then act on that. Only you can decide, Kit. But then you know that."

"Yes, I do."

"And don't underestimate what you've learned about your mother. That's a difficult thing to assimilate. Try and be in touch with your feelings about all these things. It's the only way you'll be able to reach a decision."

Kit no longer felt safe in this room. "I'd better be going."

175

At the door, Gloria reached up, putting a hand on Kit's shoulder. "Call me if you want, Kit. Any time. And I look forward to seeing you after the holidays."

"Me, too," Kit said.

Walking back to the apartment, she felt more confused than ever. Gloria was right, of course. She had to do what made her feel comfortable, couldn't see getting into a big number about it with Noj. Tom was going to wait to see her before taking any action, and clearly her mother didn't want her there early, so who was she to go barging in? This time it wasn't what *she* wanted. This time she had to think of others.

What the hell did Gloria Bell know, anyway?

9.

Sounds of high-pitched laughter came from far away.

But it wasn't far away at all. It was right there, in her ears, coming from her mouth.

Who was this boy pointing the gun at her chest?

Why it's that nice quiet Tom Nash, Esther. Who else?

Say something.

"Tom, that's real dangerous what you're doing, you know." Odd sounding voice.

Unsteady, in his hand, the pistol dipped slightly as Tom stared.

"Fun's fun," she said, wondering what in the world that meant and thinking of her mother who'd been dead for thirty years. *Fun's fun.* She'd always said that.

Smiling, Tom said, "Do you believe in a Higher Power, Esther?"

"Higher Power?" she repeated stupidly.

"Yes. You know." He gestured with the gun, twirling it in a small circle.

Esther felt everything inside her moving, grinding. "You mean, God? Well, yes. Of course. Tom, dear, why don't you put that thing away. You know I hate those guns." Rivulets of sweat ran down her sides, staining her workshirt. "Put it away for me, will you?" She wasn't sure how long her legs would hold her up. Her knees were buckling, but she held on to the ladder back chair.

"Oh, sure." Wondering why he was pointing it at her anyway, he lowered the gun, went to the cabinet, replaced it and closed the glass door.

When his back was turned her legs gave. Quickly, she sat.

Tom joined her at the table, face relaxed, smiling sweetly. "Now what were we saying, Esther?" He sipped at his hot chocolate, ignoring the dark skin on top.

She could still feel her heart thumping. "I believe you were asking me about God." What was going on here?

"Oh, yes. A Higher Power. I'd like to let you in on something.... As you know, I'm very fond of you."

She nodded, encouraging him, but unable to find her real voice.

"A new religion is coming," he whispered conspiratorially.

Lord Almighty, the boy'd been brainwashed! Carefully, she said, "Do you mean that Moon man, Tom?" How would a new religion explain what he'd done with the gun?

He frowned, blond eyebrows meeting. "Moon man?"

"You know," she said, trying for a lightness she didn't feel, "the Moonies."

"Of course not." He was indignant. "You think I'm a jerk or something?"

"Not you. Well, what religion is this?" She wondered if Anne were home and, if so, how she could get her here without alarming Tom.

"I'm not sure I should tell you now." He slumped in his chair, lip jutting out.

It was important to get the name of the cult or whatever it was. Esther felt sure of that. Anne and Cole would need to know. "You know, Tom," she said, cajoling, "you can trust me."

"Moonies," he mumbled.

She'd insulted him. "Oh, me, oh, my. Don't be so sensitive. After all, what do I know about such things? Just what I see on the TV and what I read in the papers." She took a swallow

177

of hot chocolate; her hand rattling the cup against the saucer. He didn't notice.

"Is this a new cult, Tom?" Very timidly.

"Cult?" He was angry.

"Oh, dear, stuck my foot in it again, didn't I?" Her legs began to itch and she scratched furiously. Through her heavy jeans, she couldn't feel much.

"Is that what you think . . . that I'm into one of those dumb cults? Esther, I'm not just some wimp, you know. This is different."

"Different," she repeated.

"Sure. Those cults are for losers."

"And you're no loser," she said quickly, smiling. There was a prickling at the back of her neck.

"Right."

She had to know. "Well, dear, tell me what this is all about?"

He eyed her suspiciously for a moment. Then, "It's called SOLUDA." Whispering again.

"Soluda." She saw now that his pupils were enlarged. She'd been intent before on the black and blue around his eyes, hadn't noticed. Or had they just gotten bigger?

"SOLA is the Higher Power."

What to say? How to handle this? Oh, how she wished George would come home.

"Sola." She reproduced the word. Had she ever heard it? What did it mean?

"I'm going to be Grand Duke and Kit will be Grand Duchess." He pulled small balls of wool from his blue crew neck sweater, rolled them between his fingers, dropped them on the floor.

This wasn't like Tom, Esther noted. He was fastidious. Especially in someone else's house.

"Kit knows about this, too, huh?" He'd gone crazy. How could it be?

Tom shook his head. "No, not yet. I'll tell her when she gets home."

"And your mother and father? Do they know?" All in his head. Not an organized cult, after all.

His eyes narrowed. "No. And don't tell them, Esther."

The tone was menacing. The rumble inside her started again. "Of course not, Tom. If you say not to, I won't." Crazy as a loon. God help us.

He nodded, smiled. "Good, Esther."

How could she find out if Anne was home? "Did Anne tell you to come visit?"

"What do you mean?"

"I ... I was just wondering. I mentioned you hadn't been by. I thought maybe she put you up to it."

Reaching a hand across the table, he touched the back of hers. It took every bit of control she had not to pull away.

"Darling, Esther, I don't need my mother to tell me to visit you."

She could barely look at him. Not only was his voice odd, a kind of weird whine; the words were peculiar, unlike him. It was as though someone else were speaking through him. Possessed? Nonsense.

"What's wrong?" he asked.

"Wrong? Nothing's wrong." She must be looking at him oddly. As she took in his fine blond hair, ear length; neat, straight nose beautifully flared at the nostrils; wide mouth like his mother's; white teeth perfectly even, she couldn't believe what was happening. Only the black eyes were out of whack. But any young boy could be sitting in her kitchen with black eyes. Part of being normal, wasn't it? Oh, George, please come home.

"I'm glad nothing's wrong, Esther. Do you think you'd like to belong to SOLUDA?"

What was she supposed to say? Hedge your bets, Esther. "Well, Tom, I don't know enough about it. Why don't you tell me more."

His mouth twitched.

"No, I couldn't do that. But I will eventually. Promise." He stood up.

She held her breath. What now? The gun again?

"I'd better get going. A lot of preparations need to be made, you know."

She nodded as though she understood, relief flooding through her even though she wasn't completely safe yet.

"You'd be surprised how much has to be done," he said walking toward the living room.

"I'm sure," she said. Her legs were as limp as two strands of spaghetti.

"I mean, things can't just happen on their own."

"'Course not." Her pulse quickened as he wrapped his muffler around his neck and took his green headband from his pocket.

"Well, Esther I'm glad we talked." He zipped up his parka, put an arm around her narrow shoulders.

"And don't you worry about anything, Esther. All will be revealed in good time. SOLA will find a place for you."

"Good, good," she said soothingly. Could he feel her shaking?

At the door he bent, kissed her cheek. "Take care and give George my best. I guess we'll see you Sunday."

"That's right, dear." Everything was happening in slow motion.

He put his headband in place, pulled on his gloves. "'Bye-bye."

She watched him go down the steps. At the end of the walk he turned, waved. She waved back. From this distance, you'd never know. He looked, seemed, like her old Tom. She closed the heavy oak door, pulled the bolt across and ran to the phone. Silently, she prayed that Anne was home.

There was no answer.

She let it ring a long time, waited five minutes, tried again.

Still no answer.

Hands shaking, body weak, Esther sat by the phone. She had no idea what to do. Calling Cole was not an option. He'd think she was an hysterical old woman. Oh, where in the world was Anne? And George?

Once again, she dialed.

Nothing.

Several minutes passed. Esther sat immobile, clouded by confusion. When she lifted the receiver to dial again, she couldn't even remember what she'd been thinking.

It rang and rang. Then the ringing was interrupted. Esther sat up straight, heart pounding.

"Hello."

It was Tom.

She hung up.

After a moment, she began to cry.

10.

"You want to run now, don't you?" Jim asked.

Anne's eyes were closed. She lay in the crook of his arm, head turned away from him. "I guess I do."

"It would've been a miracle if it'd been perfect the first time."

"It's not that." She stared at the bullfighting print hanging on the wall.

"I know. You're feeling guilty."

"It's my middle-class upbringing. I can't help it."

He kissed her hair. "I understand, Anne, I really do."

She wondered if all the rooms had bullfighting prints. After a moment, she said, "Jim, I can't do this again."

Pain cut across his belly. He couldn't sustain another loss. "Meaning?"

She moved away from him, reached for a cigarette. Sitting up, she pulled the beige sheet under her arms, across her breasts. "I'm simply not an adulteress. It doesn't matter what I feel for Cole or what he feels for me. I'm still married to him, living with him as his wife. As long as we're under the same roof....Jim, do you understand?"

He understood that he was losing her. His instinct was to grab his clothes, get out. Childish. "I understand what you're saying, but I can't understand why you won't leave him."

"I didn't say I wouldn't." She touched his cheek with the back of her fingers, stroked. "What I'm saying is that *until* I've told him, I can't see you again. *Until* we've decided on some other arrangement."

His pain ebbed. "You mean you're going to leave him?"

"I must."

Hoping he wouldn't cry, he said, "I want to marry you, Anne."

"You'll have to be patient. Oh, Lord, how can I say that? You've been so patient all this time. I know you won't push me."

"I won't. As long as I know that you're in my future, that there'll be an end to this sneaking around, to long periods without you.... I can wait a long time if I know that."

"After Christmas . . . the children . . . it'd be awful to disrupt things now." Her eyes implored him to understand.

He nodded, kissed her.

"After the first of the year, all right?" Her tone was questioning, but it was a statement.

"Of course."

She put out her cigarette, faced him.

They felt the excitement again. There was no time. Anne backed away.

"I have to go."

"I know." He smoothed the hair at his temples.

"I'll miss you terribly."

"I'm not pushing, darling, but will you be able to call? Of course, I'll understand if you can't." Would he really? He wasn't so sure.

"I'll find a way. You can count on that. After Christmas we'll meet—to talk."

Five days. Patience. Funny, the closer things got to where he wanted them, the less patience he seemed to have. Hang on. "As long as I know you love me," he said.

"Know it." She turned his head away from her, got out of bed.

11.

When Sara came in, Tom was sitting at the kitchen table drinking a Coke, writing in a notebook. He looked up, smiled.

Poor fat Sara. Soon she'll be at peace. "Hello, Kidlet," he said.

Sara felt an old thrill. He hadn't called her this special nickname for a long time. "Hi, Biglet," she answered. Old response. "Boy, those shiners are really something."

He was sick to death of references to his black eyes. Still, he smiled.

"Yup, they're beauties, all right." Lately, he was sweating profusely. He'd changed to a brown and green cotton shirt. It was damp already.

"Beauties," she repeated.

She wanted desperately to talk to him. About what? What could she say? Should she ask if something was wrong?

With a critical eye, Tom appraised her. Perhaps if she didn't dress in those huge sloppy shirts.

Sara felt his judgmental scrutiny. If only the floor would open up, swallow her. But it never did.

"Have a Coke," he offered.

"Dieting." Always her answer. It didn't matter that she'd had two before coming home. Quickly, she changed the subject from food. "Where's Mom?"

Tom shrugged. What would Sara think if she knew her mother was having an affair? Should he tell her?

"Not home?"

"Right." He lowered his eyes to his notebook. Looking at Sara made him sick.

For a moment, Sara thought of telling him Steven had overheard his conversation with Kit, ask him what it was about, then, afraid of his response, changed her mind. Unable to leave, rocking on one foot, her books fell from her arms, spreading themselves on the floor at Tom's feet.

He looked down. Her black three-ringed notebook split open, revealing the inside front cover. Sara could feel the heat creeping into her cheeks.

Pasted inside the cover were pictures of fashion models. Very thin models.

"Still doing that?" Tom slowly shook his head from side to side.

Swallowing hard, she answered, "They're old. I forgot they were there."

He stared at her, waiting.

Sara thought she might cry. For years she'd cut out and pasted pictures of models over the walls of her room. There'd been hundreds of them. They were how she *wanted* to look. Tom had gently urged her to remove them. It was masochistic, he said. And she felt better when she had. But lately she'd started cutting them out again, pasting them in her notebook, in her locker at school. Now he'd caught her.

His look was mean. Sara was afraid.

"I forgot to take those out," she lied.

"SOLA would kill you for that," he said calmly.

"Huh?" She bent down, knees cracking, began picking up the books, closing the cover on the offensive pictures.

"Those are new pictures, aren't they, Sara?"

The way he said *Sara* gave her a strange feeling. He'd never said it like that before. Laced with disgust. "I'll throw them away, Tom, honest."

"Pitiful," he murmured.

When she rose, books in her arms, he was again bent over his notebook, writing.

"What're you doing?" Wished she hadn't asked the minute she said it.

"Working on a project." He was writing down the tenets of SOLUDA.

She turned to leave. "Guess I'll go upstairs."

"Do you believe in anything, Sara?" Voice deep, resonant.

Stopped in her tracks. Turned around. His eyes looked odd. Pupils big. "Believe?" she asked.

"Yes, believe." He put the yellow pencil in his mouth, chewed.

Why was it so scary? She could hear her own breathing,

184

the scraping of the pencil against Tom's teeth, the pulsing of her blood. And he just sat there looking at her. Waiting.

WHAT, she wanted to scream. But she didn't. Instead, she hugged her books closer to her and started again toward the door

The crash made her stumble, books falling again. She began to cry.

Tom ran to her. "What's wrong, Kidlet? Scare ya? Ah, Sara, kid, sorry." He stroked her hair, hand heavy.

Shrinking from him, her weeping accelerated.

"I banged my fist on the table, that's all. Big deal. Sara, Sara, don't cry," he sang.

It wasn't soothing. She hiccupped.

He giggled. "Oh, now listen to that. Come on." Grabbing her by the arms he pulled. Grunted. Weak from lack of food, he couldn't budge her. Didn't really care. He dropped her arms, moved away, back to the table where he sat and drank his Coke.

Ignoring her sniffling, he said, "All I want to know, Sara, is if you believe in a Higher Power?"

After a moment, she stopped hiccupping. "You mean God?" she asked.

"If that's your choice of names." He scribbled rapidly.

"I dunno." How could someone so fat believe in God? Sara had asked God to help her thousands of times and He never had. No sooner would she ask to be stopped from eating than a chocolate bar would present itself. She hated God. Somehow, though, she felt she couldn't tell Tom that. Again, she picked up her books, piled them on the edge of the table.

"You used to believe, didn't you?" he asked.

"Yes."

"What happened?"

Sara shrugged.

"God let you down?" He smiled knowingly.

Maybe she could tell him.

The sound of the front door opening, crashing shut, silenced her. Steve and Max pushed and buffeted each other coming through the kitchen door. Max ran to Sara, threw his arms around her waist.

Sara kissed the boy, hugged him.

Too bad he'd have to go, Tom thought, staring at Max. Maybe there'd be a way to spare him. Perhaps the Duke and Duchess could make him an heir? He'd have to consult SOLA.

Steven, wary, looked at Sara, trying to pick up a clue to Tom's mood. She appeared shaken, frightened.

"Hi, Tom," Max said.

"Hi." No. He was getting soft. If he spared one, he'd start thinking he should spare them all. Everyone had to go. SOLA was pleased by this realization. Tom knew that immediately.

Steven as uncomfortable around Tom, started to leave, but was stopped by his voice.

"This is nice. Us all being together without *them*."

There was no question who *them* was. Even if the degrees of resentment, hatred or disgust differed they were all allies against their parents. Still, Steven wanted out and headed toward the door.

"Sit down," Tom said in a commanding voice.

Again Steven was stopped. The voice, although not the voice he'd overheard Tom use on the phone, was frightening. He looked at his brother.

Tom indicated the chairs around the table.

Sara and Steven exchanged a look; she gave him an almost imperceptible nod and they joined Tom, Max on Sara's lap. Like a family, Sara thought, trying to fool herself.

"I want to tell you about SOLUDA," he said. No. He heard his mind signaling.

Both Sara and Steven responded to the word, felt apprehensive.

"It's important you know before the end," Tom went on, unable to control his mouth from moving.

Find out, Sara told herself. It's only Tom. Nothing can happen. "What's soluda? What end?"

"SOLUDA is everything. SOLUDA will change the world. Nothing can stop it."

Tom rose from the table, pencil still in hand, his gaze toward the brick wall, over their heads.

They followed his line of vision. Saw nothing. Sara and Steven looked at each other, their panic full-blown.

"SOLA." Tom whispered.

Bravely, Steven said, "What's sola?"

Slowly, Tom turned away from the brick wall and looked at the children. He smiled sweetly noting the colors. Sara's outline was pink, Steven's green, Max's orange. Nice. Rainbow, almost.

Tom's smile made Sara shiver. It really was very nice. Yet something about it was scary. She felt like spiders were crawling on her.

186

Raising his arms up and to the side, Tom said, "SOLUDA will encompass. Peace to all."

Sara wanted to giggle. She thought of Tiny Tim: *God bless us, every one.* The urge to giggle vanished. A cult. Tom was in some loony cult. She'd been warned about cults. How could someone like Tom be fooled?

Steven said, "What're you talkin' about, Tom?"

"He's joined a cult. Haven't you?" said Sara.

Tom fixed his eyes on her. "Cult?" This again? What was wrong with everyone? "I'm not so frivolous, Sara," he said. Odd voice. "SOLUDA is by no means a cult. SOLUDA is...."

"Soluda, Toluda, Boluda, Poluda." Max bounced on Sara's lap, rolling his head from side to side. "Roluda, Moluda, Voluda..."

"STOP IT," Tom yelled, face reddening. "What's wrong with you? Don't you understand anything? Don't you care that there's about to be a new chapter in history?"

His voice, loud, vibrating, forced them to their feet. Sara held Max, who was beginning to cry in her arms.

"Put him down, you fat swine," Tom hissed.

Shocked, hurt, Sara obeyed. Never had Tom made a reference to her weight.

"Now get out of this kitchen," he said.

They did as he ordered. Quickly. Gladly.

Coming through the front door, Anne was hit by Sara, who flung herself in her mother's arms. The others rushed forward, Max sobbing, Steven shaking, his fair skin splotched with red patches.

"What is it?" she asked, bending down to her children, gathering them in.

"It's Tom," Sara cried, "he's crazy."

12.

Rocky's Bar & Restaurant did not live up to its name. There was no food unless one counted the bags of potato chips and smoked herring that hung from racks behind the bar and could be purchased for a quarter a bag. The front door was guarded outside by two enormous white dogs who lay on either side of the path, lazy and harmless. Inside, there were three vinyl covered tables, a dozen chairs, a fairly beat-up pool table and one pinball machine. The lighting was dim; the action all at the bar.

When Cole entered, there were four men seated there; all of them alone, silent. Above the bar, an afternoon soap droned and flickered on an old black and white television.

Cole made his way to one end of the oak bar, sat on a faded, patched red leather stool, ordered a draft beer and a packet of dried herring.

Tiny, the bartender, a beefy, flushed man in his fifties, eyed Cole suspiciously. This wasn't his usual customer. In fact, he couldn't remember the last time anyone had come into Rocky's in a suit and tie. Maybe this guy was from the IRS? Tiny couldn't make up his mind whether to treat him nice or rough. While he was debating, he served him the beer and herring.

"Ya new in town?"

"No."

"I never seen ya before, right?"

"Right."

"How come?"

"Hmmm?"

"How come I ain't never see ya before?"

"You mean in here?" Cole asked.

"Yeah, in here." Tiny gestured around the bar as though it were the Plaza.

"Because I've never been in here before."

"Oh. Yeah." He blinked. "But that's what I mean. How come ya never been in here before and now ya is?"

"Well, I don't know how to answer that exactly. I've driven by many times.... I guess I just never got around to it." Cole smiled.

Tiny stared at him as though he'd been speaking in a foreign tongue. He narrowed his eyes, crossed his arms over his massive chest, leaned forward and spoke from one side of his mouth in a confidential tone. "You official?"

"Official?"

"IRS?"

"IRS? Me? Hell, no."

Tiny liked the way he said, "hell, no," nodded his approval and walked to the other end of the bar to where another customer was asking for a refill.

Cole laughed to himself. The IRS, for God's sake. What irony. If he carried out his disappearing act, the IRS would be looking for *him*. He tore open the herring packet, pulled out the small salty fish, took a bite and washed it down with a swallow of beer. His eyes, finally accustomed to the darkened bar, took in his surroundings.

Each man stared into his own drink except for the old man at the end who talked in whispers to the bartender. Better keep his eyes on his own small place. That was the message. The way to stay out of trouble. There was nothing to look at anyway. Nothing but despair.

Two hours later Cole was feeling no pain. He'd become garrulous, engaging the now six other men in a friendly debate over American versus foreign cars. He was enjoying himself in a way he never had. Like a little sneak preview, he thought. A preview of the new life ahead of him. Free, masculine, irresponsible.

An hour later, slapping his new friends on the back, swearing he'd return, Cole made his way out of Rocky's. Weaving slightly, he crunched through the snow, past the two dog-sentinels, toward his car.

He patted his coat, feeling for his keys as he stared through the windshield. He was dizzy. Shouldn't have had the last one. Of course, he'd been buying. For all. He pulled his wallet from his pocket, opened it, removed his cash. He'd spent over fifty dollars. How was that possible? He'd been taken. Tiny'd

189

helped himself to some of Cole's change, lying loose on the bar. He opened the door angrily—one foot out, balancing. What would he say? Accuse that big bulk of stealing? Slowly, he withdrew his foot, shut the door. It served him right. He was right, had no business getting that way. Had to keep his wits about him these days.

Plans had to be made. This time he was going, no backing down. He slammed the side of his fist on the steering wheel. It hurt and he brought it up to his mouth, sucked on it.

This time he would carry through. Arizona. He'd call the airline in the morning, make his reservation.

As he started the car, he wondered why he didn't believe himself?

13.

In the kitchen, Anne stared at the top of Tom's head bent over the notebook he was frantically writing in. The other children were safely upstairs and now she had to deal with this one, her eldest. *Crazy*, Sara said. And that was all, her crying and fear making her unintelligible. Steven said something about a cult. *Crazy*.

Staring at Tom Anne saw nothing bizarre, just this rapid scrawling in his notebook. What had happened to make the others so frightened?

The telephone rang and Anne jumped. Tom started to reach for it, but she grabbed it first.

"Oh, thank God, you're home." It was Esther.

"What is it?"

"Is Tom nearby? If he is don't say anything. You understand?"

"Yes." Anne's level of anxiety rose like mercury in a thermometer. "Go on."

"Can you come over? I need to see you, talk to you. It's important, Anne."

She looked at her watch. It was getting late, but Esther sounded desperate, frightened. And it had something to do with Tom. What was happening?

Sound cheerful. Light. Don't let Tom suspect.

"Can you give me some ideas?" Anne asked casually.

In a dire voice, Esther said, "He's right there, isn't he?"

"Yes, dear, of course."

"Oh, God."

Was Esther crying? Anne understood she shouldn't indicate who it was, where she was going. "Well, Finch, I guess I can come down if you think it's that important."

"Finch? Anne, this is Esther."

"Yes, I know."

"Oh. Oh, yes. How clever you are. Oh, yes, I feel better already. Can you come right away?"

"Yes. Just hold on. 'Bye, dear." The receiver neatly slipped from her sweaty hand as she replaced it.

She couldn't leave the children alone in the house with Tom. At least not until she knew what the hell was going on.

"What are you doing, Tom?"

"Working." He smiled his smile.

The form was there, but it was absolutely hollow. Anne saw that with clarity. Feeling as though she'd been shot through with ice water, she returned an empty smile of her own. "On what?"

"A project."

"Tom, just now when I came in the children were crying and scared. What happened?"

He gave what would normally pass for a good-natured laugh. "Oh, well, Mom, I lost my temper. They were pestering me. You know. I guess I yelled at them." He shrugged, flashed the smile again.

He was lying, but there was no point in confronting him further, now. "Well, we all lose our tempers at times. No harm done." She reached out to touch his shoulder. Something in his eyes stopped her. She clumsily withdrew her hand as he returned to his notebook.

"I have to go downtown to see Finch. I'll be back soon."

"Okay."

"You want anything from town?"

"Nope."

"I think I'll take the kids with me."

"Good. Maybe I can get some work done then."

Why was he working here? Why wasn't he in his room? Well, no time to ask now.

Later.

In the car, the children stumbled over their words, telling everything they knew and felt about Tom. Steven admitted to overhearing the conversation between Tom and Kit.

"Why didn't you tell us then?" Anne asked.

"I dunno, I'm sorry." He felt like crying.

"All right," she said.

"He sounded real funny, Mom."

"How?"

"Weird."

Impatiently, she said, "Can't you be more articulate?"

"Huh?"

"You said it was creepy sounding," from Sara.

"Thanks," Anne said. What was the difference *how* he'd sounded. The fact was he'd made the call, sounded odd and lied about it. That was enough.

"Is it a cult?" Steven asked.

Sara said, "Tom says it isn't, but I think it is."

Anne looked down at Max, who was playing with a rubberband. She was glad he appeared uninterested. "It may be a cult, Sara, I don't know. Okay, here we are, everybody out."

George opened the door of the house. His eyes widened when he saw the children. After quick greetings and embraces, the children were hurried off to the television room.

In the kitchen Esther was huddled over a cup of tea. Anne had never seen her look so old, so frail.

"Esther," she said. "Oh, Esther, what is it?"

She was being punished for her affair with Jim. Anne could not stop this thought from flickering around the edges of her mind. She pounded harder at the rectangle of meatloaf. Drive the thought away. And what about the things Esther had said of Tom. Awful, too. She could barely stand to think about them. But she *had* to. Evidence was piling up. Evidence of what? Oh, Cookie, get in touch. Anne put the meatloaf in the oven, got out the salad vegetables, began to chop and pare.

She heard the front door slam. Cole. He was going to have to listen, pay attention, take some responsibilities, even though this wasn't a physical illness.

His pattern was to pick up mail on the hall table, along with the evening paper, tuck them under his arm, walk to the kitchen, ask what was for dinner, make himself a drink and go into the living room with drink, mail and paper.

Tonight, she would interrupt his routine. Continuing to chop celery, she listened for his footsteps until, surprised, she heard them go slowly up the stairs.

Damn!

A twenty-five year routine. And tonight he broke it.

The realization alarmed her. The seams of her life were splitting. She put down her chopping knife, wiped her hands on her apron, made her way to the stairs.

The water was running in their bathroom. She sat on the bed and waited. Too impatient. She knocked on the door.

"Yes?" His voice sounded odd, croaky.

"I want to talk to you."

"Not now."

"Now," she insisted.

The door crashed open.

Cole stood there, weaving, dressed only in his blue-checked boxer shorts. "What the hell do you want?"

He was drunk! That was evident. And unbelievable. She could count on one hand the times Cole had been drunk in twenty-five years.

"You're drunk."

He smiled crookedly, one hand on the door frame. "That's you all over. Always state the obvious."

"What happened?"

Shaking his head, laughing, he stumbled into the room, sat on the bed, legs outstretched. "What d'ya mean, what happened? I had a few. That some sort of crime or something?"

"No, no crime. It's just unusual, that's all."

"A lot's gonna be unusual." He lay back on the bed.

"What does that mean?"

"Nothing."

She decided not to play. Tom was more important. "I have to talk to you about Tom. He's sick."

Immediately, Cole sat up.

At the dinner table, everyone was wary of Tom. Watching carefully. Listening. Tom was oblivious to this. He was effervescent, telling stories, laughing. He knew he had every-one under control. Then *she* ruined everything.

Cult. She brought that up again.

SOLUDA. He hated hearing her say it.

He wanted to kill her there and then. Impossible. Why did she ask that? Why was everyone asking that? And how should he play it? The cult thing was what they wanted to hear, believe. Okay. That's what he'd give them.

"Well, Mom, I guess I'd better tell you."

He watched her grip tighten on her fork.

"I don't much like the word cult. I mean, it's sort of a dirty word these days." He smiled.

They were all staring at him. Ten eyes.

"Go on, dear," Anne urged.

He shrugged boyishly. "I dunno. Well, it's a group. Don't think of it as a cult."

"The group's called Soluda?" Cole asked, sober now.

"Yeah."

"What does it mean?"

"Ah, Dad, come on."

"It's secret, huh, Tom?" Steven asked excitedly, putting aside what he'd witnessed, hoping for a reasonable explanation.

"Right." He pushed his food around on his plate.

"Who's Sola?" Anne asked, gently.

"A friend. He's Spanish." He almost laughed, congratulated himself on his quick thinking.

"Will you introduce him to us?"

"Sure. When do you want to meet him? He's neat . . . you'll like him."

"What's his first name?" asked Cole, cutting a piece of meatloaf with his fork.

"Pancho." It was the only Spanish name he could think of.

"Where'd you meet him?"

"At school. He's a senior, too." They wouldn't check until after vacation. And then, of course, they couldn't! Ever.

"Why haven't you mentioned him before?"

"Say, what is this, the Inquisition?"

"I never heard of him," Sara said, then wishing she hadn't.

"And I suppose you know everyone in the senior class?" Sara said, "Guess not."

"When do you want to meet Pancho? He's gone to his

194

grandmother's for the weekend, but he'll be back Monday. Any time after that." He was thrilled by his cleverness.

Then *she* said, "Why did you lie about the phone call to Kit?"

He'd like to slit her throat, watch the blood burble out, down her neck.

"I don't know, Mom," he mumbled, lowering his head. "I guess I wanted to keep it all secret. I shouldn't've lied, I know. I'm sorry." Maybe now the stupid bitch would shut her mouth.

"Well, you've got everyone upset, Tom. You've been acting very strangely. I wish you'd **calm** down. Let's meet Pancho Sola on Tuesday."

"Sure." He took a large gulp of water.

"You're not eating, Tom."

"Not hungry. Can I be excused now?"

He watched as his parents exchanged a look.

"All right," Cole said.

"Thanks."

When all the children had left the table, Cole turned to Anne. "Feel better?"

"No," she said.

"Neither do I."

14.

He'd never felt so happy. He'd fooled them. Now they'd stay off his back. He felt as though he could fly. Ten feet off the ground.

Giddy.

High.

He pitied people who needed drugs or alcohol.

This was what they meant by natural high.

SOLA made this possible.

Only two more days.

A new thought. How could he have forgotten? He stopped pacing his room, placed his hands on the back of the moving chair. It was no longer disconcerting that everything was in constant motion. He accepted things as they were.

And he would have to accept what he'd just remembered.

Integrate.

Adjust.

But it was odd that SOLA had allowed him to forget his grandmother would be here on the twenty-second. He'd always liked her. So much nicer than his father's mother. And she cared for him. It made him sad that he'd have to kill her along with the rest.

Brought him down.

But only for a moment.

Saturday,
December 21

1.

Dorothy Clifford made sure she never saw any of her children more than twice a year.

Unless someone begged.

No one ever did.

She glanced at herself in her car's rearview mirror. Her face seemed a funny color. Good God, it wasn't turning yellow, was it? Impossible. Too soon. Much too soon. She shook the notion away.

Dorothy knew she was a good-looking woman. She wore her oyster white permanented hair short and soft around her oval face. She had dark round eyes bright as a young girl's. Her nose was narrow, and her full, wide lips were made up with a deep pink lipstick. She wore a dark brown pants suit, beige blouse. Her fur coat lay on the seat next to her.

The one thing Dorothy didn't want was to be a burden to any of her children. Widowed at the age of fifty-five, she could have become a real drain on their lives. But she'd been determined to remain independent and at the same time, supportive. Not that any of them ever asked for her support. Still, she was there for them if they needed her. She hoped they knew that.

Moving along the Garden State Parkway she thought about her children. They often filled her mind when she was doing something mechanical.

Ross, the oldest, was a lawyer, married twenty-one years with two children. Things were wonderful until the children became teen-agers. Bobby got into trouble with drugs. Stacy got pregnant during her senior year. Ross' wife, Ellen, had a breakdown and went into a hospital for nine weeks. It amazed Dorothy that such a normal family could become so dysfunctional. It must be the times. Bringing up her own children in the forties and fifties had been very different.

Liz and Doug were happy now that Liz had dealt with her alcoholism. It had been awful for awhile. And their decision not to have children had originally shocked and upset her. Now she believed Liz and Doug had been smart. They'd known what they wanted. They enjoyed their lives.

It was the same with Walter. No children. Of course, he wasn't married. At least not to a woman. He'd been living with Seth Waterman for fourteen years.

More than once Dorothy had begun to tell them she knew the true nature of their relationship, but something always stopped her. If they didn't want to admit to their homosexuality, was it her business to bring it up? Perhaps they'd be embarrassed. But in this day and age, she couldn't understand why. If she was ready to talk about it, why weren't they? Perhaps she could discuss it with Anne. But then Anne didn't know about her brother and Dorothy didn't know what her attitude was on the subject.

She felt closer to Anne than the others and was thrilled to be spending Christmas there. Even though she didn't care for Cole, it was almost always the most fun when Christmas was in Logan, Pennsylvania, with the Nashes. The children made it wonderful. Amazing all five could be so special. She'd last seen them in May for a long weekend. The only fly in the ointment was Sara. Dorothy knew the cause for her being overweight was psychological and Cole, bull-headed, wouldn't send her to a therapist. But Anne was trying to help Sara herself. Dorothy hoped she'd see an improvement.

The Nash children were Dorothy's darlings. She really didn't have a favorite. Well, maybe Tom.

Tom, the quintessential perfect son and grandson: handsome, intelligent, mannerly, affectionate, physically healthy, active in sports, charming. What grandmother could ask for more? The truth was that Dorothy prized him above the rest, with Kit running a close second.

Thinking about him, made her all the more eager to see him. This would be a grand Christmas and she wouldn't allow anything to spoil it for her. She'd not told any of her children that she had cancer, that this would be her last Christmas. She was thankful that God had leased her this time, that it was to be spent with her favorites. When the end drew near, she'd take the sleeping pills she'd been saving.

Dorothy Haines Clifford was not going to be a burden to

any of her children; not even for a day. But she'd be darned if she'd think about that now. It was Christmas, a season she'd always loved and she was going to have a good time, no matter what.

Dorothy was shaken. Sitting at the kitchen table with Anne, she listened carefully as her daughter described the events of the past few days. She'd never seen Anne so distraught. And the shock of seeing Tom with black eyes had still not worn off. She also tended to agree with her daughter that this Pancho Sola and his group couldn't be as innocent as Tom pretended.

If there was a Pancho Sola.

The tension in the Nash house was unmistakable, Dorothy'd felt it immediately. She sipped her cold coffee, reached out across the table, covered Anne's cool hand with her own.

"What can I do, darling? How can I help?"

Anne's eyes filled with tears once again. "I don't know. For years I tried to be like you, so calm, putting up with everything and then...."

"And then?"

Anne shook her head, unable to tell her mother she'd realized her way was not so hot.

"And then," Dorothy went on finishing the sentence, "you realized what a failure I'd been."

"Oh, no, Mother."

"Oh, yes. What a fool I was. Imagine, trying to pretend nothing was wrong, smoothing everything over all the time. I should have left him when you were just kids."

Anne was shocked to hear her mother talk this way.

You're surprised? Well, hindsight's a wonderful thing, darling. I was married to a drunk, oh, yes, a nice drunk most of the time, nevertheless a drunk and useless as husband and father. I didn't face the truth. I bent it, shaped it to look the way I wanted it to. For God's sake, don't you do that."

"Meaning?"

"Have you thought about sending the boy to a psychiatrist?"

Anne pushed up the sleeves of her blue sweater. "You know what Cole thinks about psychiatry."

"Do you always do what Cole wants?"

Not lately, Anne thought. "You think I should make an appointment for Tom?"

"You don't believe this cult business, and everything you've told me about him adds up to trouble. All his life, he's been a nice quiet boy and now, suddenly, he's acting in a bizarre fashion. Something's very wrong. Yes, I think you should."

Why did she care what Cole thought, anyway. What difference did it make now? "All right. I will. I'm sure I won't be able to get an appointment until after Christmas."

"Better than nothing. Until then, we'll keep our eyes on him." She smiled, patted Anne's hand.

Her mother was a wonderful looking woman. Anne hoped she'd age as well. The secret was acceptance. Her mother had never fought aging and it showed in the dignity, the inner beauty reflecting in her face.

Dorothy said, "And we'll try and have fun this weekend. Cheer up the young ones. They seem upset."

"They are."

"So let's concentrate on relaxing them. Now what's on the agenda for the rest of today?"

"The tree. Later this afternoon, we're going to buy the tree. You remember the ritual, don't you?"

Dorothy nodded.

As though she hadn't seen the nod, Anne went on. "We all pile in the car and drive out to Penntown, going from one tree seller to another, arguing the merits of the various trees." She began to cry.

"Darling, darling girl," Dorothy rose, went to her daughter. "I know, dear. I know." She put her frail arms around Anne, cradled her head against her bosom.

"No, you don't. You only know half of it, Mother."

"Then tell me. I can take it."

Anne pulled away, looked up at the waiting face. Kind. Serene. "Can you?"

Dorothy nodded.

"I'm going to divorce Cole. I'm in love with someone else." The words, Anne felt, hung between them like shocking colors.

Dorothy stroked Anne's hair. "I can take it, dear. The question is, can you?"

"With your support, I can."

"You have it." Dorothy prayed she'd live long enough to give it.

2.

Originally, the meeting had been called for eleven-thirty in the morning. He'd had to cancel because his grandmother arrived at exactly that hour. Then lunch. They were going tree buying at two-thirty. That left about forty-five minutes for the meeting.

As Tom made his way through the deep snow in the back yard, he hoped SOLA would be understanding about the change in plans. What if SOLA didn't show up?

The old shed was in view now, but there was no way of knowing if anyone was inside. Sometimes things came up. He could explain that to SOLA. Sometimes it might be more dangerous to keep to the original plans. What if Tom had come to the eleven-thirty meeting and someone had looked for him, perhaps found him here with SOLA. Then what? That would've blown everything. Surely SOLA would understand that.

But what if SOLA had been waiting for the last two hours? There'd been no way to notify SOLA of the postponement. Tom began to feel frightened. SOLA would be angry. For sure.

Outside the door to the shed, he stopped a moment, heart pounding. Had to go in. No choice. All right. He'd take whatever SOLA had to hand out.

As he reached for the door handle, it began to move. Already SOLA was making it difficult for him. Each time Tom made a pass at the handle, it moved out of his grasp.

"Please, SOLA," he called out, "please let me in."

A faint growl from inside.

Again Tom tried to open the door; again the handle eluded him.

No point in feeling angry. Did no good when it came to SOLA. Have to wait until SOLA decided to let him in. But time was running out. If he didn't make this meeting at all, there was no telling what SOLA might do.

The window.

Tom turned the corner of the small building and went to the rickety six-paned window. Amazingly, all the glass was intact. It slid up easily but banged shut when he let go. Carefully, he pushed it up again, holding it, putting one leg over the sill, then turning, bringing in his other leg, lowering himself inside. Gingerly, he let the window slide closed.

The roar was deafening.

Tom fell to the floor, his hands over his ears. Even so he could still hear.

GET UP, YOU STUPID SWINE. SOLA COMMANDS YOU. DO AS I SAY, OR YOU SHALL BE DESTROYED IN THE NAME OF SOLUDA.

Everything inside him quavered. Slowly, he raised himself to his knees, opened his eyes.

Everyone was there.

SOLA, blue gown, purple hair flowing, shimmering, stood above Tom, his arms outstretched, pointing up.

Next to him was PRINCE PLUTO. The scarlet of his gown almost too bright to look at. PRINCE PLUTO was much younger than SOLA, had long blond hair. He would have been handsome, almost pretty, if his eye teeth hadn't protruded over his bottom lip, reaching nearly to the end of his chin. PLUTO's eyes flashed orange, purple, yellow, the rays he shot forth stinging Tom's arms.

Tom gasped. It was like being attacked by a jellyfish.

BE QUIET.

SOLA's voice reverberated, shaking the shed's walls.

Tom pursed his lips, clamped his teeth tightly.

On the other side of SOLA was THE EARL OF JUPITER, thin streams of vomit running down his chin and neck. Tom smelled it; his stomach turned over. He mustn't show this. The EARL wore fuchscia.

To his right was THE LORD OF MARS, dressed in the brightest yellow Tom had ever seen. Blood dripped from all his orifices.

Left of PLUTO was THE KNIGHT OF VENUS. The turquoise satin of his robe brilliant, dazzling. Even the pus running from sores on every inch of bared skin could not detract from its splendor.

So they were all assembled.

WHAT IS YOUR EXCUSE?

Tom opened his mouth to speak; nothing came out.

YOU MUST BE PUNISHED.

Yowls, wails, groans of accord from the others.

The sounds burned his eardrums.

THE ORIGINAL PURPOSE OF THIS MEETING SHALL BE POSTPONED. PUNISHMENT SHALL SUPERCEDE. REMOVE YOUR CLOTHING.

Shrieks and grunts.

It couldn't have been more than ten degrees in the shed. Tom's nose and cheeks felt numb from the cold. What would it be like to be naked? Might as well be outside in the snow.

"All of my clothes?" he asked timidly.

ALL. AT ONCE.

There was no mistaking this command. He must undress or be obliterated. He rose as all five clapped in slow, pounding rhythm. Their animal cries accompanied the clapping. Tom tried not to look at them as he removed his clothing, but, as if hypnotized, his eyes fastened on one after another.

The long teeth of PLUTO grew longer, more yellow; green slime dropping from the ends, splashing the floor. His eyes changed colors, continued to send prickling rays shooting into Tom.

Vomit, in great rushes now came from JUPITER, plopping, gurgling. The stench was overwhelming. Tom gagged, retched with dry heaves.

Blood gushed from MARS, covering the shed floor. Tom removed his shoes and socks, and found himself standing in the hot stuff. He didn't mind that smell, found it sweet.

When he was completely naked, his clothes submerged beneath the putrid sea on the floor, he stood facing them, waiting for his punishment.

SOLA grinned, blue eyes wide, blazing. He gestured toward the festering mess at his feet.

ADD YOURS.

Tom knew what he meant. Once again, he was being asked to do it. Oh, how he hated it. He knew how bad, how wrong it was. Why did SOLA want him to do it? Because he knew how much Tom tried not to, of course.

SOLA was smart. HE knew everything, every thought.

Tom, startled, sucked in his breath.

Leering, blood smeared on his face, THE LORD OF MARS fell to his knees in front of Tom. He waggled his long pointed tongue and with his bloody hand lifted Tom's now erect penis to his mouth.

The burning sensation as MARS took Tom full in his mouth made him scream.

He undulated his hips, still crying out, his penis going in and out of the LORD's hot mouth.

Suddenly, Tom jumped.

Something was being shoved hard up his anus. He screamed again. Looking over his shoulder he saw JUPITER, his hand and arm inside Tom. In and out. In and out. He matched his rhythm to that of MARS.

The pain was excruciating; tears ran down Tom's face.

The others joined in and with their hands and tongues they kneeded and licked at his body, burning and scratching, pinching and pulling. He writed with pain. Words began to come from his mouth.

"My cock my cock so big and hard suck it fuck it suck it let me drip with sperm of all mankind I offer it up in the name of SOLUDA cock of SOLA cock of Thomas cock of the walk cock is all."

GOOD BOY, SOLA said.

3.

The lunch crowd had thinned and Jim sat at the bar, sipping a Perrier. Anne hadn't called. He tried to tell himself it meant nothing. After all, it was Saturday. On top of that, her mother arrived today. And wasn't there something about shopping for a Christmas tree?

A knot formed in his stomach. He hated the jealousy he was experiencing.

Yet it was based on something. Reality. It was Christmas time and he was alone, and it hurt.

Brushing an ash from the sleeve of his white cable-knit sweater, he thought, goddamnit to hell, this is a bitch! Maybe he should drive down to Logan, knock on the door. If Cole answered he'd say: "I'm Jim O'Neill and I'm going to marry your wife." Maybe he should just take matters into his own hands. What the hell? Was he going to sit around and mope all day waiting for the phone to ring? He wished he were a drinking man, at least he'd be able to escape into that. But Jim knew alcohol wasn't the answer. He'd had a good friend who tried to solve his problems that way and he was dead now. Like Marilyn.

He was amazed at the lack of pain he felt thinking of her, even though just the word *death* still brought her immediately to mind. Three Christmases without her. This would be the fourth. On Christmas day he'd drive to Doylestown to be with his parents, his sister, brother-in-law and their three kids. But he'd be alone.

Unconsciously, he slammed his fist on the bar.

"What's up?" Bill, the bartender, asked.

"Huh?"

"You uptight about something?"

Uptight. Jim looked at the young man, not a line on the smooth skin, not a care in the blue eyes. What did he know of life? Death? He wanted to lash out at the kid, controlled himself.

"Nothing, Bill, just thinking. Thanks for asking."

"Sure." Bill moved to the other end of the bar and busied himself washing glasses, giving his boss space.

Sitting here made Jim feel impotent. Impotency filled him with rage. Yet he'd promised Anne he'd give her time. He must have patience, trust. She'd call when she could. But he wasn't going to lose her. He wasn't going to spend another Christmas alone. Next year *he'd* take Anne and her family to buy the tree. He knew she loved him and he simply had to wait it out. Things would go in their natural order.

They had to.

Way in the back of his mind, in that far away place, he knew another loss would send him hurtling right over the edge. Continued endurance in the face of frustration was not his strong suit.

Jim O'Neill was fragile.

4.

When Tom had started walking down through the woods in the direction of the old shed, Sara and Steven were outside building an igloo next to the house. They'd been promising to make it for Max for ages and had begun it an hour before. It was going to be a surprise. Rarely did they do anything together anymore. But they were working well with each other and enjoying it. Tom's erratic behavior had brought them closer.

Seeing Tom disappear into the woods, they looked at each other.

Sara spoke first. "What d'ya think?"

Steven shrugged. "I dunno. He looks kinda...watcha call it?"

"Determined?"

"Yeah."

"Where d'ya think he's going? To the shed?"

"Maybe."

They had all, together, separately, played games in the shed as they'd grown up.

"What would he be doing in the shed in the cold?" Steven asked.

"Who knows?" Sara pulled her red plaid scarf tighter around her neck.

Their eyes met. Almost imperceptibly, they smiled. An old feeling of comraderie returned, warming them.

"Want to follow him?" Sara asked, eyes brightening.

Steven nodded.

Slowly they headed toward the woods. They didn't have

to keep Tom in sight. Safer not to. They knew they'd find him in the shed.

Cautiously, Sara and Steven inched themselves up until they could see through the window.

Tom was lying face down on the filthy floor, his hands over his ears.

Sara was frightened and took Steven's mittened hand. He didn't resist.

Slowly Tom raised himself to his knees, his back to the window. Through the glass the children heard his gasp as though he'd seen something horrible. He seemed to be listening to something, someone. He shook his head and nodded, flinched as though being assaulted. Then he spoke.

"All of my clothes?" he asked.

Sara and Steven looked at each other, then quickly back to the window. Tom was rising, his body turned slightly so they had a three-quarter view of him. His eyes were riveted on something they couldn't see. He took off his parka, flung it in a corner. Shocked, the two children watched as their brother removed each piece of clothing, throwing them, one after the other, on the floor until he was naked.

They heard him gag, a hideous sound.

Sara was embarrassed seeing her brother naked but couldn't stop watching. Steven, sensing this, said nothing.

Tom started to jump about, as though he were being attacked, flayed. He looked down at the floor as he danced around the room. Sara and Steven ducked as he turned toward them, then realized he wasn't looking out the window, wouldn't see them. They raised their heads again. Tom's penis was erect and he was pumping it up and down in his hand. He screamed, sending chills through the two frightened children.

They clutched each other.

Steven began to cry.

"Oh, Steven," Sara whispered, "should we get someone?"

He shook his head.

Tom grabbed an old toilet plunger from the corner of the shed. Horrified, they watched as he took the wooden end of the plunger and shoved it up his anus, continuing to masturbate with a frenzy, screaming again.

Sara trembled.

"My cock my cock so big and hard suck it fuck it..."

Sara backed away, pulling Steven with her, hearing the

litany humming within the shed. She couldn't watch or listen to any more.

Propelled by fear, Sara and Steven began to run, stumbling and falling in the snow, tears streaking their faces. When the house came into view, Sara stopped and collapsed in the snow. Steven dropped beside her, crying loudly. She put an arm around him even though she wanted comfort too. She was older. The responsibility to console him came automatically.

"What . . . should . . . we . . . do?" Steven squeezed out the words between sobs.

Sara shook her head. "We can't tell, Steven, never."

"But Sara, he's . . . he's. . . ."

"I know."

It was impossible to say the word. Even to think it was terrifying. Sara had to do what she did best; what she always did with difficult things.

"We have to try not to think of it. Forget it ever happened."

She began to hiccup and to experience the cold wetness of the snow. Pulling Steven up with her, she went on. "Understand, Steven? Forget it. We don't know what it's about." She felt hungry.

"But Sara . . . we got to tell someone . . . I'm scared."

"Who? Who are you gonna tell? Daddy? Mommy? Maybe Grandma? What would you say? Could you describe that?"

Steven imagined telling his father and the iciness of his extremities tuned inward. His mother was out, too. Much too embarrassing. Sara would have to tell her.

"You talk to Mom," he said.

"NO," she shouted. "Just forget it."

"Sara, please, he's. . . ."

She slapped him hard across the face, screamed NO long and loud until she frightened him into submission. When he stopped crying and her hiccups were gone, Sara wiped his face and her own, put an arm around him, insisted they sing as they walked slowly toward the house.

In the kitchen, Anne smiled at her mother as they heard the children approaching.

". . . oh, what fun it is to ride in a one-horse open sleigh."

"Some things are normal, after all," Anne said.

Dorothy gave her daughter a reassuring nod. "Of course they are," she said.

209

5.

Cole drove. Anne and Dorothy shared the front seat with him. In the back seat of the station wagon were Tom and Sara and behind the seat, sitting on the floor, were Steven and Max.

When Anne turned, looking over her shoulder in a habitual way, surveying her brood, she saw Sara squeezed against the door. Immediately, her eye went to the lock, saw it was secure. Even so, it made her nervous.

"Sara, don't lean against the door like that."

"It's locked."

"Please, dear, you never know."

Sara moved infinitessimally.

"Sara, please," Anne warned. The look on Sara's face suddenly registered.

Fear. Of what? "Is something wrong?"

"No."

"Wrong?" Tom said. "What's wrong?"

Anne's eyes darted to Tom. He was wearing dark glasses. Impossible to tell about his mood.

Steven climbed over the seat. "Comin' up," he said.

There was something odd about him, too. A false jocularity. Was that it? Anne watched him settle between Tom and Sara. There was an unusual pallid cast to his skin. Was he sick?

Tom flung his arm across Steven's shoulder. "Got all your Christmas shopping done?" he asked.

Anne couldn't deny what she so clearly saw. Steven flinched. She turned away. Obviously the children hadn't forgotten yesterday. They were still frightened of Tom. Or had something else happened? Oh, it was too unbearable. Whatever was happening would just have to go on hold. Now they were going to buy a tree just like any other family. She almost laughed.

Just like any other family! Except that she sat beside a husband whom she was going to divorce. Except that her eldest son was having a breakdown or something. Except that her other children were terrified of their brother.

Only her mother seemed at all normal. Anne looked sideways over at her mother's hands which lay in her lap. Lovely hands. Tapered fingers, strangely unwrinkled.

Oh, Mama, Anne thought, help me. Carefully, so Cole wouldn't see, Anne inched her hand toward her mother's, slipping it neatly beneath hers. Dorothy didn't turn her head or give Anne away. She squeezed her daughter's cold hand, trying desperately to transmit her love and support. Inside, a helplessness threatened to sink her.

By the time they reached the fourth Christmas tree place, they were all on edge. But this wasn't unusual; it went this way every year.

Cole wanted a short fat tree, as did Max and Sara. Steven begged for a huge tree. Anne was for a medium one, although this year she stayed out of it. She wanted the whole thing over with as soon as possible.

Usually Tom was arbitrator, reiterating the merits of each kind, mediating between the factions. This year, his attention was elsewhere. Although there was a kind of smile on his lips, almost a peaceful look, he contributed very little to the tree discussion. In the end, Anne knew Cole would win. He always did.

"This is the last place," Cole said. "I'm fed up." His eyes iced over, the blue more piercing than usual.

Sara put her arm through her father's and clung to his sleeve. "Oh, Daddy, look at that one."

"Where?"

"There. See, isn't it cute? It's so fat," she said and blushed at the sound of the word.

For once Steven found himself resisting a comment. Just like you. That's what he would have said ordinarily. But the experience they'd shared earlier sealed his lips.

"Mommy," Max said, "are we gonna put the balls on to-night?"

"Yes, darling. After dinner." She squeezed Max's shoulder.

"Won't it be fun?" Dorothy said to Max.

He nodded, grinning. Innocent. The only one.

As they untied the short fat tree from the roof of the car, Anne noticed Cole's agitation, impatience.

He ordered the boys to carry it inside instead of doing it himself as usual, and got back in the car.

"Where are you going, Cole?" Anne asked.

His angry look was unmistakable. "I have to see someone."

"Can I come, Daddy?" asked Sara.

"No."

Anne watched as he drove away, feeling something ominous in his departure.

"Let's get this show on the road," Tom said, lifting one end of the tree. Steven took the other end, Sara and Max grabbed the middle.

Anne opened the front door and the chidren passed through with the tree. When Dorothy was opposite her, they looked at one another. "I feel like I'm dying," Anne said.

6.

"**You** were gonna go off and leave me here," Steven said, glaring at Sara.

"Huh?"

"You asked Daddy if you could go with him."

"Oh, that."

Steven grimaced. "Yeah, that."

"Well, what of it?" Sara stalled, knowing she'd been wrong.

"God sake's, Sara, we need to stick together." Although feeling a bit paranoid, Steven thought he had it somewhat together now and needed to get Sara into line.

He'd smoked a joint fifteen minutes before.

It took everything she had, but she mumbled an apology to her brother and concluded with, "I wasn't thinking."

"Yeah. Look, I got an idea. I think we should call Kit." He sat on Sara's bed, leaned back against the wall.

Sara stiffened. "What for?" Kit was her nemesis. Everything she wasn't.

"Sara, we need help. We got to get Kit to come home sooner."

She would be happy if Kit never came home. The comparison was excruciating. "What can *she* do?"

"I don't know for sure, but I'd feel better if she was here."

"That's dumb."

"No, it isn't."

"Well, how do you think you could get her to come home?"

Steven wet his lips with his tongue. "We have to tell Kit about the shed."

"Are you crazy?" Even the thought made her blush.

"Sara, it's crazy not to. There's no one else we can tell."

"We decided we wouldn't tell *anyone,* Steven. What's wrong with you? We swore. Don't you remember?"

"I remember, but I've been thinking a lot and decided we gotta talk to an older person."

"Since when don't *you* know everything?" she asked, taunting him.

Steven knew he'd been a know-it-all, but the last twenty-four hours had reduced him to feeling he knew, understood nothing. He wanted to cry, but first he had to convince Sara. "Please, Sara. I'm scared. You saw him, heard him, he's crazy. Anything could happen. I mean, who knows what he'll do next?"

She thought for a moment. "But what's telling Kit going to do?"

"I just think if we tell her about what we saw...I mean we don't have to go into every awful detail...she'll come home and maybe she can tell Mom and then maybe Mom will do something."

"Like what?"

He shook his head despairingly. "I don't know. Something."

"Well, why don't we just tell Mom, then?"

"Could *you?*"

"No," Sara said. "But I don't know if I could tell Kit either."

If he had a second joint, he was sure *he* could. "I will."

"When?"

"Now. Well, in a minute. I have to go to the bathroom."

When Steven came back, they went quietly into their parents' bedroom, where the upstairs phone was.

"You stand by the door and tell me if anyone's coming."

While Sara played lookout, Steven went through the red address book on the night table until he found Kit's number.

He dialed.

The phone rang ten times before he gave up.

"We have to keep trying, Sara."

As they left the room, Steven wondered how he'd do it. He couldn't just stay stoned all day. Someone would notice. Goddamn, he thought, I might have to do it straight. He hoped he'd be able to.

7.

Jim was checking the yellow and white flowers on the tables when he heard someone in the second dining room. He went in to see. A man. No one he'd ever seen before.

"I'm sorry," he said, "the dining room won't be open until five. The bar's open, of course."

"Are you Jim O'Neill?"

"Yes." Instantly, Jim knew who it was and was surprised at his lack of anxiety.

"I'm Cole Nash." He waited for his name to register and was disappointed when he saw nothing on the man's face. It angered him. "It's my wife you've been screwing."

Jim couldn't control the blink of his eyelids. How dare Cole put it that way. "That's not true," he said, trying to sound calm.

"Don't bother, O'Neill. I know everything." He played with a button on his sheepskin jacket.

"What's everything?"

Cole narrowed his eyes, reaching for a tough effect, not a role that suited him. The best he could do was imitate what he'd seen in the movies. "Let's not play games," he said.

Part of Jim wanted to toss the guy out. But he knew Nash had rights. He would've done the same thing. Still, it made him angry. From what Anne had said, he wouldn't have expected Nash to care.

"What do you want?" he asked Cole.

"I want you to tell me what's going on." He lit a cigarette, belligerently dropped the match on the floor.

Jim watched, debated whether to rise to the bait. The verbal challenge was enough, he decided. "I thought you knew everything."

"What are your plans?"

Jim couldn't help smiling. "Is that like, what are my intentions? Honorable or not?"

"You think this is funny?"

"No. I don't."

Now that the shock of Cole Nash's appearing had waned, Jim took in the whole of the man who stood so angrily in front of him. Not a bad looking guy, tall, well-built. But something in his eyes put you off. They had no depth.

"Look, Nash, I don't know what you want me to say, but if you want to know if I'm in love with Anne, I am. If you want to know if I want her to leave you and marry me, the answer is yes. Okay?"

"Is that what she's going to do?" She wouldn't! It was enraging even to consider. The arrogance of it. The gall.

"You'll have to ask her." Unconsciously, Jim tucked his thumbs under his brown leather belt.

"I'm asking you, buster."

Buster! Right out of some grade-B movie. Suppressing his laughter, he said, "I can't speak for her."

"Have you asked her to leave me?"

"Yes."

Cole's lips formed a small defiant smile. What a fool this bastard was. Anne wasn't going anywhere.

"She'll never leave me. You don't know her."

There was nothing Jim could say. The man had hit on his worst fear. Still, Cole must feel threatened or he wouldn't have come. "Why are you here?" Jim asked. "What do you want?"

"I just wanted to see for myself. And now that I've seen, I'm sure." The smile was open now, secure.

A low blow. "Then you can get the hell out."

Cole dropped his cigarette on the floor, ground it out with his heel. "Gladly."

Standing his ground, Jim waited until he heard the heavy front door slam shut. Then walked to a window where he could see and not be seen, watched until the car drove from the lot, down the road. He shook with anger and fear.

He had to call Anne.

One of the children answered. It seemed like hours before Anne came to the phone.

"Why are you calling?" She sounded frightened. "He might have answered."

"No. I knew he wouldn't. He just left here."

Her silence didn't surprise him. He hadn't said it that way for shock value; he just couldn't think of any other way to say it. Listening to her breathe was like hearing her fear.

"Darling, don't worry. There's nothing to be afraid of," he lied.

"I didn't know he knew. What did he say?"

Jim filled her in, down playing Cole's anger.

"What should I do, Jim?"

"I have a feeling he's not planning to confront you. He doesn't think you'll leave him. If you don't want to say anything until after Christmas, I think you can still maintain that. Of course, I wish you'd jump in the car and bring all the kids and your mother here right now."

"I wish I could."

"You can."

"I can't, Jim. Things have gotten a lot worse. There's something really wrong with Tom. We're taking him to a psychiatrist on Monday."

"You could do that from here."

"Please, Jim. Don't push."

"I'm sorry." Selfish. "You're right. You've got to do it your way."

He didn't want to frighten her. And perhaps his fear was just a convenient excuse for him to push her to leave Cole now. Was he overreacting? Concocting the fear out of selfishness? What, exactly, was he afraid of?

"I'll come to you as soon as I can, Jim. I need Kit here, I guess. I need her help and support as well as my mother's. Do you think I'm awfully weak?"

"Human," he said. "Please know I'm here and loving you and willing to do almost anything you want. Do you know that, Anne? I mean if it gets to be too much."

"I know, I really do."

When he hung up, the unidentifiable fear continued to gnaw at him, finally began to take shape. Was he making it up? No. There was definitely something about Cole Nash that smelled of violence. Was it possible he was one of these guys who could go off the deep end and.... The thought was too painful to confront, but clung onto him, made him uneasy. How in God's name was he going to last through these next days without going to Logan to check?

What the hell. If Cole Nash could come here, he could damn well go there!

217

8.

Jennifer didn't tell her mother that Tom had had some sort of fit in school the day before. According to some of the kids who'd been there when it hapened, it was really creepy. Everyone was sure it was connected with the blow to his face from the basketball.

She wasn't so sure.

And neither was Jane Galloway.

"You have to face it, Jen. He's gotten to be a weirdo or something. Thank God you didn't want to have his baby or some dumb thing. Jeez." Jane rolled her brown eyes at Jennifer, her plump cheeks reddened by the cold they'd just left outside.

They sat in Jennifer's basement, listening to Porter Yates and The Truckers wail on about life being a drag unless you were stoned.

"Speaking of that, I can't spend Sunday night at your house."

"Why not?"

"He wants to see me."

"So what?"

"He says it's important."

"Listen, Jen, you have to get rid of him. Never mind Sunday night. I mean, before that."

"But, Jane, if I do, I won't have a date for the dance or your party. I mean, I'll just be dead for the holidays."

"Yeah, that's right. It's awful late. Maybe I could ask Bill Martin to take you."

"Are you kidding?"

"Sorry. Well, I see your predic. But you just have to come over Sunday. We have to plan."

218

Jennifer knew there really wasn't anything to plan. It was all arranged. What they would do on Sunday night was just go over it. Say it out loud once again. But she needed Jane's comfort. The truth was she was scared to death. What if something went wrong? She wished her mother were someone she could talk to. Like Tom's mother. He'd told her his mother was a pal. Jennifer knew if she told her mother about her pregnancy, she'd get hysterical. Punish her. And if she told her about Tom's craziness lately, she'd forbid Jennifer to go out with him.

"You hear me, Jen?"

"I don't know what to do."

"Well, I say get out of Sunday night."

"All right." Why was she such a chameleon, mimicking whoever she was with? Jane said skip Sunday, she said yes.

But what would she do if Tom insisted?

She'd go along.

Wouldn't she?

9.

They'd decided it would be awful to have a live tree, one that would be alone to wilt and die. They'd bought a small, artificial one instead. Kit made popcorn and bought cranberries. They trimmed it in the old-fashioned manner. But first a special dinner: steak, artichokes, watercress salad, brownies. With dinner, a bottle of not terribly good champagne. Then Noj read to her. A favorite story, one her mother used to read at Christmas when Kit was a child. O'Henry's "The Gift of the Magi." Would she make the kind of sacrifices there were in the story? For Noj? Was that really love?

They sat together on the old brocade loveseat they'd bought for twenty dollars at an auction. Holding hands, they stared at the tree, popcorn and cranberries lovingly strung over the vinyl branches. The voices of the Mormon Tabernacle Choir issued from twin walnut speakers, filling the room.

Noj nuzzled her neck, breath warm, sweet. What she wanted to do, this moment, was call her mother and check up. But that would bug Noj and alarm her mother.

When would she start doing things for Kit? She thought of Dr. Bell.

"Okay, what is it?" Noj asked.

She looked at him. "Huh?"

He pressed his lips together. "Don't pretend you don't know what I mean. Let's not play games. Something's upset you. I can feel it. Talk."

His staccato pace was irritating her. Inherent in it was a demand. Uncalled for, she felt.

"You want to go home, don't you?"

No use lying. He knew her too well.

"Yes," she whispered.

"I think you should. There's no point in this."

Turning toward him, she touched his cheek. "I know how disappointed you are."

"True. But what the hell, babe, it's either my disappointment or your resentment."

"And my anxiety," she added.

He squeezed her arm in agreement. "When?"

"Tomorrow." She knew he was thinking about the party with his professor. "Night," she amended, hating herself for capitulating this way. So it was a compromise. So what? "If I leave around seven, I'll get there about one. I'll be all packed and go directly from the party."

Noj bit at his lower lip, a frown forming between his brows. "What?" she asked.

"It worries me to think of you driving alone at night."

"Oh, for Christ's sake!" Aggravated, she pulled away, and busied herself rolling up the sleeve of her silk blouse.

"Is it so out of line for me to worry about you?"

She threw up her hands in a gesture of helplessness, then slapped them down onto her thighs. "I'd rather leave in the morning, Noj, in the daylight, but I'm staying to go to your damn party because I know it's important to you."

"The hell with the party. Go in the morning." He stood up, went to the stereo, turned it off.

Now what? She shouldn't have said that about the party. It put her in a no-win situation. "You're sulking."

"No, I'm not." He turned around, gave her a fake smile.

"You know you want me to go to the party with you," she said.

"Of course I do. What's wrong with that?"

"Nothing." She patted the empty seat.

"Exactly." He joined her again. "Look, Kit, just because I want you to stay doesn't mean I get what I want. You want to go home, you go. I'll survive."

She could have killed him. Instead, she ran a hand over his hair. "I want to go to the party with you, Noj. I'll be all right driving at night. It's no big deal. I've done it in the past."

"Are you sure?"

"Yes. I won't tell the family I'm coming then. They'd worry. It's better if I just arrive."

"I have a dexie you can take before the trip."

"Fine." She wouldn't take it. Drugs scared her.

Noj put an arm around her shoulders. "I don't want you leaving later than seven."

"I won't."

He kissed her. The phone rang and Kit tried to pull away. "Noj please."

"Forget it," he said.

"I can't." She pulled out of his embrace, but when she reached the phone, it was dead.

"Damnit," she said. "It could have been important."

"If it is, they'll call back." He held out his arms.

"Maybe it was my family." Absently, she sat back down.

"Oh, come on, Kit. Drop it."

"But maybe it was."

"If it was and it's important, they'll call back."

"I guess." He was right. She was being neurotic.

10.

Dinner passed without incident. Cole still hadn't mentioned his meeting with Jim. There'd been no opportunity. Anne would bring it up later, when they were alone, when they were done with the tree.

Christmas music played on the radio.

"...later on, we'll conspire..." Julius LaRosa crooned.

And Steven and Sara sang, "...later on we'll *perspire* as we dream by the fire..." Collapsing in giggles.

Anne, catching her mother's eye, smiled across the room. For a moment, she could pretend all was normal. She clung to these rare moments like a drowning women, which she was. Cole plugged in the tree lights. The hanging of the balls and other ornaments could begin.

Tom was in his room dressing for the dance. The atmosphere downstairs was more relaxed than it had been all day.

"Let Max put on the first ball," Sara said.

"Good idea," said Anne. "C'mon, darling, pick one."

Max chose a shiny green one, hanging it on the lowest branch.

The others applauded, then picked their own ornaments to hang.

When they were both on the back side of the tree, Steven whispered to Sara, "What'll we do if we don't get another chance to call tonight?"

"Try tomorrow, I guess."

They had tried twice more. Once just before the tree trimming had begun. Each time, Steven had had a few tokes to give him courage. He was flying pretty high now, but the general excitement was covering it. "I hope tomorrow's not too late."

222

"What's that mean?" Sara asked, eyes wide.

"I don't know," he said and giggled.

"What's so funny?" Anne asked.

"Nothing," they said in unison.

When Tom came down he said, "Let me hang one on the tree, so I'm part of it."

Anne looked at her son. With the exception of the black eyes he appeared normal. The blue velour shirt from L. L. Bean matched his eyes; his jeans were clean, neat. He'd washed and combed his hair, as always. Could she be wrong? Maybe everything was going to be all right after all. Then she remembered Esther's panic. The talk of Soluda and Pancho Sola. The fear on her children's faces.

C'mon, Cookie, he's a mess and you know it. This is an isolated moment. Whatever is happening to him, he goes in and out of it. They watched as Tom hung a wooden drum. Anne noticed the other children stayed away from him, pulling back as he passed near them.

"There," he said, still smiling, turning to face them. "Now it's my tree, too. Well, I'm off."

"I'll walk you to the door," said Anne.

"Good."

As they headed for the foyer, he put his arm around her waist. "G'night all."

They said goodnight.

"Whoops." Tom let go of his mother, returned to Dorothy. "It's not every night I get to kiss my grandmother goodnight."

He planted a firm kiss on her cheek, squeezed her shoulders. "Have a good night, sweetheart."

"You, too," Dorothy said, eyes slightly misty.

Cole said, "Take it easy driving, Tom."

"Sure thing."

Oh, God, Anne thought, it's all right out of a forties movie. Perfect. And just as unreal as they were.

In the foyer, she watched as Tom put on his parka, scarf, headband, gloves.

"Tom," she said cautiously, "are you feeling all right?"

"Sure, Mom, why do you ask?"

She gently touched the blue-purple flesh around his eyes. But it really wasn't why she worried.

"Oh, those. Don't worry. I'm fine. Go on back and trim the tree. Have fun. I'm going to."

His smile made everything seem right again. He kissed her cheek. "I love you, Mom."

"I love you, too." She kissed him back and he was gone. Was it irresponsible to let him go out? Why hadn't she said no?

Cookie, you *know* why.

Fear. Afraid of his reaction. Afraid of what he might say or do if thwarted. Oh, yeah, right out of a forties movie!

11.

Tom had begged SOLA to let him get through the dance without an episode. So far, so good. A few kids might be avoiding him, but most had either forgotten his so-called fit or didn't care. After all, he was still president of the senior class and captain of the basketball team.

Jennifer seemed odd, though. Or something. Usually she wanted lots of physical contact, but tonight she was really staying away—or was it his imagination? Never mind. He was grateful. He had no desire to touch her.

Tom was a terrific dancer. Especially when he did the Hustle, but tonight would be the last night he'd ever dance this or any other dance. SOLA said there wasn't time for dancing. Under the rule of SOLUDA, dancing would be outlawed.

So Tom gave the Luxo, a new dance, his all, and tried hard not to notice that Jennifer's body was outlined in bright orange. Ignored the fact that everything in the gym was in motion—tables, chairs, bleachers, decorations, even the twelve-foot Christmas tree. Paid no attention to the fact that all the guys in the band were covered in a phosphorescent pink haze.

He just kept dancing. And he was as good as ever. He knew this by the applause when the dance was over. It didn't matter what he saw or heard. He could control things now.

He was gaining a kind of power he'd never had before, never anticipated. SOLA was being very good to him.

He wasn't going to go over the edge tonight. Nothing was going to tip his hand or jeopardize K-Day.

Jane Galloway's party was a shambles. Her parents weren't home: out on a party of their own. Booze and drugs were in plentiful supply. Everyone was stoned. Everyone but Tom and Jennifer.

Tom didn't need anything, didn't approve. He told Jennifer that as long as she was with him, he wouldn't permit her to get high. She said he was a chauvinist pig. He said he was being sensible. The truth was he didn't give a damn what she did. But if he brought her home high, it was possible the Wheelers might be mad, refuse to let her go out with him the next night.

Then he couldn't end Jennifer's life. He would anger SOLA. Ruin the schedule.

After about an hour, Tom and Jennifer left the party. When they pulled up in front of Jennifer's house, she was sitting against the door on her side, sulking. They'd said nothing all the way home. He could have killed her. But not yet.

He tried not to let her orange glow hurt his eyes. It was important to appease her. She couldn't break tomorrow's date.

"It's because I love you, Jen," he said softly.

"But *everyone* was doing it." She stared straight ahead.

"Why do you always want to be a sheep?"

"Oh, Tom, you sound like somebody's mother. Sometimes I wonder how you ever got to be so popular. You're such a nerd."

"Thanks."

"Well, you are. God!"

"There are things you don't understand, Jennifer."

She looked at him. He was staring straight ahead through the windshield. His voice sounded peculiar. Maybe Jane was right. Maybe she should dump him. New Year's Eve wasn't everything.

"About tomorrow night, Tom," she began.

His head snapped around to face her, eyes narrowed, and Jennifer was chilled by his look.

"We're on, aren't we?"

She knew she mustn't break the date now. Let him think

225

what he wanted. She'd never felt so scared. "Sure we're on. I just wondered what time."

"Eight-thirty. My parents are having some neighbors over and I have to hang around for awhile. Okay?"

"Sure," she said.

"Good." Maybe he should kill her now. But there'd be an investigation. He'd be the last to have seen her alive, the likeliest suspect. He might be questioned, detained, even caught. No way he could choke the life out of this bitch tonight.

"Honey, I have to go in," said Jennifer. She desperately wanted to get away from him.

"Okay."

They kissed, though each one felt nauseated from the contact. Jennifer got out of the car.

"See you tomorrow night," he said.

"Right." She ran up the path to her door. Not for a million dollars, she thought. No way.

Tom drove off. No matter what happened she would not elude him on K-Day. He was determined. There was nothing she could do, nothing at all, to escape her execution.

Power was his.

12.

"You're a goddamned slut," Cole said.

Anne sat on the edge of the bed. "Please lower your voice, Cole. I don't want to wake Mother." The guest room was adjacent to theirs.

"I'll bet you don't," he spat. "Maybe I should just tell her. Maybe I should just walk right in there and tell her what her favorite daughter is."

Tired, Anne said, "Oh, don't be so prosaic."

"You're really something." Straddling a chair, he stretched out his legs, arms crossed on the back. He was enjoying this. He didn't really give a damn what she did. But playing the role was fun. Nothing hurt.

"Why did you go see Jim?" It was strange talking to Cole about Jim.

"You've got to be kidding. Don't I have any rights?"

"No, you don't. Not any more, Cole." Her mouth felt dry.

"You in love with this guy?" Things weren't going the way he'd planned. Anne wasn't frightened, threatened.

"Yes." So there it was. Now, she'd have to speak of divorce. So much for waiting until after the holidays. If he decided to leave before Christmas, she and her mother would manage somehow.

Her answer wasn't a surprise to Cole. He'd guessed as much. Anne wasn't the type to have an affair. Nevertheless, he felt compelled to go on with the charade of outraged husband. He was always playing some role lately. Anything but the real Cole Nash. Whoever *he* was.

Cole pushed up the sleeves of his maroon sweatshirt. "Are you planning to divorce me?"

She took a deep breath. "Yes."

"And when had you thought you'd let me in on your little secret?"

"I was planning to wait until after Christmas."

Great. Just great. He would've been gone. Now what? Was there any point in going through all that trouble?

"I thought it'd be best to try and get through Christmas. For the sake of the children."

He nodded, thinking not of his children but of his escape plans.

"I still think it's best," she said, staring at a worn place in the flowered carpet she'd never noticed before.

Alimony. Good reason to stick to his plans. "You going to marry this joker?" A muscle jumped in his cheek.

"Yes." It was the first time she'd let herself be sure. A kind of calm spread through her. She supposed it was relief.

If she married O'Neill, there wouldn't be alimony. What about child support? Yes. Better disappear. Wait. He began to smile.

"Why are you smiling?"

"Because you're so absurd." Hardly the reason. If he disappeared, she wouldn't be able to marry O'Neill for seven years. Not until Cole was declared legally dead. He could've laughed out loud. The last laugh.

"You're up to something," she said, worried.

"Like what?"

"I don't know. Would you contest the divorce?"

"No."

She was weary, wanted sleep. "All right, Cole. I don't know what you're up to and I don't care."

"I'm up to nothing." You'll care, he thought.

"Do you agree not to say anything to the children until after the holidays?"

"Sure." By Monday afternoon, he'd be gone.

"Can we live civilly until then? I'd prefer we slept in the same room until we tell them."

"Fine." Rising, he walked to the bureau for a pair of fresh pajamas. Should he have given her a harder time? Called her some more names? Knocked her around a bit maybe? No. He'd played it just right. It was best the way he had it planned. Let her think he was going to be reasonable. Then sock it to her with his vanishing act. The bitch.

Anne wondered what Cole had in store for her. It couldn't be so easy, but she was too tired to try and second-guess him. As long as he was willing to get through the holidays quietly, peacefully. That was the main thing. Tomorrow they'd try to have a normal day. Tomorrow night they'd have their Christmas with Esther and George. That was as much as she could deal with right now.

The front door slammed. She listened as Tom came up the stairs and into his room. Her last piece of tension dissolved. Now that Tom was home, everyone was safe.

13.

Tom's headache was blinding.

He sat on the floor in the middle of his room. The last night he would do this. By this time tomorrow night the killing would almost be over. Only a little more than twenty-four hours before he became Duke.

And then he'd be allowed to sleep again.

Tonight he'd pray to SOLA for the necessary strength to carry out His will. It was after midnight. K-Day was here. Beginning.

Sunday,
December 22

1.

"Who are you calling?" Anne asked.

Sara had looked away from the door for only a moment.

Steven, startled, guilty, quickly replaced the phone in its cradle, but not before he heard Kit say, "Hello, hello?"

"Steven? Did you hear me?"

"Yes, Mom." God's sake. What now?

"Who are you calling? Why do you look so guilty? Both of you."

Steve couldn't think, he was so stoned.

"Oh, Mom," Sara said. "It's Christmas time. You shouldn't be asking questions." Sara felt proud of her quick thinking.

Anne hesitated a moment, and then said, "The Durhams are here. Will you come down soon?"

"Just gotta take care of something," Steven said, confident now.

"All right," said Anne, smiling. "Better late than never."

When she was gone, Sara and Steven looked at each other and sighed.

Steven said, "She answered. We got her." He dialed again, but this time the phone rang and no one answered.

"I don't believe it," he said.

"Oh, Steven."

"She's gone out."

"What now?"

He put down the phone. Shook his head. "We'll try whenever we can. But she's probably out for the night. Won't be home until late."

"So we'll try again tomorrow."

"What for? Isn't she leaving tomorrow?"

"Oh, yes," came Sara's reply. "I guess if we don't get her later, that's it. Should we tell Mom, then?"

"Nah. It'll work out the way it should. Tom's going out tonight. Kit'll be home tomorrow evening for sure. It'll be all right."

They left the bedroom, patting each other for reassurance. Both showing a brave face. Both scared.

2.

Kit looked gorgeous. She wore black velvet pants, a white silk blouse with long puffy sleeves, black crepe scarf tied once around her throat, the two long ends trailing down over her breasts to her waist.

Professor Block wasn't the only man in the room who couldn't take his eyes off her. Noj had ambivalent feelings about this. He was proud, but it also pissed him off. She could never go anywhere without the lascivious attention of men.

"What can you expect when you look like that?" he'd said to her.

"And what should I do about it? Pull my hair back in a bun, put on thick-lensed glasses, wear hideous army-navy surplus stuff? Why should I have to look rotten when I like nice things? Why is it my responsibility to keep the hounds away?"

He knew she was right. Yet, sometimes, he found himself wishing she wouldn't wear certain clothes. Tonight he'd wanted her to look good. Block was his most important professor and Noj knew he liked the ladies. He wasn't sure exactly how Kit's looking beautiful would affect his relationship with Block, but he felt it couldn't hurt. And in knowing that, he was ashamed. Almost like being a pimp.

Looking across the room, he watched as Adam Block made

his way toward Kit, who was talking to three male graduate students. Block joined the group; within moments, the others drifted away. Would Block try and make a date with her? What would she do? Kit wasn't against seeing older men; she'd told Noj all about the Mancinelli affair. His gut turned over as he watched her laugh at something Block said.

Kit was shocked when Professor Block asked if he could see her after the holidays. She was also not interested. He was an extremely handsome man, sexual, charismatic, but she wasn't even tempted. In that instant, she knew how much she loved Noj.

"I'm flattered," she said, "but I'm very involved."

"With Noj Hampton?" Block asked.

"Yes."

"Lucky man." Block touched the gray hair at his temple, smiled ruefully.

"I'm the lucky one." She looked at her watch. Six forty-five.

"Going somewhere?"

"Yes. I'm leaving for home. Logan, Pennsylvania. As a matter of fact, if you don't mind, I'm going to use your bedroom to change into my driving clothes." She put down her drink, adjusted the black scarf, evening the ends.

"Can I come?"

"To Logan?"

"To the bedroom."

"Only if you bring Mrs. Block." She smiled, walked away.

Block watched her go. She was unreal. He hadn't wanted anyone so much for ages. He'd have to remember to give Hampton a hard time next term. Just for the hell of it.

Sitting in the dark in Kit's car, Noj held her tightly, not wanting her to leave. They kissed, his tongue deep in her mouth. Only Noj was aroused. Kit was anxious to go, already ten minutes off schedule. Besides, the hang up phone call she'd received right before leaving for the party had disturbed her. She found it ominous. Nevertheless, Kit wanted to be on her way.

"Noj." She began to extricate herself.

"I love you," he said.

"Me, too."

"What did Block want?" he whispered in her ear.

"Nothing," she lied.

"You interested in him?"

She pushed him away. "Of course not."

234

"I saw the way you looked at him."

"Oh Christ, Noj, is this the way you're going to send me off?"

"Can you deny that you were flirting?"

"Yes, I can. I have to leave. It's getting late." She felt completely joyless.

"Why are you running from this conversation?"

She shook her head. "Oh, Noj, please. You'll kill us if you don't get over your jealousy. I'll tell you the truth. He asked to see me and...."

"I knew it." He slammed the dashboard with his palm.

"Wait. I told him no. I told him I was very involved with you."

"The fucker." He hit it again.

"You're not listening, Noj. Damnit, you don't care what I said or did, do you?"

He was spinning out of control. "You led him on, didn't you?"

"Get out, Noj. I have to go."

"Why the hell do you have to try and turn on every man you meet?"

"Get out," she said tersely.

He stared at her, eyes going cold. "You make me sick." He opened the car door, jumped out, slammed it shut.

"Thanks," she said to the empty seat.

Driving away, she didn't look back. Noj was just using this thing with Block. He didn't want her to leave. Couldn't bear to part nicely. Maybe he'd miss her too much. Good God! She didn't have to go all the way to Vienna to figure that one out! The hell with him. She was going to concentrate on the trip, getting home safely.

She switched on the radio. *I'll Be Home for Christmas* floated into the car. Kit hummed along with the music, then sang the words.

She felt better already.

3.

Anne knew it had taken courage for the Durhams to come over tonight. She probably should have let them off the hook. But that hadn't even occurred to her until she looked at Esther sitting on the couch with her mother, still in a state of shock. The pallor of her skin a blue-white, usually bright, eyes now dim, mouth twitching slightly at the corners, the ever-present smile gone. Anne could have wept, knowing the cause.

She looked over at George, seemingly comfortable in the rose wingback chair. He was a stocky man, recently heading toward paunchiness. His skin was a rusty color, treated by the elements. The fringe of hair he still had was brown, with no gray. George's eyes were brown, heavily hooded. His nose, short and stubby, centered over deep red lips, the color of his flannel shirt. He had old man ears, long and flappy, tufts of dark hair poking from the earholes. Taking his face as a whole, it looked as though it were cracking, the lines so deeply etched. He was intent on keeping up a facade tonight, laughing and joking with Cole and the younger children.

They had exchanged presents and Tom seemed his old self; charming, witty, grateful for the shirts he received from Esther and George. There'd been one awkward moment when George forgot the true state of affairs, slipped automatically into old banter.

"Hope you like those shirts, boy. I tried to persuade Esther to get a target gun, but she said, 'not on your life.'"

The words hung in the air, clanging against each other. George's face drained of blood when he realized what he'd said. But Tom broke the tension.

"No offense, George, but I'd rather have these terrific shirts any day." Sweet smile cutting through everything.

Anne could see in Esther's eyes what she herself thought. Could the whole gun incident have been misinterpreted? But it *had* happened. No denying it. Yet for the last twenty-four hours, Tom seemed so normal. Perhaps whatever it was, was over.

"So, Cole, should we make an ice fishing date over the holiday?" George asked, pulling on an earlobe.

"Sounds good." Cole dipped his hand into a bowl of nuts.

"You taking the twenty-sixth and twenty-seventh?"

"Yes."

"Good. How about Friday then?"

"Fine." Cole sipped his eggnog, trying not to smile. He'd be long gone by then, soaking up sun instead of trudging through snow with this old fart. Looking at George made him think of his own parents. Until now he hadn't really considered that he'd never see them again. Trying to dredge up some feeling about his loss, he came up empty.

But the loss of his children was different. It had taken him by surprise. To never see their sweet faces again. How could he have thought he wouldn't care? Sometimes he felt he didn't know himself at all. Sad to miss how they'd change, grow, become people. But it was him or them, and if he stayed, he felt he'd die. He had nothing left to give them.

Again he thought of Stuart and Clara. Father and Mother. Stranger and Stranger. All these years he'd tried to get their attention, failed, and now he was leaving. Would they notice that he was gone? He knew the answer. Barely. Acceptance was his at last.

Tom had gone upstairs, changed into one of his new shirts. Thin brown and green stripes, two buttons on the cuffs. Underneath a dark green turtleneck. His brown corduroy jeans were neatly pressed, his Frye boots shined.

"Well, don't you look nice," Dorothy said. She'd yet to see any of Tom's odd behavior. She could take him at face value. The darling boy she'd always known.

"This is a super shirt, Esther. Thanks again." Smiling at her, Tom felt overwhelmed by the aqua light which shone from a band around her head. He wondered if it was a signal that he should spare her. SOLA would make it clear when the time came.

"Glad you like it," Esther said, in a small voice. She hoped Tom wouldn't touch or kiss her.

237

"Got a heavy date, huh?" George asked, winking.

Tom winked back. Give him what he wanted. Normal. Nice.

"Is it still that sweet girl, Jennifer?" Dorothy asked.

"That's her." His grandmother had three eyes. All were moving. He said a silent prayer to SOLA, asking him to hold off on all this. After all, he had to drive.

"Are we going to see Jennifer this Christmas?" Anne wondered if the girl had noticed a change in Tom. Maybe she should give her a call in the morning.

Tom smiled. "Sure. She'll be over Christmas day." In her coffin, he thought.

"Where are you going tonight? Party?" Anne asked.

He shook his head. "Movies. The Cameo is playing *The Rocky Horror Show* early tonight."

"I thought you saw that," Steven said.

"Twenty-two times," Tom answered proudly.

There was general laughter, and Dorothy said, "I can't imagine seeing a movie twenty-two times."

And you never will, thought Tom. "Well, it's the way *we* do it. I got to be going."

Methodically, like the good boy he'd always been, he went around the room, shaking hands, kissing, saying goodnight.

4.

For the first time since he'd opened the Inn, Jim wished he served on Sunday nights. It would've taken his mind off his problems. But the customers would be all gone by now, anyway. They dined early on Sunday nights in Pennsylvania. Besides, it was beginning to snow. Heavy, small flakes. And from his window above the dining room, Jim watched as they began to cling to the pavement.

Lighting a cigarette, he sat near the window, watching the snowfall's soothing rhythm. Anne had called early that morning, telling him Cole had confronted her. She'd told Cole she was finished, but they'd decided to go on as usual until the holidays were over. Jim supposed it was the right thing, under the circumstances. All his reasons for thinking Anne should kick Cole out now were selfish. It was easy for him. After all, what did he know about kids?

Jesus! He was going to be stepfather to five! Well, the older two wouldn't be a problem. Tom would be at college, and Kit was a grown woman. But what about the three younger ones? No point in worrying about that now. Enough to worry about. Oh, yeah? Like what? What in hell did he have to worry about?

Jim stubbed out his cigarette. Anne had told Cole the truth. The guy had accepted it. Still Jim was uneasy. He couldn't shake a feeling of impending doom. Nonsense. Still, every moment that ticked by made him more anxious.

Anne had promised to call again when everyone was in bed. Only then would he feel calmer.

There were hours to go.

5.

Tom turned the car into the Durham driveway, flicked off the lights, killed the motor. He walked the short distance to the back of the house. Snow had begun to fall. He was glad the footprints and tire tracks would be covered.

Framing the back door were small panes of glass about half a foot wide and a foot long. With his gloved fist, he broke the pane level with the doorknob. Carefully, he picked out the remaining shards, reached through, turning the knob to open the door. The Durhams had left on the lights. As always.

Snow melted from Tom's shoes onto the brick kitchen floor. He crossed the room to the gun case, reached for the handle. It was locked.

Tom heard SOLA growl.

"Don't worry," he said and picked up the poker from beside the firepace. Standing well back, he smashed the glass, returned the poker to its place.

There were many guns to choose from. At the top were rifles. Three. Two unwieldy. Below these were the pistols. George had been collecting them for years. All the way back to the First World War. There was an early Colt .45, its long barrel a gray-green, the handle brown wood. Tom rejected it as fragile.

Next to it was a more solid-looking gun. George had often lectured him about the various guns, despite Esther's objections. He knew this was a Browning FN. A British automatic used in the Second World War. It was the gun for him. He guessed he'd known it all along. Carefully, he lifted it from its place, surprised by its weight as the nose dipped downward. George had said it weighed two pounds, but it seemed heavier.

Gripping it properly, a thrill shot through him. The butt felt good in his hand. He set it on the counter, opened the drawer below the case. Ammunition was stored neatly, box after box, clearly marked. In a moment, he found the 9mm cartridges meant for the Browning. There were two full boxes. The beauty of the Browning was that it took 13 cartridges in a magazine, more than twice as much as the average automatic. Tom removed the magazine, loaded it, slammed it back into the butt. The rest of the ammunition he shoved in his deep parka pockets. He stuck the gun into his waistband, under his belt, and left the house.

Outside, he abandoned his original plan to cut the phone wires. It would be unfortunate if the phone were reported out of order too early. Plenty of time to cut them later. At the end of the driveway, he turned the car left and headed toward the Wheelers'.

No matter that Jennifer had called earlier and broken their date. He didn't need a date to kill her. He wondered who else would be at her house. He hoped her parents didn't have company because then he'd have to kill them all.

6.

Noj sat in his car, motor running. Ass. Unbelievable that he'd behaved the way he had. Stupid. Childish. Just because she was leaving, something he'd known about for a long time. Of course, she left twelve hours or so before the time she'd originally planned, but was he really such an infant?

Good Christ, what kind of a therapist was he going to make if he behaved like this, and was his ego so delicate that he couldn't take the slightest competition? Besides, she wasn't even interested in Block.

Dr. Safier had told him to get used to this if he was going to be involved with a woman who looked like Kit. Men were bound to be attracted. Some would try to take her away from him. What was important, Safier had said, was how he and Kit handled it.

Well, he sure had handled it, all right!

Now what? He wouldn't be able to speak with her until tomorrow afternoon. It wouldn't be fair to wake her in the morning. She wouldn't even get home until one or two. He had a better solution. He'd drive to Logan. Kit had a half hour start on him. Even if he stopped back at the apartment, maybe he could catch up with her.

Pulling away from the curb, he smiled. No matter when he arrived, it would be a gesture she couldn't ignore. He'd only stay until morning, not wanting to interfere with her family, then drive on to New York and out to Southold, Long Island, where his family waited for him.

Or maybe Kit would ask him to stay another day. His family didn't expect him until the twenty-fourth anyway. It would be fun to spend the day with the Nashes. Besides, he'd like to hear about Tom's cult activities firsthand.

It was a terrific decision.

7.

Cruising by the Wheeler house, Tom breathed a sign of relief. No extra cars in front. The family was alone. He parked the car on Orchard Street, around the corner. The gun was tucked securely in his pants, under his parka, as he walked the two blocks.

Snow collected on his hair and shoulders. He blinked flakes from his lashes. The doorbell glowed pink, then green. It tried to move away from his forefinger. At last he managed to pin it down. The chimes were loud, hurting his ears. He covered them with his hands.

Annette Wheeler opened the door. Her mouth opened slightly, closed. "Why, Tom." She was obviously surprised.

Smiling, he said, "Good evening, Mrs. Wheeler." And stepped inside, taking advantage of her confusion.

Annette backed up as Tom closed the door behind him.

"It's snowing," he said, brushing some from his arms.

"Yes." Shs looked at the melting flakes on his head. "I thought Jennifer called you."

He ignored this. "Where is she?"

"She's out."

His smile faded. "Out? But we have a date."

Annette cleared her throat. An intangible fear was closing in.

"Jennifer told me she broke the date with you, Tom. She's gone out."

Annette had insisted when Jennifer finally reported all

242

the odd things Tom had been saying and doing. She'd gone to Jane's as planned.

"Is she still getting ready? She's always late." He removed his gloves, slapped them against his sleeve.

"Gordon," Annette called, voice cracking. Her husband would straighten this out.

From somewhere deep within the house, Tom heard SOLA.

FIX THIS.

Gordon Wheeler, tall, thin, his chiseled face Lincolnesque, appeared in the doorway between the den and living room, his plaid shirt sleeves rolled up, *Time* magazine in one hand. "What's up, Tom?"

Trying to sound calm, yet give Gordon a clear signal, Annette said, "Tom's come for his date with Jennifer. I've told him she's gone out." She slipped her hand through her husband's arm.

"That's right, Tom. I thought Jennifer broke the date with you."

Tom said nothing. The brilliant white glow bordering Gordon Wheeler burned Tom's eyes. From an inside pocket, he removed his wraparound sunglasses, put them on. "Would you call Jennifer, please?"

"She's not here," Gordon said, feeling frightened.

"Call her anyway."

"She's out, Tom," came the reply, sounding brave. Why the glasses? he wondered.

Inside his mind, Tom begged SOLA for instructions. Probably he should kill them. Then he heard it.

LEAVE THIS PLACE, SOLA said.

Of course. If he killed them, Jennifer would come back, report it. He might be deflected from his more important mission.

COME BACK LATER. GET ALL THREE AFTER THE OTHERS ARE DEAD.

Yes, Tom thought. Naturally.

"You hear me, Tom?" Gordon was saying.

"Sir?"

"Are you all right?"

He removed the glasses, smiled sweetly. "Of course." He had to take a chance that Jennifer hadn't called him in front of her mother. "Jen didn't break the date. I wonder why she told you she did?"

Annette Wheeler was sure her daughter had, but something told her to play along. "Well, I'm sorry, Tom, I'll give her hell for not telling you. That was terrible. She just had to...." She stopped. She didn't want Tom to know Jennifer was at Jane's. "Go to her grandmother's," she finished.

Good. She hadn't heard Jennifer call. "Guess I'll be on my way." He turned toward the door. "Merry Christmas."

When he was gone Annette Wheeler ran for the phone. "What are you doing?" Gordon asked.

"I'm calling the Nashes. They have to be told."

Outside, Tom thought about snipping the Wheelers' phone wires, then rejected the idea. It could foul things up. He'd do it later. The snow was coming down faster.

Turning his car around, he headed toward the Durhams. His next assignment.

8.

The reception on Kit's car radio was lousy. She snapped it off. Maybe it would improve later.

On the road for two hours, she was sorry she hadn't waited until morning. Snow definitely threatened. It had been stubborn, pig-headed to leave when she did. What difference could her middle of the night arrival make? Except to alarm everyone. And, of course, to annoy Noj.

It was hard enough making this trip, not knowing exactly what she'd find at home. Her mother was having an affair. Tom was probably into some religious cult. Surely the others were being affected in some way.

Suddenly, there was an explosion like a gunshot. In the second before the car swerved out of control, she realized it was a blowout. She tried desperately to remember what to do as the car pulled and bucked to the left. Although she hadn't seen another car for the last fifteen minutes, now one approach, its headlights signaling possible death. As hard as she could, Kit turned the wheel to the right. The old car vaulted toward the shoulder of the road as she applied pressure to the brake.

Narrowly missing her, the driver of the oncoming car honked frantically, his horn expelling a final outraged cry as he disappeared behind her. Carefully negotiating the width of the shoulder, Kit brought the car to a stop and sat gripping the wheel for several moments before she could let it go. Every part of her body shook. Blood slammed in her ears.

Outside it was quiet. The silence eerie. Her breathing slowed; she slumped in the seat. Wanting to cry, she chastized herself. Too much like a helpless female. She knew she had to get out, find the jack and change the goddamn tire.

"Oh, shit," she said aloud.

It was beginning to snow.

9.

"Oh, no you're not," Gordon Wheeler said, grabbing the phone from his wife.

"Why not, Gordon?" she was startled. "There's something very wrong with him. Surely, you could see that."

"Yes, I saw it."

"Well, then?"

Gordon took the phone gently from his wife's hand, replaced it in the cradle.

"We don't even know these people, Annette."

"What's that have to do with it?" She lit a cigarette.

"I just don't like being a butt-insky."

She blew a puff of smoke into the air. "I know Jennifer broke the date with him. I just know it."

"Look, he's gone. Let's forget it." He rolled the *Time* magazine in his hands.

She reached for the phone again. "I'm calling Jennifer."

"What in hell for?"

"I want to know for sure if she broke the date. If she did and Tom still came here, then there is something very, very wrong and we should call his parents."

He put his large hand over hers, roughly. "No. You're not calling Jennifer. You're always checking up on the kid and...."

"There's a reason...."

"I don't give a damn, Annette. When she comes home tomorrow, we'll ask her. If she did tell him...well, we'll talk about calling the Nashes then."

"Not good enough, Gordon. I want you to promise me if she called him, you'll definitely call the Nashes."

He thought it over. Tomorrow he could convince her it was really none of their business. "All right."

"Promise?"

"Yes, yes. Let's have a drink. That kid shook me up."

They walked away from the phone.

10.

George Durham threw the bolt on his front door, locking Esther and himself securely inside.

"I never thought I'd say this, but I'm glad that's over." Esther hung her duffel coat on the peg next to George's mackinaw.

"I know what you mean. The tension's so thick you could cut it with a knife."

Esther shook her head sadly, began pulling off her snowboots. "Makes me feel real bad."

"Maybe when they get Tom to the doc on Monday it'll be better. Let me help you, girl." George tugged at her boot as she held fast to the brass doorknob. "'Course, I don't hold much with those head doctors."

"Sometimes it's necessary. And you have to admit, George, something's wrong with that boy's head."

"I guess. There you go."

Esther slipped her feet into the red and white fur booties she kept near the door. "Want some hot chocolate?"

"I'm pretty full. Well, all right." George loved sitting with his wife at the kitchen table, sipping something, talking over the day.

"Come on, then." She took his hand. They walked, like lovers, through the living room to the kitchen.

Esther, slightly ahead of George, gasped first. He echoed her almost immediately.

"Hello," Tom said, feet crossed on the kitchen table in front of him, the gun pointed directly at them. "Come on in. Make yourselves at home."

He grinned, white teeth gleaming, cheeks flushed.

"What the hell's this?" George asked in a dry voice. Was that his Colt .45?

"Just a simple welcome home committee of one."

Protectively, George stepped in front of Esther. He narrowed his hooded eyes spotting the smashed gun case. It *was* his gun. "What's going on here, boy?"

Esther thought of her children, wondered if she'd see any of them again.

"Sit down," Tom ordered, his voice deeper now.

"Gimme that gun." The boy had no business playing with one of the prizes of his collection.

"Please, George," Esther whispered, "be careful."

"SOLA wants you to sit down," Tom said.

"Who?" George barked.

"It's his friend," said Esther.

"What friend?"

"George, let's do what Tom and his friend want."

Angry the situation was clearly out of his control, George banged into a chair across the table from Tom. Esther sat down next to him.

"Thank you," Tom said gently.

Glancing over Tom's head, George noticed two empty places in the case. His Browning FN was also missing. Damn that boy!

247

"Do you want to tell us about your friend, Tom?" Esther's hands danced in her lap as though they had lives of their own.

"Do you believe in SOLUDA?"

What was the right answer? Her life hung in the balance; she was sure of that. A wrong answer might end it. Pressing her lips firmly together, she prayed silently for guidance.

"Esther?" Tom said.

"Why don't you tell me more about it so I can decide."

"Oh, Esther, I wish things could be different." Tom sounded plaintive, wistful. "There's no question in George's case. But you.... ah, well."

George felt his insides twisting into knots. It rankled having this punk kid holding them at bay. And with *his* 1873 Colt. He always hated the feeling of helplessness, had done everything he could all his life to avoid it. Dependency was anathema to George.

"What's this about, Tom? Let's get on with it."

Tom grinned. Imagine wanting to get on with your own death?

11.

Steven couldn't sleep. Maybe he'd had too much pot. Maybe not enough. He listened to the even, steady breathing coming from Max in the other bed.

He wished like hell they'd gotten through to Kit. They'd tried twice more and gotten no answer. Now it was too late.

Even though he'd told Sara there was nothing to worry about, that Kit would be home soon enough, he really didn't believe it. Not that he had any evidence. It was just a feeling. And what could she do anyway? For that matter, what *would* Kit do when they told her? Call the police? National Guard?

Go to sleep. He rolled over on his side and began counting sheep. It was no good. Another joint? Why not, it might work. He was getting nowhere fast this way. A joint might do it.

12.

Tom, the gun still trained on them, reached down next to his chair without taking his eyes from the two old people and brought up a coil of rope. "Esther, dear, SOLA wants you to tie George in the chair." He held the rope out to her.

"I don't know how you mean," Esther said, tears clouding her vision.

"If you don't tie your husband to that chair, I'm going to blow your brains out." He smiled sweetly.

Suddenly, George realized the seriousness of their situation. "Do as he says, Esther." There was a chance the boy would leave them alive if they cooperated. "Please, do as he says."

"Very good," from Tom.

Esther, legs shaking, rose from her chair and took the rope from Tom. Edging around the table, she arrived at where George was sitting.

"Move the chair out from the table. Over there." Tom gestured with the gun to the center of the room.

George obeyed.

"All right now, start with his wrists, behind his back. I'll guide you." A kindly teacher to a new student.

George put his arms behind him, around the back of the chair, wrists together. Tom explained patiently as Esther, crying, followed his directions. He made her pull the knots tight, his old boy scout training paying off. Ten minutes later, when she tied the final knot around her husband's ankles, Tom was convinced George was secure.

"Now you sit."

He put another chair about fifteen feet away from George, facing him. With the rope that was left, he tied Esther into the chair.

"Very good," he said when he finished.

"Now what?" George asked.

Tom pulled a knife from his belt. He'd taken it from a drawer, under the pine counter. It was a boning knife. Sharp. Gleaming with reflected light.

Esther, when she saw it, began to cry openly. She wished she could speak, say the right thing, but only tears would come.

Tom walked behind George. Waited. Heard the command. THROAT.

"Perhaps you'd like to close your eyes, Esther."

She looked at him curiously, not understanding. In the moments she took to fathom his statement, she watched transfixed, while Tom reached from behind her husband, and in one swift, streaking motion, slit his throat.

George's eyes widened, popped. His mouth opened, forming an "O." No sound came forth, except for a slight gurgling. He arched his body, chest thrusting forward, hands and feet straining against his bonds. Before George slumped forward, Tom registered the surprised expression in the man's eyes.

Esther's crying annoyed him.

"Shut up," he ordered.

She tried. Still the sobs slipped out. Staring at the body of her dead husband, Esther tried to believe it was a dream, a trick. George would laugh in a moment and he and Tom would tell her they were just playing. How had they worked out the blood? She watched the stain grow, darkening George's red shirt.

Enough, Tom thought. And turned the gun toward Esther, the long, narrow barrel pointed at the middle of her forehead. When the gun exploded, he was surprised to see he'd been off. It blew away her face. Dead center. From the back of her head some gray pulpy stuff flew out hitting the wall behind her.

Watching the glutinous mass slide down the wall, Tom decided it was probably her brains. From his back pocket he took a clean white handkerchief and wiped down the gun. With a pencil through the trigger guard, he picked it up as he'd seen it done in countless movies. Gently, he replaced the Colt in the gun case.

Next he went to the sink, washed off the knife, George's blood making pink water, now gone down the drain. Carefully, he dried the knife and returned it to the drawer.

GOOD BOY.

Tom nodded.

Things were going nicely.

Careful not to touch anything, he went out the way he'd come in and headed toward his car.

Home again, home again, jiggity-jig!

13.

Kit always had trouble taking no for an answer. For awhile, standing in the snow, staring at her crippled car, she believed absolutely that it could be fixed. But after futilely trying to will the snow to stop and the tire to repair itself, she had to admit defeat. It would be impossible to change a tire in this weather.

Two choices. Either signal someone to stop by putting flares around the car—thank God, Noj had insisted she buy them—or take the flashlight and start walking. She chose the latter.

Unfortunately, she'd have to leave her large suitcase and Christmas gifts for the family behind. Strapping on her backpack, she congratulated herself for having the forethought to bring it. Then locked the doors, set the flares in place, switched on the flashlight, set off on the snowy highway. She prayed for two things: that a car would come along soon, that the driver would be a woman. At the least, a man with his family. She'd flash her light on the driver before getting in. If it was a man alone, she'd keep on walking. Of course, out here, alone, if the driver wanted, he could force her to get in. Or kill her. Or whatever else he might have in mind. She didn't have to think about that, Kit decided. She had to accept her total loss of control. Her immediate future was in the hands of the Fates.

14.

"**Where** are you?" Jim asked.

"I'm home," Anne said.

"I mean, where are you calling from?" Hearing her voice sent relief rushing through him.

"I'm in the bedroom."

"Where's Cole?"

"He's watching a movie." Remembering that Jim had never been inside the house, she added, "Downstairs in the television room. My mother's in bed, Tom's out on a date and the other kids are asleep."

"I love you, Anne."

"I love you, darling."

"How are things going?"

"All right, I guess."

"You guess?"

"I don't know. There's a certain tension in the air, unease. I suppose that would be natural."

"Do you think he could get violent?"

"Tom?" Her response surprised her. Jim's question had touched something on another level.

"Cole," he corrected.

"Oh. Well, no. I don't know. I hadn't thought about it. I don't think so." She recalled the other night when he'd tried to force himself on her. "He's been quite calm since our talk. I think he's relieved. He seems to be walking around with a kind of smile on his face, as though he has a secret or something."

There was a cold, prickling sensation below Jim's hair at the base of his neck. He didn't like what she'd said.

"A secret?"

"Oh, I don't know." She laughed. "I'm probably imagining it."

"Anne," he said, trying to sound calm, "don't you usually trust your instincts?"

"I usually do."

"Darling, I don't want to alarm you but do you think it's safe to stay in the house with him? Look...the man's going to lose his entire family. Couldn't that send him off the deep end? It happens, you know."

"Not Cole," Anne said quickly.

"Why not Cole?"

How could she tell Jim it was her eldest son she feared, not her husband? Yet she was going to share the rest of her life with this man. "All right, Jim, the truth is I *am* afraid. I'm afraid that...."

There was an odd sound on the line. A click. Had Cole picked up? Jim was afraid to speak. If Cole *was* on the other line and heard Jim's voice, it might provoke him. He'd wait until Anne spoke again. But there was no sound. And then the dial tone.

Shaking, he dialed Anne's number, not thinking what he'd do if Cole answered. The line was busy. Frantically, he dialed again. Busy.

He dialed the operator. "I'd like to check a number, to see if it's busy or out of order. I was just cut off in the middle of a conversation."

"Is this an emergency, sir?"

"As a matter of fact, it is."

"What is the number?"

Jim gave it to her and lit a cigarette, hands trembling, while the operator tried the number. It was busy.

"I'll have to check further, sir."

Squeaks. Buzzes. Someone picked up.

"This is the Old Hickory exchange, Miss Barber speaking. May I help you?"

Jesus! He went through the speech again.

"Is this an emergency, sir?"

"You're damned right it is."

A beat of silence. Then Miss Barber's voice again. "Hold on, please."

253

Jim carried the phone while he paced the room, cigarette dangling from his lips.

"Sir?"

"Yes?"

"KL 5-8439 is out of order."

"Why would that be?"

"I really don't know. You'll have to call the repair office in the morning. The number is...."

"Could the snow have knocked the lines out?" He tripped over the phone cord. "Damn."

"I'm sorry, sir. Please call the repair office in the morning. Do you wish the number?"

"Can't you make a guess?" he begged, foolishly.

"A guess?"

"Oh, never mind." He slammed the phone back in its cradle. Then picked it up and dialed Anne's number again on the off-chance that Miss Barber had been wrong. She wasn't.

At the window, he saw the snow coming down evenly, consistently, but no harder than it had been an hour before. He was thirty miles away from Anne; maybe the storm was worse there. There was no telling what kind of weather might knock out phone and electricity. Sometimes the slightest storms put both out of commission.

At any rate, he was out of contact with Anne. He didn't like it. But what the hell could he do about it? He couldn't very well go there. Maybe he should drive into Old Hickory, get a room for the night. At least he'd be closer. But that was ridiculous.

He flopped into his easy chair. There's nothing to do, he told himself. Nothing to do.

But in some part of his brain, some small part, he didn't buy that at all.

15.

The beak-nosed woman, black eyes fiery, told the young, blonde pretty one, her sauce was not Italian. Cole sipped his wine. His mind shut out the commercial, turned inward. Arizona to Palm Beach to Canada.

Another country would be best. Toronto. She'd never find him there. One thing for sure, he'd never marry again. No wife. No kids.

Gray light signaled the movie had come back on. *Gilda.* Rita Hayworth. Maybe he'd find a number like Rita. He liked redheads. Shit! What the hell was this? A feeling of mourning. He blinked. Tears slid down his cheeks. He was crying. Silently. Of course.

He drained the glass of wine, trying to blot out the reality he'd just glimpsed, but it didn't work. Goddamnit. He had known it all along? No matter. He knew it now.

Cole Nash wasn't going anywhere.

Not now.

Not ever.

16.

After Tom cut the telephone wires to his house, he walked calmly to the window of the den. He'd seen the flickering light from the television. Peeking through the bottom half of the window, he watched his father sitting alone drinking, staring at the tube. Perfect. The back door was open. He stepped quietly into the kitchen.

SOLA was with him.

Everything was going according to schedule. Except the mix-up with Jennifer, but he'd take care of that. Standing in front of the knife drawer, he listened to the house.

Silent, except for its usual squeaks and creaks.

Carefully, he opened the drawer, removed the knife and laid it on the counter. He took off his parka, and headband, put them on a chair. Next his shirt and pants. So far he'd been lucky. Not gotten any blood on them. But why take chances? He folded the shirt, neatly placing it with his other clothes. He hung his jeans over the back of the chair. His sunglasses remained in place on his nose.

The black handle of the Browning nestled coldly in his left hand. With his right hand, he picked up the long sharp knife and tip-toed toward the den.

17.

The phone was dead. If it was dead from the weather, there was no point going downstairs. Nothing Cole could do. Besides, she'd have to explain who she'd been talking to at that hour. And if the phone was dead because Cole had done something to it, she absolutely didn't wish to confront him.

But why would he do that? Anne knew Jim would be worried. Wished there were a way she could go over to Esther's and call him. If she slipped out the back door, Cole wouldn't even know she'd gone. But if it was the weather, Esther's phone was undoubtedly out of order, too. And she had this strange feeling it would be dangerous to leave her room.

Slowly, she eased herself up from the bed, walked over and locked the door. On the bed again, she sat, waiting.

For what? She wondered.

18.

When Noj saw Kit's car parked at the side of the road, he had the same kind of reaction he'd had when he learned of John Kennedy's assasination. He'd been fourteen then, shopping for his mother at the local A & P. The principal of Southold High had died and the school was closed. As he pushed the basket up an aisle, the sound system blared. A rendition of *Once in Love with Amy* was interrupted by a newscaster.

Part of his mind took in what the newscaster was saying. Something about Dallas, the President, gunshots. He wasn't really listening. Wouldn't it be weird, he thought fancifully, if an American President were shot at? It was at least five minutes before the newscaster's information registered.

Passing Kit's car, he thought, 'wouldn't it be awful if something happened to Kit's car?' This time it only took thirty seconds before his brain understood, recorded the data. The car he'd seen, with a flare in front and back, *was* Kit's car. He slowed to a stop.

In a few moments, he'd carefully turned around and was heading back toward it. He parked across the road, left his motor running, lights on.

Her car was empty. He tried the doors. Locked. Peering into the back seat, he could see her large red suitcase. He ran across the road, turned off the motor of his car and took the keys. He had a key to her car on his ring. He opened the door, removed the suitcase, locked the car again.

Starting his car, Noj wondered how long ago she'd had the flat and if she'd been picked up yet. He would have to drive carefully, but quickly.

It was essential that he be the one to find her.

19.

Only the top three-quarters of Cole's head appeared above the back of his chair. Tom stood behind him, knife poised, naked chest glistening with sweat. Using the gun would be simple. He could easily blow off his father's head. But the sound would alarm the others upstairs. In the grander scheme of things, the knife was called for. He could reach over his father and with his left arm grab him around the neck, plunge the knife in his chest. Tricky, yet the only way.

Tom took a silent step closer.

Something odd passed over Cole, something unnameable, something that made him turn. He jumped up. For a second, he didn't recognize the almost naked boy wearing sunglasses, knife held high, a strange pull to his mouth. My God.

The chair between them, Cole said, "Tom?" It was all he could manage.

"Yes, Cole? What is it?" Tom grinned, voice odd, high-pitched.

The boy's words sickened him. "What's up? What are you doing?"

"What's it look like, Cole?"

Tom had never called him by his first name before. Cole watched him lower the knife, keeping it poised at his side. Then he saw the gun in Tom's other hand. Jesus!

"Where'd you get that gun?"

If he kept talking to his son this way, as though asking where he'd gotten a new football, maybe he could dispel the ominous atmosphere filling the room.

"I got it at the Durham's, Cole."

"Why are you calling me that?"

"Isn't that your name?" He giggled.

"George gave you that gun?" He wished he could see behind the sunglasses.

Tom's voice deepened. "Did I say he gave it to me? No. SOLA made the arrangements."

"Sola? You mean that friend of yours Pancho Sola?" Cole was stalling.

"SOLA is my father. *You* are shit."

It was shocking to hear Tom talk this way. He wondered if he should try and jump the kid?

"What do you want?" he asked softly.

"Your life," Tom answered coolly.

Cole believed his son. He watched as Tom leveled the gun at him. His thoughts were in shards. Couldn't grab hold of anything.

"Step to the side," Tom ordered.

Cole obeyed. The chair no longer separated them. Nothing but six feet of space. If he jumped, lunged, Tom might have time to pull the trigger. What other chance did he have?

"Turn around," Tom ordered. If he tried to stab his father in the chest Cole could fight him. Might, in fact, win.

Cole knew any chance of survival was over if he complied with Tom's command, but what else could he do? He tried words.

"Listen to me, Tom. You're sick. You need help. Give me the gun and the knife."

Tom laughed. "Turn around."

Turning, Cole thought of the Jews in Germany going to the ovens. Eternal hope.

First it was cold. Then it burned. A searing pain in the middle of his back. Cole fell to his knees, realizing the knife had plunged between his shoulder blades, had been pulled out again. He couldn't believe that this was it. The end of his life. Surely it was a nightmare. Someone, something would save him. Stuart or Clara? Never. He fell over on his side, then onto his back. He opened his eyes. He wanted to look at his assassin.

Above him, legs apart, knife held tightly in his right hand as it dripped blood, his blood, Tom grinned at him. Watching, as though it were happening to someone else, unable to yell for help, he saw Tom drop to his knees beside him, raise the knife high in the air. As it came down, he involuntarily shut his eyes. Then felt it enter his body.

Tom heard the grunts and cries of this terrible man as over and over he brought down the knife, blood spurting everywhere. After the final thrust, he leaned back and listened for SOLA.

GOOD BOY.

20.

Jim couldn't stand it. Not knowing, not able to make contact, was driving him nuts. If it hadn't been so late, he would have called Anne's friend at the bookstore, asked her to go to the house, check. But you just didn't call strangers and alarm them after midnight. He had to accept that the storm had knocked out the phone lines in Logan.

Logan. The Galloways. Of course, Jim had friends in Logan. If the Nash phone was out because of the storm, the Galloway phone would be out, too. They lived about a mile apart, on the river. At least it would tell him something.

Jim lifted the receiver. What if Bob or Sally Galloway answered? What would he say to them at this hour?

The truth was the Galloways' answering would leave only one real possibility. Someone had cut the Nashs' line.

Jim dialed the Galloway number. There was static, then ringing.

"Hello," It was the sleepy voice of Bob Galloway. "Hello?"

As Jim hung up the phone with one hand, he opened his night table drawer with the other, and stared at the shiny black pistol which lay inside.

21.

The snow was coming down in layers now, sheets. Kit was tired. It was becoming harder and harder to walk. Cold crept through her fur-lined boots and a feeling of dampness stole over her toes. It seemed as though she'd been trudging along for hours. Her legs ached and the exposed flesh around her eyes was numb. She'd wrapped her muffler over nose and mouth, and tucked the ends into the hood of her parka. Occasionally, she slipped off the road onto the shoulder, fell. If only she could rest, but she knew she mustn't.

Her situation was perilous. In all the time she'd been walking, only one car had passed. Either the driver hadn't seen her or was afraid to stop. What if no one stopped? She couldn't ignore the pulling in her legs, the dizziness, the nausea that was beginning. And the tiredness.

Suddenly she was falling. She heard herself whimper, like a child, she thought. She dragged her body up and, sitting, staring into the black, snow quickly covering her, she realized she'd lost both her flashlight and backpack. She extended a hand, felt around her. She knew she wasn't trying very hard, but she couldn't. Maybe in awhile. Right now, she had to rest.

As she lay on her snowy pillow, feeling strangely warm, Kit knew she was going to die. Tentacles of fear reached every part of her body. Someone was crying. Someone was telling her to get up. She couldn't, and closed her eyes.

22.

He shouldn't have smoked that last joint. Now he was scared. Hearing things. Maybe those sounds were always there. After all, he wasn't usually awake at this hour.

Steven got out of bed, crossed the narrow separation between his bed and Max's, stood looking down at his sleeping brother.

Angel.

How odd he should think that. Usually, he thought of his little brother as a brat. But right now, lying on his back, arms up and framing his head, sweet smile on his face, all Steven could think was *Angel*. He leaned down and shook his shoulder. Max moaned. Again he shook him.

This time Max opened his eyes. Blinked. "Wha?"

"Wake up, Max." He didn't know why he was waking him. Not really. Company?

Max started to turn over, but Steven held him. "You have to get up."

"Why?" He rubbed his eyes.

"Because." Steven wanted to cry. Then he said, "We have to get dressed."

"You're crazy. It's night."

"I know. But isn't it fun?"

Max thought for a moment. "No. I'm sleepy."

Steven tore off his pajama top then his bottoms. He reached for a sweatshirt. "See, I'm getting dressed." He had no idea why he was doing this.

Max sat up. "Steven, what's wrong?"

"We're going to play run-away." He thought about climbing out on the roof in the snow, then down the tree. Everything inside him trembled. He'd never be able to do it. Too stoned. Why should he have to anyway? His thinking was way off. Still, he continued to dress. "Get dressed."

"I don't wanna."

A bright idea came to Steven. "I love you, Max. You're my best friend and I want you to do what I say. Okay."

"You're not mad at me anymore for breaking your plane?"

"Nah."

"I'm your best friend?" His eyes were shining.

"That's right."

Max jumped from the bed and went for his clothes. He'd waited a long time to hear Steven say those words.

23.

Somewhere in the distance, inside the house, Anne heard sounds. Not ordinary house sounds; not people talking. Unidentifiable, alarming noises. Something moved under the bedspread. Anne squealed, jumped up.

Coco poked her head from beneath the covers. Anne's body relaxed as though it were deflating. Smiling, she picked up the cat, held her close. Coco purred. After a few minutes, she heard footsteps coming up the stairs. They were almost familiar. Something off about them. She put down Coco, who rubbed against her legs. The sound of Anne's own breathing was so loud it almost obliterated the footsteps which had gotten to the top of the stairs, and were coming down the hall toward her room.

Jesus, she thought, an intruder. Paralyzed, she watched as the doorknob turned first to the right, then to the left. When she heard the voice, she was stunned. Then afraid.

"Mom, open up, will you?" Tom said.

But they weren't his footsteps. Did he have someone with him and he'd walked on tip-toe himself? Pancho Sola?

"Mom, you in there?"

"Are you alone?" she asked, voice quaking.

"Alone? Sure."

Why didn't she believe him? Why was she so afraid to open that door? "Where's your father?"

After a moment Tom said, "He's downstairs in the TV room. Open the door, will you? I want to talk to you."

Anne swallowed, took a deep breath. He's your son, for God's sake, she reprimanded herself. No need to act so crazy. All right, he's had some difficulty the last few weeks, but he sounds perfectly fine. Her guilt was making her paranoid. No two ways about that. But she couldn't stop herself from asking.

"What were those noises I heard?"

"Noises? Oh, must have been the tube. He's got some old movie on. Loud, too."

Of course. She relaxed, walked to the bedroom door and unlocked it, smiling.

Cole's eyes opened. Drowning, he thought. Swim to shore.

Painfully, inch by inch, he crawled across the rug of the television room toward the livingroom, wondering how he'd fallen into the river.

"Hello, Mom." Tom, returning her smile, pointed the gun at Anne.

She backed into the room as he entered, wanting to scream. She'd been right. What was he doing with this gun? Where were his clothes? What was that blood on his chest, legs? Oh, God, what?

"It's all over," he said. "SOLA's time is here. There'll be no more sin, no more whores like you. I know everything about you and the innkeeper." He pushed back the sunglasses with a forefinger.

"Oh, Tom, you don't understand." Somehow he'd gotten things mixed up. "Tom, darling, let me explain, let me help you." Her legs shook. She wondered if he could see it.

"SOLUDA will make everyone calm. I will become Duke and Kit the Duchess. The rest of you must go." He grinned. "Too bad about the kids, I guess, but that's the way SOLA wants it."

Too bad about the kids. Anne repeated the words to herself. Oh, my God.

"Tom, you can't. You don't mean you're going to kill them,

do you? Oh, no, Tom listen...listen, you're sick, you don't understand, you...." She started to walk toward him, arms outstretched.

He stopped her with a forward jut of the gun. "You have nothing to say. Only SOLA tells me what to do."

Anne was crying. "Tom, let me talk to him. Please. I'll do anything." Where was this Sola?

He laughed. "What you're going to do is what I tell you. SOLA speaks to you through me. I am his channel."

"Please don't hurt the children, Tom. Please." There was no Sola. No cult. Her son was insane.

Hadn't she read about this somewhere? The son who kills his family. But this doesn't happen to you, not to your son, not to your family. Intolerable. Couldn't be.

"All right, enough of this crap. Let's move." He stepped to the side, motioned her with the gun to move in front of him.

"Where are we going?" she asked, her voice weak, timid.

"To see your mother and blow out her brains."

24.

Noj felt sick. He'd been driving for a long time. There was no sign of Kit. He prayed she'd been picked up but didn't believe it. He hadn't seen one other car in an hour. Maybe he'd missed her.

He stopped, turned the car around. Felt he should go back. Cover the same territory. Slower.

After ten minutes he was convinced he'd made a mistake. Besides, she wouldn't be on that side of the road. He turned around again. Creeping along, one hand on the wheel, he leaned sideways, trying to see the edge of the road.

He almost passed it. A dark lump, like a pile of refuse.

He hit the brakes, pulled the emergency, was out of the car almost before it stopped. When he reached the lump, he fell to his knees.

"Jesus," he said.

It was Kit. He slapped her cold stiff cheeks, Nothing. He tried to lift her, fell. Scrambling up, he found her arms, began to pull and drag.

25.

The gun was like a magnet. As though hypnotized, Jim stared at it. He watched his hand reach out, taking the gun from the drawer. Like a sleepwalker, he moved through the rooms. From the coat stand near the door, he removed his goosedown jacket, wool hat. His gloves were on the table, along with his keys. Placing the gun in his right hand pocket, he went out the door, down the stairs, into the cold, snowy night.

His good old car started immediately. As he pulled out into the highway, he told himself he was nuts. And then, as clearly as if she were sitting right next to him, he was sure he heard Marilyn say: No, you're not, Jim. Hurry!

26.

Dorothy had been wakened by strange noises in the house. She didn't want to interfere. She'd just lie here quietly until she fell back asleep. When her bedroom door opened, she just reached out, snapped on the light.

Anne came through the door first. Tom, wearing only his briefs and a pair of sunglasses, was behind her, holding a gun at Anne's head. There was blood on him.

"Oh, Mama," her daughter cried.

Slowly, Dorothy slid up against the wall. What to say? Do? Sentences flew through her brain, all of them absurd.

Anne wanted to fling herself on her mother's bed, beg her to save them. Surely, Mother could make it all right again. But, immediately, Anne knew her mother could no more save her than she could save her own children. At that moment, the realization hit her fully. Unless she killed this boy, this son, he was going to kill her other children.

"Morning, Grandma," Tom said. "SOLA wants you."

Dorothy ran her tongue over her dry lips.

"Sola?" Her voice caught low in her throat. "Is that your friend, dear?"

Tom laughed.

"Please, Tom," Anne tried to run toward him. He pushed her back into position.

"I wish," Tom said, "that you could understand. I know you can't. You think I'm cruel, a fool. Actually, I'm kind. Kind of a rind. In the end, that is."

Dorothy wondered why he was rhyming, why he used this voice with a weird tenor quality?

"SOLA is everything. I must do what I'm told. Good as

gold. You've always wanted me to be a good boy. Now I am. Like Uncle Sam."

Without a single doubt, Dorothy knew these were her final moments. Her grandson was going to kill her. Funny that she wasn't afraid. Of course, her time was almost over anyway. Perhaps God had chosen this way so she wouldn't feel pain. But what of the others? Her daughter? Her grandchildren? Oh, Lord, No. Now panic took hold of her with crushing force.

"Thomas, you mustn't." So ineffectual.

"But I must, Grandma, that's exactly it. I must. Please trust. For the good of SOLUDA." And he squeezed the trigger.

The gun's report seemed to split the room apart. Anne screamed, automatically shutting her eyes. When she opened them she saw her mother slumped to the side, a red blotch spreading across the front of her pink nightgown.

"Mama! Oh, my God!" She ran to her. "Mama, no, please." Despite her hysteria, she could see at once her mother was dead. She fell to her knees at the side of the bed, her head in her mother's dead lap. Patiently, Tom waited. This was part of the whore's punishment. She would watch all the executions; she'd be the last to go. That was the way SOLA wanted it.

Downstairs, Cole Nash died, on his stomach, six feet from the front door. His last thought was of his mother and father, wondering if they'd cry.

27.

It was funny because when Steven heard the bang it was almost a relief. Almost as though he'd been expecting it. The scream was the frightening thing. Methodically, to himself,

Steven said, that noise was a gunshot and the scream was a lady. But what lady?

Max was holding Steven around the waist, breathing funny. Crying? Steven knew they had to get out. He also knew he'd never make it. He had no balance. The kid had to go alone. "Don't cry, Max. Remember what I said before?"

"What was that noise?" Max asked.

No point trying to pretend. "We're in trouble. You got to save us, Maxy."

"Huh?"

He went to Max's drawer, took out a heavy sweater and put it over the sweater the boy already had on. A pair of extra gloves were in another drawer. He gave them to Max, then wound the boy's head with a woolen scarf. Best he could do. His real outer garments were downstairs. Steven walked Max to the window, opened it. Cold air and snow rushed in. Jesus, Steven thought, Max might fall, but it was the only chance.

"Listen carefully," Steven said. "You got to go out and down like always. When you get to the ground, you got to go to Esther and George's and tell them we're in danger. Tell them to get help, call the police. You'll be a hero, Maxy."

Max was whimpering. "I can't. I'm afraid. You go."

He had to tell the truth. "Max, I'm stoned. I have no balance. I'll fall."

"But so will I. I never did it in the snow."

"You gotta try. Your boots will grip. Please, go."

"I'm afraid," Max cried.

Steven put his arms around him, hugged hard and started crying. "Oh, please, Max. For me."

Max knew this was his chance to help Steven. He'd be his friend forever if he did it. "Okay. I'll try."

He put a foot out on the roof, then another. Steven watched. Max slid down the roof, losing his grip. The tree branch rested on the roof. Max grabbed it, crying, and he held fast. Slowly, he made his way down the branch, inch by inch. Then he was out of sight.

Steven shut the window, slumped to the floor, and waited.

28.

At five past one, Kit opened her eyes. The second time she'd come to and found Noj beside her. This time the car was moving. Again, she shuddered, realizing how close she'd come to death. If Noj hadn't come after her, she would have died in the snow. Frozen to death. The thought made her sick.

But now she was going to live! God, how precious life was. So it took a close call to make her realize that. So what? Some people never knew it. She was lucky. A second chance. And thank God for Noj. She'd never fight with him again. Life was too short.

Kit touched his thigh.

"Snow's a bitch." He wiped the inside of the window with his gloved hand. "Think we should find a motel until morning?"

It wasn't the first time he'd made the suggestion. And it was probably sensible. But Kit wanted to get home *now*.

"Noj, please, darling. I didn't almost freeze to death to get home tomorrow. Let's just get there, okay?"

"Okay, babe."

If the snow didn't get worse, and if nothing else untoward happened, they could be there in another two hours.

Soon enough.

29.

Tom's patience ran out. He pressed the gun in Anne's ribs.

"Get up," he commanded.

The cold, hard object in her side cut off Anne's tears. Slowly, she rose, turned, faced her son.

"Tom, you can't."

"Let's go see the children," he said gaily.

She wanted to vomit. "Kill me instead," she begged.

"Oh, I'm going to, don't worry. But later. These are SOLA's instructions." He flashed his even white teeth in a grin.

"Who's Sola?" she said stalling. "I know he's not this Pancho person." Nausea swirled inside her, rising, gagging.

"SOLA is everything." He gestured with the gun. "Move along. Have no fear, mother dear."

Should she try to jump him, grab the gun?

"Hurry." He tapped her arm with the tip of the black barrel.

Anne recoiled. If she grabbed for it the gun could go off. She'd die, save no one. It was better to wait. An opportunity would arise. God wouldn't let her children die. But her mother. And.... Cole was dead, too. She knew it as surely as if she'd seen his dead body.

"Where's Cole, Tom?"

"I told you, in the television room. Like a broom." He wished he'd quit rhyming. He hated it.

"Is he dead?"

"Very."

The confirmation was like a two-by-four he'd slammed against the back of her knees. She must have been harboring the idea that Cole, like the National Guard or the Mounties, would come at the last moment, save them all. But there *was* no Cole. She was the only adult left.

Out in the hall, walking toward Sara's room, Anne's brain skidded and slid over ideas, plots, rejecting them all as too dangerous, no help to her babies.

"Open the door," Tom ordered. He prayed to SOLA to be relieved of the rhyming.

Anne obeyed, still hoping for a miracle. The light was on, Sara was huddled in the corner, an old stuffed teddy bear clutched in her arms. For a split second Anne thought she would pass out. Forcing her head to clear, she told herself, I am the adult. I must stay strong until the end. It's coming soon.

"Hello, darling, come to Mother."

Sara didn't move.

"Hello there, Sara," Tom said.

Sara looked at him, wondered why he was naked and whose blood covered him. She decided she was going crazy. She didn't see what she saw, hear what she heard. She was crazy as a loon. She smiled.

"Let's go." Tom motioned with the gun, calling her to him. "We're going to go see Steven and Max."

The smile faded. She wasn't crazy. He was here. All bloody. With a horrible gun. "Mom?"

"Do what he says," Anne told Sara.

The procession of three headed down the hall to the boy's room. Again Tom ordered Anne to open the door and again she obeyed, now knowing what else to do. Immediately, Anne felt the cold in the room. Steven, fully clothed, sat on the floor near the window. With her eyes, Anne searched the room for Max. She couldn't see him anywhere.

"Where's Max?" Tom asked.

"Gone," Steven said.

Tom's eyes narrowed. What was going on here? SOLA had said nothing about Max not being here. But things fell into place for Anne. The cold made sense. Somehow Max had gone out that window. But where to? And how? And why hadn't Steven gone? She looked at him sitting there, eyes wide, strange.

Steven was glad he was stoned. Glad he was going to die stoned. Glad Max got away. But maybe he wouldn't die. Maybe Max would get to Esther and George in time. How long had it been since Max had left? Hours? Minutes? As usual, his time sense was completely gone.

"Where's Max?" Tom demanded. He leveled the gun at Steven.

"Steven," Anne said, urging him to answer.

"Gone," came the laconic reply.

Anne had to think quickly seeing the look on Tom's face. "Sola told Max to go," she said, desperate.

Tom turned to look at his mother. What did she know? The thought that SOLA might speak to his mother confused him. "SOLA spoke to you?" Tom realized he hadn't rhymed for a bit. SOLA was kind.

She took a chance. "Yes."

"You lie," he shouted. But he wondered. Hadn't the thought of sparing Max been discussed? Would SOLA tell his mother and not tell him? But then the ways of SOLA were mysterious.

Anne knew she had to try and convince Tom of this, stall. Perhaps Steven had had the foresight to send Max to get help. Maybe someone would come.

"I'm telling the truth. SOLA has spoken and taken Max away."

"Why?" Now he had her.

Good Christ, what was the right answer?

From Steven, "We should've told, Sara, oh, yeah, we should've told."

Tom swiveled toward the boy.

Anne opened her mouth to ask, told what? Realized it didn't matter. Besides, Tom had been distracted from his question to her.

"Told what?" Tom asked.

Sara began to whimper, moving to a corner of the room, teddy bear still clutched in her arms. Again, distracted by Sara's whimpering, Tom turned to look at her. Then he said, "Sit on the bed, Mother. You too, Steven."

Slowly, Steven rose from his position on the floor and stood unsteadily.

"Come here," Anne said to him, thinking, I'm calling my child to the slaughter. What in God's name could she do? Steven walked across the room, sat on the bed next to Anne. Anne held him around the shoulders, his small body feeling more vulnerable than ever. Ah, Cookie, comfort your son, your daughter, that's all you can do.

"Sara, darling, come here."

"No," Tom commanded. He raised the gun, pointed it at Sara in her corner.

"Please, Tom." Anne clutched Steven. What could she do? One for one? Besides, he wasn't going to, he wouldn't, he....

Sara, eyes wide, looked straight into the eye of the gun. "Tom? Is it because I'm fat?"

"Yes," he answered and fired twice into his sister's face.

30.

Several times, Jim almost turned back. The snow was coming down in solid sheets and he decided maybe he was crazy. What was he going to do once he reached the Nash house? Then, suddenly, he was off the side of the road. Stuck.

Fortunately he kept a shovel on the floor in the back, and as he dug his way out, he again wondered what he'd do on his arrival.

Sweat ran down his chest as he lifted the last pile of heavy snow. He threw the shovel in the back, got in, eased the car up onto the road. The snow was thinning out.

He knew he was foolish, going to ring their bell in the middle of the night. Jim lit a cigarette, laughed at himself. Oh, well, better safe than sorry. He'd soon see that everyone was alive and well in the Nash household.

And that would be that.

31.

It was cold and he was tired. And very scared. Max had never been outside at this hour of the night. Maybe bears would come. He ran a few steps on the road, slipped, fell. Then he got up, brushed himself off. Steven said to go to Esther's and George's and that was what he was gonna do.

Maybe wolfs. He was sure he heard them howling. But he couldn't run, he'd fall. Don't be a 'fraidy, he told himself. Maybe tigers. Nah, no tigers here.

Turning the bend, he saw the Durham house. And coming from the back there was a light. He wondered if Esther would give him hot chocolate.

32.

Steven's screams could be heard far from the house. But there was no one to hear. Anne held him to her breast, stroked his fine hair.

Anne's brain rejected Sara's death as it rolled over her in waves. She fought passing out, knowing she had to hold on, had somehow to save Steven. Or die trying. But he'd be so frightened without her, so much more frightened in those moments after she'd gone. Still, she had to try. The thought of her own death seemed merciful. There was no way she could live now. Even if she survived this bloodbath, she'd be dead spiritually. She felt her life ebbing away, as though blood were seeping from her. As though he'd already pulled the trigger.

The thought of Jim entered her conciousness for a moment. Just long enough to acknowledge that she loved him. Was she being punished? No. It was not that.

Good-bye, my darling.

In an instant, she pushed Steven away from her, hard, fast, catapulting from her seat on the bed, Steven's screams ringing in her ears. Leaping at Tom, as though she were flying, feet leaving the floor.

As it entered, the bullet burned her throat. Only then did she understand the sound she'd heard days ago. The firing of Tom's gun. Anne fell to the floor, her hands sliding down his naked chest and legs. She wanted to laugh. It wasn't days ago. It was now. What was now? She hit the floor, rolled onto her back.

I'm reading this in the paper, she thought. Blood filled her throat, gagged her. She coughed once, spit. Ah, Cookie, it-was-so-goddamned-short. Anne's eyes closed as her last breath gurgled and hissed.

Steven's screams continued like an alarm. Persistent. Unrelenting. They hurt Tom's head. Stepping over his mother's body, he lifted the gun high in the air and crashed the butt down into the crown of Steven's head. Over and over and over, hammering, thudding, until the boy was still, lying sideways, brains and blood covering the gingham spread.

It was over.

He'd done SOLA's bidding.

Standing in the middle of the room, he waited to hear SOLA's sanction, the commendation he'd earned, but nothing came. Time passed. Still nothing.

He decided it would come later. All in SOLA's own time. Now he needed to clean up.

In the bathroom, he washed and dried the gun and set it on the toilet seat. He threw back his head in the shower, letting the hot water wash away blood from his body. Afterwards, he went downstairs to get his clothes. Going through the living room to the kitchen, he didn't notice the body of his father near the front door.

Dressed again in his new shirt and jeans, gun tucked securely in his belt, he went back to the boy's room. He found he no longer needed the sunglasses as he surveyed his work.

Three bodies.

It was good work.

Why didn't SOLA speak?

SOLA worked in mysterious ways. Tom must be patient, wait in this room. He'd hear when SOLA was ready. He sat in Steven's desk chair. Coco jumped in his lap. Gently he stroked her as she settled into a round ball.

Facing the open door, waiting for SOLA, he hummed to himself, trying not to smell the sickly sweet odor of blood.

33.

"**Watch** out!" Kit yelled.

Noj swerved, the car skidded, turned around and around, came to a stop.

"My God," he whispered. "What was it?"

"A child," she said. Quickly she opened the door, and got out, Noj following.

Huddled on the side of the road was the child, whimpering. Kit ran over and the child looked up. Max.

"Omigod," she said, almost falling over. Then she pulled him into her arms. Noj was beside her.

"My brother," she mumbled, "my little brother."

"George, Esther," the boy said.

Noj and Kit looked at one another. Something was very wrong. Noj scooped up the cold, shaking boy and they ran back to the car.

34.

It was ten after three and the lights were on. Lots of them.
Jim turned off his motor as he looked at the Nash house. He
got out of the car, quietly closed the door, started up the path.
On the porch, he listened. There was no sound. He reached
out and tried the door. It was open. Taking the gun from his
pocket, he carefully pushed open the door. Cole's body was
the first thing he saw. He gasped, stepped around the body.
It never occurred to him to leave, call the police. He thought
only of Anne. He had to save her. He heard a noise from
above and realized the murderer could still be in the house.
No matter. He had to get to Anne.

Silently he crossed the room to the stairs.

Tom rose from his chair, removed the gun from his belt,
pulled back the hammer. Someone was here. Someone was
coming up the stairs. Was it SOLA?

At the top of the stairs, Jim listened. A faint sound reached
him. Heavy breathing. He followed the sound to a room with
an open door. What was that strange sweet smell? It frightened him, but his need to find Anne drove him beyond his
fear.

He counted to three, then jumped into the open doorway,
gun out in front.

A blond, angelic looking boy said, "SOLA, at last you've
come."

35.

Max kept crying. When they pulled up in front of the house, Kit saw the strange car.

"Whose?" Noj asked.

"I don't know."

"Jesus. Let's go for the police."

But Kit was out of the car and running across the snow covered lawn, up the steps, across the porch. She reached for the doorknob, opened it and saw Cole's body. She opened her mouth to scream, but the sound of the gunshot stopped her and she fell to her knees.

Noj was beside her, lifting her, dragging her away, back across the porch, down the steps, through the snowy lawn, to the car.

"Get help," he said tonelessly, "police."

"Omigod, omigod, omigod."

It was all Kit could say.

Tuesday,
January 7

Noj waited in the car. It was the way she wanted it. Always so damn independent. Well, he loved that about her, didn't he? Sometimes. He smiled. Sometimes.

Looking out the window, he saw her coming down the hospital steps. A beautiful, brave woman. He would be her family now. He and Max.

Leaning across the front seat, he opened the door for her. She looked tired, worn. And why not? Good God.

"Hi, babe."

"Hi." She tried to smile.

"How was it?"

"Awful."

"Did he talk to you?"

She shook her head. "Just stares straight ahead."

"Is there any hope for him?"

"The doctor doubts it. The shock was too great. But he thinks what really sent him over the edge was..." she swallowed hard, "killing Tom in cold blood like that."

"Poor bastard. What else could he do?"

She nodded.

"Let's go," she said.

Noj started the car, headed out of the parking lot.

If only she could have gotten through to Jim O'Neill. She wanted to tell him she understood. Forgive him for killing her poor, sick brother. The autopsy had shown nothing. The doctors said it was probably a chemical break. Caused by? They didn't know. She looked over at Noj. At first, she'd hated him. If it hadn't been for him, she would have come home earlier, saved everyone. But then she had to admit the truth. He'd actually saved her life. Tom would have killed her, too.

In her mother's date book was the psychiatrist appointment. For Monday, the twenty-third. Kit knew she would have gone along with that had she come home early. What else could she have done?

Mom, oh, God, Mom. She started to cry.

Noj reached across, touched her hand. "It's okay, darling, cry."

Daddy, Steven, Sara, Grandma, Esther, George. How could it be? But it was. At least she had Max.

They pulled onto the highway, heading back to school.

"Do you think Max will be all right?" she asked.

"Well, your uncle's a good man, isn't he?"

"Yes, of course."

"Kids bounce. Listen, I've been thinking. In June, when we graduate, will you marry me, Kit? I know this is a funny time to ask but, will you? We could take Max to live with us."

It was a generous offer, she thought. But she was far too shattered to consider it now. Maybe later.

"Oh, Noj, I just, I can't.... Oh, God." She sobbed.

"Okay, okay, babe, don't worry about it. Just know the offer's good any time."

She nodded through her sobs. When she stopped crying, she lay her head back against the seat, eyes closed. I will recover, she thought. People do. But I'll never be the same.

All right. I'll never be the same, but God Almighty, I'm alive. For a moment, she felt guilty. And then she didn't.

NEW FROM FAWCETT CREST

THRILLS ✦ CHILLS ✦ MYSTERY
from FAWCETT BOOKS

CURRENT BESTSELLERS
from POPULAR LIBRARY